About the

Lynne Graham lives in Northern Ireland and has been a keen romance reader since her teens. Happily married, Lynne has five children. Her eldest is her only natural child. Her other children, who are every bit as dear to her heart, are adopted. The family has a variety of pets, and Lynne loves gardening, cooking, collecting all sorts and is crazy about every aspect of Christmas.

A *USA Today* and *Wall Street Journal* bestseller, **Robin Covington** loves to explore the theme of fooling around and falling in love in her books. A Native American author, she proudly writes diverse romance where everyone gets their happily ever after. Robin is an unapologetic comic book geek, hoards red nail polish and stalks Chris Evans. She is thoroughly obsessed with her Corgi, Dixie Joan Wilder (Yes – *the* Joan Wilder).

Chantelle Shaw enjoyed a happy childhood making up stories in her head. Always an avid reader, Chantelle discovered Mills & Boon as a teenager and during the times when her children refused to sleep, she would pace the floor with a baby in one hand and a book in the other! Twenty years later she decided to write one of her own. Writing takes up most of Chantelle's spare time, but she also enjoys gardening and walking. She doesn't find domestic chores so pleasurable!

Opposites Attract Collection

March 2025
Love in Paradise

April 2025
Medics in Love

May 2025
Rancher's Attraction

June 2025
Workplace Temptation

July 2025
On Paper

August 2025
Forbidden Love

Opposites Attract:
On Paper

LYNNE GRAHAM

ROBIN COVINGTON

CHANTELLE SHAW

MILLS & BOON

All rights reserved including the right of reproduction in whole or in part in any form. This edition is published by arrangement with Harlequin Enterprises ULC.

This is a work of fiction. Names, characters, places, locations and incidents are purely fictional and bear no relationship to any real life individuals, living or dead, or to any actual places, business establishments, locations, events or incidents. Any resemblance is entirely coincidental.

Without limiting the author's and publisher's exclusive rights, any unauthorised use of this publication to train generative artificial intelligence (AI) technologies is expressly prohibited. HarperCollins also exercise their rights under Article 4(3) of the Digital Single Market Directive 2019/790 and expressly reserve this publication from the text and data mining exception.

® and ™ are trademarks owned and used by the trademark owner and/or its licensee. Trademarks marked with ® are registered with the United Kingdom Patent Office and/or the Office for Harmonisation in the Internal Market and in other countries.

First Published in Great Britain 2025
by Mills & Boon, an imprint of HarperCollins*Publishers* Ltd
1 London Bridge Street, London, SE1 9GF

www.harpercollins.co.uk

HarperCollins*Publishers*
Macken House, 39/40 Mayor Street Upper,
Dublin 1, D01 C9W8, Ireland

Opposites Attract: On Paper © 2025 Harlequin Enterprises ULC.

The Dimitrakos Proposition © 2014 Lynne Graham
Seducing His Secret Wife © 2021 Robin Ray Coll
Wed for the Spaniard's Redemption © 2019 Chantelle Shaw

ISBN: 978-0-263-41744-9

This book contains FSC™ certified paper and other controlled sources to ensure responsible forest management.

For more information visit: www.harpercollins.co.uk/green

Printed and Bound in the UK using 100% Renewable Electricity
at CPI Group (UK) Ltd, Croydon, CR0 4YY

THE DIMITRAKOS PROPOSITION

LYNNE GRAHAM

CHAPTER ONE

'BEARING IN MIND the history of the company's expansion and success, it *is* a most unjust will,' Stevos Vannou, Ash's lawyer, declared heavily in the simmering silence, a wary eye locked to the very tall, dark and powerfully built male across the office.

Acheron Dimitrakos, known as Ash to his inner circle, and Greek billionaire founder of the global giant DT Industries, said nothing. He did not trust himself to speak. Usually his control was absolute. But not today. He had trusted his father, Angelos, as far as he trusted anyone, which was to say *not* very much, but it had never once crossed his mind that the older man would even consider threatening the company that Ash had single-handedly built with the bombshell that his last will and testament had become. If Ash didn't marry within the year, he would lose half of the company to his stepmother and her children, who were already most amply provided for by the terms of his father's will. It was unthinkable; it was a brutally unfair demand, which ran contrary to every honourable scruple and the high standards that Ash had once believed the older man held dear to his heart. It just went to show—as if Ash had ever had any doubt—you couldn't trust anybody, and your nearest and dearest were the most likely to plunge a knife into your back when you were least expecting it.

'DT is *my* company,' Ash asserted between compressed lips.

'But regretfully not on paper,' Stevos countered gravely. 'On paper you never had your father transfer his interest to you. Even though it is indisputably the company that *you* built.'

Still, Ash said nothing. Cold dark eyes fringed with ridiculously long black lashes locked on the sweeping view of the City of London skyline that his penthouse office enjoyed, his lean, darkly handsome features set in hard, forbidding lines of restraint. 'A long court case disputing the will would seriously undermine the company's ability to trade,' he said eventually.

'Picking a wife would definitely be the lesser evil,' the lawyer suggested with a cynical chuckle. 'That's all you have to do to put everything back to normal.'

'My father knew I had no intention of ever marrying. That is exactly why he did this to me,' Ash ground out between clenched teeth, his temper momentarily escaping its leash as he thought of the utterly unhinged woman his misguided father had expected him to put in the role. 'I don't want a wife. I don't want children. I don't want *any* of that messing up my life!'

Stevos Vannou cleared his throat and treated his employer to a troubled appraisal. He had never seen Acheron Dimitrakos betray anger before or, indeed, any kind of emotion. The billionaire head of DT Industries was usually as cold as ice, possibly even colder, if his discarded lovers in the many tabloid stories were to be believed. His cool, logical approach, his reserve and lack of human sentiment were the stuff of legend. According to popular repute when one of his PAs had gone into labour at a board summit, he had told her to stay and finish the meeting.

'Forgive me if I'm being obtuse but I would suggest that any number of women would line up to marry you,' Ash's companion remarked cautiously, thinking of his own wife, who threatened to swoon if she even saw Acheron's face in print. 'Choosing would be more of a challenge than actually finding a wife.'

Ash clamped his mouth shut on an acid rejoinder, well aware the portly little Greek was out of his depth and only trying to be helpful even if stating the obvious was more than a little simplistic. He knew he could snap his fingers and get a wife as quickly and easily as he could get a woman into his bed. And he understood exactly why it was *so* easy: the money was the draw. He had a fleet of private jets and homes all over the world, not to mention servants who waited on him and his guests hand and foot. He paid well for good service. He was a generous lover too but every time he saw dollar signs in a woman's eyes it turned him off hard and fast. And more and more he noticed the dollar signs *before* he noticed the beautiful body and that was taking sex off the menu more often than he liked. He needed sex as he needed air to breathe, and couldn't really comprehend why he found the greed and manipulation that went with it so profoundly repellent. Evidently somewhere down inside him, buried so deep he couldn't root it out, there lurked an oversensitive streak he despised.

It was worse that Acheron knew exactly what lay behind the will and he could only marvel at his father's inability to appreciate that the woman he had tried to push Acheron towards was anathema to him. Six months before the older man's death there had been a big scene at his father's home, and Acheron had steered clear of visiting since then, which was simply one more nail in the coffin of the proposed bride-to-be. He had tried to talk to his stepmother about the problem but nobody had been willing to listen to common sense, least of all his father, who had been sufficiently impressed by the lady's acting ability to decide that the young woman he had raised from childhood would make his only son the perfect wife.

'Of course, perhaps it is possible that you could simply ignore the will and *buy* out your stepmother's interest in the company,' the lawyer suggested glibly.

Unimpressed, Ash shot the older man a sardonic glance. 'I will not pay for what is mine by right. Thank you for your time.'

Recognising the unmistakable note of dismissal, Stevos hastily stood up to leave while resolving to inform his colleagues of the situation immediately to sort out a plan of action. 'I'll put the best business minds in the firm on this challenge.'

Jaw line clenched as hard as a rock, Ash nodded even though he had little hope of a rescue plan. Experience told him that his father would have taken legal advice as well and would never have placed such a binding clause in his will without the assurance that it was virtually foolproof.

A wife, Ash reflected grimly. He had known since childhood that he would never take a wife and never father a child. That caring, loving gene had passed him by. He had no desire for anyone to grow up in his image or follow in his footsteps, nor did he wish to pass on the darkness he kept locked up inside himself. In fact, he didn't even like children, what little contact he had had with them simply bearing out his belief that children were noisy, difficult and annoying. Why would any sane adult want something that had to be looked after twenty-four hours a day and gave you sleepless nights into the bargain? In the same way why would any man want only one woman in his bed? The *same* woman, night after night, week after week. Ash shuddered at the very suggestion of such severe sexual confinement.

He recognised that he had a decision to make and he resolved to act fast before the news of that ridiculous will hit the marketplace and damaged the company he had built his life around.

'Nobody sees Mr Dimitrakos without an appointment *and* his prior agreement,' the svelte receptionist repeated frigidly. 'If you don't leave, Miss Glover, I will be forced to call Security to have you removed from the building.'

In answer, Tabby plonked her slight body back down on the plush seating in the reception area. Across from her sat an older man studying documents from a briefcase and talking urgently in a foreign language on his cell phone. Knowing she looked like hell did nothing for her confidence in such luxurious surroundings but she hadn't had a full night's sleep for some time, she no longer owned any decent clothes and she was desperate. Nothing *less* than desperation would have brought her to DT Industries seeking an interview with the absolute seven-letter-word of a man who had summarily refused to take any responsibility for the child whom Tabby loved with all her heart. Acheron Dimitrakos was a selfish, arrogant pig and what she had read about his womanising exploits in one of her clients' glossy scandal-sheet magazines had not improved her opinion. The man who had more money than Midas had turned his back on Amber without even expressing a desire to meet with Tabby as his co-guardian, or checking out the little girl's welfare.

The call to Security by Reception was duly made in clear crystalline tones undoubtedly intended to scare

Tabby off before the guards arrived. Her small face stiff, she stayed where she was, her slight body rigid with tension while she frantically tried to think up another plan of approach because gatecrashing Acheron's office wasn't going very well. But it wasn't as if she had had a choice, although she acknowledged that the situation was very serious indeed when such a callous personality became her last hope.

And then fate took a hand she wasn't expecting and she wasted a split second simply staring when she saw the tall dark man from the magazine pictures striding across Reception with a couple of suited men following in his wake. Tabby flew to her feet and raced after him. 'Mr Didmitrakos...Mr Dimitrakos!' she launched, stumbling over the syllables of his wretchedly complicated surname.

And at the exact same moment as her very tall and commanding quarry paused by the lift wearing an expression of sheer disbelief at her approach, the security guards came at a literal run, muttering fervent apologies to the man in front of her!

'I'm Amber's other guardian, Tabby Glover!' Tabby explained in feverish haste as both her arms were suddenly grabbed by the two men with him and she was yanked back a step from her proximity to him. 'I need to see you...I tried to get an appointment but I couldn't even though it's desperately important that we talk before the weekend!'

Security really was in need of sharpening up if they allowed him to be cornered on the top floor of his own building by a crazy woman, Ash reflected in exasperation. The young woman was wearing a worn jacket, track pants and trainers, her fair hair tied up in a high ponytail, pale shadowed face bare of make-up. She was small and plain, not at all the kind of woman who would have attracted his attention...although no sooner had he decided that than he noticed her remarkable blue eyes, which were an unusual violet in shade and dominated her pinched features.

'Please!' Tabby gasped. 'You can't be this selfish—nobody could be! Amber's father was a member of your family—'

'I have no family,' Ash informed her drily. 'Escort her out,' he told the security officers, who took over from his bodyguards in restraining Tabby even though she hadn't put up a struggle. 'And make sure this doesn't happen again.'

Taken aback that he wouldn't even give her five minutes of his time, that he betrayed no recognition even of Amber's name, Tabby was momentarily silenced. Then she swore at him like a fishwife, angrily employing language that had never left her lips before. In response, his brilliant dark eyes glittered with a raw angry hostility that momentarily shocked her because that cool front he wore evidently concealed much murkier depths.

'Mr Dimitrakos...?' Another voice interposed, and Tabby turned her head in surprise to see the older man who had been seated near her in the waiting area.

'The child—you'll recall your late cousin's guardianship request, which you turned down a couple of months ago?' Stevos Vannou hurtled forward to remind Acheron Dimitrakos in a quiet, respectful undertone.

An inconsequential memory pinged in the back of Ash's shrewd brain and drew his straight black brows together into a frown. 'What of it?'

'You selfish bastard!' Tabby raked at him, outraged by his lack of reaction and the consequences that his indifference to Amber's fate were about to visit on the child. 'I'll go to the press with this...you don't deserve anything better. All that wretched money and you can't do anything good with it!'

'*Siopi!* Keep quiet,' Acheron told her sternly in Greek and then English.

'And you and whose army is going to make me?' Tabby snapped back, unimpressed, the fighting spirit that had carried her through many years of loss and disappointment rising to the fore again to strengthen her backbone.

'What does she want?' Acheron asked his lawyer in English as if she weren't there.

'I suggest we take this back into your office,' Stevos remarked on a loaded hint.

Savage impatience gripped Ash. Only three days earlier he had returned from his father's funeral and, without even allowing for his grief at the older man's sudden death from a heart attack, it had turned into a very frustrating week. The very last thing he was in the mood for was a drama about some child he had never met and couldn't have cared less about. Troy Valtinos, oh, yes, he could remember now, a third cousin he had also *never* met, who had unexpectedly died and, in doing so, had attempted to commit his infant daughter to Ash's care. An act of sheer inexplicable insanity, Acheron reflected in exasperation, thinking back incredulously to that brief discussion with Stevos some months earlier. He was a childless single male without family back-up and he travelled constantly. What on earth could anyone have supposed he would do with an orphaned baby girl?

'I'm sorry I swore at you,' Tabby lied valiantly in an effort to build a bridge and win a hearing. 'I shouldn't have done that—'

'Your mouth belongs in the gutter,' Acheron breathed

icily and he addressed the security guards, 'Free her. You can take her out when I'm done with her.'

Tabby gritted her teeth together, straightened her jacket and ran uncertain hands down over her slender denim-clad thighs. Ash briefly studied her oval face, his attention lingering on her full pink mouth as a rare flight of sexual fantasy took him to the brink of picturing where else that mouth might be best employed other than in the gutter. The stirring at his groin put him in an even worse mood, reminding him of how long it had been since he had indulged his healthy libido. He knew he had to be in a very bad way if he could react to such an ignorant female.

'I'll give you five minutes of my valuable time,' Acheron breathed with chilling reluctance.

'Five minutes when a child's life and happiness hang in the balance? How very generous of you,' Tabby replied sarcastically.

Roaring rancour assailed Acheron because he wasn't accustomed to such rudeness, particularly not from women. 'You're insolent as well as vulgar.'

'It got me in the door, didn't it? Politeness got me nowhere,' Tabby traded, thinking of the many phone calls she had made in vain requests for an appointment. As for being called cheeky and vulgar, did she really care what some jumped-up, spoilt snob with loads of money thought about her? Yet her brain was already scolding her for her aggressive approach, telling her it was unwise. If she could get around the freeze front Acheron Dimitrakos wore to the world, he was in a position to help Amber while she was not. As far as Social Services were concerned, she could not be considered a suitable guardian for Amber because she was single, had no decent home and was virtually penniless.

'Start talking,' Ash urged, thrusting the door of his office shut.

'I need your help to keep Amber in my custody. I'm the only mother she's ever known and she's very attached to me. Social Services are planning to take her off me on Friday and place her in foster care with a view to having her adopted.'

'Isn't that the best plan in the circumstances?' Ash's lawyer, Stevos Vannou, interposed in a very reasonable voice as though it was an expected thing that she should be willing to surrender the child she loved. 'I seem to remember that you are single and living on benefits and that a child would be a considerable burden for you—'

Acheron had frozen the instant the phrase 'foster care' came his way but neither of his companions had noticed. It was a closely guarded secret that Ash, in spite of the fact his mother had been one of the richest Greek heiresses ever born, had once spent years of his life in foster care, shifted from home to home, family to family, enduring everything from genuine care to indifference to outright cruelty and abuse. And he had never, ever forgotten the experience.

'I haven't lived on benefits since Amber's mother, Sonia, passed away. I looked after Sonia until she died and that was why I couldn't work,' Tabby protested, and shot a glance brimming with offended pride at Acheron's still figure. 'Look, I'm not just some freeloader. A year ago Sonia and I owned our own business and it was thriving until Troy died and she fell ill. In the fallout, I lost everything as well. Amber is the most important thing in my world but, in spite of me being chosen as one of her guardians, there's no blood tie between Amber and me and that gives me very little real claim to her in law.'

'Why have you come to me?' Ash enquired drily.

Tabby rolled her eyes, helplessly inflamed by his attitude. 'Troy thought you were such a great guy—'

Ash tensed, telling himself that none of what she had told him was any of his business, yet the thought of an innocent baby going into foster care roused a riot of reactions inside him drawn from his own memories. 'But I never met Troy.'

'He did *try* to meet you because he said his mother, Olympia, used to work for your mother,' Tabby recounted.

Acheron suddenly frowned, straight black brows pleating as old memories stirred. Olympia Carolis, he recalled very well as having been one of his mother's carers. He had not appreciated when the guardianship issue had arisen that Troy was Olympia's son because he had only known her by her name before marriage, although if he stretched his memory to the limit he could vaguely recall that she had been expecting a child when she left his mother's employ. That child could only have been Troy.

'Troy was frantic to find a job here in London and you were his business idol,' Tabby told him curtly.

'His...*what*?' Ash repeated with derision.

'False flattery won't advance your cause,' Stevos Vannou declared, much more at home in the current meeting than he had been in the last, for the matter of the will would require considerable research of case law to handle.

'It wasn't false or flattery,' Tabby contradicted sharply, angry with the solicitor for taking that attitude and switching her attention back to Ash. 'It was the truth. Troy admired your business achievements very much. He even took the same business degree you did. That and the fact he saw you as head of his family explains why he put you down as a guardian in his will.'

'And there was I, innocent that I am, thinking it was

only because I was rich,' Acheron breathed with sardonic bite, his dark deep drawl vibrating down her spine.

'You really are a hateful, unfeeling creep!' Tabby slammed back at him tempestuously, fiery emotion ablaze in her violet eyes. 'Troy was a lovely man. Do you honestly think he realised that he was going to die at the age of twenty-four in a car accident? Or that his wife would suffer a stroke within hours of giving birth? Troy would never have taken a penny from anyone that he hadn't earned first.'

'Yet this lovely man left both his widow and child destitute,' Ash reminded her censoriously.

'He didn't have a job, and Sonia was earning enough money at the time through the business we owned. Neither of them could possibly have foreseen that both of them would be dead within a year of having that will drawn up.'

'But it was scarcely fair to name me as a guardian without prior discussion of the idea,' Acheron pointed out drily. 'The normal thing to do would have been to ask my permission first.'

Rigid with tension, Tabby made no comment. She recognised that he had a point but refused to acknowledge the direct hit.

'Perhaps you could tell us without further waste of time exactly what you imagine Mr Dimitrakos could do to help you?' Stevos Vannou sliced in, standing on the sidelines and thoroughly disconcerted by the sheer level of biting hostility erupting between his usually imperturbable employer and his visitor.

'I want to ask Mr Dimitrakos to support my wish to adopt Amber.'

'But is that a realistic goal, Miss Glover?' the lawyer countered immediately. 'You have no home, no money and no partner, and my own experience with Social Services and child-custody cases tells me that at the very least you need a stable lifestyle to be considered a suitable applicant to adopt.'

'What the heck does having or not having a partner have to do with it?' Tabby demanded defensively. 'This past year I've been far too busy to waste time looking for a man.'

'And with your approach it might have proved a considerable challenge,' Acheron interposed without hesitation.

Tabby opened and closed her lush mouth in angry disconcertion and took a seething step closer to the Greek billionaire. 'You accused me of having no manners? What about your own?' she snapped in outrage.

Studying the two adults before him squabbling and insulting each other much as his own teenaged children did, Stevos averted his attention from them both. 'Miss Glover? If you had had a partner it would certainly have made a big difference to your application. Raising a child today is a challenge and it is widely believed that *two* parents generally make that easier.'

'Well, unfortunately for me a partner isn't something I can dig up overnight!' Tabby exclaimed, wishing the wretched man would think of something other than picking holes in her suitability to adopt Amber. Didn't she have enough to worry about?

A germ of a wild idea leapt into Stevos's brain, and he skimmed his insightful gaze to Acheron and addressed him in Greek. 'You know, you could both help each other...'

Ash frowned. 'In what possible way?'

'She needs a stable home and partner to support her adoption application—you need a wife. With a little compromise on both sides and some serious legal negotiation, you could both achieve what you want and nobody would ever need to know the truth.'

Acheron was always quick on the uptake but for a split second he literally could not believe that Stevos had made that speech, could even have *dared* to suggest such an insane idea. He shot a disdainful glance at Tabby Glover and all her many obvious deficiencies and his black brows went skyward. 'You *have* to be out of your mind,' he told his lawyer with incredulity. 'She's a foul-mouthed girl from the back streets!'

'You've got the money to clean her up enough to pass in public,' the older man replied drily. 'I'm talking about a wife you *pay* to be your wife, not a normal wife. If you get married, *all* your problems with regard to ownership of the company go away—'

In brooding silence, Acheron focused on the one massive problem that would not go away in that scenario— Tabby Glover. *Not wife material* screeched every one of his sophisticated expectations, but he was also thinking about what he had learned about Troy Valtinos and his late mother, Olympia, and his conscience was bothering him on that score. 'I couldn't marry her. I don't like her—'

'Do you *need* to like her?' Stevos enquired quietly. 'I shouldn't have thought that was a basic requirement to meet the terms of a legal stipulation to protect your company. You own many properties. I'm sure you could put her in one of them and barely notice she was there.'

'Right at this moment the first thing on my agenda has to be the child,' Acheron startled his lawyer by asserting. 'I want to check up on her. I have been remiss in my responsibilities and too quick to dismiss them.'

'Look...' While Stevos was engaged in giving Ash an

alarmed look at that sudden uncharacteristic swerve of his into child-welfare territory, Tabby had folded her arms in frustration and she was glowering at the two men. 'If you two are going to keep on chatting in a foreign language and acting like I'm not here—'

'If only you were not,' Ash murmured silkily.

Tabby's hands balled into fists. 'I bet quite a few women have thumped you in your time!'

Shimmering eyes dark as sloes challenged her, his lean strong face slashing into a sudden smile of raw amusement. 'Not a one...'

Amber, Tabby reminded herself with painful impact, her heart clenching at the thought of the child she adored. She was here to ask for his help for Amber's sake, and Amber's needs were the most important consideration, not how objectionable she found the despicable man. His charismatic smile struck her like a deluge of icy water. He was incredibly, really quite breathtakingly, handsome and the fact that he found her amusing hurt. Of course, Tabby had never cherished many illusions about her desirability factor as a woman. Although she had always had a lot of male friends, she'd had very few boyfriends, and Sonia had once tactfully tried to hint that Tabby could be too sharp-tongued, too independent and too critical to appeal to the average male. Unfortunately, nobody had ever explained to Tabby how she could possibly have survived her challenging life without acquiring those seemingly unfeminine attributes.

'You want to meet the child?' Stevos stepped in quickly before war broke out again between his companions and wasted more time.

A sudden smile broke across Tabby's face like sunshine, and Acheron studied her intently, scanning her delicate features, realising that there could be an attractive female beneath the facade of bolshie belligerence. He liked women feminine, really, *really* feminine. She was crude and unkempt and the guardian of Olympia's granddaughter, he reminded himself doggedly, striving to concentrate on the most important element of the equation. And that was the child, *Amber*. He cursed the fact that he had not known of the connection sooner, cursed his own innate aversion to being tied down by anything other than business. He had no relatives, no loving relationships, no responsibility outside his company and that was how he liked his life. But not at the expense of basic decency. And his recollection of Olympia, who had frequently been kind and friendly to a boy everyone else had viewed as pure trouble, remained one of the few *good* memories Ash had of his childhood.

'Yes. I want to see the child as soon as possible,' Acheron confirmed.

Tabby tilted her head to one side, taken aback by his change of heart. 'What changed your mind?'

'I should have personally checked into her circumstances when I was informed of the guardianship,' Acheron breathed grimly, angry with himself for once at the elaborate and very protective support system around him that ensured that he was never troubled by too much detail about anything that might take his mind off business. 'But I will take care of that oversight now and be warned, Miss Glover, I will not support your application to adopt the little girl unless I reach the conclusion that you *are* a suitable carer. Thank you for your help, Stevos, but not for that last suggestion you made...' Sardonic dark eyes met the lawyer's frowning gaze. 'I'm afraid that idea belongs in fantasy land.'

CHAPTER TWO

'I COULD'VE DONE with some advance warning before you came to visit,' Tabby remarked thinly, after giving the uniformed chauffeur the address of the basement flat where she was currently staying, courtesy of her friend, Jack.

Jack, Sonia and Tabby had become fast friends and pseudo-siblings after passing their teenaged years in the same foster home.

Tabby eased slowly into the leather upholstered back seat of Acheron's unspeakably fancy limousine and studiously avoided staring starstruck at her surroundings but, dear heaven, it was a challenge not to stare at the built-in bar and entertainment centre. She had, however, enjoyed a mean moment of glorious one-upmanship when she sailed out of the front doors of the DT building with the doors held open by the same security guards who had, the hour before, manhandled her on the top floor.

'Obviously a warning would've been unwise. I need to see how you live without you putting on a special show for my benefit,' Acheron responded smoothly, flipping out a laptop onto the small table that emerged at the stab of a button from the division between front and back seats.

Tabby gritted her teeth at that frank admission. Any

kind of fake special show was not an option open to her in the tiny bedsit that she was currently sharing with Amber. It was purely thanks to Jack, who was a small-time builder and property developer, that she still had Amber with her and had not already been forced to move into a hostel for the homeless and give up Sonia's daughter. It hurt that her long-term friendship with Sonia counted for nothing next to the remote blood tie Acheron Dimitrakos had shared with Troy. What had they been? Troy's gran had been a cousin of Acheron's mother, so Acheron was what…a third cousin or something in relation to Amber? Yet Tabby had known and loved Sonia since she was ten years old. They had met in the children's institution where they were both terrorised by the older kids. Tabby, having grown up in a violent home, had been much more used to defending herself than the younger girl. Sonia, after all, had once been a loved child in a decent family and tragically orphaned by the accident in which her parents died. In comparison, Tabby had been forcibly removed by the authorities from an abusive home and no longer knew whether her parents were alive or dead. There had been a few supervised visits with them after she was first taken away, many attempts to rehabilitate her mother and father and cobble the family back together, but in reality her parents proved to be more attached to their irresponsible lifestyle than they had ever been to their child.

Acheron Dimitrakos worked steadily at his laptop, making no effort to start up a conversation. Tabby compressed her generous mouth and studied him. She knew he had already decided that she was a rubbish person from the very bottom of the social pile. She knew he had taken one look and made judgements based on her appearance...and, doubtless, her use of bad language, she conceded with a sneaking feeling of shame.

But then she doubted he knew what it felt like to be almost at the end of your tether. He was so...self-possessed, she decided resentfully, her violet gaze wandering over his bold bronzed profile, noting the slight curl in his thick black hair where it rested behind his ear and the extraordinary length of his dense inky-black eyelashes as he scrutinised the screen in front of him. Imagine a boyfriend with more impressive lashes than you have yourself, she ruminated, unimpressed, her soft mouth curling with disdain.

It annoyed her that he looked even more gorgeous in the flesh than he had in the magazine photographs. She had believed the photos must've been airbrushed to enhance his dark good looks but the evidence to the contrary was right before her. He had high aristocratic cheekbones, a perfectly straight nose and the wide, sensual mouth of a classic Greek statue. He was also extremely tall, broad-shouldered, narrow-hipped and long-legged—in fact, he was graced with every attractive male attribute possible.

Not a nice, caring person though, she reasoned staunchly, determined to concentrate on his flaws. Indeed, thinking of how he had outright refused to take any interest in Troy and Sonia's daughter, it was a challenge to understand why he should be suddenly bothering to come and see Amber now. She decided that she had made him feel guilty and that, after all, he *had* to have a conscience. Did that mean that he would support her application to adopt Amber? And even more importantly, would his opinion carry any weight with Social Services?

Acheron could not concentrate, which annoyed the hell out of him. Tabby Glover never sat still, and the constant movements of her slight small body on the seat beside him were an irritating distraction. He was too observant, he thought impatiently as he noted the bitten nails on her small hands, the shabbiness of her training shoes, the worn denim of jeans stretched taut over slender thighs, and he suppressed a sigh. He was out of his depth and although he had told Stevos to return to his office he was not enjoying the course he had set himself on. After all, what did he know about a young child's needs? Why did he feel guilty that he had already made up his mind to the hard fact that this young woman was not a fit sole guardian for a baby girl?

When the car came to a halt, Tabby slid out of the limo and bounced down the steps to stick her key in the front door of the basement flat. *Here goes,* she conceded nervously as she spread wide the door.

Ash froze one step inside, aghast at the indoor building site that comprised her accommodation. There was scaffolding, buckets and tools lying around, wires dangling everywhere, plasterboard walls. Tabby thrust open the first door to the left of the entrance.

Acheron followed her into a small room, packed with furniture and a table bearing a kettle and mini-oven and scattered with crumbs. Baby equipment littered almost every other surface. A teenage girl was seated on the bed with work files spread around her and when she saw Tabby she gathered up her files with a smile and stood up to leave. 'Amber's been great. She had a snack, enjoyed her bottle and she's been changed.'

'Thanks, Heather,' Tabby said quietly to the girl who lived in the apartment above. 'I appreciate your help.'

The child was sitting up in the cot wedged between the bed and the wall on one side. Acheron surveyed the child from a safe distance, noting the mop of black curls, the big brown eyes and the instant dazzling smile that rewarded Tabby's appearance.

'How's my darling girl?' Tabby asked, leaning over the cot to scoop up the little girl and hug her tight. Chubby arms wrapped round her throat while curious brown eyes inspected Acheron over Tabby's shoulder.

'What age is she?' Ash enquired.

'You should know,' Tabby said drily. 'She's over six months old.'

'Do the authorities know you're keeping her here?'

A flush of uneasy colour warmed Tabby's cheeks as she sat down on the bed because Amber was getting heavier by the day. 'No. I gave them Jack's address. He's a friend and he bought this apartment to renovate and sell on. He's allowing us to stay here out of the goodness of his heart. He hasn't the space for us at his own place.'

'How can you live in such a squalid dwelling with a young child and believe that you're doing the best you can for her?' Acheron condemned.

'Well, for a start, it's not squalid!' Tabby flared defensively and hurriedly rose to set Amber back into her cot. 'It's clean. We have heating and light and there's a fully functional bathroom through that door.' She pointed a hand to the opposite wall, and the gesture fell down in effectiveness because her arm shook and she hurriedly lowered it again. Tears were suddenly stinging the back of her eyes, and her head was starting to thump with the onset of a stress headache. 'For the moment I'm just doing the best I can but we're *managing*.'

'But you're not managing well enough,' Ash stated curtly. 'You shouldn't be keeping a young child in accommodation like this.'

Her brow pulsing with the band of tension tightening round it, Tabby lifted her hands to release the weight of her hair from the ponytail. Acheron watched a torrent of long blonde hair fall down to her waist and finally saw something he liked about her appearance: blonde hair that was natural unless he was very much mistaken, for that pale mass had no dark roots or streaky highlights.

'I'm doing the very best I can,' Tabby countered firmly, wondering why he was staring at her, her self-conscious streak on override, her pride still hurting from the 'squalid' comment.

'And how are you supporting yourself?' Acheron asked with a curled lip.

'I'm still cleaning. I didn't lose all my clients when I had to close my business down, and those I kept I'm still working for. I take Amber with me to the jobs. Most of my clients are out at work anyway so her coming with me doesn't bother them,' she admitted grudgingly. 'Take a look at her. She's clean and well fed and happy. We're rarely apart.'

Ash assimilated the information with a grim twist of his expressive mouth. 'I'm sorry, but your best isn't good enough. Nothing I've seen here will convince me otherwise. You don't have a proper home for the child. You're clearly living on the poverty line—'

'Money isn't everything!' Tabby protested. 'I love her and she loves me.'

Ash watched the slender blonde lean over the cot rail to gently stroke the little girl's head and saw the answering sunny smile that the gesture evoked. No such love or tenderness had featured in his childhood experience, and he fully recognised the fact, but he was also bone-deep practical and not given to changing his mind mid-course. 'Love isn't enough on its own. If you had a supportive family to back you and a proper home to raise her in I might feel differently, but you on your own with her in this dismal room and dragging her out with you to cleaning jobs is *wrong*,' he pronounced with strong conviction. 'She could do better than this, she *should* have better than this and it is *her* needs and not your own that you should be weighing in the balance.'

'Are you saying that I'm selfish?' Tabby prompted in disbelief, because she had given up so much that was important to her to take care first of Sonia, after she had suffered her first stroke, and ultimately her baby daughter.

Beneath the shocked onslaught of eyes the colour of rain-washed amethysts, Acheron's stubborn jaw line clenched hard and his mouth compressed. 'Yes. You have obviously done the best you can and given her continuity of care since her mother's death but now it's time for you to step back and put her best interests ahead of your own personal feelings.'

The tears glistening in Tabby's eyes overflowed, marking silvery trails on her cheeks, and for the first time in years Acheron felt like a real bastard and yet he had only told the truth as he saw it. *I love her and she loves me.* Yes, he could see the strength of the bond before him but it couldn't cover up the cracks in the long-term struggle for survival he saw for them both. Olympia's grandchild deserved more. Yet how did he put a price on the love and then dismiss it as if it were worthless?

'What age are you?' he pressed.

'Twenty-five.'

'I should've dealt with this situation when it first came up,' Acheron acknowledged grimly, thinking that she was surely far too young and immature to take on such a burden and that he should have taken immediate action to resolve the situation the instant the guardianship issue arose. It was his fault that Tabby Glover had been left to struggle on with the child while becoming more and more dangerously attached to her charge.

'Not if it meant parting Amber and me sooner,' Tabby argued. 'Can't you understand how much I care about her? Her mother and I became best friends when we were kids, and I'll be able to share my memories of her parents with her when she's old enough to want that information. Surely there's something you could do to help?'

But on a personal level, Acheron didn't want to be involved. He always avoided emotional situations and responsibilities that fell outside company business, and it had been that very detachment that had first roused his late father's concern that his only son should have set himself on such a solitary path.

Tabby searched Acheron's handsome features, marvelling at his masculine perfection even as she appraised the glitter of his dark-as-jet eyes and the hard tension round his wide, sensual mouth. 'I'll do anything it takes to keep her...'

Acheron frowned, his brow furrowing. 'What's that supposed to mean?'

'What do you think? I'm desperate to keep Amber. If you have any suggestions on how I can be a better parent to her, I'm willing to listen and take advice,' Tabby extended with the new-found humility of fear.

'I thought you were offering me sex,' Acheron confided bluntly.

'Seriously?' Tabby gasped in shock at that misconception. 'Does that happen to you a lot? I mean...women... just offering?'

Acheron nodded cool confirmation.

Her violet eyes widened in astonishment and she lifted her head, pale blonde hair cascading in a silken tangle round her shoulders with the movement. In the space of a split second she travelled from *possibly* pretty to decidedly beautiful in Acheron's estimation, and desire kindled; a desire he neither wanted nor intended to act on. His body was stubborn, though, and the pulse of heaviness at his groin was utterly disobedient to his brain, throwing up outrageous images of her lying on his bed, that lovely swathe of hair spread over his chest, that lush mouth gainfully employed in pleasuring him. He gritted his perfect white teeth, suppressing the outrageous fantasy, furiously conscious of the child's innocent presence and his unprecedented loss of self-discipline.

'Women just offer themselves? No wonder you're so full of yourself,' Tabby remarked helplessly, aware of the tension in the atmosphere, but unsure of its source as she stared back at him. She liked looking at him, didn't know why or exactly what it was about those lean sculpted features that fascinated her so much. But as she collided with his stunning dark-as-midnight gaze, liquid warmth surged between her legs and her nipples tightened, a message even she couldn't ignore or deny. He attracted her. The filthy rich Greek with his dazzling good looks and hard-as-granite heart *attracted* her. How foolish and deceptive physical chemistry could be, she reflected ruefully, embarrassment colouring her pale cheeks.

I'll do anything it takes to keep her... And suddenly Acheron, rigid with the force of his self-control, was reasoning with a new and unfamiliar sense of freedom to think outside the box and he was thinking, Why not? Why the hell not? Possibly Stevos's bright idea had not been as off the wall as it had first seemed. He and this strange girl both wanted something from each other, and he could certainly ensure that Amber benefitted from the deal in every way, thereby satisfying his uneasy conscience where the child was concerned.

'There *is* a way you could keep Amber with you.' Ash dangled the bait straight away, as always impatient to plunge to the heart of the matter.

Tabby leant forward where she sat, wide violet eyes intent on him. *'How?'*

'We could apply as a couple to adopt her—'

Thoroughly disconcerted by that unexpected suggestion, Tabby blinked. 'As a couple?'

'With my backing it could be achieved but we would need to be married first,' Ash delivered smoothly, deciding there and then that he would not admit the truth that he would have a great deal riding on the arrangement as well. That acknowledgement would tip the power balance between them and he refused to take that unnecessary risk and find himself being blackmailed. The less she knew, the less power she would have.

Astonishment was stamped on her small oval face. *'Married?'*

'For the sake of the adoption application. I should think that the most traditional approach would have the likeliest and quickest chance of success.'

'Let me get this straight…you're saying you would be willing to marry me to help me get permission to adopt Amber?' Tabby breathed in frank disbelief.

Acheron dealt her a sardonic look. 'Naturally I'm not suggesting a proper marriage. I'm suggesting the legal ceremony and a joint application to adopt her. We would then only have to give the appearance that we are living below the same roof for as long as it takes to complete the proceedings.'

So, not a real marriage, a *fake* one, she mused, but even so she was still transfixed by the concept and the idea that he might be willing to go to such lengths to help her. 'But why would you do that for us? A couple of months ago, you simply dismissed the idea that you could have any obligation towards Amber.'

'I wasn't aware then that she was Olympia Carolis's grandchild—'

'Olympia...who?' Tabby queried blankly.

'Troy's mother. I only knew her by the name she had before she married. I knew her when I was a child because she worked for my mother and lived with us,' Acheron volunteered with pronounced reluctance. 'I lost all contact with that side of the family after my mother died. But I liked Olympia. She was a good woman.'

'Yet you don't have the slightest true interest in Amber,' Tabby commented with a frown of incomprehension. 'You haven't even tried to hold her.'

'I'm not accustomed to babies and I don't want to frighten her,' Acheron excused himself glibly and watched her process his polite lie. 'I should've taken a greater interest in the child when I was first informed that I was one of her guardians. Your situation would not have reached crisis point had I accepted that commitment and taken my share of the responsibility.'

His admission of fault soothed Tabby, who had not been prepared for that amount of candour from him. He had made a mistake and was man enough to acknowledge it, an attitude that she respected. He had also moved a step closer to the cot and Amber, always a friendly baby, was beaming up at him in clear expectation of being lifted. But his lean brown hands clenched into taut stillness by his side, and she recognised that if anyone was frightened it was not Amber, it was *him*. Of course, he was an only child, and she assumed he had had little contact with young children because his rigid inhibited stance close to the baby spoke loudly for him.

'So, you've changed your mind and you think I should adopt her?'

'Not quite that,' Ash declared levelly. 'If we go ahead with this, I will be on the spot to oversee Amber's welfare and if I'm satisfied that you're a capable mother, I will release her fully into your care after we divorce. Naturally I will also ensure that when we part you have a proper home to raise her in.'

In other words, she would be on probation as a parent for the duration of the fake marriage, which was not good news on her terms. But Acheron Dimitrakos had to *really* care about what happened to Amber to be willing to get so involved and make such a sacrifice as marrying a stranger for the child's benefit alone, she thought ruefully, suddenly ashamed of her prejudices about him.

He would be killing two birds with one stone, Ash decided with satisfaction, solving all his problems in one decisive act. He would choose a discreet location for the ceremony but at the same time, if anyone was to be expected to believe that they were a couple and the marriage genuine, she would have to undergo a major makeover first.

'I'll take you home with me now,' Acheron pronounced. 'Bring the baby...leave everything else. My staff will pack your possessions.'

'Are you joking? Walk out the door with a strange man and move in with him?' Tabby breathed in stark disbelief. 'Do I look that naive and trusting?'

Acheron studied her levelly. 'You only get one chance with me and, I warn you, I'm not a patient man. I can't leave you and the child living here like this and, if we decide to go ahead with the marriage and adoption plan, there are things to be done, forms to be filled in without further waste of time.'

Tabby leapt up. As he shifted his feet in their highly polished leather shoes and elevated a sleek black brow in expectation he emanated impatience in invisible sparks, filling the atmosphere with tension. He thought he was doing her a favour and that she ought to jump to attention and follow his instructions and, because that was true, she wasn't going to argue with him. In fact, just for once, she was going to keep her ready tongue glued to the roof of her mouth and play nice to keep him happy and willing to help. Yes, she would trust him, but common sense suggested that a male as rich and gorgeous as he was had many more tempting sexual outlets than a woman as ordinary as she was.

'OK...' Tabby stuffed nappies and bottles and a tub of formula milk into the worn baby bag, and threaded Amber's chubby arms into a jacket that was slightly too small before strapping her into the car seat that she had had no use for since she had had to sell her car.

Acheron was already on his phone to his PA, telling her to engage an emergency nanny because he had no plans to trail the baby out shopping with them. The deal was done, only the details had to be dealt with now and he was in his element.

Ash stayed on the phone for the first ten minutes of their journey, rapping out instructions, making arrangements, telling Stevos to make a start on the paperwork. For the first time in a week he felt he was back in control of his life and it felt good. He stole a reluctant glance at Tabby, engaged in keeping Amber occupied by pointing out things through the windows. The awareness that Tabby Glover was going to prove very useful to him compressed his hard mouth because he was convinced that she would be difficult.

'Where are you taking us?' she asked, still in something of a daze after that discussion about adoption and marriage. She was scarcely able to credit that her and Amber's luck had turned a magical corner because Acheron Dimitrakos bore not the slightest resemblance to a fairy godmother.

'Back to my apartment where we will drop off... Amber,' Acheron advanced warily.

'And who are you planning to drop her off with? Your staff? *That's* not going to happen,' Tabby began forcefully.

'I have organised a nanny, who will be waiting for us. We will then go shopping to buy you some clothes.'

'Amber doesn't need a nanny and I don't need clothes.'

Acheron treated her to a scornful dark appraisal that burned colour into her cheeks. 'You're hardly dressed suitably. If we're to put on a convincing act, you need clothes,' he contradicted.

Anger flared in her violet eyes and her head turned sharply. 'I *don't* need—'

'Just say the word and I'll return you both to your clean and comfy basement,' Acheron told her in a lethally quiet tone of warning.

Tabby sucked in a sudden deep breath and held it, recognising that she was trapped, something she never ever allowed herself to be because being trapped meant being vulnerable. But if she said no, refused to toe the line, she would lose Amber for good. There would be no coming back from that development because once Amber was removed from her care, she would be gone for all time.

Had Acheron Dimitrakos been right to censure her selfishness in wanting to keep Sonia's daughter as her own? It was a painful thought. She hated to think that he could know better about anything but she knew that outsiders often saw more clearly than those directly involved. All she had to offer Amber was love, and he had said love wasn't enough. But Tabby valued love much more highly because she hadn't received it as a child and had often longed for the warm sense of acceptance, well-being and security that a loving parent could bestow. Only time would tell if Amber herself would agree that Tabby had made the wisest decision on her behalf.

Amber hugged Tabby in the lift on the way up to Acheron's apartment, the little girl clinging in reaction to Tabby's increasing tension. Acheron stood poised in the far corner of the mirrored compartment, a comfortable six feet three inches of solid masculine detachment. Tabby studied him in growing frustration, noting the aloof quality in his gaze, the forbidding cool of his lean, strong face. He was so unemotional about everything that he infuriated her. Here she was awash with conflicting emotions, terrified she was doing the wrong thing, putting her feelings rather than Amber's needs first…and whose fault was that? She had not doubted her ability to be a good mother until Acheron Dimitrakos crossed her path. Now she was facing the challenge of also surrendering her pride and her independence to meet his expectations.

'I don't think this is going to work,' she told him helplessly. 'We mix like oil and water.'

'A meeting of true minds is not required,' Ash imparted with sardonic bite. 'Stop arguing about every little thing. That irritates me.'

'A nanny is not a little thing. Who is she?'

'A highly trained professional from a reputable source. I would not put the child at risk.'

His intense dark eyes challenged her, and she looked away, her cheeks burning, her mouth dry, her grip on

Amber still a little tighter than it needed to be. For a split second she felt as though Amber were the only sure element left in the world that he was tearing apart and threatening to rebuild. He intimidated her, a truth that made her squirm. Yet he was willing to help her keep Amber, she reminded herself doggedly, and that should be her bottom line. Whatever it took she should bite the bullet and focus on the end game, not how bad it might feel getting there.

'Won't the sort of marriage you suggested be illegal?' she heard herself ask him abruptly. 'You know, a marriage that's just a fake?'

'Why would it be illegal?' he countered with icy cool. 'What goes on within any marriage is private.'

'But our marriage would be an act of deception.'

'You're splitting hairs. No one would be harmed by the deception. The marriage would simply present us as a conventional couple keen to adopt.'

'You're hopelessly out of date. Lots of couples don't get married these days,' Tabby pointed out.

'In my family we always get married when it comes to child-rearing,' Acheron told her smoothly.

That's right, remind me that I'm not from the same world! Tabby thought furiously, a flush of antagonism warming her face as embarrassment threatened to swallow her alive. Her parents had not been married and had probably never even thought of getting married to regularise her birth.

Her gaze strayed inexorably back to him until she connected with smoky dark deep-set eyes that made her tummy lurch and leap and heat rise in her pelvis. There was just something about him, she thought furiously, dragging her attention from him as the lift doors whirred open and she hastily stepped out into a hallway, something shockingly sexy and dangerous that broke through her defences. She did not understand how he could act like an unfeeling block of superior ice and still have that effect on her.

CHAPTER THREE

THE NANNY, COMPLETE with a uniform that suggested she belonged to the very highest echelon of qualified nannies, awaited Acheron and Tabby in the spacious hall of Acheron's apartment and within minutes she had charmed Amber out of Tabby's arms and borne her off.

'Let's go,' Acheron urged impatiently. 'We have a lot to accomplish.'

'I don't like shopping,' Tabby breathed, literally cringing at the prospect of him paying for her clothes.

'Neither do I. In fact, usually the closest I get to shopping with a woman is giving her a credit card,' Acheron confided silkily. 'But I don't trust you to buy the right stuff.'

Mutinously silent as she slid back into the waiting limousine in the underground car park, Tabby shrugged a slight shoulder, determined not to battle with him when it was a battle she could not win. Even so, he could dress her up all he liked but it wouldn't change the person she truly was. No, she would be sensible and look on the clothing as a necessary prop for their masquerade, another move in what already felt more like a game than reality because in no realistic dimension did a girl like her marry a guy as rich and good-looking as him.

A personal shopper awaited them at Harrods where,

surprisingly enough, Acheron appeared to be in his element. Tabby did not attempt to impose her opinions and she hovered while Acheron pointed out what he liked and the correct size was lifted from the rail. She soon found herself in a changing cubicle with a heap of garments.

'Come out,' Ash instructed impatiently. 'I want to see you in the pink dress.'

Suppressing a groan, Tabby snaked into the classy little cocktail frock, reached down to flip off her socks and walked barefoot out of the cubicle.

Acheron frowned as she came to a halt and he strolled round her, staring at her slight figure in surprise. 'I didn't realise you were so tiny.'

Tabby gnawed at her lower lip, knowing she had skipped too many meals in recent months, painfully aware that she was too thin and that what delicate curves she had possessed had shrunk along with any excess body fat. 'I'm a lot stronger than I look,' she said defensively.

Acheron studied her doll-like dimensions with unabashed interest, his narrowed gaze running from her fragile shoulders down to her pale slender legs. He could've easily lifted her with one hand. He liked curves on a woman yet there was an aesthetically pleasing aspect to the pure delicacy of her build. Her breasts barely made an indent in the bodice of the dress and her hips made no imprint at all. Yet with that tousled mane of long blonde hair highlighting her pale oval face and bright violet eyes, she looked unusual and extraordinarily appealing. He wondered if he would crush her in bed and then squashed that crazy thought dead because sex would naturally not be featuring in their agreement. As she turned away, he froze, taken aback by the sight of the colourful rose tattoo marring the pale skin of her left forearm.

'That dress won't do,' Acheron told the assistant thinly. 'She needs a dress with sleeves to cover that.'

Gooseflesh crept over Tabby's exposed skin, and she clamped a hand over the skin marking she had forgotten about. Beneath her fingers she could feel the rougher skin of the scar tissue that the tattoo pretty much concealed from view, and her heart dropped to the pit of her stomach, remembered feelings of bitter pain and heartache gripping her in spite of the years that had passed since the wound was first inflicted. She had made the clear considered choice that she could live better with the tattoo than she could with that constant reminder of her wretched childhood catching her unawares every time she looked in the mirror. Of course, the skin ink wasn't perfect because the skin surface beneath it was far from perfect and the tattooist had warned her of the fact in advance. As it was, the rose, albeit a little blurred in its lines, had done the job it was designed to do, hiding the scar and providing a burial place for the bad memories. Only very rarely did Tabby think about it.

'How could you disfigure your body with that?' Acheron demanded in a driven undertone, his revulsion unhidden.

'It's of a good luck charm. I've had it for years,' Tabby told him unsteadily, her face pale and set.

The personal shopper was already approaching with a long-sleeved dress, and Tabby returned to the cubicle, her skin clammy now with the aftermath of shock—the shock of being forced back, however briefly, into her violent past. The rose was her lucky charm, which concealed the vivid reminder of what could happen when you loved someone unworthy of that trust. So, he didn't like tattoos; well, what was that to her? She put on the new dress, smoothed down the sleeves and, mustering her self-possession, she emerged again.

Acheron stared her up and down, his beautiful face curiously intent. Heat blossomed in her cheeks as he studied her with smouldering dark eyes, his tension palpable. Desire flickered low in her pelvis like kindling yearning for a spark, and she felt that craving shoot through every fibre of her body, from the dryness of her mouth to the swelling sensitivity of her nipples and the honeyed heat between her thighs. It made her feel light-headed and oddly intoxicated, and she blinked rapidly, severely disconcerted by the feelings.

'That will do,' he pronounced thickly.

She wanted to touch him so badly she had to clench her hands into fists to prevent herself from reaching out and making actual contact. She felt like a wasp being drawn to a honey trap and fiercely fought her reactions with every scrap of self-control left to her. Don't touch, *don't touch*, a little voice warned in the back of her head, but evidently he was listening to a different voice as he stalked closer and reached for her hands, pulling them into his, urging her closer, forcing her fingers to loosen within his grasp.

And Tabby looked up at him and froze, literally not daring to breathe. That close his eyes were no longer dark but a downright amazing and glorious swirl of honey, gold and caramel tones, enhanced by the spiky black lashes she envied. His fingers were feathering over hers with a gentleness she had not expected from so big and powerful a man and little tremors of response were filtering through her, undermining her self-control. She knew she wanted those expert hands on her body exploring much more secret places, and colour rose in her cheeks because she also knew she was out of her depth and drowning. In an abrupt movement, she wrenched her hands free and turned away, momentarily shutting her eyes in a gesture of angry self-loathing.

'Try on the rest of the clothes,' Acheron instructed coolly, not a flicker of lingering awareness in his dark deep voice.

Hot-faced, Tabby vanished back into the cubicle. Evidently he pressed all her buttons, and she had to stop letting him do that to her, had to stand firm. Of course he was sexy: he was a womaniser. He had insulted her with that crack about her tattoo and had then somehow switched that moment into something else by catching her hands in his and just looking at her. But she wasn't some impressionable little airhead vulnerable to the merest hint of interest from an attractive man, was she? Well, she *was* a virgin, she acknowledged grudgingly, as always stifling her unease about that glaring lack in her experience with men. After all she had not intentionally chosen to retain her virginity; it had just happened that way. No man had ever succeeded in making her want to get that close to him, and she had no plans to share a bed with someone simply to find out what it was like.

And then Acheron Dimitrakos had come along and turned everything she thought she knew on its head. For, although he attracted her, she didn't like him and didn't trust him either, so what did that say about her? That she had a reckless streak just like her long-lost and unlamented parents?

Tension seethed through Acheron. What the hell was the matter with him? He had been on the edge of crushing that soft, luscious mouth beneath his, close to wrecking the non-sexual relationship he envisaged between them. Impersonal would work the best and it shouldn't be that difficult, he reasoned impatiently, for they had nothing in common.

He watched her emerge again, clad in cropped wool trousers, high heels and a slinky little burgundy cashmere cardigan. She looked really good. She cleaned up incredibly well, he acknowledged grudgingly, gritting his teeth together as his gaze instinctively dropped to the sweet pouting swell of her small breasts beneath the clingy top.

He had done what he had to do, he reminded himself grimly. She was perfect for his purposes, for she had as much riding on the success of their arrangement as he had. Thankfully nothing in his life was going to change in the slightest: he had found the perfect wife, a non-wife…

He left Tabby alone with the shopper in the lingerie department and she chose the basics before heading for the children's department and choosing an entire new wardrobe for Amber, her heart singing at the prospect of seeing the little girl in new clothes that fitted her properly. The chauffeur saw to the stowing of her many bags in the capacious boot of the limousine, and she climbed in beside Acheron, who was talking on the phone in French. She recognised the language from lessons at school and raised her brows. So, that was at least *three* languages he spoke: Greek, English and now French. She refused to be impressed.

'We'll dine out tonight,' Acheron pronounced, putting the phone away.

'Why the heck would you want to do that?' Tabby demanded in dismay at the prospect.

'If we want to give the appearance of a normal couple, we need to be seen out together. Wear that dress.'

'Oh…' Tabby said nothing more while she wondered what social horrors dining out with him would entail.

She had never eaten out in a fancy restaurant, having always cravenly avoided such formal occasions, intimidated by the prospect of too much cutlery and superior serving staff, who would surely quickly spot that she was a takeaway girl at heart.

Two hours later, having showered and changed, Acheron opened the safe in his bedroom wall to remove a ring case he hadn't touched in years. The fabled emerald, which had reputedly once adorned a maharajah's crown, had belonged to his late mother and would do duty as an engagement ring. The very thought of putting the priceless jewel on Tabby's finger chilled Acheron's anti-commitment gene to the marrow, and he squared his broad shoulders, grateful that the engagement and the marriage that would follow would be one hundred per cent fake.

'Fine feathers make fine birds' had been one of her last foster mother's favourite sayings, Tabby recalled as she put on mascara, guiltily enjoying the fact that she had both the peace and the time to use cosmetics again. Make-up had been one of the first personal habits to fall by the wayside once she took on full-time care of Amber. But the nanny had been hired to work until eleven that night, leaving Amber free to dress up and go out like a lady of leisure. A *lady*? She grimaced at the word, doubting she could ever match that lofty description, and ran a brush through her freshly washed hair before grabbing the clutch that matched the shoes and leaving the room.

Acheron's apartment was vast, much bigger than she had expected. Tabby and Amber had been relegated to rooms at the very foot of the bedroom corridor, well away from the main reception areas as well as the principal bedroom suite, which seemed to be sited up a spiral staircase off the main hall. Acheron Dimitrakos lived like a king, she conceded with a shake of her head, wide-eyed at the opulence of the furnishings surrounding her and the fresh flowers blooming on every surface. They truly did come from different worlds. But the one trait they shared, she sensed, was an appreciation of hard slog and its rewards, so she hoped he would understand why she needed to continue to work.

'Put it on,' Acheron advised in the hall, planting an emerald ring unceremoniously into the palm of her hand.

Tabby frowned down at the gleaming jewel. 'What's it for?'

'Engagement ring...marriage?' Acheron groaned. 'Sometimes you're very slow on the uptake.'

Tabby rammed the beautiful ring down over her knuckle and squinted down at it, her colour high. 'I didn't know we were going for frills. I assumed you would choose more of a basic-package approach.'

'Since we'll be getting married pretty quickly and without a big splash our charade needs to look more convincing from the outset.'

'I'm already living with you and wearing clothes you bought for me,' she parried flatly. 'Isn't that enough of a show?'

'Many couples live together without marrying, many women have worn clothing I paid for,' Acheron derided. 'What we have has to look more serious.'

The restaurant was dimly lit and intimate and their table probably the best in the room. Certainly the attention that came their way from the staff was so constant that Tabby found it almost claustrophobic. Having studiously ignored her during the drive while talking on his phone, Acheron finally allowed himself the indulgence of looking at his bride-to-be. Her blonde mane tumbled round her shoulders framing a vivid and delicate little face dominated by violet eyes and a lush fuchsia-tinted mouth. He couldn't take his eyes off that mouth, a mouth modelled to make a man think of sin and sinning.

'How am I performing so far as your dress-up doll?' Tabby enquired mockingly to take her mind off the fact that she had still not established which knife and fork to use with the salad being brought to them.

'You answer back too much but you look amazing in the right clothes,' Acheron conceded, startling her with that compliment. 'So far I'm very satisfied with our bargain, and you can be assured that I will play my part.'

As he reached for one fork she reached for another and then changed course mid-movement, her gaze welded to his lean brown hands. *Just copy him*, her brain urged her.

'I've applied for a special licence. The legalities should be in place in time for the ceremony to be held on Thursday,' Acheron delivered. 'My lawyer is making all the arrangements and has contacted Social Services on our behalf with regard to our plans for Amber.'

'My word, he's a fast mover,' Tabby remarked breathlessly.

'You told me you didn't want the child to go into foster care,' he reminded her.

Her skin turned clammy at that daunting reminder of the unknown destination that would have awaited Amber had Tabby not gained his support. 'I don't but there are things we still haven't discussed. What am I supposed to do while we're pretending to be married?'

A winged ebony brow lifted. '*Do*? Nothing. You concentrate on being a mother and occasionally a wife. I will expect you to make a couple of appearances with me at public events. That is the sole commitment you have to make to me.'

'That's great because I want to start up my business again…in a small way,' Tabby admitted abruptly.

His handsome features clenched hard. 'No. That's out of the question. The child deserves a full-time mother.'

Tabby couldn't believe her ears. 'Most mothers work—'

'I will cover your financial requirements,' Acheron delivered with unquenchable cool. 'For the foreseeable future you will put the child's needs first and you will not work.'

Tabby gritted her teeth. 'I don't want to take your money.'

'Tough,' Acheron slotted in succinctly.

'You can't tell me what I can and can't do.'

'Can't I?'

Tabby's pulse had quickened until it felt as if it were beating in the foot of her throat, obstructing her ability to breathe and speak. Frustrated rage lay behind her choked silence as she stared across the table at him, her small face taut and pale. He was pulling strings as if she were a puppet. And wasn't she exactly that?

A chill settled over her rage, safely enclosing it. He was willing to help her to adopt Amber and she was stuck with his outdated idealistic attitude whether she liked it or not. Yes, she could walk away from him but if she did so she would also be walking away from the child she loved. And that, Tabby reflected hollowly, she could not do.

Amber had tugged at Tabby's heartstrings from the day she was born and Sonia was too weak, having suffered her first stroke within hours of the birth, even to hold her daughter. Consequently, for as long as Tabby needed Acheron's support she would have to conform to *his* expectations. Facing and accepting that ugly frightening truth had to be one of the most humbling experiences Tabby had ever known because it ran contrary to every tenet she had lived by since adulthood. The threat of no longer being in full charge of her life genuinely terrified Tabby.

'You seem to have lost your appetite,' Ash remarked, watching her move the food around her plate without lifting anything to her ripe pink mouth.

It was a steak cooked rare, not the way she liked it. But then she had coped with the menu being written in pretentious French simply by making the exact same menu choices as he had.

'You killed my appetite,' Tabby countered thinly.

A forbidding look flitted across his chiselled features. 'If restarting your business means that much to you, you should give up your desire to adopt a child, who will need much more of your time than you could give her as an independent businesswoman.'

Well, that certainly put his point of view across, Tabby conceded ruefully, sipping her water, ignoring the full wineglass beside it. She never touched alcohol, didn't trust the effect it might have on her, feared it might even awaken a craving she might find hard to control. She couldn't argue with Acheron Dimitrakos because setting up her business again *would* demand a great deal of her time. She compressed her lips, reasonably certain she could've coped without short-changing Amber but questioning for the first time whether or not that would have been fair to the child she loved. After all, she had personally never enjoyed the luxury of being a full-time mother and perhaps it would be more sensible to give that lifestyle a shot rather than dismissing it out of hand.

'Are we on the same page?' Acheron Dimitrakos asked impatiently over the cheese and crackers.

Mouth full at last of something she wanted to eat, Tabby nodded while trying not to imagine what it would feel like to be financially dependent on a man for the first time in her life.

As they emerged from the restaurant, Acheron banded an arm round her stiff spine, and she blinked in bewilderment at the daunting acknowledgement that they were literally surrounded by photographers. 'Smile,' he instructed her flatly.

And, hating it, she did as she was told.

'What was that all about?' she demanded once they were driving away.

'Public proof of our relationship,' Acheron supplied drily. 'There'll be an announcement of our engagement in *The Times* tomorrow.'

What relationship? Tabby thought with wry amusement. He said jump, she said how high? That was not a relationship, it was a dictatorship, but possibly he didn't know the difference.

The plaintive cry roused Acheron from a sound sleep. He listened for a while but the noise continued. After a moment, he rolled out of bed with a curse on his lips and reached the bedroom door, before groaning out loud and stalking back to rummage through a drawer and extract a pair of jeans. He hated having guests. He hated any interruption to his usual routine. But Tabby was a better option than a real wife, he reminded himself with satisfaction, and a good deal less likely to develop ambitious ideas about hanging on to her privileged position.

He pushed open the door of the nursery and saw the baby in the cot. It was kicking its arms and legs in furious activity, its little face screwed up as it loosed a wail that would have wakened the dead. Only, apparently, not her wannabe adoptive mother. Ash hovered by the cot, his wide, sensual mouth on a downward curve. The baby sat up in a flash and looked expectant, even lifted its arms as if she expected him to haul her to freedom. It looked far too lively for a baby supposed to be sleeping.

'No more crying,' Ash decreed firmly. 'I don't like crying.'

The baby's arms lowered, its rosebud mouth jutting out in a pout while its bright brown eyes studied him uncertainly.

'You see, crying gets you nowhere,' Ash explained helpfully.

Another heartbroken sob emanated from the baby. She looked incredibly sad and lonely, and Ash stifled a groan.

'Aren't you going to lift her? She needs comforting,' Tabby murmured from the doorway, studying the little tableau of inflexible male and needy baby. It was infuriating to register that she couldn't take her eyes off him when he was wearing only a pair of jeans. He had a six-pack that could have rivalled a top athlete's and his lean, muscular bronzed chest was state-of-the-art perfection, showcasing a male body that could have played a starring role in any female fantasy.

'Why would I lift her?' Ash enquired with a raised brow, flashing her a glance and noticing in that one brief look that she was wearing a pale nightdress that revealed more than it concealed of her tiny body while she stood with her back turned to the light in the corridor. He glimpsed delicate little pink nipples and a pale shadowy vee between her thighs, and his body reacted with instantaneous arousal.

'Because if you expect our adoption application to impress the powers-that-be, you need to be confident that you can handle Amber.'

'I will be perfectly confident if the situation demands that of me, but at this hour of the day it would be very unwise to remove her from the cot,' he declared. 'She's there for the whole night. It's two in the morning, in case you haven't noticed. Why raise her hopes by lifting her?'

Amber released another howl and, gripped by frustration, Tabby marched over to the cot, swept up the little girl and settled her without ceremony into Ash's arms. 'If she has a nightmare she needs comforting. She needs to know someone is there for her and a little cuddle usually soothes her.'

Amber was as shocked as Acheron to find herself in his arms. Wide brown eyes anxiously observed him. 'Cuddle?' Ash almost whispered the word in appalled disbelief. 'You actually expect me to cuddle her?'

CHAPTER FOUR

With a gasp of irritation, Tabby removed Amber from his awkward hold and pressed her close. 'Skin-to-skin contact is important,' she demonstrated, kissing Amber's hot brow.

'I'm not doing the kissing stuff either,' Acheron breathed witheringly.

'Then smooth her hair, rub her back, make her feel secure in other ways,' Tabby advised ruefully. 'Stop being so resistant to my suggestions.'

'And how do you suggest I do that? With a personality transplant?' Acheron derided. 'I'm no good with kids. I have no experience of that sort of affection.'

'It's never too late to learn,' Tabby told him with determination, settling Amber carefully back into his arms. 'Hold her closer, pet her. And please don't tell me you have no experience of petting women.'

'I don't pet them. I have sex with them. This is not an appropriate conversation to have around a child!' Acheron bit out in exasperation.

Picking up on his annoyance, Amber whimpered. He spread his fingers across her back in an uneasy rubbing motion.

'Bring her closer,' Tabby urged, approaching him to

tuck the baby into the curve of his shoulder. 'She's not going to bite.'

Acheron could never recall feeling quite so tense or uncomfortable. He knew what she wanted from him but he didn't want to do it. Then he thought of DT Industries, which would be one hundred per cent his only after the wedding, and he held the baby against him, deeming it a sacrifice worthy of such a result.

'And talk to her,' Tabby suggested.

'What about?' Acheron demanded with perfect seriousness, freezing as the baby nestled close of its own volition, disconcerted by the alien warmth and weight of her as she dug little hands into the flesh of his shoulder.

'Stocks and shares if you like. It doesn't matter at this age. It's the sound and tone of your voice that matters,' Tabby explained.

Acheron mumbled a Greek nursery rhyme.

'And if you walk around the room with her, it might make you feel more relaxed.'

Acheron gritted his teeth and started to tell the baby exactly what he thought of Tabby in Greek, careful to keep the antagonism out of his voice. Amber looked up at him with big trusting brown eyes, and he marvelled at her ability to award that amount of trust to a complete stranger. If the baby could try, he could as well even if it did stick in his throat to be listening to Tabby's instructions and following them. She maddened him, he acknowledged grimly, gently rubbing Amber's back as he talked. The baby slowly rested its head down on his shoulder.

'Give her to me,' Tabby murmured. 'She's going back to sleep.'

'And so ends lesson one,' Acheron mocked as she settled Amber back into the cot and covered her again.

Only it was not the child he was watching but Tabby. The pale grey silk glimmered in the dull light from the corridor, splaying across her thighs, outlining the plump little curves of her derriere as she bent over the cot rail, prominent nipples visible against the flimsy fabric as she straightened again.

Acheron was hard as a rock by the time he completed that far from fleeting appraisal. 'You might want to cover up more around me,' he commented. 'Or is this a come-on?'

Her violet eyes flew wide as she faltered at the doorway, and she flashed him an incredulous glance back over a narrow shoulder. 'Do you think you're irresistible or something?'

Acheron strode over to the doorway. 'You can't be that innocent. Men are fairly predictable when there is so much bare skin on display.'

'I am not on display,' Tabby countered furiously, crossing her arms defensively over her lightly clad length, sharply disconcerted by the idea that he could see her body beneath the nightie. 'When I came in I had no idea you would be in here.'

Acheron closed a hand around her wrist and tugged her into the corridor, shutting the door behind him. 'I like what I see,' he informed her softly.

Tabby stared up at him with fulminating force, noting the dark shadow of stubble outlining his stubborn jaw line and how that overnight growth enhanced his sheer masculinity. 'But I'm not offering myself.'

'No?' Acheron dipped his handsome head and nibbled at the corner of her inviting mouth, invading with his tongue as soon as she parted her succulent lips. Without further ado, he hauled her up against him, hands weaving across her slender back and then sliding up to glance over the taut peaks of her breasts in a caress that made her shiver.

That single kiss had unholy pulling power. Tabby bargained with herself to continue it. One second, just *one* second more to feel the hungry plunge of his tongue that raised a riot of damp heat low in her body and then his hands, dear heaven, his hands skimming, brushing the tender tips of her breasts before cupping her urgently sensitive flesh. 'No,' she told him shakily.

'No?' Wine-dark eyes glittered down at her, and her swollen mouth ran dry because she wanted another kiss, wanted the wildness she experienced beneath his skilled hands, wanted more with a ferocity that terrified her. Long fingers splayed to her spine, tipping her into revealing contact with the erection that his jeans could not conceal. 'We could have fun for an hour or two.'

'Do I strike you as that easy?' Tabby prompted tightly, outraged by the tone of his proposition. Did he think she was flattered by the idea of being his entertainment for a couple of hours? A quick and easy sexual convenience because there was no more appealing prospect available?

His stunning eyes narrowed. 'I don't make judgements like that about women. I'm not sexist. I enjoy sex. I'm sure you do as well.'

'You're wrong,' she began heatedly, thinking he was little different from the men who, having bought her a drink, had assumed that they were entitled to her body and could not comprehend her reluctance. Sex as a leisure-time pursuit was not her style.

'If you haven't enjoyed sex before then you've been with the wrong men,' Acheron assured her silkily, running a caressing finger along the ripe curve of her lower lip, and the breath feathered deliciously in her throat, a ripple of treacherous, unwelcome response quivering through her slender length.

'You're a class act in the persuasion stakes,' Tabby told him very drily, stepping back out of reach, fighting the unexpected chill of separation from the allure of his warm, vital body. 'But it's wasted on me—though I'm a virgin, I'm well aware that a man will tell you practically anything to get you into bed.'

'A...*virgin*?' Ash echoed in an astonished undertone, disbelief clenching his taut dark features. 'Seriously? Or is that a hook to pull me in deeper?'

Tabby slowly shook her head and then surrendered to laugh out loud. 'You are so suspicious of women it's not real. I don't want to pull you into anything. In fact, I think it would be a very bad idea for us to get that involved.'

'I wasn't thinking of involvement...I was thinking of sex,' Acheron traded smoothly. 'A simple exchange of pleasure.'

Tabby noted the way he even had to separate involvement from the act of sex and registered that he was positively phobic when it came to the concept of commitment. He did not want her to misunderstand what was on offer: a bodily exchange of pleasure, nothing more, no strings whatsoever. 'Goodnight,' she said gruffly, turning on her heel.

'A virgin...*seriously*?' Acheron breathed in her wake, the dark deep richness of his accented drawl vibrating through her in the stillness of the silent apartment.

Tabby turned her head slowly back to him. 'Seriously.'

Acheron frowned, dark brows drawing together, and stared at her, his eyes gleaming golden with curiosity and fascination in the overhead lights. 'But why?'

'I've never wanted to.' *Until now*, a little voice piped up in her brain, for that passionate kiss and the carnal caress of his well-shaped hands had roused more hunger in Tabby than she had ever felt in her life. A fierce physical hunger that she sensed could easily get out of hand.

'You wanted *me, hara mou...*' Acheron murmured with assurance as she walked away from him, blonde hair streaming down her back like a pale flowing river highlighting the curve of her bottom.

Tabby knew she should say nothing, but she couldn't resist the little devil inside herself that he provoked and she turned her head again, succumbing to temptation to murmur softly, 'But obviously...not enough.'

That crack might have affected some men like a challenge, Acheron mused broodingly as he strode back to his room for a cold shower, but he was not one of those men because logic had always ruled his libido. If he slept with her it would clearly get messy, and he hated messy relationships and didn't tolerate them for longer than it took to delete such women's numbers from his phone.

He reminded himself of the dire consequences of his last reckless encounter, and it was even worse that Tabby was still a virgin. He found that hard to credit but could not see any advantage in her telling such a lie. A woman who was still a virgin at twenty-five had to have *very* high expectations of her first lover for why else would she have waited so long? He would not be that man, would never fit that framework or meet the demands she would make. He had been warned and from now on he would keep his distance….

Tabby screened a yawn and settled Amber down on the rug at her feet. So far, it had been a very boring morning. Acheron's lawyer, Stevos, had arrived with a bundle of documents, which had been painstakingly filled in, and now he was engaged in explaining the pre-nuptial contract to her clause by painful clause. Naturally Acheron wanted to protect his wealth, and discussing the terms of divorce before they even got as far as the wedding would have been depressing had she been in love with him, but she wasn't in love with him and couldn't have cared less about his money.

'But I don't need anything like that amount of cash to live on after the divorce,' Tabby protested worriedly. 'I know how to live well on a small budget and even a quarter of that amount would be more than generous.'

'You're supposed to be out for all you can get,' Acheron chipped in helpfully from his restive stance by the window. 'Sign the contract and forget about it. Once you've lived in my world for a while, you'll find your tastes have changed and that you want more.'

Tabby slung him a look of resentment. 'I only want Amber out of this arrangement. I'm not going to turn into a greedy, grasping manipulator overnight either!'

'Mr Dimitrakos simply wants you and the child to enjoy a secure and comfortable future,' the lawyer interposed soothingly.

'No, Mr Dimitrakos wants to buy my loyalty and my loyalty is not for sale!' Tabby replied with spirit. 'I very much appreciate what he is doing to help me keep Amber in my life and the very last thing I will do is take advantage of his generosity in any way. Please accept that.'

'Sign,' Acheron slotted with raw impatience. 'This nonsense has taken up enough of my morning.'

'You mustn't forget to be present at the visit from the social worker this afternoon,' Stevos reminded him doggedly.

Stevos planted another document in front of Tabby when she had signed the first. 'It's a standard confidentiality agreement, which will prevent you from talking about the terms of your marriage to anyone outside this office.'

'That it's a big fat fake has to stay a secret,' Acheron interposed bluntly.

Suppressing a sigh, Tabby signed and then glanced up to watch Acheron as he talked to his lawyer in Greek. He was wearing a dark grey suit with a very subtle pinstripe and a purple shirt and he looked…absolutely amazing, as if he had stepped live out of a glossy magazine shoot. Sleek, sophisticated and breathtakingly handsome, he instantly commanded her gaze whenever he came within sight. There was no harm in looking at him and appreciating the view, she told herself ruefully. He was like a beautiful painting she could admire without needing to own, particularly as any woman with ideas of ownership where Acheron Dimitrakos was concerned was, in Tabby's opinion, in for a very rough ride.

They had shared the breakfast table in his dining room earlier that morning but the table was literally *all* they had shared. He had read his newspaper while she tended to Amber and munched toast, struggling to eat as quietly as a mouse in a cat's presence. It had proved neither sociable nor relaxed and she had already decided to eat her meals in the kitchen from now on.

'One of my assistants is going to take you shopping now for a wedding dress,' Acheron divulged as Tabby bent to lift Amber off the rug before she got her little hands on his shoelaces. 'And we will have to engage a nanny to take care of Amber when we're busy.'

Tabby straightened. 'I don't want a wedding dress… or a nanny.'

Scorching dark eyes assailed hers. 'Did I ask for your opinion?'

'No, but you're getting it, no extra charge.'

'A wedding dress is not negotiable.'

'Nothing's negotiable with you!'

Dark eyes flared sensual gold. 'If you were willing to try a little harder to please, you might be surprised,' he murmured huskily.

He was thinking about sex again: she *knew* it by the look in his eyes and the husky tone of his voice. Colour burned up hotly over her cheekbones as she dealt him a quelling glance.

'I'll be honest about this—I don't want to waste a wedding dress on a phony marriage. It just seems wrong,' Tabby admitted, lifting her chin. 'I want to save the white wedding dress for the day I do it for real.'

'Tough,' Acheron responded obstinately, moving closer. 'This may be a rush wedding but I want it to look as normal as possible and few women choose to get married without frills.'

Amber held out her arms to him and smiled.

'Cuddle her,' Tabby instructed, dumping the little girl into his startled arms. 'Practice makes perfect and, just as I have to look convincing at the wedding, you have to look convincing as an adoptive father-to-be this afternoon.'

Amber yanked at Acheron's silk tie with gusto and an appreciative grin suddenly slashed his mouth, shocking both his companions. 'Amber really doesn't give a damn about anything but attention and what amuses her in the moment.'

'A baby's needs are simple,' Tabby agreed wryly, striving not to react to that intensely charismatic smile of his, which made her want to smile back like a dream-struck idiot. Just looking at him, amusement falling from his features, she felt slightly light-headed and her tummy hollowed as if she were travelling downhill at breathtaking speed on a roller coaster. 'The nanny?'

'A necessity when you will have other calls on your time,' Acheron pronounced. 'Be practical.'

Tabby breathed in deep, reluctant to argue with him when the social services interview was to take place within a few hours. She took Amber back into her arms and strapped her into her buggy where the little girl screwed up her face and complained vehemently.

'She knows what she wants,' Acheron remarked. 'You will need to be firm as she gets older.'

'Obviously.'

'And you might find it a challenge to wear that wedding dress for real for some man when you already have a child in tow,' Acheron delivered with lethal cool. '*I* don't date single parents.'

'Tell me something that surprises me,' Tabby urged witheringly. 'You're too selfish, too concerned about protecting your own comfort level.'

'I just respect my limitations.'

'Nonsense. You can't stand the idea of having to consider someone else's needs before your own,' Tabby traded.

'So, what am I doing now in marrying you?' Acheron demanded curtly.

'You're righting the wrong you committed a couple of months ago when you refused to be Amber's guardian and no doubt that makes you feel so unselfish and perfect you think you're one hell of a guy!'

Listening to that exchange, Stevos was staring in shock at Tabby and her colour was high when she released the brake on the buggy and wheeled it out of the door.

Acheron's PA, Sharma, greeted her in the outer office and took her straight out to a limo for the shopping trip.

Tabby was surprised to be taken to an exclusive and very fashionable wedding boutique rather than a department store, but appreciated that with the time available it would be a challenge to come up with a sophisticated dress that fitted the bill. While Sharma played with Amber, Tabby tried on gowns, finally selecting the least fussy available and choosing the accessories suggested by the attentive proprietor. That achieved, she returned to Acheron's apartment and rang Jack to tell him that she was getting married and to invite him to the civil ceremony the following day.

'Is this a joke?' Jack asked.

'No. It is kind of sudden but I know exactly what I'm doing. Acheron wants to adopt Amber with me.'

'You've kept this very quiet. How long have you been seeing him for?' Jack enquired ruefully.

'A while. I didn't know it was going to turn serious or I'd have mentioned it sooner,' Tabby fibbed, wishing she could just have told the truth.

'It'll solve all your problems,' Jack pronounced with satisfaction. 'I've been really worried about you and Amber.'

Acheron turned up just in time for the interview with the social worker and swiftly proved a dab hand at twisting the truth, contriving to make it sound as if they had known each other far longer than they had. The older woman was so palpably impressed by Acheron and his incredible apartment that she asked few searching questions.

An hour later Tabby was feeding Amber and stealing bites from her own meal in the kitchen when Acheron appeared in the doorway, his expression thunderous. He swept up the highchair with Amber in it and turned on his heel.

'What on earth are you doing?' Tabby cried, racing after him.

Acheron set the chair down at one end of the dining table. 'We eat in here together. You do not eat in the kitchen like a member of my staff. That will not support the impression of a normal married couple.'

'I shouldn't think any of your staff could care less where we eat!' Tabby replied.

'But you need to be more cautious about appearances,' Acheron spelled out the warning grimly. 'Any one of my staff could sell a story to the tabloids and blow a massive hole in our pretence of being a couple.'

Tabby fell still. 'I never thought of that. Can't you trust your employees?'

'Most of them but there's always a rotten apple somewhere in the barrel,' Acheron answered with cynical cool.

Tabby nodded and returned to the kitchen to fetch her meal. He thought of every pitfall from every possible angle and it shook her that he had evidently already suffered that kind of betrayal from someone close to him. It was little wonder that he continually expected the worst from people, she reflected ruefully.

'Why were you eating in the kitchen?' he enquired as she settled at the table.

'I know you like your own space,' Tabby said quickly.

'You're not comfortable eating with me. I noticed that in the restaurant the first night,' Acheron commented, resting level dark eyes on her rising colour. 'You'll have to get over that.'

'Yes, but it was a strain that first night,' Tabby admitted, grudgingly opting for honesty. 'I couldn't read the menu because my French isn't up to it. I didn't even know which cutlery to use.'

A stab of remorse pierced Acheron. It had not even occurred to him that she might feel out of her depth at his favourite restaurant. 'Cutlery isn't important, *hara mou*—'

'Believe me, it *is* when you don't know which utensil to use.'

'In future, *ask*.' Acheron compressed his wide, sensual mouth, irritated that he had been so inconsiderate of the differences between them. 'I'm not…sensitive. I won't pick up on things like that unless you warn me. By the way, Sharma has engaged last night's nanny to work for us. I've also secured permission for us to take Amber abroad.'

'Abroad?' Tabby exclaimed. 'What are you talking about?'

'We're heading to Italy after the wedding. I have a house there. It will be easier to keep up the newly married act without an audience of friends and acquaintances looking on,' Acheron pointed out with irreproachable practicality.

Tabby woke early the next morning. Well, it was her wedding day even though it bore no resemblance to the very special event she had once dreamt the occasion would be. For a start, Sonia would not be there to play bridesmaid as the two women had always assumed she would, and momentarily Tabby's eyes stung with tears because sometimes the pain of losing her best friend felt like a wound that would never heal. She reminded herself that she still had Jack, but Jack was a man of few words and his girlfriend, Emma, was uneasy about his friendship with Tabby. As a result Tabby kept contact with Jack to the minimum. With a sigh, she rolled out of bed to go and tend to Amber and get dressed.

The nanny, Melinda, was in Amber's bedroom. Tabby had forgotten about the nanny, forgotten that she was no longer the only person available to care for the little girl, and Amber was already bathed, dressed and fed. A little pang of regret assailed Tabby because she had always enjoyed giving Amber her first peaceful feed of the day. But Sonia's daughter still greeted her with uninhibited love and affection, and Tabby buried her nose in the little girl's sweet-smelling hair and breathed deep, reminding herself why she was marrying Acheron and meeting his every demand. Amber was worth almost any sacrifice, she conceded feelingly.

The ceremony was to be held at an exclusive castle hotel, and Tabby was amazed at how much it had been possible to arrange at such speed. Then she reminded herself that Acheron's wealth would have ensured special attention and she scolded herself for being so naive.

Sharma had arranged for a hairstylist and a make-up artist to attend her at the apartment, and Tabby hoped that their professional skill would give her at least a hint of the glossy sophistication that Acheron's female companions usually exuded. As quick as she thought that, she wondered why his opinion should matter to her. Was it simply a matter of pride?

Sharma helped lace Tabby into her dress while the stylist adjusted the short flirty veil attached to the circlet of fresh flowers attached to Tabby's hair.

'With those flowers on your head you look like the Queen of Summer...' Sharma burbled enthusiastically. 'Mr Dimitrakos will be blown away.'

It dawned on Tabby for the first time that she was dealing with someone who thought she was about to attend a genuine wedding and she flushed with discomfiture, quite certain that the last thing Acheron would be was 'blown away'.

'And watching the boss go to so much trouble to get married in such a hurry is *so* romantic,' Sharma continued. 'I used to think he was so...er, cold, no offence intended...and then I saw him with the baby and realised how wrong I was. Of course fatherhood does change a man...'

And Tabby registered that Sharma had, not unnaturally, added two and two to make five in her assumption that Acheron was Amber's father. 'Actually, Amber is the daughter of my late best friend and Acheron's cousin,' she explained, deeming it wiser to put the other woman right on that score.

Grim-faced, Acheron paced while he awaited the arrival of the bridal car. He was very tense. It might be a fake wedding but with the arrival of his stepmother, Ianthe, and two of her adult children along with several good friends, it felt unnervingly real and he was already fed up with making polite conversation and pretending to be a happy bridegroom. Unhappily, a wedding without guests would not have been a very convincing affair, he reminded himself impatiently, and at least the woman whose attendance would have been least welcome had failed to show up. Stationed by the window of the function room adorned with flowers for the ceremony, he watched as a limousine embellished with white ribbons that fluttered in the breeze drew up at the hotel entrance.

Tabby stepped out in a sleek bell of rustling white fabric and petticoats, little shoulders bare, her veil and glorious streamers of golden-blonde hair blowing back from her oval face. Acheron's expressive mouth hardened even more, a nerve pulling taut at the corner of his lips. She looked as dainty and delicate as a doll and utterly ravishing, he noted in exasperation, cursing his all-too-male response to so feminine and alluring an image. Tabby didn't just clean up well, in Stevos's parlance; she cleaned up spectacular, Acheron conceded wryly, only absently registering the emergence of the new nanny clutching Amber, who was looking similarly festive in a candy-pink dress and matching hairband.

Tabby was guided straight into the ceremony where music was already playing. Her apprehensive glance took in the sea of faces and then lodged on Acheron and stayed there as if padlocked. *Whoosh!* She could feel all her defences being sucked away by the pure power of his compelling presence. He stared back at her, making no pretence of looking forward to the registrar, his stunning dark eyes golden and bright as sunlight in his lean face and so gorgeous he made something low in her body clench tight like a fist. Knees a tad wobbly, she walked down the short aisle between the seated guests and stilled by his side, the words of the brief ceremony washing over her while she frantically reminded herself that finding Acheron attractive was a one-way trip to disaster and not to be risked lest it should somehow threaten Amber's future as well.

He slid a ring onto her finger and she did the same for him. Afterwards, he retained his grip on her hand, ignoring her attempt to tug gently free, and suddenly there was a crowd of people round them murmuring congratulations, and introductions were being made.

His stepmother was a decorative blonde with a shrill voice and she had a son and a daughter by her side, both of whom seemed rather in awe of Acheron, which gave Tabby the impression that he had never been a true part of his father's family. Jack appeared with his girlfriend, Emma, and the other woman was friendlier than Tabby had ever seen her. Tabby chatted at length to Jack and turned only to find Acheron studying her, his handsome mouth compressed.

'Who was that?'

'Jack's an old friend and the only person I invited,' she proclaimed defensively.

'How much did you tell him?' Acheron enquired grimly.

'I told him nothing,' Tabby responded, wondering what his problem was. 'He thinks this is all for real.'

Drinks were being poured and toasts made by the time a tall, curvy brunette in a sapphire-blue suit swept into the room without warning.

Someone close to Tabby vented a groan. The brunette marched up to them like a woman on a mission and shot an outraged look at Acheron's stepmother, Ianthe. 'Mother, how could you take part in this insane charade when it goes against *my* interests?' she demanded loudly. 'I should have been the bride here today!'

'Let's not go there, Kasma,' her brother, Simeon, advised sheepishly. 'We're here to celebrate Ash's wedding, and I know you don't want to spoil the day by creating a scene.'

'Don't I?' Kasma struck an attitude, furious dark eyes glittering bright. She was a very beautiful woman with a great figure, a perfect face and a torrent of long dark hair, Tabby noted in a daze of agitation. 'Tell me, what has *she* got that I haven't, Acheron?' she demanded in a fierce tone of accusation.

Amber was starting to cry and Tabby took the opportunity to step out of the drama to join Melinda, the nanny, at the back of the room. After all, family squabbles and bitter ex-lovers were none of her business. Had Acheron had an affair with his stepsister? By the looks of it, it had been a rash move to utilise his charisma within the family circle, and she could understand why he had said on the first day that they met at his office that he had *no* family. His late father's family spoke to Acheron as politely as the strangers they so clearly were. Evidently he had never lived with them, which made her wonder who he *had* lived with when he was younger because Tabby was convinced she remembered his very famous mother's death being announced on television while she herself was still only a child.

Tabby took Amber into the baby-changing room, thinking that the histrionic Kasma would, with a little luck, be gone by the time she returned to sit down to a late and much-needed lunch.

But she was to have no such luck. No sooner had she finished undressing Amber than the door opened to frame Kasma's lush shape. 'Is that child Ash's?' she asked drily.

Tabby changed Amber, who was squirming like mad and craning her neck to look at the visitor. 'No.'

'I didn't think so,' Kasma said snidely. 'Ash has never been the daddy type.'

Exasperation kindling, Tabby straightened her shoulders and turned her head. 'Look, I don't know you and I'm busy here—'

'You know why Ash married you, don't you?' the brunette continued thinly. '*I* should have been Ash's bride. No one understands him as well as I do. Unfortunately for all three of us, he's too stubborn and proud to accept being forced to do what he should have done long ago.'

'I don't need to know what you're talking about,' Tabby told her uncomfortably. 'It's really none of my business.'

'How can you say that when by marrying Ash you're winning him a fortune?' Kasma demanded resentfully, her mother's vocal shrillness feeding into her sharp tone. 'According to the terms of his father's will if he stayed single until the end of the year he would lose half of *his* company to *my* family! And, of course, anyone who knows how Ash feels about his company would know that he would do virtually *anything* to protect it...even marry a totally unsuitable nobody from nowhere to maintain the status quo!'

CHAPTER FIVE

KASMA'S ACCUSATION RANG in Tabby's ears like a nasty echo during the flight to Italy. After the brunette's departure, lunch had proceeded quietly but Tabby had not had the advantage of a private moment in which to question Acheron. She had intended to raise the subject during the flight but Melinda was looking after Amber at the back of the cabin and she did not feel that she could speak freely.

Was it possible that Acheron had had a far more self-serving motive to marry than he had admitted? Tabby deemed it perfectly possible when she compared his refusal of all responsibility for Amber only months earlier with his sudden change of heart. Why on earth hadn't she been more suspicious of that rapid turnaround of his? He had to think she was as dumb as a rock, she thought painfully, feeling betrayed not only by his lack of honesty but also by her own gullibility. What terms had been included in his father's will? How could he possibly lose half of a company that belonged to him? And if Kasma's information was correct, why hadn't Acheron simply told Tabby the truth?

And the answer to that question could only be *power*, Tabby reflected with steadily mounting anger. As long as Tabby had believed that Acheron was doing her a favour for Amber's sake she had been willing to meet his every demand because she had been grateful to him, believing that he was making a big sacrifice even if theirs was only a fake marriage. But what if it wasn't like that at all? What if Acheron Dimitrakos had needed a conformable wife just as much as she needed the support and stability that would enable her to adopt Amber? That very much changed the picture and made them equals. But Acheron had never been prepared to treat Tabby as an equal. Acheron preferred to dictate and demand, not persuade and compromise. Well, those days were gone if Kasma had told her the truth…

'You're very quiet,' Acheron commented in the car driving them through the Tuscan countryside. She had changed out of her wedding gown before leaving London, and he had felt weirdly disappointed when he saw her wearing the violet dress he had personally chosen for her in London instead. The fabric and long sleeves were too heavy for a warmer climate and there was a flush of pink on her face in spite of the air conditioning. The colour, however, brought out the remarkable shade of her eyes and somehow accentuated the succulent fullness of her pink mouth.

Acheron breathed in slow and deep, dropped his gleaming gaze only for it to lodge on a slender knee and the soft pale skin beneath, which only made him wonder if her skin would feel as silky to the touch as it looked. He gritted his teeth, cursing his high-voltage libido. It had never once crossed his mind until now that, even with the options he had, a platonic relationship might still be a challenge, but evidently he was suffering from sexual frustration. Why else would he find her so appealing?

'I'm enjoying the views,' Tabby proclaimed stiltedly, so angry with him that she had to bite her lower lip before she started an argument while still trapped in the car with him. 'Where exactly are we going?'

'A villa in the hills. Like most of my properties it once belonged to my mother but I had it renovated last year.'

Despite her anger, curiosity stirred in Tabby. 'Your mother died when you were still quite young, didn't she?' she remarked.

His lean bronzed features clenched hard, dark golden eyes screening. 'Yes.'

The wall of reserve he used as a shield cast a forbidding shadow over his expressionless face. 'I lost my parents quite young too,' Tabby told him, rushing to fill the uneasy silence with an innate sensitivity towards his feelings that annoyed her. 'I went into foster care. That's where I met Jack and Amber's mum, Sonia.'

'I didn't realise you'd been in foster care,' Acheron breathed flatly, well aware she would not have had the escape route from that lifestyle that had eventually been granted by his inherited wealth.

'Well...' Tabby responded awkwardly, colliding with impenetrable midnight eyes heavily fringed by spiky black lashes and fighting a sensation of falling...and falling...and falling. 'They weren't the happiest years of my life but there were some good times. The last foster home I was in was the best and at least the three of us were together there.'

That appeared to be the end of that conversation as Acheron compressed his lips in grim silence while Tabby fought that light-headed sensation and struggled to focus on her anger. So, Acheron Dimitrakos was gorgeous and he kept on making her hormones sit up and take notice but he was also a skilled manipulator and deceiver and only a complete fool would forget the fact. In addition, it had not escaped her notice that he really wasn't interested in learning anything about her background and who she was as a person. But then had he ever seen her as a person in her own right? Or simply as someone he could easily use?

The car turned off the road and purred up a sloping driveway to the very large ochre-coloured stone building sprawling across the top of the hill. Tabby had to tense her lower lip to prevent her mouth from dropping open in comical awe because what he called a villa *she* would have called a palace. A fountain was playing a rainbow of sparkling water droplets down into a circular pool in the centre of a paved frontage already embellished with giant stone pots of glorious flowers. As she climbed out into the early evening sunshine, a flicker of movement from a shrubbery attracted her attention and a white peacock strutted out, unfurling his pristine feathers. The light caught his plumage as he unfurled it like a magnificent silver lace fan. The peacock posed, head high, one foot lifted, his confidence supreme in spite of his aloneness.

'You remind me of that bird,' Tabby muttered as the car carrying Amber and her nanny with the bodyguards drew up behind them.

Acheron raised an ebony brow enquiringly.

Embarrassed, Tabby shrugged. 'Never mind. Could we have a word in private?' she asked then.

'Of course,' he said without expression, but she didn't miss the frowning glance he shot in her direction as she moved to speak to Amber and her nanny. The little girl was fast asleep though, and a last feed and an early night were clearly what she most needed after a long and exhausting day.

The hall of the villa was breathtaking. Gleaming stretches of marble flooring ran below the arches that separated the reception areas. Tabby had never seen so many different shades of white utilised in a decor or anything so impractical for a household with a child in tow. Of course they would not be staying for long, she reminded herself, and Amber wasn't yet mobile so all the sharp-edged glass coffee tables and stylishly sited sculptural pieces on pedestals would scarcely endanger her.

'Very impressive,' she pronounced while Melinda followed the housekeeper up the wrought-iron and marble staircase.

'I have a few calls to make,' Acheron informed her and he was already swinging away, a tall, broad-shouldered male in a beautifully cut lightweight suit made of a fine fabric that gleamed in the light flooding through the windows.

'We have to talk...'

Over the years, far too many women had fired that same phrase at Acheron and had followed it with dramatic scenes and demands for more attention that he found abhorrent. His powerful frame tensed, his lean, strong face shuttering. 'Not now...later.'

'Yes...*now*,' Tabby emphasised without hesitation, violet eyes shimmering with anger, for she was not going to allow him to rudely brush her off as if she were the nobody from nowhere and of no account that Kasma had labelled her. If she toed his line and treated him like a superior being she would soon be thinking the same thing about herself.

'What is this about?' Acheron enquired coldly.

Tabby walked very deliberately out of the hall into the area furnished with incredibly opulent white sofas and slowly turned round, slim shoulders straight, chin lifted. 'Is it true that to retain ownership of your company your father's will required you to take a wife before the end of the year?'

His stubborn jaw line clenched. 'Where did you get that story from?' he asked grittily and then he released his breath with a measured hiss of comprehension. 'Kasma... *right*?'

'It's true, then,' Tabby gathered in furious disbelief. 'She told me the truth.'

'The terms of my father's will are nothing to do with you,' Acheron stated with chilling bite, his dark eyes deep and cold as the depths of the ocean.

But Tabby was in no mood to be intimidated. 'How dare you say that when getting married must've suited you every bit as much as it suited me? Didn't you think I deserved to know that?'

Acheron gritted his even white teeth together in a visible act of restraint. 'What difference can it possibly make to you?'

'I think it makes a *huge* difference!' Tabby slung back at him, violet eyes darkening with seething resentment. 'You made me feel as if you were doing me an enormous favour for Amber's benefit.'

'And wasn't I?' Acheron slotted in, utilising a tone that was not calculated to soothe wounded feelings.

'And you can stop being so rude right now!' Tabby launched at him, that derisive tone and superior appraisal of his lashing her like an offensive assault. 'Yes, Acheron, it *is* rude to interrupt and even more rude to look at me as if I'm some bug on the ground at your feet! I was completely honest with you but you, and no doubt your lawyer, deceived me.'

Eyes smouldering gold, Acheron was having trouble holding on to his temper. 'How you were deceived? I did exactly as I promised. I married you, I helped you to lodge an adoption application and I have ensured your future security. A lot of women would kill for one half of what I'm giving you!'

Her slender hands closed into irate fists. She wanted to pummel him as he stood there, the king of all he surveyed, cocooned from ordinary mortals and decent moral tenets by a level of wealth and success she could barely imagine. 'You are so arrogant, so hateful sometimes I want to hit you and I'm not a violent person!' Tabby hastened to declare in her own defence. 'Do you honestly not understand why I'm angry? I was frank with you. There were no lies, no pretences, no evasions. I believe I deserve the same respect from you.'

His wide, sensual mouth curled. 'This doesn't feel like respect.'

'Is this how you normally deal with an argument?'

'I don't have arguments with people,' Acheron responded levelly.

'Only because people probably spend all their time trying to please and flatter you, not because they always agree with you!' Tabby snapped back in vexation. 'For someone who appears very confrontational, you're actually avoiding the issue and refusing to respond to my natural annoyance.'

'I don't wish to prolong this argument, nor do I see anything natural about your annoyance,' Acheron admitted curtly. 'I don't make a habit of confiding in people. I'm a very private individual, and my father's will certainly falls into the confidential category.'

'I had the right to know that I didn't need to be grateful and submit to your every demand because you were getting even more out of this marriage than I was!' Tabby condemned, refusing to be sidetracked by a red herring like his reserve. 'You used my ignorance like a weapon against me!'

'The will was a matter of business and was of no conceivable interest to you,' Acheron stated in a raw undertone.

'Don't talk nonsense. Of course it was of interest to me that you had as much need to get married as I did!' she flashed back at him. 'It levels the playing field.'

'As far as I'm concerned, there *is* no playing field because this is not a game!' Acheron countered angrily. 'I married you and now that you're my wife, you're trying to take advantage of your position.'

Her violet eyes widened and she planted her tiny hands on her hips, just like a miniature fishwife getting ready to do battle, he decided, torn between grudging amusement and exasperation. 'Take advantage? How am I taking advantage? By standing up to you for once? By daring to state *my* side of the case?' she hissed back at him with simmering rancour.

Acheron strode forward, planted two hands over hers and hauled her up into the air before she could even guess his intention. He held her there, entrapped. 'You don't have a side of the case to argue, *moraki mou*—'

Enraged by his behaviour, Tabby glowered down at him. 'If you don't put me down, I'll kick you!' she launched at him furiously.

In response, Acheron banded her closely to his big powerful length, ensuring that her legs were as trapped as her hands. Dark golden eyes fringed by heavy black lashes held hers fast. 'There will be *no* kicking, *no* hitting, *no* bad language—'

'Says who?' Tabby bit out between gritted teeth.

'Your husband.' Acheron frowned as though that aspect had only just occurred to him and he was as much amused as irritated by the reality.

It was as if she were a firework and he had lit her

up inside. Rage blazed through Tabby. 'You are *not* my husband!'

Unholy amusement lit Acheron's eyes, whipping up the lighter tones she had noticed before and giving him an extraordinary appeal that made her mouth run dry and her tummy perform acrobatics. 'Then what am I?'

'A rat with a marriage certificate!' Tabby snapped at him informatively.

Acheron gave her a look of mock sympathy. '*Your* rat because you're stuck with me.'

'Put…me…down!' Tabby ground out fiercely. 'Or you'll regret it!'

'No, I much prefer this set-up to you shouting at me from across the room.'

'I was not shouting!'

'You were shouting,' Acheron repeated steadily. 'That is not how I conduct disputes.'

'I don't give a monkey's about how you like to conduct your disputes!' Tabby fired back.

It was those sparkling eyes, that incredibly succulent and inviting mouth of hers, Acheron mused abstractedly, conscious that she somehow hauled fiercely on every libidinous hormone he possessed and fired him up like a horny teenager. He didn't understand it, didn't care, didn't think he needed to, but without conscious volition he drew that tempting mouth up to his and crushed it under his, and the taste of her was as rich and fragrant and luscious as juicy strawberries on a summer day.

'No… No,' Tabby's dismayed objections, voiced as much to her wayward self as to him, were swallowed up by the hot, hungry pressure of his erotically charged mouth on hers.

Nobody had ever kissed Tabby as he did with all the passion of the volatile nature he kept under wraps, but which she sensed every time she was with him. He demanded and teased and the force of his sensual lips on hers followed by the invasive plunge of his tongue was unbelievably exciting and sexy.

He was very, *very* sexy, she acknowledged dimly, as if it was an excuse, and as he hoisted her higher to get a better grip on her slight body he let go of her hands and, instead of using them to get free of his hold, she balanced one on a broad shoulder and delved the fingers of the other into the springy, luxuriant depths of his black hair. With a guttural sound low in his throat he brought her down on something soft and yielding and then sealed her fast to the hard, driving length of his powerful frame.

And even as a faint current of alarm blipped somewhere in the back of Tabby's head she was aware of how much she loved feeling his strong, muscular body over and on hers. In fact, her every skin cell was leaping and bouncing with pent-up energy long before his fingers closed over the slight thrust of her achingly sensitive breast, and she strained up breathless and bound by a new tide of sensation. Indeed, desire had infiltrated her with such powerful effect that she scarcely knew what she was doing any more. Nothing had ever felt more necessary; nothing had ever felt more thrilling than the hot, hungry stimulation of his mouth and his hands. Spasms of excitement were quivering through her in a gathering storm. But then other sounds suddenly cancelled out those physical responses: a stifled gasp linked to the rattle of china and the sound of hastily receding footsteps.

'My goodness, what was that?' Tabby exclaimed, dragging her mouth from beneath his to find that she was lying on a sofa beneath him. *Beneath him*, her brain repeated, and her body went into panic mode when she collided with smouldering dark golden eyes and pushed at his shoulders, wriggling out from under his weight at frantic, feverish speed.

'Let's go to bed,' Acheron husked, closing long brown fingers over hers.

And it's just that simple and casual for him, she told herself angrily, furious that she had not contrived to resist him. She perched at the far end of the sofa, smoothing her tumbled blonde hair back from her brow, a slight tremor in her hands and her face so hot with mortification she could have boiled eggs on it. 'No, let's not…it would mess up things.'

'The bed would be more comfortable than the sofa,' Acheron declared single-mindedly.

'I'm not talking about *where*…I'm saying *no*, we're not going to do that!' Tabby slung back at him in frustration, wincing at the nagging bite of separation from his lean, hard body, fighting the ache of longing between her thighs with defiant determination. No way was she planning to be one more in a no doubt long line of easy women for Acheron, a mere female body to scratch an itch for a male unaccustomed to doing without sexual satisfaction.

Acheron sprawled back at the other end of the sofa, long powerful thighs spread so that she noticed, really couldn't help noticing, that that little tussle with her body had seriously aroused his. Her face burned even hotter and her tummy hollowed just looking at the prominent bulge at his pelvis, reactions to a physical craving she had never experienced before assailing her in an unwelcome wave.

All of a sudden and no thanks to Acheron for the lesson, she was realising why she was still a virgin. No other man had ever attracted her enough to make her drop her guard and yearn for sex. Sex, yes, that was all it would be, straightforward, unvarnished sex, not something a sensible woman would crave, and she was very sensible, wasn't she? *Wasn't she?* It really bothered her that even while thinking along those lines and carefully realigning her defences she was still fully engaged in appreciating the pure male beauty of Acheron's lean bronzed face and long, powerful body.

'You want me,' Acheron breathed a little raggedly. 'I want you.'

'Weird, isn't it…? I mean, we can't even be civil to each other,' Tabby pronounced shakily, still as out of breath as he was, recalling that wild entanglement and the fierce need he had sent powering through her and then suppressing the uncomfortable memory before standing up, smoothing down her dress with careful hands.

'Yet you burn me up, *hara mou*,' Acheron breathed huskily, springing upright with easy grace.

Tabby turned her head away. 'Let's not talk about that…you and me? It would be a very bad idea. We have as much in common as a cat and a dog. I'd like to see my room,' she completed, moving back with determination towards the hall.

'I'll show you. We've frightened off the staff,' Acheron volunteered with an unconcerned laugh. 'I think that noise was someone bringing us coffee and we were seen.'

'Yes, I can imagine what they saw,' Tabby cut in stiltedly, wishing he would drop the subject.

'Well, that's at least one person who will believe that we're genuine honeymooners,' Acheron replied nonchalantly, refusing to take the hint as he led the way up the marble staircase.

'But we're *not*,' she reminded him doggedly.

'You're not a very flexible personality, are you?'

'You'd roll me out like pastry if I was,' Tabby quipped. 'I'm still mad at you, Acheron. You took advantage of my ignorance.'

'I'm an alpha male, programmed at birth to take advantage,' Acheron pointed out with unapologetic cool. 'But you called me on it, which I wasn't expecting.'

He pushed open double doors at the end of the corridor and exposed a small hall containing two doors. 'That's my room.' He thrust open one door and then the second. 'And yours...'

Tabby worried at her full lower lip. 'Do we have to be so close?'

'I don't sleepwalk,' Acheron murmured silkily. 'But you're very welcome if you choose to visit.'

'I won't be doing that.' Tabby strolled in the big room, glancing into the en suite that led off and then into a dressing room to slide open a wardrobe, only to frown at the garments packed within. 'Didn't your last girlfriend take her clothes with her?'

'Those are yours. I ordered them,' Acheron explained. 'You'll need summer clothes here.'

Tabby spun back to study him with simmering violet eyes. 'I'm not a dress-up doll.'

'But you know that all I want to do is *undress* you, *moraki mou*.'

Tabby went pink again and compressed her lips.

'You blush like a bonfire,' Acheron remarked with sudden amusement as he strode off to make use of another door on the opposite side of the room that evidently led to his suite.

Tabby thought about turning the lock and then decided it would be petty, for surprisingly on that level she trusted him and had no fear that he might try to take what she was not prepared to offer. If she withstood his appeal, she was quite certain he would withstand hers and find some far more amusing and experienced quarry to pursue. Unfortunately, she didn't like the idea of him with another woman in the slightest and she told herself off for that because she knew she couldn't have it both ways. Either they were together or they were not; there was no halfway stage to explore.

Acheron stripped off for a cold shower. He was still ragingly erect and wondering when a woman had last turned him down. He couldn't remember, and the shock of Tabby's steely resolve still rankled. But it was a timely warning to steer clear, he reflected impatiently, his sensual mouth twisting as he stifled the urge to fantasise about having her tiny body wrapped round him while he satisfied them both. If she attached *that* much importance to sex, he definitely didn't want to get involved because sex meant no more to him than an appetite that required regular satisfaction.

Tabby rifled through the new wardrobe he had acquired for her without even mentioning his intent. She tugged out a long cotton dress that looked cool and, more importantly, covered up anything that she imagined a man might find tempting. If he kept his hands off her, she would keep her hands off him. She worried at her lower lip with her teeth. She had wanted to rip his clothes off him on that sofa, and the incredible strength of the hunger he had awakened still shocked her in retrospect. But nothing more was going to happen, *nothing*, she stressed inwardly with more force than cool. She could handle him, of course she could. He might be a very rich, very good-looking and very manipulative male but she had always had a good gut instinct about how best to look after herself.

Buoyed up by that knowledge, Tabby got changed, freshened up and went off to find out where the nursery had been set up.

CHAPTER SIX

'It's time you told me something about yourself,' Acheron declared, settling back into his seat and cradling his wineglass in one elegant hand.

Tabby was ill at ease. The grand dining room and the table festooned with flowers and fancy dishes for the first meal they were to share as a married couple made her feel like Cinderella arriving at the ball without a prince on hand to claim her. He had watched her watching him to see which cutlery to use, and the awareness had embarrassed her, making her wish that she had never confessed her ignorance. 'What sort of something?'

Acheron raised an ebony brow. 'Let's be basic—your background?'

He was so relaxed that he infuriated her, sheathed in tight faded denim jeans and a black shirt left undone at the throat. She had assumed he would dress up for dinner much as aristocrats seemed to do on television shows and, if she was honest, that was probably why she had picked the long dress. But instead of dressing up, Acheron had dressed *down* and, maddeningly, he still looked amazing, black hair curling a little from the shower, stubborn jaw line slightly rough with dark stubble, lustrous dark eyes pinned to her with uncompromising intensity and she couldn't read him, couldn't read him at all, hadn't a clue what he was thinking about.

'My background's not pretty,' she warned him.

He shrugged a shoulder in dismissal of that objection.

Tabby clenched her teeth and stiffened her backbone. 'I imagine my conception was an accident. My parents weren't married. My mother once told me they were going to give me up for adoption until they discovered that having a child meant they could get better housing and more benefits out of the welfare system. They were both druggies.'

Acheron no longer seemed quite so relaxed and he sat forward with a sudden frown. *'Addicts?'*

'I warned you that it wasn't pretty. Their drug of choice was whatever was cheapest and most easily available. They weren't parents in the normal sense of the word, and I don't think they were even that keen on each other because they had terrible fights. I was simply the child who lived with them,' Tabby proffered tightly. 'And I got in the way…frequently because children have needs and they didn't meet them.'

Acheron forced his shoulders back into the chair, his astonishment at what she had told him concealed by his impassive expression. He almost told her then and there in a revelation that would have been unprecedented for him that they had much more in common than a cat and a dog.

'Have you heard enough?' Tabby enquired hopefully.

'I want to hear it *all*,' Acheron contradicted levelly, slowly comprehending the base level of painful isolation and insecurity from which that chippy, aggressive manner of hers had undoubtedly been forged. Tabby had been forced at an early age to learn to fight for her survival, and that he understood.

'I was the kid in the wrong clothes at school...when they got me there, which wasn't very often. Then my father started to take me with him as a lookout when he burgled houses,' she confided flatly, hating every word she was telling him but somehow needing him to know that she could handle her troubled, crime-infested childhood and indeed had moved far beyond it. 'Social Services got involved when he was caught in the act and eventually, because I was missing so much school and my parents were incapable of looking after me properly, I was put into care.'

'As was I,' Acheron admitted gruffly. 'I was ten years old. What age were you?'

Tabby stared back at him wide-eyed. '*You*...were in care? But your parents must have been *so* wealthy.'

'Which doesn't necessarily mean that they were any more responsible than yours,' Acheron pointed out drily. 'Believe me, my mother's money didn't protect me, although it did protect *her* until the day she died from an overdose. Her lawyers rushed her out of the country before she could be prosecuted for neglecting me.'

'What about your father?' Tabby prompted sickly, still shaken and appalled that he, who seemed so very assured and rich and protected, could ever have lived within the care system as she had. All at once she felt guilty about the assumptions she had made.

'His marriage to my mother only lasted about five minutes. When she got bored with him she told him that the child she was expecting—*me*—was the child of her previous lover...and he believed her,' Acheron explained flatly. 'He couldn't have afforded to fight her for custody in any case. I met him for the first time when I was in my twenties. He came to see me in London because a relative of his had noticed how very alike we looked in a newspaper photograph.'

'So what did your mother do with you?' Tabby asked, sipping at her glass of water.

'Very little. The trust who controlled her millions paid for a squad of carers to look after her and keep her worst excesses out of the newspapers. She was addicted to drugs too,' Acheron divulged tautly. 'But once I was no longer a baby none of her staff had a direct mandate to look after me, and my mother was, all too frequently, high as a kite. So I was left to my own devices, which eventually attracted the attention of the authorities. I had no other relatives to take responsibility for me.'

Painfully aware of the grim memories shadowing his eyes and the sad knowledge that his father could not have been waiting in the wings to take charge of him, Tabby stretched her hand across the table without even thinking about it and rested it down on his, where his long, elegant fingers were braced on the tablecloth. 'I'm sorry.'

His arrogant dark head came up at a combative angle even as he lifted his hand to close it round hers, glancing down at their linked hands in virtual bewilderment as if he couldn't quite work out how that connection had happened. Dark colour crawled up to accentuate the high cheekbones that gave his face such strength and definition. 'Why would you be sorry? I imagine I got off lighter than you. I suspect you were physically mistreated...?'

Her oval face froze. 'Yes,' she almost whispered in confirmation.

'I only met with physical abuse *after* I entered the care system. I was an obnoxious little brat by then, semi-feral and may well have deserved what I got,' Acheron volunteered between gritted teeth.

'No child deserves pain,' Tabby argued.

'I endured two years of complete hell and innumerable different homes until my mother died and the trustees rescued me. I was sent off to boarding school for what remained of my childhood.'

Tabby's heart squeezed tight and her throat thickened at the awareness that just like her he had grown up knowing nothing of the love and security of a happy home and committed parents. She had been *so* wrong about him and it shamed her that she had been so biased purely because his late mother had been a famous Greek heiress. 'You never forget it…how powerless and lost you feel,' she framed unevenly.

Acheron looked across the table at her, his stunning dark golden eyes glittering. 'You leave it behind you, move on,' he told her squarely, suddenly releasing her hand.

'Yes, but it's always there somewhere in the back of your mind.' Starstruck even as she yanked her hand back, she collided with his eyes and the rare warmth of connection there and it made her feel not as if she was falling but instead flying high as a bird, breathless and thrilled.

'Not if you discipline yourself,' Acheron asserted smoothly.

'Tell me about your father's will,' Tabby urged, already dreading the return of the cold reserve that was beginning to clench his lean, darkly handsome features again.

'Some other time. We've raked over enough personal stuff for one evening…surely?' A sleek black emphatic brow lifted, the force of his will bearing down on her from the lambent glow of his beautiful lustrous dark eyes.

And Tabby, who was usually like a nail stuck to a magnet when in the grip of curiosity, quelled her desire to know more, conceding that, for a male as famously reticent as he was, he had been remarkably frank with her when he hadn't needed to be, for she knew of no stories referring to his dysfunctional upbringing that had ever appeared in the media. She swallowed back her questions and lifted a fork to attack the dessert that had been brought to the table.

'I'm crazy about meringue,' she confided. 'And this is perfectly cooked, crunchy on the outside, soft inside.'

A flashing smile crossed his wide, sensual mouth. 'A little like you, then? All fight on the surface and then all tender when it comes to another woman's child?'

In receipt of that rare smile, she felt her heart race. 'I only want Amber to have all the things I never had.'

'An admirable ambition. I've never had the desire to reproduce,' Acheron admitted, watching the tip of her tongue flick out to catch a tiny white crumb of meringue that could not possibly have tasted any sweeter than her lush mouth. Just like that he was hard as a rock again, imagining what else she might be able to do with her tongue, and the heavy pulse of mounting need at his groin was infuriating. It made him feel out of control and, because he despised that kind of weakness in any part of his life, he gritted his teeth and battled for restraint.

'I've never been the broody sort,' Tabby burbled, licking the fork before dipping it into the delicious dessert again, uncomfortably aware of the dark golden swoop of his gaze following her every move. 'But I was with Sonia when Amber was born and then I had to look after her the first few weeks until Sonia was strong enough after her stroke to leave hospital. I'm afraid that by that stage I was committed heart, soul and body to Amber...our attachment just happened and then Sonia had the second stroke and died immediately.' She paused, clashed with his caramel-shaded eyes and felt her mouth run dry. 'Please stop staring at me.'

'Then stop playing with the fork,' Acheron suggested huskily. 'Naturally I'm picturing you spread across the table as an infinitely more appealing main course than the one I've eaten.'

Surprised colour sprang into her face, and she dropped the fork with a clatter. 'Do you ever think of anything but sex?'

'And you're not thinking about it too?' Acheron derided thickly, studying her with burning intensity.

And the pink in her cheeks burned hotter than ever because he was perfectly correct. His raw masculine virility called to her on a visceral level. The table between them felt like a barrier she wanted to push out of the way. She wanted things she had never wanted before. She wanted to taste that intriguing little triangle of brown male skin visible below his throat, kiss a path along that stubborn jaw line, *touch*, explore. And even worse the mere thought of such experimentation made the blood race through her veins, her nipples tighten and push against her bodice while a liquid sensation of squirming warmth flowered between her thighs. *So, this is lust*, she told herself sharply. *Grow up and deal with it like a woman, not a frightened little girl.*

Acheron thrust back his chair and vaulted to his full commanding height of well over six feet. 'Come on...'

'No, sit down,' Tabby told him shakily, very much afraid that she knew exactly where he wanted her to go and even more afraid that she was ready to say yes, for never in her life had she ever felt anything as powerful as the primitive longing he awakened in her.

'Don't look at me like that and then try to tell me what to do, *hara mou*. It doesn't work,' Acheron advised, strolling round the table to move behind her and tug out the chair with her still seated in it.

'One of us has to try to be sensible,' Tabby protested in desperation.

Acheron bent down and scooped her out of the chair as if she were a child. *'Why?'* he queried thickly, his warm breath fanning her throat. 'We're not hurting anyone. We're both free agents. We can do as we like—'

'That's not how I live.'

'You've trapped yourself in a cage of irrational rules because that makes you feel safe,' Acheron countered, striding across the hall with her still cradled in his arms. 'But I can keep you safe too…'

Only he could still hurt her, just as easily as he could silence her arguments and sweep her literally off her feet, Tabby acknowledged feverishly even as her fingers reached up of their own accord to skate admiringly along the clean, hard line of his jaw. 'You don't make me feel safe.'

'But then you don't trust anyone,' Acheron countered with a swift downward glance at her anxious face. 'Neither do I. Even so, I *can* promise you that I won't lie to you.'

'Not much of a comfort when you could give tips to Machiavelli on how best to get your own way by nefarious means,' Tabby traded, provoking a surprised laugh from Acheron as he mounted the stairs. She knew decision time had come and gone and she wanted his mouth on hers so badly that it literally hurt even to think about it.

He lowered her to the carpet to open the first door, grabbed her hand as though he was afraid she would run off last minute and virtually dragged her into his bedroom. 'Now, I finally have you where I want you. Can you believe that this is our wedding night?'

'But it isn't…we're not really married.' Tabby leant back against his bedroom door, taut with tension because she was sincerely out of her comfort zone and could scarcely breathe for nerves. 'Let's not kid ourselves about that. Neither one of us ever had any plans to make this a proper marriage. I may be wearing a wedding ring but it's meaningless.'

Acheron didn't know a single woman of his acquaintance who would have reminded him of that fact at that precise moment, or who would have come to his bedroom without a carefully set agenda of ambitious and mercenary acquisition in mind. In the strangest possible way, Tabby was a breath of fresh air in his life, he reflected, uneasy with the thought.

'I know.' Like a hunter stalking a wary doe, Acheron approached and closed both of his hands over hers to pull her forward into his arms. 'But nothing that feels as exciting as this could possibly be meaningless,' he traded huskily.

'It's only hormones.'

'Says the woman who hasn't a clue what's going to be happening in that bed,' Acheron teased, feathering his mouth hungrily over the soft, silky contours of hers and making her shiver.

'Of course I know what happens…' But she still didn't quite know what she was doing there with him, breaking her rules of self-protection by letting him get that close, risking the vulnerability she always shunned. 'It's just sex,' she told him staunchly.

'It will be amazing sex,' Acheron predicted, skimming the straps down on her dress, pressing his hungry mouth to a slight-boned shoulder while pressing her close, letting her feel the hard-packed urgency in his lean body while reminding himself that he would have to go slow.

'I love your confidence,' Tabby whispered half under her breath.

'I thought it annoyed you.'

Tabby stretched up on tiptoe to link her arms round his neck and tug his handsome dark head down to her level. 'Shut up,' she told him helplessly, entrapped by dark eyes blazing like a banked golden fire across her face.

Acheron hoisted her off her feet and brought her down at the foot of the bed to flip off her shoes. 'I don't want to hurt you,' he admitted.

'If it hurts, it hurts,' Tabby said prosaically, determined not to surrender to apprehension because, with the single exception of her deep attachment to Amber, she had never felt as much as he made her feel either emotionally or physically. She supposed she was suffering from some kind of idiotic infatuation with him but assumed it would fade as time went on. 'Is this a one-time thing?' she asked him abruptly.

Engaged in slipping off her shoes, Acheron glanced back at her, amusement playing attractively about the wilful, passionate set of his mouth. 'You can't plan everything in advance, Tabby.'

'I do,' she told him tautly. 'I always need to know exactly where I am and what I'm doing.'

And his mouth claimed hers slow and deep and hungry and the tight knot of anxiety inside her unfurled because, in that moment, her senses locked to his, her body screaming with eagerness for more...more...more, and she couldn't stay focused the way she usually did. He unzipped the dress and extracted her from its folds with an ease and exactitude that briefly chilled her because she discovered she couldn't bear to think of him with the other lovers who must have honed his skills.

'What's wrong?' he prompted, more attuned to her than she had expected, instantly picking up on her renewed tension.

Perhaps she was, at heart, a terribly jealous, possessive person, she reasoned in mortification, troubled by her thoughts and wondering how she could possibly know what she was like when she had never enjoyed a deeper relationship with a man. There she perched, shivering a little in spite of the warmth of the room, suddenly conscious that she was clad only in bra and knickers and that her body was far from perfect.

'Nothing's wrong,' she breathed while he continued to study her troubled face with a frown. *'All right!'* she exclaimed as if he had repeated the question. 'I was just thinking that you're very smooth at stripping clothes off a woman!'

And Acheron burst out laughing, revelling in that honesty, appreciating that she would simply say whatever she thought without considering its impact and instead saying only what he might want to hear. That quality was another rarity in his world. 'Thank you…I think,' he teased.

'And you're still wearing too many clothes,' Tabby protested, all too aware of her own half-naked state as she struggled not to recall that she had really tiny breasts and was pretty skinny everywhere else where it was said to matter to a man. After all, regardless of her deficiencies, he wanted her. That was a certainty that buoyed her up as she watched dark golden eyes flare over her with unashamed desire and appreciation.

He laughed and shed his shirt, kicked off his shoes with the complete unselfconsciousness of a male who had never been inhibited in a woman's presence or constrained by the fear that a woman might not admire what he had to offer. Her throat ran dry as he unveiled the superb expanse of his bronzed torso, exposing the lean, ripped muscles of his six-pack. Poised there, black stubble darkening his handsome jaw, eyes glinting, hair tousled by her fingers with his jeans hanging low on his narrow hips as he unzipped them, he was as gorgeous as a tiger in his prime: glossy and strong and beautifully poised.

She tried and failed to swallow when she saw the tented effect of his boxers, the all too prominent evidence of his readiness outlined by the fine fabric. When his long, elegant hands began to sweep off that final garment she averted her attention and reached back awkwardly to unhook her bra, peeling it off before scrambling below the linen sheet to rip off her knickers in an effort to seem a little more in control than she was.

'I want you *so* much, *koukla mou*,' Acheron growled, yanking the sheet off her from the foot of the bed so that she sat up again, wide-eyed and thunderously aware of her nakedness. 'I also want to see you, *watch* you—'

'There's not a lot to see!' she gasped, her small body crowding back against the banked-up pillows.

Acheron locked a hand round one slender ankle and pulled her very gently down the bed. 'What I see is beautiful,' he breathed thickly, his hungry scrutiny skimming from the tangle of blonde curls at the apex of her thighs to the glorious hint of secret pink beneath and the mouth-watering swell of her breasts topped by prominent pale pink nipples. In one movement he was up on the bed by her side.

'I'm not.'

'Don't want to hear it!' he interrupted, long fingers fisting in the tumble of her golden hair to hold her still as he skated his mouth back and forth over her lips until they parted and his tongue speared inside, delving and exploring with a thoroughness that deprived her of breath and sanity. He could kiss, oh, yes, he could kiss, and then his fingers teased very gently at her straining nipples and he lowered his mouth there, catching a painfully sensitive peak between his lips and plucking it with a tugging intensity that made her nipple throb and arrowed heat straight down into her pelvis.

She trembled, and her spine arched as he pressed her flat on the mattress, dividing his attention now between the distended buds, suckling on her, flicking his tongue back and forth until the tingles of awareness rose like a tide to engulf her. She trembled, insanely aware of the gathering of heat and moisture between her thighs and the intolerable ache building there along with the desperate desire to be touched.

'You're very responsive,' Acheron purred, studying her with heavy-lidded eyes the colour of melted toffee set between the twin fringes of his black lashes. He skimmed a hand down her thigh, stroked her between her legs, and her hips shifted up in supplication. He possessed her swollen mouth again with carnal hunger before he sent a finger delving into her hot, damp heat.

A sound of helpless keening pleasure was wrenched from Tabby. All of a sudden everything she was feeling was centred in that one tormentingly sensitive area of her body. He settled his mouth to her throat and nuzzled a leisurely trail along the side of her neck, awakening nerve endings she had not known she possessed. What she could not understand was that in the space of minutes she had travelled from not being very sure of what she was doing to craving what he was offering with every straining sinew in her body.

'If at any stage you want me to stop, just say so, *koukla mou*,' Acheron husked.

'Wouldn't that be very difficult for you?' she whispered, her hand smoothing down over his muscled chest to discover the thrusting power of his erection.

'I'm not a teenager. I can control myself,' Acheron

growled, arching up into her hand as she traced the velvet-smooth hardness of his shaft while marvelling at the size of him. In that field, he had more than she had expected, more width, more length, and she didn't want to think about how on earth he could make them fit as nature had intended. With a slight but perceptible shudder of reaction he relocated her stroking fingers to his muscled abdomen and added, 'As long as you don't do too much of that.'

Satisfied that she could affect him as much as he affected her, Tabby lay back only to release a whimper of startled sound as he circled her clitoris with expert fingers, unerringly striking the exact spot and the exact pace that would drive her over the edge fastest. Her heart was racing when he shifted down the bed, slid between her thighs and employed his mouth there instead. She had known about that, of course she had known, and had never thought she could be that intimate with any man but the insane pleasure he gave her drove all such logic from her mind, and she gasped and writhed and cried out. Enthralled by an exquisite torture of sensation that built and built, her body leapt out of her control altogether and jerked spasmodically into an intense climax that left her weak.

In the aftermath, Acheron rose up over her, lean, dark features taut and flushed with hunger, and she could feel the wide, blunt tip of him at the heart of her, pushing, precisely stretching her inner sheath until a sudden sharp pain made her cry out in surprise, and he froze in place.

'Do you want me to stop?' Acheron prompted raggedly.

'No point now.' Tabby could see he was in no condition to stop, could feel him hard and pulsing and alien inside her. In any case, the pain of his invasion had already faded and the ache of hollow longing he had roused still lingered. She wrapped her arms round him, instinctively urging him on, fingers smoothing across the bronzed satin of his broad back.

'You're so tight,' he rasped, shifting with an athletic lift of his lean hips to surge into her again, deeper, further, harder in a technique that met every physical craving she hadn't known she had. 'I'm incredibly turned on.'

The flood of sensation returned as he withdrew and plunged back into her again, ensuring that she felt every inch of his penetration. The intensity of sensation shocked her and the powerful contracting bands in her pelvis turned her into a fizzing firework of wild excitement. He moved faster and she clung, riding out the electrifying storm of passion with a heart that seemed to be thumping in her eardrums. The explosion of raw pleasure that followed stunned her as the inner convulsions of her body clenched her every muscle tight as a fist. He vented a shuddering groan of completion while the waves of delight went on and on and on, coursing through her thoroughly fulfilled body.

In a dazed state of abstraction, Tabby lay in the tumbled bedding afterwards, watching Acheron stride across the room to retrieve something before vanishing into the bathroom, from which she soon heard the sound of running water. The instant their encounter had finished, the very moment he had attained release, he had rolled away from her and made no effort to touch her again. She was painfully aware of how much she would have liked him to hold her close in a caring, affectionate way that acknowledged their new intimacy and it disturbed her that she should feel so hurt by his withdrawal. After all, she wasn't looking for, or expecting, love or commitment, was she? No, she wasn't that naive.

She had slept with Acheron because for the very first time she had felt a fierce desire to experience that extra dimension with a man. But his swift departure from the bed had disappointed her, leaving her feeling ridiculously used and rejected. That was silly, she told herself firmly, because when it came to what they had just done he had not taken advantage of her in any way. Indeed, to some degree she was willing to acknowledge that *she* had taken advantage of *him* the moment she had estimated that he would undoubtedly possess the erotic skills that were most likely to ensure that she received pleasure from her first experience. That didn't, however, entitle him to forgiveness for disappointing her in the sensitive aftermath of sex.

Slithering out of bed, Tabby swiftly got dressed, finger-combing her tangled hair back off her damp brow before she approached the bathroom door.

A towel linked round his narrow bronzed hips, Acheron was in the act of stepping out of the shower cubicle.

'A-star for the sex, F for failure for the follow-up,' Tabby pronounced with scorn, mentally blocking out the lean, powerful vibrancy of his commanding presence. Yes, Acheron Dimitrakos was gorgeous but in her scheme of things that was unimportant in comparison to the way he treated her.

CHAPTER SEVEN

IN RECEIPT OF that attack, Acheron stiffened in astonishment and angled his arrogant dark head back, his black-as-jet eyes gleaming with angry incomprehension even as his attention lingered on how astonishingly lovely Tabby looked fresh from his bed with her long blonde hair in a waving, tousled mass round her shoulders, her small face warm with self-conscious colour and her ripe pink mouth still swollen from his kisses. Even as he fought to think clearly, his reaction to that view and those thoughts was instantaneous and very physical. 'What the hell are you talking about?'

'The instant you had your satisfaction you leapt out of bed and abandoned me as though I was suffering from some horrid contagious disease,' Tabby condemned. 'Not an experience I would be tempted to repeat—you made me feel like a whore!'

'That's melodramatic nonsense,' Acheron fielded with derision, willing back his increasing arousal with every fibre of his self-discipline.

'No, I don't think it is. You couldn't even bear to hold me close for thirty seconds,' Tabby reminded him doggedly. 'Well, I think it's sad that the only way you feel comfortable physically touching anyone is in a sexual way.'

Acheron cursed in Greek. 'You don't know me as well

as you think you do. But I warned you that I didn't do cuddling.'

'You think that excuses you?' Tabby asked with scornfully unimpressed eyes of violet blue dominating her flushed and furious face. 'It doesn't. It simply shows you up as selfish and inconsiderate, and I deserved better.'

'I don't fake affection for anyone just because it's the acceptable thing to do,' Acheron bit out between clenched teeth. 'And I have so little practice at it, I would feel foolish and uncomfortable!'

And that was the most strikingly truthful thing he had told her about himself to date, Tabby reckoned, stunned by the raw honesty of that irate reply. Indeed his admission of ignorance and discomfiture squeezed her heart like a clenched fist. Without even thinking about what she was doing, she closed the distance between them, deliberately invading his personal space to stretch her arms round his neck and look up at him.

'Practise on me,' she urged quietly. 'I practised on Amber. I wasn't a very touchy-feely person either before I got to hold her for the first time.'

Acheron swallowed hard, insanely aware that she was making a platonic approach and quite impervious to the reality that below the towel he was still ragingly erect. He didn't want to hug her as though she were his friend; he wanted to shag her senseless. But he knew that option wasn't in the ring at that moment and he closed his arms round her slowly and lifted her to the other side of the big bathroom. 'You shouldn't have got dressed again,' he scolded.

'I assumed we were done,' Tabby confided bluntly.

Acheron bent down and lifted the hem of her dress to take it off over her head. Totally disconcerted, Tabby froze there for a split second, her arms crossed defensively across her bare breasts. 'What are you doing?'

Acheron hooked a finger into her knickers and jerked them down, lifting her again into his arms to trail them off. 'I may have leapt out of bed but I *was* thinking about your comfort,' he breathed as he lowered her down into the warm embrace of the scented water filling the bath. 'Now lie back and relax.'

Thoroughly disconcerted, Tabby surveyed him in wonderment. 'You came in here and ran a bath for me?'

'I hurt you...I thought you'd be sore,' he breathed huskily as he lit the candles in the candelabra by the sink and doused the lights.

'It was just one of those things, not your fault.' But Tabby reddened and sank deeper into the soothingly warm water, resting her head weakly back on the cushioned padding on the rim. In truth she *was* sore, that part of her so tender she was now uncomfortably aware of her pelvic area. What a pair they were, she thought morosely. He couldn't do ordinary affection and she couldn't do sex.

There was a pop as Acheron released a cork from a champagne bottle and sent bubbling golden liquid down into a pair of goblets.

'Where did that come from? And the candles?' she pressed weakly.

'Honeymoon couple, wedding night? The staff had all the trimmings waiting in the bedroom... It would be a shame not to use them,' Acheron remarked, perching on the side of the bath to offer her a glass of champagne.

'No, thanks. I never drink,' she said stiltedly.

Acheron thrust the glass into her hand. 'Unless you have a drink problem, one glass isn't going to do any damage.'

Her small fingers tensed round the stem. 'No, I don't have a problem but my parents did.'

'That doesn't mean you have to avoid it altogether.'

'I always like to play it safe,' Tabby confided, taking a small sip of the champagne, tiny bubbles bursting below her nose and moistening her skin.

'I'm more of a risk-taker. I enjoy excitement,' Acheron traded wryly.

'I think I could've worked that out for myself.'

Acheron compressed his mouth, his eyes semi-concealed by his black lashes. 'I didn't stay in bed with you because I didn't want you to have unrealistic expectations of our relationship.'

She grasped what he meant immediately and wished she didn't, a tiny pang of hurt pinching somewhere down deep inside her. He didn't want her getting the idea that there was anything more complex between them than straightforward sex. 'I may be inexperienced but I'm not stupid,' Tabby told him with pride.

'And I'm not good with words if I gave you that impression,' Acheron acknowledged grimly. 'Tabby, I don't have conversations like this with women. I've never met a woman like you.'

'Are we *still* talking about me being a virgin?' Tabby asked in a small voice.

'I'm accustomed to women who know the score.'

'I know it too,' Tabby breathed, skimming a glance across his hard-edged profile, her chest tightening with a sense of constraint. 'I'm a very practical person.'

Acheron scanned her small, tight face, the set grip of her tiny hands over her raised knees as he read the valiant defensiveness she used as a screen and his stomach hollowed out at the prospect of hurting her. He had never felt that way around a woman before and he didn't like it at all. She might be fragile but she had made a choice, just as he had done, and they were both adults, he reminded himself impatiently as he straightened again.

At the same moment, Tabby sat up abruptly and set down the champagne flute, water sloshing noisily around her slight body. 'Oh, my goodness, what am I doing in here? I can't stay! The baby monitor is in my bedroom.'

'Melinda will take care of Amber's needs. Relax,' Acheron urged.

'Melinda can't be expected to work twenty-four hours a day. I told her I'd take care of Amber at night,' Tabby countered as she rolled onto her knees, concern for Amber overcoming her self-consciousness, and began to stand up. 'Pass me a towel—'

'No, you stay where you are,' Acheron instructed, his hand closing over her shoulder to press her back into the warm water again. 'I'll collect the monitor and check on Amber as well.'

Her violet eyes widened. '*You*...will?'

Acheron strode back into the bedroom to retrieve his jeans and wandered back to the doorway, dropping the towel with total unselfconsciousness to pull on the jeans. 'Why not? You've already shown me what to do with her if she's crying.'

'I wasn't expecting you to help,' Tabby commented. 'It's my job, not yours, after all.'

'Our arrangement isn't that clear cut. This is a joint venture when it comes to me requiring a wife and you requiring an adoptive father figure,' Acheron reminded her, turning on his heel.

Stiff with uncertainty, Tabby lay back in the warm water and sipped the champagne while still feeling thoroughly confused by Acheron's behaviour. She had got him wrong when she condemned him for abandoning her immediately after sex. But then, had the simple act of sex put him into a particularly good mood? Could a man be that basic? In consideration of her needs, he had run her a bath before he went for his shower. Now he was actually off to check on Amber for her as if the child was something more than the extra baggage she had assumed he deemed her to be. At the same time, however, he had also clearly felt the need to spell out the lowering message that the only thing between him and Tabby was sex. As if she didn't already know that!

Acheron was the ultimate womaniser, steering clear of involvement and commitment. And why shouldn't he? common sense asked. A young, handsome, wealthy male was in high demand in the world of women and had no need to settle on only one. In addition, Acheron had issues but then who didn't after such a childhood as they had both undergone? In remembrance, Tabby suppressed a shiver. He had probably learned just as she had that if you kept everyone at arm's length you didn't get hurt.

But Tabby had moved on from that self-protective stance when she first opened her heart to friendship with Sonia and then Amber and finally understood how much more warm and satisfying life could be with love and loyalty in it. She knew she had lost her business and her first home because she had chosen to personally care for Sonia and Amber but she had no regrets about the choices she had made.

Amber was now her sole responsibility, she recalled, while wondering what she was doing lying back in a luxury bathtub drinking champagne when the baby she loved might be in need of her. In an instant she had clambered dripping out of the bath and swathed herself in a big warm towel, hurriedly patting herself dry before reaching for her dress again. It was time to get back to the real world, she told herself urgently, and there was nothing 'real world' about lounging around lazily in Acheron's opulent bathroom.

Acheron groaned when he heard the baby crying through the monitor. The little plastic speaker was set on the dressing table and as he studied it he became aware that something had been written on the mirror.

'Go home, whore!' someone had printed with what looked like a red felt-tip pen.

Bemused, nerves still jumping at the sound of the baby crying, Acheron hesitated only a moment before striding into the bathroom to snatch up a towel, dampening it and walking back to wipe the mirror clean again before Tabby could see it. For a split second he paused, brooding over the disturbing awareness that only his household staff had access to the bedroom and that one of them clearly wasn't trustworthy. But why leave such a message for Tabby to find? he questioned furiously. She was his wife, his legal wife with every right to be in his house. Who would target Tabby? His handsome mouth down-curved: Kasma was the most likely suspect. Pure rage blazed in Acheron as he dug out his cell phone, called his head of security and brought him up to speed on the development. His temper uneven, he strode off to take care of the baby. She was only a baby, he told himself bracingly, of course he could handle one tiny baby without help.

Amber was sitting upright screaming at the top of her voice, her little face red as fire. Acheron hovered a few feet from the cot. 'Nothing's that bad,' he told Amber in what he hoped was a soothing tone.

Amber lifted up her arms expectantly.

'Do I need to come that close?' Acheron asked uneasily. 'I'm here. You're safe. I assure you that nothing bad is going to happen to you.'

Amber fixed bewildered brown eyes on him, tears

rolling down her crumpled face, and lifted her arms again in open demand.

Acheron released his breath on a slow measured hiss and moved closer. 'I'm no good at the cuddling stuff,' he warned her ruefully, reaching down to lift the child, who startled him by wrapping both arms tightly round his throat and hanging on as firmly to him as a monkey gripping a branch.

An exhausted sob sounded in his ear, and he splayed a big hand across the little girl's back and shifted his fingers in a vague circular motion aimed at soothing her fears. A vague shard of memory featuring a woman's face momentarily froze him where he stood. He didn't recall what age he had been but he had certainly been very small when the woman had come in the night to comfort him, rocking him in her arms and singing to him until he stopped crying. Had that woman been Olympia, Amber's late grandmother and his own mother's former carer? Who else could it have been? Only Olympia had ever shown him concern and treated him as if he was something other than a nuisance part of her well-paid job.

'I owe you,' he told Amber heavily and he rearranged her awkwardly in his arms and began to rock her, suppressing that rare memory of the past with the profound discomfort that such images always brought him. 'But even for you I can't sing.'

Amber startled him by smiling widely up at him, showing off her two front teeth, and he smiled back before he even knew what he was doing.

And that was how Tabby saw them when she came to a halt in the doorway: Acheron with a tousled black curl falling over his brow, his haunting dark eyes locked to Amber while the most glorious smile lifted his wide, sensual mouth. Barefoot and bare-chested, well-worn jeans hanging low on his lean hips, he looked both extravagantly handsome and unusually human at the same time. Her breath feathered in her throat and her mouth ran dry because that smile was pure sensual dynamite.

'Let me take her,' she proffered quietly. 'I'll put her back in bed.'

'We were managing fine,' Acheron announced, not without pride in the accomplishment as he settled Amber into Tabby's arms. 'Obviously she's not very choosy.'

'Well, you're wrong there. She can actually be quite choosy and can be difficult with some people,' Tabby admitted as she rested Amber down on the changing mat and deftly changed her before placing the child back into her cot, gently stroking her cheek when she grizzled. 'It's bedtime, sweetness. We don't play at bedtime.'

'I'll organise cover for the nights,' Acheron remarked as she joined him in the corridor.

'That's not necessary.'

'You can still go to her if you want but you can't be dragged out of bed *every* night,' he told her drily.

'I'm still the woman who wants to be her mother. It's my duty to be there for her,' Tabby reminded him gently. 'I don't want other people looking after her all the time.'

'Be reasonable.' Acheron paused outside the two doors that led into their separate bedrooms. 'Are you joining me for what remains of the night?'

The ease with which he asked the question disconcerted Tabby because she had assumed that once his lusty curiosity was satisfied she would no longer be of interest to him. His approach both pleased and annoyed her. 'I'm afraid if I did join you, there would have to be rules,' she murmured awkwardly, her hand closing on the handle of her own bedroom door.

'Rules?' Acheron repeated in wonderment. 'Is that your idea of a joke?'

'No, I rarely joke about serious stuff,' Tabby countered gently. 'If you want to hear the rules, ask me.'

'I don't do rules,' Acheron ground out between gritted teeth. 'Perhaps it has escaped your attention, but I'm not a misbehaving child!'

Tabby closed the door quietly in his face.

She had donned one of her slinky new nightdresses before the door opened again. She scrambled hastily below the top sheet and looked across the room enquiringly.

'What bloody rules?' Acheron slung at her, poised hands affixed to his lean hips, his hard-muscled abdomen prominent.

'One,' Tabby enumerated. 'Any relationship we have has to be exclusive and if you plan to stray you have to tell me and finish it decently. No secrets, no sneaking around on me.'

Acheron surveyed her with wild golden eyes of increasingly wrathful incredulity. 'I don't believe I'm hearing this!'

'Two,' Tabby continued unconcerned. 'You treat me with respect at all times. If I annoy you, we have it out but not around Amber.'

'You're absolutely out of your mind,' Acheron breathed with unsettling conviction while he studied her with seething, dark golden eyes. 'And I married you.'

'Three,' Tabby pronounced woodenly, although her colour was high and her hands clenched into fists by her side. 'I'm not a toy you can pick up and put down again whenever you feel like it. I'm not the entertainment when you're bored. If you treat me well, I will treat you equally well, but if you don't…well, all bets would be off then.'

'Na pas sto dialo!' Acheron murmured wrathfully. 'It means, go to hell, and take your precious rules with you!'

Tabby didn't breathe again until the door had snapped closed behind him and then she lay back in bed, her body feeling heavy as a stone dropped from a height, her tummy rolling like a boat on a storm-tossed sea. Well, that was one way of getting rid of Acheron without losing face, one way of ensuring he was forced to see her as an equal. What else could she have said? Sliding willy-nilly into a casual sexual affair with no boundaries was not her style and with a man as volatile as he was it would be a sure recipe for disaster. But now that the ultimate womanising, free-spirited man knew that she would make major demands, he would be careful to avoid her from now on.

And what sort of idiot was she to feel sad about that fact? She would get over her silly notions about him—of course she would, because there was really no other option open to her. He wanted one thing, she wanted another, so it was better to end it before it got messy and painful and humiliating. Better by far...

In the middle of the night, Acheron went for a cold shower. His erection wouldn't quit and he was still in an unholy rage. Rules, blasted rules. Was he suddenly back at school? Who did she think she was dealing with? Even more crucially, *what* did she think she was dealing with? Did she assume he had got into that bed and somehow signed up for the whole relationship charade? Trust a woman to take a concept as simple as sex and complicate it!

Even so, he was as furious with himself as he was with her. He had suspected that her naivety would lead to problems and he knew he should have listened to his misgivings. But just as the hot blood pulsing through his tense, aching body wouldn't stop, his desire for her had proved unrelenting. He'd had to know what she was like and he'd found out and, even worse, she had been amazing and no sooner had he stopped than he wanted to go again…and again…and again. His even white teeth clenched hard. That fast he was recalling the hot clenching of her tight little body around him, an explicit memory that did nothing to cool his overheated libido.

'So, who's the cutest little baby in the world?' Tabby chattered the next morning while Amber waved her spoon in the air, cheerfully responding to the warm, loving gush of Tabby's appreciation.

Acheron suppressed a groan and slung himself down into a chair by the dining table on the terrace. Baby talk at breakfast time, one more thing she had brought into his life that was not to his taste. First thing in the morning he liked sex and silence and since he had had neither he could not be expected to be in a good mood, he reasoned impatiently. The sight of Tabby in a little red strappy top and shorts that exposed far too much bare creamy skin for his delectation didn't help. Even a glimpse of the tattoo on her arm as she swivelled in her seat failed to switch off the ever-ready pulse at his groin.

Tabby tried to scan Acheron without being obvious about it, sending little flips of her eyes in his direction with her lashes quickly dropping again. He was *so* beautiful; it was surely a sin for a male to be so beautiful that she was challenged to stop staring at him. Even the awareness of the lingering tenderness between her legs couldn't dull her appreciation of that long, lean, powerful frame of his, gracefully draped in the chair like a work of art to be admired. The sunlight glittered over his black springy curls, and she wanted to run her fingers through his hair, stroke that stubborn jaw line set like granite until she awakened that wonderful smile again. Disconcerted by her treacherous thoughts, Tabby twisted her head away, resisting temptation.

Amber extended both arms in Acheron's direction and beamed at him. 'Not right now, *koukla mou*,' he murmured. 'Have your breakfast first.'

That he had acknowledged Amber's presence but not hers aggravated Tabby. Last night she had only been a body but this morning she was evidently invisible into the bargain. 'Good morning, Acheron,' she said curtly.

'Kalimera, yineka mou,' Ash murmured silkily, noting the fiery brightness of her extraordinary violet eyes as she settled her gaze on him. 'Did you sleep well?'

'Like a log,' Tabby lied, wondering why he brought out a mean streak in her that she had never known she had.

A maid poured his coffee, and the rich aroma flared her nostrils, inexplicably reminding her that Sonia had become preternaturally sensitive to certain smells when she first fell pregnant with Amber and an edge of panic suddenly sliced through Tabby's surface calm. 'Last night…' she prompted abruptly, waiting with a rapidly beating heart and hot cheeks for the maid to retreat. 'You *did* use protection, didn't you?'

Magnificently nonchalant in the face of that intimate question, Acheron widened lustrous, dark golden eyes in mocking amusement. 'You think I would be stupid enough to neglect such a precaution?'

'I think in the heat of the moment if you wanted something enough you would take risks,' Tabby admitted tautly.

Acheron lifted a winged ebony brow and cocked his handsome head in Amber's direction. 'Not if it meant risking the acquisition of one of those,' he declared. 'Passion doesn't rule me.'

'Or me,' she echoed half under her breath. As she leant forward to help Amber clear her plate, her breasts stirred beneath her tee with the movement, pushing her unbearably sensitive nipples against the fabric, and made her think that a bra would have been a better idea than going without. Particularly in Acheron's radius.

The same view was not wasted on Acheron either, who recalled the precise pout of her delicate flesh and his almost overpowering desire to eat her alive. While the smouldering silence at the table stretched, the nanny entered and removed Amber from her chair to bear her off for a bath.

Acheron dragged in a deep, cooling breath of the sunshine laden air, knowing that, for the sake of peace and better understanding, he had to challenge Tabby's misconceptions. 'Your rules?' he mused with a dismissive shrug of one broad shoulder. '*My* rules? I never ever get involved with clingy, needy women.'

Coming at her out of nowhere, that statement crashed down on Tabby like a brick dropped on glass and her head flew up, violet eyes wide. 'Are you calling me clingy and needy?'

'What do you think?'

Tabby sprang out of her chair, the feet of it slamming back noisily across the tiles underfoot as she stabbed her hands down on the table for support. Anger had gripped her in a stormy surge. 'How dare you? I've never been clingy or needy in my life with a man!'

'Yet your first move is to try and hedge me round with rules. You want reassurance and promises about a future that is unknown to both of us,' Acheron reasoned with cold precision. 'I don't own a crystal ball.'

'I don't like the way you operate!' Tabby vented fiercely.

'Yet you know nothing about me. For years I've been exclusive in my affairs and I don't move on without saying so when I lose interest,' Acheron declared lazily, rising upright to study her, his brilliant, dark eyes hard and glittering. 'It is offensive that you should condemn me for lies and infidelity on the basis of your assumptions about my character.'

'You're so smooth...I wouldn't trust a word that came out of your mouth!' Tabby hurled at him accusingly, refusing to acknowledge that he had a point.

'Now who's guilty of prejudice?' Acheron riposted with soft sibilance. 'What do you find most offensive about me? My public-school education, my wealth or my lifestyle?'

Ferocious resentment held Tabby rigid where she stood, her small face taut and flushed with indignation, but it was the soft pink fullness of her lush mouth that welded Acheron's attention there. 'What I find most offensive is your certainty that you know best about *everything*!'

'I do know that we are poles apart and that this arrangement will work most efficiently if we stick to the original agreement we made.'

Tabby's tummy flipped as though she had gone down in a lift too fast, sheer strain locking her every muscle into tautness. 'You should've kept your blasted hands off me!' she slammed back.

Acheron flashed her a grim appraisal from his stunning golden eyes, and his mouth twisted sardonically. 'Sadly, I *couldn't*...'

And with that final admission, Acheron strode back into the air-conditioned cool of the villa and left her alone to contemplate the truly fabulous view. The rolling green

Tuscan hills stretched out before her marked out in a colourful patchwork of woodland, olive groves and vineyards. She snatched in a deeply shaken breath, the hot air scouring her lungs. He wanted them to return to the sensible terms of their platonic agreement, which was exactly what she had believed she wanted. Why, then, when she had achieved her goal, did she feel as though she had lost the battle? Indeed, instead of feeling relieved and reassured by his logical approach to their differences, she felt ridiculously hurt and abandoned…

CHAPTER EIGHT

Tabby rolled the soft ball back to Amber where the child sat below the dappled shade of an ancient spreading oak tree. Amber rolled over and crawled to the edge of the rug, a look of glee in her bright eyes as she scanned the wide green expanse of freedom open before her.

Tabby marvelled at the speed with which the little girl had learned to embrace independent movement. One minute she had been rolling over and over again to explore further afield and the next she had perfected crawling. At just over seven months old she was a fairly early developer but she had always been a physically strong baby who met every developmental guideline in advance, and Tabby wasn't really surprised that Amber had discovered how to get around without adult assistance ahead of time. As she watched the little girl pulled a blade of grass and stuck it in her mouth.

'No...no,' she was saying while retrieving the grass when Melinda strolled up and offered to give her a break.

'Yes, and you're welcome,' Tabby confided ruefully. 'She's much more of a handful now, and I wouldn't mind a little break to sunbathe and read.'

'We can manage that. I'm going to put her in the buggy and take her for a walk,' the blonde nanny told her smoothly. 'I just love it here.'

Tabby glanced at the younger woman, wondering why she found it such a challenge to like her and feeling rather guilty about the fact. After all, Melinda was great with Amber, a diligent worker and friendly. Perhaps it was the hungry little glances she often saw Melinda aiming at Acheron that had prevented Tabby from bonding more with the other young woman. It was not that she was jealous, Tabby reasoned uneasily, simply that she wasn't comfortable with a woman prepared to show that much interest in the married man who employed her. In any case, and to be fair to all parties concerned, Acheron had shown not the smallest awareness of Melinda's curvaceous blonde allure.

'Any idea when we'll be leaving here yet?' Melinda asked as she gathered up Amber's toys and stuffed them in a bag.

'Not yet, sorry…my husband hasn't decided how long we'll be staying,' Tabby replied, wryly impressed by the way that possessive label slid off her tongue. But that, she had learned, was the easiest way to refer to Acheron in front of the staff.

Yet he was as much a husband as a caged tiger in a zoo would be, she conceded unhappily, lifting her book and her sunglasses and heading for the cool courtyard in which the pool was situated. For the past week she had barely seen Acheron, who confined himself to his office most of the day and often half the night to work. Even when he was around his phone was always ringing and his single-minded focus on business was exactly what she should have expected from a goal-orientated alpha male.

Occasionally he would join her for a cup of coffee at breakfast time and he generally put in a rather silent appearance at the dinner table, eating quickly and then politely excusing himself. He was a cool and distant companion at those meals and there was never so much as a hint of sexual awareness in either his looks or his conversation. It was as though that wild bout of passion on their wedding night was the product of her imagination alone, but Tabby still found it a distinct challenge to revert to treating him like a stranger and that embarrassed her, denting her pride and her belief in her own strength and independence because no woman of character should continue to crave the attention of a man set on treating her like the wallpaper.

Yet amazingly, infuriatingly, Acheron was playing an entirely different ball game with Amber. Melinda swore that Acheron never passed the nursery door without coming in to talk to and play with her charge and Amber had already learned to make a beeline for Acheron whenever he was in her vicinity. In fact, when it came to Acheron, Amber took her welcome for granted. Maybe Acheron's ego was flattered by the amount of attention Amber gave him. Maybe he was even belatedly discovering that he actually liked and enjoyed the company of children? How could she possibly know what motivated his interest? Tabby had not got through a week of virtually sleepless nights without acknowledging that she knew very little at all about Acheron Dimitrakos. Her husband was a mystery to her in almost every conceivable way.

Acheron stood at the window and groaned at the sight of Tabby arranging her slim pale body on a lounger like an exhibition banquet for the starving. A purple bikini cupped her rounded little breasts and slender hips and every shift of her slim thighs drew his considerable attention. He shifted uneasily, struggling to rein back the heavy pulse of arousal that was making his nights so long and frustrating.

Although he had kept watch, as he told himself a protective husband should do, he had yet to see Tabby go topless to eradicate the risk of tan marks. He frowned, not wanting her to show that amount of naked flesh when there were always staff roaming the grounds. It was very strange, he acknowledged in bewilderment, that in spite of the fact he thought it was a very old-fashioned attitude, which he would not have admitted even under torture, he didn't like the idea of anyone but him seeing any part of Tabby bare. He thought that there was a very weird possessive streak in him somewhere and blamed it on the surprising fact that he had become his wife's first lover.

His wife, a label he had never thought he would use, he conceded hard-mouthed, his dark eyes hooded and unusually reflective. Had Tabby genuinely been his wife, however, she would have been in his bed throughout the long hot hours of the afternoon abandoning herself to the demands of his passion and losing herself in the release he would have given her. As his body hardened afresh under the onslaught of that X-rated imagery he cursed bitterly under his breath.

Regretfully, Tabby had all the flexibility of a steel girder: he could do the rules or he could do cold showers. There would be no halfway measures, no get-out clause with her. It would be all or nothing and he knew he *couldn't* do it, couldn't walk that line and change himself to suit when he knew there was no future in it. It wouldn't be fair to her. Yet right at that precise moment Tabby's rules had more pulling power than a ten-ton truck.

That evening, Tabby selected a drop-dead gorgeous blue dress from the closet. Over the past week she had worn a different outfit every day, reasoning that the clothes were there and there was little point wasting them. In any case it would be downright silly to choose to overheat in the jeans and tops that were virtually all she had left of her own clothes since her life first began to unravel after she had lost her own home. Back then she had had to surrender an awful lot of her possessions, whittling her collection of clothing and objects down until she retained only what mattered most and what she could carry.

She tossed the dress on the bed, put on her make-up and brushed her hair, not that how she looked mattered when Acheron was treating her as though she were someone's maiden aunt. But then Acheron *wasn't* the reason why she took the trouble to dress up, she reminded herself staunchly. She did it for her own self-esteem and the knowledge that behaving, at least on the outside, like a rich honeymoon bride was part of her role. Clothed, she eased her feet into perilously high heels and surveyed herself critically in the mirror, mouth momentarily drooping while she wished she were taller, curvier and more striking in appearance…like Kasma? The Kasma whom Acheron never, ever mentioned? But then what business was Kasma of hers? The fiery fury, ignited only a week before by the discovery that Acheron would benefit as much as she did from their marriage, had drained away. After all, she had married Acheron for only one reason: to become Amber's adoptive mother, and all she needed to focus on now was getting through their little charade of a marriage as smoothly and painlessly as possible. Worrying about anything else, *wanting* anything else was unnecessarily stressful and stupid.

Acheron was crossing the hall when Tabby reached the head of the marble staircase. Obeying instinct, she threw her head back and straightened her spine even as she felt perspiration break out across her skin. There he was, sleek, outrageously good-looking and sophisticated even when clad in jeans and an open-necked shirt. Her heart went bumpety-bumpety-bump like a clock wound up too tight, and she gripped the bannister with an agitated hand to start down the stairs. Unfortunately for her, her leading foot went down, however, not onto a step but disorientatingly into mid-air and she tipped forward with a shocked cry of fright, her hand slipping its light hold on the stair rail, her whole body twisting as she tried to halt her fall so that her hip struck the edge of a hard marble step and her ankle was turned beneath her.

'I've got you!' Acheron bit out as the world steadied again.

Mercifully Tabby registered that she was no longer falling but that pain was biting all the way from her hip down her leg…no, not her leg, her ankle. She adjusted as Acheron swept her up into his arms with too much enthusiasm and her leg swung none too gently and she couldn't bite back the cry of pain that was wrenched from her throat. 'My ankle…'

'*Thee mou*…you could've been killed falling on these stairs!' Acheron breathed with a rawness that took her aback, striding back down into the hall with his arms tautly linked round her slight body. He called out in Greek until one of his security staff came running and then he rapped out instructions.

Against her cheek she could feel the still-accelerated pounding of his heart and she wasn't surprised that he was still high on adrenalin because he must have moved faster than the speed of light to intercept her fall. She felt quite queasy at the realisation that but for his timely intervention she might have fallen all the way down the marble staircase and broken her neck or at the very least a limb or two. Relief that she had only wrenched her ankle and bruised herself filtered slowly through her. 'I'm OK... Lucky you caught me in time.'

Acheron laid her down with exaggerated care on a sofa and squatted athletically down to her level. 'Did you feel anyone push you?' he asked, brilliant dark heavily fringed eyes locked to her face.

She was astounded at the tenor of that question; her violet eyes rounded. 'Why would anyone push me down the stairs?' she asked weakly. 'I lost my balance and tripped.'

Acheron frowned. 'Are you certain? I thought I saw someone pass by you on the landing just before you fell.'

'I didn't see or hear anyone.' Her brows pleated and her lashes screened her eyes, the heat of embarrassment washing away her pallor because she knew exactly *why* she had tripped but wild horses wouldn't have dragged the confession from her. 'Yes, of course I'm certain.'

If she hadn't been so busy admiring Acheron and trying to pose like a silly teenager to look her very best for his benefit, she would never have missed her step, Tabby was reflecting in deep, squirming chagrin.

'I'm afraid I have to move you again...I'll try not to hurt you,' Acheron told her, sliding his hands beneath her prone length. 'But I have to get you into a car to get you to a doctor.'

'For goodness' sake, I don't need a doctor!' Tabby exclaimed in growing embarrassment.

But over the next couple of hours while she was subjected to every possible medical examination at the nearest hospital, she might as well have been talking to a wall because Acheron refused to listen to a word she said. Furthermore, far from behaving like the cool, reserved male she was accustomed to dealing with, Acheron was clearly all wound up although why he was, she had no idea. He paced the floor outside her examination cubicle, talked to her through the curtain to check she was all right and not in too much discomfort, insisted on an X-ray being done while virtually ignoring the doctor who assured him that she was suffering from nothing more serious than some nasty bruising and a sprained ankle. Even more embarrassing, his security team spread out round them on full systems alert as if awaiting an imminent rocket attack on the casualty department.

'Ah...very much the adoring and anxious husband,' the middle-aged doctor chuckled in his ignorance.

If only the man knew how wrong he was, Tabby thought unhappily, feeling like a wretched nuisance and a malingerer taking up valuable medical attention when really there was nothing very much amiss with her.

If Tabby had died, it would have been *his* fault. Acheron brooded on that thought darkly, rage and guilt slivering through him in sickening waves and like nothing he had ever felt before. But then he had never been responsible for another life before and, though he would have liked to have thought otherwise, he believed that his wife was very much *his* responsibility. Naturally he was appalled by the suspicion that someone who worked for him might have attempted to hurt his wife. Having seen the rude message left on her bedroom mirror, he was unimpressed by her conviction that she had simply had an accident. In the split second it had taken for Tabby to lose her balance and topple she might not even have noticed that someone had lightly pushed her or tripped her up.

He was even more frustrated that his security staff had failed to come up with anything suspicious on any member of the villa staff. Acheron's mouth twisted. Unfortunately the Tuscan villa had rarely been used, hence the renovation the previous year and the hire of employees who were a new and unknown quantity and whose dependability would only be confirmed by the test of time. His lustrous eyes hardened and his stubborn mouth compressed into a tough line of determination. Tabby's safety was paramount and as he was very reluctant to frighten her with his suspicions. The wisest strategy would be to immediately vacate the villa and seek a more secure setting. That decision reached, Acheron gave the order, refusing to back down even when the chief of his security pointed out that such a move would entail rousing the baby from her bed as well. Regardless of the drawbacks of his plan, Acheron could hardly wait to get Tabby and the baby away from the Tuscan villa, which now, to his way of thinking, seemed a tainted place. He watched the doctor bandaging her swollen ankle, annoyance still gripping him that he had failed to prevent her from getting hurt.

'Sorry about all this.' Tabby sighed in the limo as they left the hospital.

'When you have an accident you don't need to apologise for it. How are you?' Acheron pressed.

'A bit battered and sore—nothing I won't quickly recover from,' Tabby responded with a smile. 'It'll certainly teach me to be more careful on stairs from now on.'

Acheron was quietly stunned. No woman of his acquaintance would have neglected to make a huge fuss over such an incident by exaggerating their injuries and demanding his sympathy and attention. Tabby, however, characteristically downplayed the episode and asked nothing of him, an acknowledgement that only increased his brooding discomfiture with the situation.

'Where on earth are we going?' Tabby enquired as he lifted her out of the limo and stowed her in the wheelchair already waiting for her use. 'Is this the airport?'

'Yes, we're flying to Sardinia,' Acheron said casually.

'Seriously? I mean, like *right now*?' Tabby stressed in disbelief. 'It's ten o'clock at night.'

'Amber and her nanny are already on board the helicopter, as is your luggage,' Acheron admitted.

There were many things Tabby could have said but she was fighting a dropped jaw and had already learned to think twice before she spoke her mind around Acheron. She clamped her lips firmly together and assumed that he was bored at the villa and that the evident appeal of a change of surroundings had persuaded him to act on impulse. Not only was he dragging Amber out of bed, but he was also forcing Tabby to travel when she was exhausted and in pain. Her lush mouth down-curved: he was being selfishly inconsiderate but she supposed that was normal behaviour for a male accustomed to thinking only of his own needs.

The helicopter was very noisy and Tabby, who hadn't eaten since lunchtime, was almost sick with hunger. She insisted on taking Amber from Melinda, though, and soothed the overtired baby herself. She was surprised when Acheron eased the drowsing child from her arms and settled her on his lap instead. Amber looked up at him, stuck her thumb back in her mouth and closed her eyes again, seemingly content with the exchange. Tabby must've dozed off at that point because she wakened confused by the bright light on her face and the jabs of pain from her ankle as Acheron carried her into a house.

'How do you feel?' he enquired again, stunning gaze sweeping her pale, taut face.

'I'll be fine—'

'Don't be a martyr—you look like death warmed over,' he countered impatiently. 'You're going straight to bed, *yineka mou*. I've organised food as well.'

A bed and a meal sounded very appealing to Tabby at that moment. He mounted a staircase and a faint breeze cooled her cheekbone. Her lashes swept up on a tall open window framed by pale fluttering draperies just as Acheron laid her down on a ginormous bed and began to carefully ease the bedding from beneath her. It struck her that for once he was being very kind and that set her teeth on edge.

'Why are you being so nice to me all of a sudden?' Tabby demanded abruptly.

That single question said so much that Acheron didn't want to hear just then that he almost groaned his frustration aloud. Leave it to Tabby, he thought ruefully. Leave it to Tabby to say what nobody else dared to say to Acheron Dimitrakos. He breathed in slowly. 'You're hurt.'

'You don't do rules and I don't do pity,' Tabby told him, tilting her chin in challenge.

'You're my wife.'

'Not really.'

'*Enough* my wife that I want to treat you like one,' Acheron contradicted almost harshly.

Tabby screened eyes blank with incomprehension and she was horribly tempted by an urge to slap him. He should have come with a dictionary or some sort of instruction manual that explained how he worked because once again she was all at sea as to what went on his complex and infuriating head.

'I want to make you feel better,' Acheron announced.

'No pity parties here, please.'

'I haven't behaved very well,' Acheron muttered in a harsh driven undertone. 'I am trying to make amends.'

'Pity's pity,' Tabby told him, unmoved by that argument.

Acheron came down on the bed beside her. There was

something wild about the glitter in his seething golden eyes as he gently knotted one hand in the fall of her golden hair and closed his mouth hungrily over hers. He sent a jolt of such savage hunger rocketing through her that she froze in sheer fright.

'Does that feel like pity?' he growled.

Tabby made no comment because she could barely breathe. She wanted him to do it again and for longer and was only just able to keep her hands off that lean, powerful body so very close to hers for the first time in a week. One little touch and he made her feel like a sex addict ready to run scarily out of control. In sudden retreat, she dropped her head and then mercifully they were interrupted by the entrance of a woman carrying a tray.

'You need to eat,' Acheron told her unnecessarily.

With his assistance, Tabby leant back against the pillows and lifted the knife and fork. She literally didn't *dare* look at him again, couldn't trust herself that far, knew that she couldn't risk reliving that burning, driving sensation of sexual need in his presence. Hungry though she undoubtedly was, she had to force herself to eat because the sheer level of tension holding her taut was suppressing her appetite. She ate in silence while Acheron paced restively round the big room, constantly drawing her eyes until she remembered that she couldn't afford to look, and in fact had to blank him out to stay in control. And what did that say about her? Was she really that weak that she couldn't withstand him? This guy who had virtually ignored her for the past week? The same one who had slept with her and then backed off at supersonic speed? Shame engulfed her, increasing the exhaustion she had been fighting to contain.

The tray was removed from her lap. Her lashes

drooped, eyes so heavy she literally couldn't hold them open any longer.

'Get some sleep,' Acheron urged, and for once she was in the mood to obey.

Tabby awoke with a piercing need to go to the bathroom, eyes flickering open on darkness and a strong feeling of disorientation. She struggled to sit up and gasped in dismay at the pain that shot through her ankle while she stretched out a wildly flailing hand in search of a bedside light. Mercifully she found the switch attached to a hanging wire, and light illuminated the bedroom a scant second before the male lying on a sofa against the wall leapt upright.

'Ash?' she whispered in disbelief. 'What are you doing in here?'

Acheron was bare-chested and barefoot, low-slung denim jeans clinging to his lean hips. Her startled gaze clung to the muscled expanse of his magnificent bronzed torso and then flicked guiltily higher to take in the dark stubble masking his lower jaw and the unnerving intensity of eyes that glittered like black diamonds in the low light. 'I couldn't leave you in here alone.'

'Why not?' Tabby queried, her face hotter than fire as she forced herself to swivel her hips and shift her good leg off the edge of the bed. 'Why would you sleep on a sofa for my benefit?'

'What on earth are you trying to do?' Acheron demanded, striding across the room.

'I need the bathroom,' she breathed between gritted teeth, mortification rolling over her like a tidal wave.

'You are so stubborn, *koukla mou*. Right now, you need help and I didn't want to put a stranger in here with you,' he admitted impatiently, pushing the walking stick resting against the bedside cabinet into her hand and then slowly pulling her upright to take advantage of its support. 'Now go slow or you'll hurt yourself.'

But Tabby had already worked out that there was no way of moving her leg without her ankle hurting her and she simply clenched her teeth and got on with it, tears stinging her eyes as she hobbled clumsily towards the connecting door he had already opened for her benefit.

Acheron groaned something in Greek and carefully scooped her up into his arms to carry her into the bathroom and gently settle her down on the stool by the vanity unit. 'Pain's always worse in the middle of the night. You'll feel better tomorrow,' he predicted. 'Shout when you're ready to go back to bed.'

Reckoning that there would be two blue moons in the sky before she willingly asked for his help, Tabby studied her tousled reflection in the mirror in cringing horror. She was still wearing the make-up she had put on for dinner the night before and she had panda eyes, sleep creases on her cheek and hideously messy hair. How come he looked gorgeous in the middle of the night but she looked like the Bride of Dracula?

She glanced down and fingered the skimpy nightdress she now wore and swallowed back a groan. Acheron must've undressed her. So what? He had already seen her naked, she reminded herself doggedly, so he had seen nothing new and it was very silly to be embarrassed about it. Levering herself upright, she took care of necessities and then made use of the facilities to clean herself up as best she could. Feeling considerably fresher but pale and stiff with the amount of pain her every movement had made her suffer, Tabby hobbled back out of the bathroom.

Acheron was waiting to scoop her up and deposit her back on the bed.

'I still don't understand what you're doing here with me,' she said weakly, perspiration breaking out on her brow.

'There're only three bedrooms in the main house. I knew you wouldn't want Amber staying away from you in the staff quarters and Melinda needed the third room,' Acheron explained drily.

'There's *only* three bedrooms?' Tabby remarked in amazement. 'You really didn't plan this move very well, did you?'

Acheron dealt her a fulminating appraisal in seething silence. 'It's three in the morning…let's talk about it tomorrow.'

Tabby watched him move back towards the sofa and released her breath on a reluctant sigh. 'Oh, for goodness' sake, share the bed… It's as big as a football pitch. I'm sure we can manage to avoid each other.'

Acheron swung round, his surprise unfeigned, but he said nothing. He switched out the light, and she lay very still in the darkness, listening to the sound of his jeans coming off and trying very hard not to picture what he looked like without them. The sheet moved, the mattress depressed and she forced herself to relax. She was safe as houses with him, she told herself wryly. Acheron was powered by reason, not emotion, not passion. He knew they were a match made in hell.

It was dawn by the time Tabby woke again. Soreness and stiffness assailed her with her first involuntary movement, and she screwed up her face in silent complaint. She turned her head only for her breath to hitch at the sight of Acheron lying asleep only inches away from her. His hair, rumpled into ebony curls, stood out in stark contrast to the white pillow case, his black lashes luxuriant fans that rimmed his strong cheekbones, his wilful passionate mouth full and relaxed. She couldn't stop staring at him. The sheet was wrapped round his hips, the corrugated musculature of his bronzed chest and abdomen exposed as well as a long, powerful, hair-roughened thigh. The pure haunting beauty of his perfectly sculpted body grabbed her by the throat and shook her inside out while heat pooled in her pelvis. She wanted to touch him; she wanted to touch him so badly it hurt to be denied.

His lashes swept up and he stretched slowly and languorously, long, taut muscles defined like ropes below his smooth brown skin. *'Kalimera, yineka mou.'*

Tabby arched a brow. 'Which *means*…?'

'Good morning, wife of mine,' Acheron translated with rich amusement lightening his dark eyes.

'I'm not yours,' Tabby hissed back faster than a striking rattler.

A lean brown hand lifted and wound slowly and carefully into the tumbled fall of her blonde hair, his glittering dark golden eyes hot as boiling honey on her skin. 'How else would you describe yourself? You married me and then you accepted my body into yours. Don't you appreciate that that means that we legally consummated our union?'

Seized by chagrin and confusion, Tabby stiffened. 'I…I…'

He covered her mouth with his, lingering to nibble teasingly at her full lower lip before moving on to taste her with explosive eroticism. A chemical reaction took place inside her, her body jerking in response while within seconds a giant mushroom of heated hunger and longing surged up inside her, blowing her best intentions to hell. Helpless in the grip of that sensual offensive, she kissed him back and his tongue drove deep between her lips with a raw sexual charge that roared through her like a rocket attack.

'Ash?' she mumbled when he freed her long enough to breathe again.

He stared down at her with lancing impatience, every line of him rigid with tension. 'To hell with your rules,' he growled in a tone of decision, his broad chest vibrating against her swollen breasts. 'I only play by my own.'

Those words were still ringing in her ears when he slid his hands underneath her and lifted her slowly onto her side. 'What are you doing?' she gasped.

'I'm making what we both need possible,' Acheron rasped in her ear, his warm breath fanning her neck as he buried his mouth in the sensitive slope between neck and shoulder while his hands slid up from her waist to cup her achingly tender breasts. 'As you're in no condition to run away, shout loud if you want to say no.'

In stark disconcertion her violet eyes opened to their fullest extent and locked onto the sofa he had occupied the night before. She had invited him into the bed in the first place. Had he assumed her body was included in the offer? Or was he just as entrapped as she was by the chemistry between them? Naturally that latter interpretation pleased her more but, in the midst of her pondering, long fingers plucked at the straining peaks of her breasts and actual thought became too much of a challenge.

Acheron tasted the soft white skin of her throat and the sweet scent of her enclosed him, heightening his arousal to an almost unbearable extent. In need of release he pressed his throbbing erection against her bottom, and she gasped and leant back into him while he lifted her nightdress to caress the swollen bounty of her small, taut breasts, paying special attention to her plump pink nipples. 'I love your breasts,' he told her thickly. 'They fit perfectly into my hands, *moli mou*.'

Every tiny muscle straining as she trembled, Tabby looked down at the fingers, so dark against her paler skin, expertly caressing her. Sharp biting arrows of need were spearing down between her legs where her indescribably sensitive flesh was tingling. She shifted and a faint sound of discomfort was wrenched from her as she accidentally moved her ankle.

'Lie still,' Acheron urged. 'You don't need to do anything. Let me do all the work.'

Her desire was already so strong that she wanted to scream, wanted to tell him what to do and to do it quickly. The shock of the thought and a vision of his reaction cooled her teeming thoughts. But she hadn't known, hadn't ever dreamt that a kiss and a little intimate touching could send her temperature shooting from zero to overload and she knew that she was finally understanding the very basic reason why he had become her first lover. He burned her up like a lightning strike, awakened a craving that overwhelmed her defences.

His hand shimmied down over her thigh, flirting, teasing more intimate areas without delivering on the promise. She ached, she actually ached deep down inside where she felt hollow and desperate, her entire being locked to the playful passage of that provocative hand. Fingertips traced her hidden core, stroking nerve endings that were impossibly delicate. She dragged in a sustaining breath while he nibbled an enervating path down the side of her extended throat. 'In a minute I'm going to kill you,' she swore shakily.

'No, you're going to ask me to do it again.'

'You really don't suffer from low self-esteem,' she noted even more unevenly, her breath catching in her convulsing throat as a fingertip brushed her clitoris, and flame leapt through her entire core.

'Not between the sheets...no,' Acheron agreed silkily.

'You've been told you're wonderful?'

'Many times. I'm filthy rich. Telling me I'm rubbish in bed—even if it's true—wouldn't be profitable,' he advanced with cynical cool.

Consternation seized Tabby. 'That's *awful*—'

'Awful,' he mimicked, stroking the most sensitive spot on her whole body so that she jackknifed back against him with a startled yelp.

'I don't want your money,' Tabby exclaimed helplessly. 'I just want your body!'

A stark little silence fell, and she squeezed her eyes tight shut in horror. *I didn't say that, I couldn't possibly have said that!*

'I've got no objections to that goal,' Acheron husked, biting at her ear lobe with erotic intent, ostensibly undeterred by her claim. 'It's earthy and honest...why not?'

He touched her again and her mortification drowned in a sea of shivering response. She lay back against him, tiny muscles twitching, soothed by the heat and strength of him even as that amplified physical contact heightened her awareness. With immense delicacy he stroked the seam of her femininity and then slid inside where she was warm and wet and, oh, so needy. She quivered, pitched straight to a high of longing that she couldn't quell or even control. He sank a finger inside her, and she jerked and gasped as he plunged slowly in and out, raising her temperature to boiling point, making her squirm and shift, forgetting even the twinges of pain in her ankle.

'Hot, tight, ready,' Acheron growled hungrily in her ear as she arched back into his lean, hard body, instinctively seeking the fulfilment that only he could give while he angled away from her to don a condom. 'I've been fantasising about this for days.'

'Days?' she parroted in surprise as he lifted her undamaged leg to spread her open for him.

'Every night since that first night, every day I saw you in that teeny tiny bikini, *glyka mou*,' Acheron confided, tilting her forward, long fingers tightening their hold on her slender thigh as he entered her with a groan of intense masculine satisfaction.

A muffled scream of pleasure was torn from Tabby's throat as her body was forced to adjust to his size, her inner channel stretching to the brink of insane pleasure.

'All right?' Acheron murmured thickly.

'Well, I wouldn't want you to answer your phone right now!' Tabby admitted shakily, her heart thundering, her blood racing, her whole body thrumming with sensation as he eased back and then slammed into her again, jolting her with wicked pleasure.

'No boundaries!' he ground out forcefully. 'No boundaries between us!'

She couldn't think, couldn't speak for the intensity of what he was making her feel. He tugged her head back and took her mouth with passionate, driving need and the taste and heat of him scorched her all the while the slow, sure thrust of his engorged shaft stimulated her senses to an unbearable peak of excitement. Her hips writhed. The pace quickened. The heat built. She was crying out, sobbing she knew not what when her wayward body finally clamped down convulsively on him and she soared over the edge in a frenzied crescendo of release that took her by storm.

Ecstasy was still rippling through her weak body in small blissful waves when he wrapped his arms round her and kept her close.

'You're amazing,' he husked.

'You too,' she whispered, exhaustion pinning her to the bed.

'And we're going to do this over and over again,' Acheron decreed with lethally sexy assurance. 'No more cold showers, no more separate beds, no more posing in teeny tiny bikinis I can't rip off.'

'Sleepy,' she framed apologetically.

'Sleep…you're going to need all your energy,' he said.

CHAPTER NINE

WHEN TABBY WOKE for the fourth time in twelve hours, she was totally disorientated and she blinked in the strong sunlight flooding through the French windows. A split second later, she sat up and checked her watch to discover that it was mid-afternoon.

My goodness, she had slept half the day away! In guilty dismay, she clambered awkwardly out of bed, learning that Acheron had got it right when he had suggested she would feel better in the morning. Her hip still ached like the very devil but the pain in her ankle had become more bearable. Curious to see her surroundings, having arrived in complete darkness the night before, she limped over to the French windows with the aid of her stick and went out onto the sunlit balcony to stand at the rail.

A craggy cove stretched out below her, the towering rocks encircling a stretch of pure white sand lapped by a turquoise sea so clear she could see the ocean bottom. The lush tree-filled gardens ran right to the edge of the beach. It was absolutely idyllic and very beautiful but Tabby's attention was drawn straight to the couple standing together in the rippling surf. Amber's pram was parked in the shadow of the rocks and Melinda, clad in a minuscule red bikini that exaggerated her bountiful curves, was talking with apparent urgency to Acheron, whose lean, powerful body was sheathed only in trunks.

It was an unexpectedly intimate and disturbing sight, and Tabby couldn't take her eyes off the couple, jealousy spearing through her with an immediacy that appalled her. She jerked in dismay and snatched in a startled breath when Melinda rested a hand down on Acheron's arm. To his credit the contact only lasted for a second because he took an immediate step back from the forward blonde and with a brief final word strode back across the sand towards the house. Tabby hobbled back hurriedly indoors to get dressed, her brain struggling to encompass what she had seen at the same time as she accepted that, yet again, the very foundations of her relationship with the man she had married had been demolished and everything had changed.

Sexual desire had stimulated that change, she conceded, shame slivering through her. *No boundaries*, Acheron had proclaimed with passion and he was certainly correct on that score: the rules she had tried to impose had been blown right out of the water along with her nonsensical belief that she could resist him. Even more pertinently, seeing Melinda touch Acheron had inflamed her with ferocious possessiveness and the sort of angry jealous feelings she had never before experienced. What did that say about her intelligence? What was she letting him do to her? Where were these violent conflicting emotions coming from? She was behaving like a lovesick idiot! Was that the problem? Had lust first sucked her in and then left her childishly infatuated with him?

Opening her as yet still packed cases, she extracted underwear and a long, loose sundress before stepping into the bathroom to freshen up. The whole process took her much longer than usual having to wash her hair in the sink, which was a challenge, and left the bathroom floor swimming by the time she had finished. When she finally emerged after mopping dry the floor, however, she felt more like herself with clean, tidy hair and a little make-up applied.

Acheron strolled into the bedroom and there Tabby was; captured in a patch of sunlight, long golden hair rippling down to softly frame her delicate features, her tiny body sylphlike in a pale blue dress that reflected her amazing eyes, which were currently pools of anxious troubled violet that evaded his. She was *so* open, *so* honest in her reactions, it literally shocked him. Nothing was concealed; nothing was hidden from him. His broad chest tightened as he expelled his breath and gritted his teeth. He could not begin to imagine how frighteningly vulnerable that lack of concealment and reserve made her. If he didn't act first, she was undoubtedly about to unleash a rash volley of accusations and questions about their renewed intimacy, which threatened to put them both right back where they had started after their car crash wedding night and her proclamation of her unnecessary rules.

'Tabby,' he murmured evenly, noting avidly that he could see the little points of her deliciously prominent nipples showing below the fine material of her dress as well as the slender outline of her shapely legs. An overpoweringly strong urge to claim her again assailed him.

'Ash,' she said breathlessly, studying his lean, darkly handsome features with a sinking heart because that fast she was out of breath and dizzy just looking at him. 'We need to talk.'

'No, we don't, *glyka mou*,' Acheron contradicted with stubborn assurance as he drew closer. 'Let's do this my way. We don't talk, we especially *don't* agonise over anything. It is what it is and we just enjoy it for as long as it lasts.'

He had snatched the confused words out of her mouth before she had even collected her thoughts enough to speak. She suspected that his solution was vintage Acheron in the field of relationships—say nothing, do nothing and the problem will go away. 'I wasn't about to agonise over anything,' she protested, swaying slightly because she found it hard to stand still for long and had to grip the walking stick in a tighter hold.

He closed hands round her forearms to steady her and slowly trailed his hands down to her waist. 'You can't help yourself.'

As she looked up at him, her lush full lips tingled and she was conscious of a sensation like prickling heat curling low in her pelvis. He angled his mouth down and kissed her with intoxicating urgency.

'Oh...' she said in breathless surprise at the development, her body humming into ready awareness with an enthusiasm that disconcerted her.

He lifted her dress slowly, brazen dark golden eyes locked to hers, daring her to object. Anticipation pierced her, sharp as a lance, liquid heat pooling between her thighs. His gaze not once leaving hers, he found her with his fingers, eased below her lace-edged panties and stroked and that fast she was hotter than the fires of hell, leaning up against him for support, making no objection when he gently lowered her back onto the bed. The stick fell forgotten on the floor.

'I only just got up,' she exclaimed, her surprise unconcealed.

'You should've waited here for me, *glyka mou*,' Acheron told her sibilantly.

'I can't believe you want me again already.' Tabby studied him with confused and wondering eyes.

'The instant I look at you I want you,' Acheron admitted in a slightly raw undertone because there was a lack of control and a weakness in such a truth that deeply disturbed him.

'Not the very first time you saw me,' she reminded him stubbornly.

'You swore at me...not your finest hour, *glyka mou*,' he mocked. 'Now that I know you, it wouldn't bother me at all or make me stop thinking that you're the hottest woman on the planet.'

Eyes wide with astonishment, Tabby was transfixed by that statement. 'You really mean that?'

'*You have to ask*? Here I am throwing you down on the bed to ravish and you have to ask how much I want you? I can't wait to get you horizontal and that's not OK,' Acheron groaned, yanking off her panties with scant ceremony and splaying her legs with a voracious hiss of all-male satisfaction, fully appreciating the pink glistening femininity he had exposed. 'No, don't spoil the view,' he censured when, hot-cheeked, she tried to scissor her thighs together again. 'I like to look and I *love* to appreciate.'

Tabby forced herself to remember that while he peeled off his trunks, revealing his long, thick erection. Heat rolled through her, moisture gathering at the heart of her along with a soul-deep yearning that should have terrified her. She realised that she was acting on instinct, not even pausing to think about what he had said, skipping the *agonising* as he had phrased it because what woman wished to be viewed in that light?

'*Thee mou*, hot, hot, hot,' Acheron rasped as he came down on top of her, punctuating every word with a passionate kiss and hands that traced every erogenous zone she possessed until her impatience steadily rose to match his.

Only then did he sink into her hard and fast, muttering something in Greek before he paused to press his lips to her brow. 'Am I hurting you?' he grated uneasily.

'Only if you stop,' she traded helplessly, her whole body clenching round him as possessively as her arms, hands smoothing over his satin-smooth back, clenching there, nails curving inward as he ground into her, and she cried out in helpless delight. Excitement rose in an unstoppable tide, and she lost the self she knew in it, living from one glorious moment of intense sensation to the next until the great gathering storm became too much to contain and the passion swept her off the heights down into the ecstatic rippling aftermath.

'Well, there wasn't much finesse about that,' Acheron remarked, cradling her up against him in a damp tangle of limbs. 'My apologies.'

'No need,' Tabby countered, pressing her mouth softly to his chest, revelling in the hot, musky smell of his skin and the closeness that he was embracing. 'It was another ten out of ten.'

'You're *grading* me now?' he demanded in obvious horror.

'If you drop down to a five or lower, I'll warn you,' Tabby teased, smiling because she felt amazingly light-hearted while she was studiously engaged in not agonising. The minute she forgot his maxim though the real world immediately flooded back and, assailed by those whirling doubts, insecurities and unanswered questions, she became tense again and marvelled that she had so easily suppressed what she had seen.

'I saw you with Melinda on the beach,' she told him

baldly, putting it right out there without holding back and judging her words and their effect.

Acheron's big powerful frame stiffened and he tilted her head back to study her troubled face. 'I'm bringing another nanny in to work with Melinda, who will eventually replace her. I've already made the arrangements. I don't want Amber upset by too sudden a change in staff,' he volunteered.

Tabby was wildly disconcerted by the announcement but relieved to know that Melinda would soon be moving on, while being impressed and touched that he had also been careful to consider Amber's need for consistent care. 'You're planning to sack Melinda?'

'She's on a temporary contract. We can let her go any time we like but I'd prefer to dispense with her services in the usual way. She knows a little too much about our marriage for my comfort.'

Frowning at that admission, Tabby prompted, 'What do you mean?'

'Melinda is clearly aware that we were using separate bedrooms at the villa. When we were on the beach she offered to share Amber's room so that I could take over hers,' Acheron explained grimly.

Wings of hot pink reddened Tabby's cheeks. Annoyance and embarrassment that their unconventional sleeping arrangements had evidently attracted the attention of the staff engulfed her. 'Perhaps she was planning to do a little wandering during the night once you were conveniently close. She *was* coming on to you, wasn't she?'

Lean, extravagantly handsome features impassive, stunning dark eyes screened, Acheron nodded. 'It happens.'

Tabby looked up at him, weak with relief that he had told her the truth without fanfare or fuss. 'Often?'

Acheron released a rueful chuckle at the innocence of that question. 'All the time. If I ignore it, it usually dies a natural death but Melinda doesn't take hints...possibly because she's already reached the conclusion that ours is not a normal marriage. She *could* take that information to the press, laying me open to a potential charge that I only married you to circumvent my father's will.'

Tabby grimaced. 'We'll have to work harder at being a more convincing couple. Share a room, spend time together, fake it up to behave more like a honeymoon couple is expected to behave.'

'But it doesn't have to be fake now,' Acheron pointed out with lazy assurance.

But in her heart she would know it *was* fake, Tabby reflected painfully. He gave her great sex but he wasn't offering to give her anything more. Maybe that was the only kind of giving he knew—short-term physical stuff with a built-in time limit, she conceded fairly, not wanting to judge him just because he was different. After all, was she any more evolved in the field of relationships? She wanted him *so* much, wanted his attention as much as Amber did, was willing to do whatever it took to hold that attention. But she was not willing to admit even to herself that he was also stirring up emotions that she was afraid she couldn't handle.

'Why did your father write a will that forced you to get married when you didn't want to?' Tabby asked quietly, knowing that that was the heart of the matter and the mystery that he had so far avoided explaining.

'In a nutshell? He wanted me to marry Kasma,' Acheron told her tersely, his beautiful mouth hardening. 'And I don't *ever* want to talk about that.'

With difficulty, Tabby swallowed an irritated comeback on that omission, knowing such a response would only reinforce his reserve and make him dig his stubborn heels in even harder. She could leave the thorny question of Kasma to one side for the moment and concentrate on other aspects. 'But surely your father knew how you felt? How close were the two of you?' Tabby persisted.

A tiny muscle pulled taut at the corner of his unsmiling jaw. 'I only met him in my late twenties,' he reminded her drily. 'I suppose it was more of a business relationship than most. His company was struggling. He asked me for advice. I went in to help and ended up taking over.'

'Didn't he resent that?'

'Not at all. He wasn't much of a businessman, more of a family man desperate to give his loved ones a secure future.'

'That was your stepmother and her children?'

Acheron compressed his lips. 'My father married her when her kids were very young and raised them as his own but I didn't meet them until about eighteen months before he died.'

'Why not?' Tabby asked in surprise.

'His family weren't relevant to me or to our relationship. They were strangers. There was no blood tie and I've never had a family, so I was very wary about getting involved in that side of his life. As things turned out, I was right to be wary and to have kept my distance for as long as I did,' he pronounced with dark finality.

A silence full of undertones enclosed them in the aftermath of that assurance, adding to Tabby's discomfiture. She was trying desperately to work out what his past relationship with his stepsister, Kasma, had entailed. Obviously there had been an affair that left the beautiful brunette with expectations that Acheron was not prepared to fulfil. Presumably the affair had ended badly with bitterness on both sides. Had some tragedy occurred? Had

Kasma fallen pregnant or some such thing? Mightn't that explain why his late father had got such a bee in his bonnet about Acheron marrying his stepdaughter? Certainly the other woman had believed very strongly that she was the only woman who should become Acheron's wife. Was Kasma in love with him? Or was she more fixated on his money and his status? But regardless of why Kasma wanted Acheron, what did it matter when *he* didn't want *her*? Tabby asked herself irritably, weary of suspicions that were winding up her tension for no good reason. If it was that simple though, why couldn't he just say so?

'I wish you didn't keep secrets. I wish you were more frank and straightforward about things,' she admitted before she could think better of it.

'You're so honest sometimes you terrify me, *glyka mou*,' Acheron confided ruefully. 'And if this honeymoon is going to work, we will each have to compromise our most cherished ideals.'

Acheron peered down at the red-rose tattoo adorning Tabby's slender arm with a frown and stroked a finger gently across it. 'The skin underneath feels rough and the design is already blurred. The tattooist must have damaged your skin.'

Tabby gritted her teeth, relaxation abandoned as she yanked her arm free of his light hold. 'Don't touch me there.'

Lustrous dark golden eyes scrutinised her from below inky-black lashes. 'Why not?'

'Are we about to have *another* one of those conversations in which you suggest that I go for laser treatment to have it removed?' Tabby condemned, her small face taut and pale as she decided it was time to tell him the truth, which would surely conclude his interest in the subject.

'If you must know, I won't have it removed because it's covering up an ugly scar. In fact, the scar was there first. The tattooist did a marvellous job but he couldn't have made the ink design perfect when my skin was far from perfect to begin with.'

His lean dark features were frowning now. 'What sort of a scar?'

'Take it from me...you really don't want to know,' Tabby told him warningly, pulling away from him to scramble to her feet in the shade of the pine trees that overhung the pinkish pale sand. After checking that Amber still lay splayed out on her blanket in sleeping abandonment, her olive-skinned chubby limbs protruding starfish fashion from her white *broderie anglaise* playsuit, her rosebud mouth soft and relaxed, Tabby stalked on down the beach, a slight figure clad in shorts and a bikini top.

Acheron, she thought, her hands knotting into fists, her teeth grinding together in angry frustration. There were times she wanted to throw him into the sea from a great height. She had thought *she* was the nosy one but he didn't quit once he was on a trail either. Even worse, he was a domineering perfectionist. Although he wasn't planning to spend the rest of his life with her and Amber, he still wanted to persuade her that she should have the tattoo removed and he was as relentless as a steam roller running down a hill. At breakfast he had asked her if she would be happy for Amber to get something similar done, and Tabby had been betrayed into looking in dismay at Amber's smooth soft forearm and Acheron, being Acheron, had noticed that revealing appraisal.

'So, you *do* regret getting it done,' he had exclaimed with satisfaction.

Yes, Acheron had some infuriating traits, she acknowledged, but over the past month in Sardinia he had also been a highly entertaining companion, a very sexy lover and a patient and caring father figure for Amber. At that moment, Tabby couldn't begin to work out how an entire four weeks had flashed past faster than the speed of light. The first week had been a challenge while she was still hobbling round with a stick and pretty much sentenced to passing her time at the beach house. But once her ankle had healed, they had begun to go out and about.

Snapshots of special moments they had shared filled her memory with more comforting images. They had climbed the massive staircase to the Bastione terrace to see the amazing panoramic view of the rooftops of Calgiari. While she was still wheezing from the climb and overheated from the sun, he had told her that there was actually a lift but that he had assumed that she would enjoy the full tourist experience more. It had taken several cocktails and the cooling effect of the lovely breeze on the terrace before she had forgiven him, and if she was truthful her resistance had only truly melted when he slid long brown fingers into hers in the lift on the way down again.

They had made an evening visit to Castelsardo, a beautiful village dominated by a magical citadel all lit up at night, to enjoy live music in the piazza. Amber had adored all the noise and bustle going on around her and Acheron had enjoyed the baby's bright-eyed fascination.

The following night, however, they had sought out more adult fun, dancing until dawn at the Billionaire club where Tabby had felt distinctly overshadowed by the number of gorgeous women, sleek and deadly as sharks, cruising for a wealthy hook-up. That Ash had acted as if he only had eyes for her and had kissed her passionately on the dance floor had done much to lift her self-esteem.

Memory after memory was now tumbling inside Tabby's head. For forty-eight hours they had sailed a yacht round the national park of La Maddalena, a group of protected and largely uninhabited islands teeming with flora and wildlife. The last night they had skinny dipped in a deserted cove and made love until the sun went down. Exhausted, she had wakened to find Acheron barbecuing their evening meal, stunning dark golden eyes smiling lazily at her and making her heart somersault like a trapeze artist.

Of course, they had done all the usual things as well, like strolling round the famous boutiques on the Costa Smeralda, an activity or a lack of activity that Acheron was astounded to discover bored his bride to tears.

'But you *must* want me to buy you something,' he had protested. 'You *must* have seen something you liked. You do realise that the only thing I've bought you since we arrived is that bed linen?'

Tabby had seen the exquisite bed linen in an upmarket handicrafts shop and her childhood memories of being clumsy with a needle and thread had given her a true appreciation of the amount of skill involved in producing such beautiful embroidery. That had been a purchase to treasure, a gift she truly loved, and only later had it occurred to her that she would never see that winter-weight linen spread across a bed that she shared with Acheron and that it would inevitably adorn a bed she slept in alone. Once the summer was over, their marriage would be history.

But then while she had known they would be faking their honeymoon and had dutifully posed with him for a persistent paparazzo, who had followed them round Porto Cervo, she had not appreciated the lengths Acheron might go to in making their relationship look genuine from the inside and the outside. So, if occasionally she got a little confused and thought about him as if he *were* her real husband, who could blame her for making that mistake?

Or for falling madly and irrevocably in love with him during the process, she reasoned wretchedly. After all, no man had ever treated her as well as he did, no man had ever made her so happy either, and only he had ever made love to her several times a day, *every* day, as if she were indeed the hottest, sexiest woman on the planet. Naturally her emotions had got involved and she suppressed them as best she could, knowing that the last thing Acheron required from her was angst and a broken heart, which would make him feel guilty and uncomfortable.

It wasn't his fault she had fallen for him either. It certainly wasn't as though he had misled her with promises about the future. In fact, right from the outset she had known that there was no future for them. He had never made any bones about that. Once they had succeeded to legally adopt Amber, their supposed marriage would be left to wither and die. Tabby would make a new life with the little girl she loved while she assumed Acheron would return to his workaholic, womanising existence. Would she ever see him again after the divorce? As she confronted that bleak prospect an agonising shard of pain slivered through Tabby and left a deep anguished ache in its wake. Would Acheron want to retain even the most distant relationship with Amber? Or would he decide on a clean break and act as if Amber didn't exist?

Acheron crossed the beach, noting how Tabby's figure had rounded out once she was eating decent food, recalling with quiet satisfaction that she no longer bit her nails—small changes that he valued.

'How did you get the scar concealed by the tattoo?' he demanded obstinately, interrupting Tabby's reverie and shooting her back to the present by wrapping both arms round her from behind, carefully preventing her from storming off again. 'Were you involved in an accident?'

'No…it wasn't an accident,' Tabby admitted, past recollections making her skin turn suddenly cold and clammy in spite of the heat of the sun.

He was being supportive, she reminded herself doggedly, guilt biting into her former annoyance with him. When Amber had cried half the night because she was teething and her gums were sore, Acheron had been right there beside her, helping to distract the little girl and calm her down enough to sleep again. She had not expected supportiveness from Acheron but his interest in Amber was anything but half-hearted. When it came to childcare, he took the rough with the smooth, serenely accepting that children weren't always sunny and smiling.

The new nanny currently working with Melinda was called Teresa, a warm, chattering Italian woman whose main source of interest was her charge. Within a week the English nanny would be leaving to take up a permanent position with a family in London.

'Tabby…I asked you a question,' Acheron reminded her with deeply unwelcome persistence. 'You said you didn't get the scar in an accident, so—'

Dredged from the teeming tumult of her frantic attempt to think about just about anything other than the past he was trying to dig up, Tabby lifted her head high and looked out to sea. 'My mother burned me with a hot iron because I knocked over a carton of milk,' she confessed without any expression at all.

'Thee mou…' Acheron growled in stricken disbelief, spinning her round to look at her pale set face and the yawning hurt still lingering in her violet eyes.

'I was never allowed to be with either of my parents

unsupervised again after that,' she explained woodenly. 'My mother went to prison for burning me and I never saw either of them again.'

Bewildered by the great surge of ferocious anger welling up inside him, Acheron crushed her slight body to his, both arms wrapping tightly round her. For some reason he registered that he was feeling sick and his hands weren't quite steady, and in that instant some inexplicable deep need that disturbed him was making it impossible for him not to touch her. 'That must've been a relief.'

'No, it wasn't. I loved them. They weren't very lovable people but they were all I had,' Tabby admitted thickly, her dry throat scratching over the words as if she was reluctant to voice them. She had learned as a young child that loving gestures would be rejected but now more than anything in the world she wanted to wrap her arms round Acheron and take full advantage of the comfort he was clumsily trying to offer her, only that pattern of early rejection and knowledge of how abandonment felt kept her body rigid and uninviting in the circle of his arms.

'I understand that,' Acheron breathed in a raw driven undertone. 'I rarely saw my mother but I still idolised her—'

'What a pair we are!' Tabby sniffed, her tension suddenly giving way as tears stung her eyes and overflowed, her overloaded reaction to having had to explain and indeed relive what she never, ever talked about to anyone.

Acheron stared down at her tear-stained visage, pale below his bronzed skin, his strong facial bones forbiddingly set. 'I can't bear to think of you being hurt like that, *yineka mou*—'

'Don't...don't talk about it!' Tabby urged feverishly. 'I try never to think about it but every time I saw the scar in the mirror as a teenager, I remembered it, and sometimes people asked what had happened to me. That's why I got the tattoo…to cover it up, hide it.'

'Then wear that tattoo with pride. It's a survival badge,' Acheron informed her with hard satisfaction. 'I wish you'd explained weeks ago but I understand now why you didn't.'

'Oh, for goodness' sake, let's talk about something more cheerful!' Tabby pleaded. 'Tell me something about you. I mean, you must have *some* happy childhood memories of your mother?'

Acheron closed an arm round her slight shoulders to press her back across the beach towards Amber. 'The night before my first day at school she presented me with a fantastically expensive pen engraved with my name. Of course, I was only allowed to use a pencil in class but naturally that didn't occur to her. She was very fond of flamboyant gestures, always telling me that only the very best was good enough for a Dimitrakos—'

'Maybe that was how she was brought up,' Tabby suggested quietly. 'But you still haven't explained why that pen made you happy.'

'Because generally she ignored me but that particular week she was fresh out of rehab and engaged in turning over a new leaf and it was the one and only time she made me feel that I genuinely mattered to her. She even gave me a whole speech about education being the most important thing in my life…that from a woman who dropped out of school as a teenager and couldn't read anything more challenging than a magazine,' he told her wryly.

'Do you still have the pen?'

'I think it was stolen.' He sent her a rueful charismatic smile that tilted her heart inside her chest and interfered with her breathing. 'But at least I have that one perfect moment to remember her by.'

* * *

Acheron could not relax until he had commissioned a special piece of jewellery for Tabby's upcoming birthday, which surprisingly fell in the same week as his own. That achieved, he worried about having taken that much trouble over a gift. What was wrong with him? What sort of man went to such lengths for a wife he was planning to divorce? *Keep it cool*, a little voice chimed in the back of his uneasy mind. But it had proved impossible to play it cool when confronted with the harsh reality of Tabby's childhood experiences, which had had the unexpected effect of showing Acheron that he had a good deal less to be bitter about with regard to his own. His mother had been a neglectful, selfish and inadequate parent but even at her worst he had never doubted that she loved him. And possibly, but for the malicious machinations of a third party, his father might have learned to love and appreciate him as well...

The constant flow of such unfamiliar thoughts assailing him kept him quiet over dinner. Aware of Tabby's anxious gaze, he was maddened by the knowledge that he wasn't feeling like himself any more and that, even in the midst of that disorientating experience, withdrawing his attention from her could make him feel guilty. Never a fan of great inner debates, or even in the habit of staging them, he was exasperated and bewildered by the emotions Tabby constantly churned up inside him. *She was too intense*, too rich for his blood. He needed to take a step back, he decided abruptly; he needed some distance, and the instant he made that decision he felt better and back in control again.

'I have to go away on business for a couple of days,' Acheron volunteered as he strode out of the bathroom, a towel negligently wrapped round his lean, muscular body. His black hair tousled and damp, his lean, devastatingly handsome face clean-shaven, he looked amazing and Tabby's mouth ran dry before she could even process what he had said.

Realising that he was leaving her, Tabby went rigid and then scolded herself because he had done very little work in recent weeks and could hardly be expected to maintain that lifestyle indefinitely. No, she had been spoilt by his constant company and had to learn fast how to adapt to his absence. Was that why he had been so quiet and distant over dinner? Had he worried about her reaction? Well, it was time to show him that she was strong and not the complaining type.

'I'll miss you, but we'll be fine,' she responded lightly.

Acheron ground his teeth together, having expected her to object or even offer to travel with him. This was definitely a moment when he had believed she would cling and make him feel suffocated. He watched her clamber into bed, slender as a willow wand, the modest nightdress concealing the hot, secret places he loved, and lust kicked in so fast he felt dizzy with it. Lustrous dark eyes veiling, he discarded the towel, doused the lights and joined her. *Not tonight*, he thought grimly, as though he was fighting a battle; tonight he could get by without her.

Eyes sparkling in the moonlight, Tabby rolled over to Acheron's side of the bed and ran delicate fingers hungrily across a hair-roughened thigh while her hair trailed over his pelvis.

Acheron closed his eyes in despair. He could always lie back and think of Greece. If he said no like a frightened virgin, he would probably upset her, and there was no point doing that, was there? Why risk upsetting her? She found his swelling shaft with her mouth, and his hips shifted upward in helpless encouragement. It crossed his mind that the divorce might upset her because she acted as if she was fond of him, looked at him as if he was special, dived on him in bed if he didn't dive on her first, never missed a chance to put her arms round him...although strangely *not* this afternoon on the beach when he had put his arms round her in an effort to offer sympathy for what his thoughtless questions had made her cruelly relive. A particularly strong wave of pleasure blanked out the subsequent thought about *why* she might not have responded, yet another thought he didn't want to have. All that sentimental stuff, he thought grimly—he never had been any good at that. He had probably been clumsy.

Afterwards, Acheron didn't hold her the way he usually did, and Tabby felt cold inside and abandoned. She curled up on her side, hating him, loving him, wanting him, fretting and reckoning that love was the worst torture in existence for a woman. There was no point always wanting what he wouldn't give her, didn't even *want* to give her, she reflected painfully. Their divorce was not only written in the stars but also written into a pre-nuptial contract from which there would be no escape.

And maybe he still had feelings for Kasma, whom he would not discuss although she had on several occasions worked the conversation helpfully round in that direction to give him an easy opening. But trying to get Acheron to talk about something he didn't want to talk about was like trying to get blood out of a stone. In her experience though, people only avoided topics that embarrassed or troubled them, so his failed relationship with Kasma must have gone deep indeed to leave behind such conspicuous and quite uncharacteristic sensitivity...

The following morning, Tabby drifted out of sleep to discover that Acheron had made an early departure and without leaving even a note. She spent a quiet day with Amber and it was the next day before the silence from Acheron began to niggle at her. He didn't have to stay in touch when he was only planning to be away forty-eight hours, she conceded ruefully, and she was not so needy that she required him to check in with her every day. But as she lay in the bed that felt empty without him the day stretched before Tabby like a blank slate, shorn of anticipation, excitement and happiness.

Thoroughly exasperated with her mood, she went for a shower and got dressed in the bathroom, emerging to catch a glimpse of her reflection in the tall cheval mirror across the bedroom and wonder why she couldn't see it properly. As she automatically moved closer to see what was amiss with the mirror she realised that someone had written something on it, and she frowned at it in bewilderment.

He's using you! Tabby was gobsmacked. Why would anyone write that on their mirror for her to see? Clearly it was meant to be personal, and presumably Acheron was the 'he' being referred to. What on earth did it mean? Whatever, it really spooked her that someone had come into their bedroom while she was in the bathroom and left a message presumably intended to shock and insult her. After all, only someone in the house could have had access to their room and that knowledge made gooseflesh blossom on her exposed skin.

Without hesitation she lifted the house phone and asked to speak to Ash's security chief, Dmitri. Almost before she had finished speaking, Dmitri joined her in the room to see the mirror for himself. If his forbidding expression was anything to go by, he took the matter very seriously. Dmitri, however, was a man of few words and she left him to it and went downstairs for breakfast.

CHAPTER TEN

'CAN I ASK you where you're planning to go?' Melinda asked with a sunny smile, joining her at the breakfast table, which she never dared to do when Acheron was around.

'Into Porto Cervo to shop,' Tabby admitted. 'I'm looking for a birthday present.'

'There's some great jewellery boutiques...try the Piazzetta delle Chiacchere,' Melinda advised helpfully.

Tabby nodded, feeling guilty about how much she disliked the curvaceous blonde who would, by the end of the week, mercifully be gone from the household to take up her new appointment. Since Teresa's arrival and increasing involvement with Amber, Melinda seemed to spend a lot of time hovering unnecessarily and watching their comings and goings. Once, Tabby had even suspected that the blonde was eavesdropping on her and Acheron. No doubt the nanny had now registered that their detached marriage had developed into something closer. Or was that only her own wishful thinking at work? Tabby wondered heavily.

Acheron had been gone only one day and she felt bereft. That was a pretty poor show for a strong, independent woman, she conceded shamefacedly. She missed him so much, and her outlook wasn't improved by her recollection of his unusual behaviour on that last night they had spent together. He had been silent and moody, extraordinarily uninvolved when she had made love to him, saying nothing, doing nothing, in fact, acting like a right—

'Miss Barnes?' Dmitri appeared in the doorway. 'Could I have a word with you?'

'*Right* now?' Melinda prompted with a sparkling smile that seemed wasted on the granite-faced older man.

'Now would be a good time,' Dmitri responded evenly.

Tabby left Teresa in charge of Amber, having decided that dragging the little girl out to trail round the shops during the hottest part of the day would be unwise. The message was still on the mirror when she walked past into the bathroom to renew her lipstick and it made her shiver. *He's using you.* Well, as far as their marriage was concerned they were using each other, she told herself doggedly. Although things had changed drastically once they began sharing a bed in reality. Was Acheron only sleeping with her because that intimacy added to the illusion of their having a normal marriage? After all, if he was seen out by the paparazzi with another woman while he was supposed to be a happily married new husband, it wouldn't look good. So, was she being used on that basis? But how could she call it using when she was in love with him and wanted him to make love to her? Did that make her a silly lovelorn fool? Or was *she* taking equal advantage of *him*?

From the instant Dmitri phoned him and broke the news, Acheron hadn't been able to stay still or think with his usual logic. Gripped by insane impatience and mounting concern, he just wanted to get back to Sardinia and stand watch over Tabby and Amber. Unfortunately for him, getting a last-minute slot for the jet to take off in

Athens and jumping the queue took longer than he had envisaged. He cursed the fact that he had left them behind in the first place, cursed his conviction that he should protect Tabby at all costs from what Kasma might do next.

Why had he chosen to leave Tabby when he actually wanted to be with her? What did that say about him? That he couldn't recognise his own emotions and was prone to running away from what he couldn't understand? Feelings had never been so intense for him before and he had been torn between a kind of intoxication at the fire of them and a kind of panic at knowing he was out of control. He had never allowed that to happen to him before but he'd had no choice. He had jumped on the panic as an excuse and now he was paying the price. Thee mou, *if anything was to happen to them*, he brooded darkly, his fists clenching aggressively just as his pilot signalled him from across the VIP lounge that they were good to go.

'I really do believe that your husband would prefer you to stay in today,' Dmitri informed Tabby quietly.

Unfortunately, Tabby was in no mood to be grounded like a child and marvelled that Acheron could even think he could give out orders that way through Dmitri, particularly when he had taken off himself at such short notice. What was it? Why was he trying to keep her on the home front? Some sort of control issue on his part? And poor Dmitri was embarrassed to have to say such a thing to her; she could see it in the older man.

'I'm sorry but it's really important that I go out today,' she said levelly. 'I have something I have to buy.'

'Then I'll accompany you and I'll drive, Mrs Dimitrakos,' Dmitri responded with determination.

For the sake of peace, Tabby nodded agreement but knew she was going to have to have a discussion with

Acheron with regard to the intense security presence he maintained in their lives. Was it really necessary that they be guarded and watched over every place they went? Was there a genuine risk of their being robbed or kidnapped? Was there some kind of specific threat out against Acheron?

'You'll be very bored,' she warned Dmitri as she settled into the passenger seat of the SUV and watched another car full of security men follow them out of the entrance to the beach house with wry acceptance.

'It's not a problem. I'm used to going shopping with my wife,' Dmitri told her calmly. 'She can stare at one shop window for ten minutes before she's satisfied she's seen everything.'

Tabby knew she would be even more of a drag because she didn't even know what she was planning to buy and was hoping to be inspired by something she saw. What did you buy for the man who had everything? The massive monthly allowance he had awarded her, however, had piled up in her bank account and thanks to his generosity she had got to spend very little of it, so she had plenty to spend.

Dmitri following behind her, Tabby prowled through the exclusive boutiques and jewellery outlets. Acheron wasn't the sort of guy who wore jewellery. He wore a wedding ring and occasionally cuff links and that was all. But short of copping out by buying him another silk tie when he already had a rail of them, what was she to give him for his thirty-first birthday? Mulling over that thorny issue, she saw the pen. Actually *the* pen was the only possible description for a pen that bore a world-famous designer label. It would cost a fortune, she reckoned. But equally fast she recalled the pen his mother had bought him and decided that the cost was less important than what it meant, although why she was so keen to buy a significant gift for a man who couldn't even be bothered to phone her, she couldn't explain. Maybe it was the desolate thought that the pen might survive with him a lot longer than their marriage and act as a reminder of what they had once shared. Depressing, much? She scolded herself impatiently for her downbeat thoughts.

She bought the pen and arranged for it to be inscribed with his name and the date. She had to make use of the platinum credit card he had given her to make the purchase and, while trying to act as if she spent such sums all the time, she was secretly horrified at spending so much money and worried that Acheron would think she had gone mad. Pale and shaken after that sobering experience, she told Dmitri that she wanted to go for a coffee. He led the way to an outdoor café and insisted on choosing a seat a couple of tables away from her.

She had just bought the most expensive pen in the history of the world, she reflected guiltily, and when he saw the bill he might well freak out and regret telling her that her card had no upper limit. She was sipping her latte slowly, savouring the caffeine, when a shadow fell across her table.

Kasma settled her long elegant body down smoothly into the seat opposite. 'You've been so unavailable you've forced me into all this cloak and dagger stuff,' she complained.

Totally taken aback by the other woman's appearance, Tabby stared at the beautiful brunette with wide, questioning eyes. 'What on earth are you doing here?'

'You're here, Ash is here...where else would I be?' Kasma asked, rolling big dark eyes in apparent disbelief at the question. 'I refuse to believe that you're so stupid that you can't accept that Ash belongs with me.'

'Miss Philippides...' Dmitri broke into the conversation, standing straight and tall beside Kasma's chair. 'Please leave—'

Kasma slung him a defiant glance. 'We're in a public place and I can go where I please on this island. We're not in Greece now.'

'May I suggest then that *we* leave, Mrs Dimitrakos?' Dmitri continued, regarding Tabby expectantly.

Tabby breathed in deep. 'When I've finished my coffee,' she murmured, determined to hear what Kasma had to say since she sure as heck wasn't going to receive any information from Acheron.

Grim-faced, Dmitri retreated to an even closer table.

'I believe in getting straight down to business,' Kasma informed her. 'How much money do you want to walk out on this absurd marriage?'

Dumbstruck, Tabby stared at the older woman. 'You can't be serious.'

'Oh, I'm always serious when it comes to Ash. We belong together and he would have married me, *not* you, had my stepfather not foolishly tried to force the issue in his will,' Kasma contended confidently. 'You must know how proud Ash is.'

'Staying here, entering into this dialogue is a very bad idea, Mrs Dimitrakos,' Dmitri leant closer to spell out.

Kasma shot a vicious burst of Greek at the older man and the look on her face was downright scary. With the sudden suspicion that Dmitri's advice to retreat from the scene might well be the most sensible move, Tabby lifted her bag, settled some money on the table for the bill and stood up. Before she walked away, however, she had something to say. 'No matter how much money you offered me I wouldn't walk out on Acheron,' she murmured tautly. 'I love him.'

'Not as much as I love him, you bitch!' Kasma launched at her in a seething shout of fury that shook Tabby rigid.

Cupping her elbow firmly in his hand, Dmitri walked her away from the café at a fast pace. 'Kasma Philippides is a dangerously unstable woman. Your husband has a restraining order out against her on Greek soil and she's not allowed to approach him or make a nuisance of herself there. You can't talk to her. You can't reason with her. We've learned that the hard way.'

'Ash should've warned me. If he'd warned me, I would've walked away immediately,' Tabby protested defensively. 'I could see that she was obsessed with him at the wedding but I didn't understand how much of a problem she was in his life.'

'He wasn't expecting her to follow you here. He had no idea she was on the island. By the way, he's flying back as we speak.'

Relief swept Tabby. He would finally have to tell her the whole story. But he had had to take out a legal restraining order to keep Kasma at a distance? What had driven him to take his father's stepdaughter to court? That must have taken some nerve, particularly while his father was still alive. Had Kasma been acting like some sort of psycho stalker?

They were driving along the coast road when she noticed that Dmitri kept on looking worriedly in the driving mirror. Tabby glanced over her shoulder to notice the bright red sports car behind them. The driver had long dark hair just like Kasma's.

'She's following us,' Dmitri told her flatly. 'Make sure your belt is safely fastened. I may have to take evasive manoeuvres but I've already alerted the police.'

'Evasive manoeuvres?' Tabby gasped when there was

a sudden jolt at the rear of the car. 'She's trying to ram us? Is she crazy in that tiny little car?'

Dmitri didn't answer. His concentration was on the road because he had speeded up. Tabby's heart was beating very, very fast as she watched in the mirror as the red car tried to catch up with them again. They were zooming round corners so fast that Tabby felt dizzy and she was still watching Kasma's car when it veered across the road into the path of another car travelling the other way.

'Oh, my word, she's crashed...hit someone else!'

Dmitri jammed on the brakes and rammed into Reverse to turn and drive back. He leapt out of the SUV. The team from the other security car were already attending to the victims of the crash, carrying the passenger to the verge, the driver, still conscious, stumbling after them. The red sports car had hit a wall and demolished part of it. Tabby slowly climbed out, her tummy heaving as she approached the scene of frantic activity. Dmitri was talking fast on his phone as he approached her. 'Stay in the car, Mrs Dimitrakos. You don't need to see this. Miss Philippides is dead.'

'Dead?' Tabby was stunned, barely able to credit that the woman who had been speaking to her only minutes earlier could have lost her life.

'She wasn't wearing a belt—she was thrown from the car.'

'And the people who were in the other car?' Tabby asked.

'Very lucky to be alive. The passenger has a head wound and the driver has a leg injury.'

Tabby nodded and got back slowly into the SUV, feeling oddly distanced from everything happening around her. That sensation, which she only vaguely recognised as shock, was still lingering when she gave a brief statement at the police station with a lawyer sitting in, volunteering information she couldn't understand in the local language. That completed, she was stowed in a waiting room with a cup of coffee until Acheron strode through the door. He stalked across the room, emanating stormy tension, and raised her out of her seat with two anxious hands.

'You are all right? Dmitri swore you were unhurt but I was afraid to believe him,' Acheron grated half under his breath, his lean, darkly handsome features taut and granite hard as he scanned her carefully from head to toe.

'Well, I was fine until you made me spill my coffee,' she responded unevenly, setting the mug down and rubbing ineffectually at the splashes now adorning her pale pink top. 'Are we free to leave?'

'Yes, I've made a statement. *Thee mou*,' Acheron murmured fiercely. 'Kasma had a knife in her bag!'

'A *knife*?' Tabby repeated in horror.

'But for Dmitri's presence she might have attacked you!' Acheron lifted a not quite steady hand and raked long brown fingers through his luxuriant black hair. 'I was so scared when I heard she'd come here, I felt sick,' he confided thickly.

'She's dead,' Tabby reminded him in an undertone.

Acheron released his pent-up breath and said heavily, 'Her brother, Simeon, is on his way to make the funeral arrangements. He's a decent man. I hope you don't mind but I've asked him to stay with us.'

'Of course, I don't mind. No matter what's happened, your father's family deserve your consideration and respect.'

'Melinda's flying back to London,' Acheron volunteered. 'She was responsible for the messages on the mirror.'

'Messages...there was *more* than one?' Tabby queried in consternation.

Acheron told her about the message he had seen at the villa in Tuscany and how Dmitri had instantly worked out that Melinda had to be the perpetrator when the nanny did it a second time. Confronted that same morning after breakfast by Dmitri, Melinda had confessed that Kasma had approached her in London and had offered her a lot of money to leave the messages and to spy on Acheron while keeping Kasma up to date with information on where they were staying. It was Melinda who had warned Dmitri that Kasma was actually on the island, news that had alarmed Acheron into making an immediate return.

The fountain of questions concerning Kasma that had disturbed Tabby earlier in the day was, by that stage, returning fast, but the haunted look in Acheron's lustrous dark eyes and the bleak set of his bronzed face silenced her. He escorted her out to a car, and she slid in, appreciating the air-conditioned cool on her overheated skin.

'I have a lot to explain,' Acheron acknowledged flatly and then he closed his hand over hers.

In a reflexive movement, Tabby rejected the contact and folded her hands together on her lap. 'After the way you behaved that last night and the fact that you haven't been in touch since, I think holding hands would be a bit of a joke,' she said bluntly. 'You don't need to pretend things you don't feel to pacify or comfort me. As you noted, I'm unhurt. It's been a horrible day but I'll get over it without leaning on you.'

'Maybe I want you to lean on me.'

Tabby raised a brow, unimpressed by that unlikely suggestion. 'I'd prefer to fall over and pick myself up. I've been doing it all my life and I've managed just fine.'

Acheron compressed his wide, sensual mouth. 'I

should have explained about her weeks ago but the subject of Kasma rouses a lot of bad memories...and reactions,' he admitted with curt reluctance.

'Kasma's the reason you thought someone might have pushed me down the stairs at the villa,' Tabby grasped finally.

'Maybe she made me a little paranoid but she did destroy my relationship with my father before he died.'

'And that's why he wrote that crazy will,' Tabby guessed.

'I told you that I only met my father's family about eighteen months ago. I only agreed in the first place because it seemed to mean so much to him. What I didn't mention before is that the week before that dinner engagement took place at his home, I met Kasma *without* knowing I was meeting Kasma,' he told her grittily.

Tabby frowned. 'Without knowing it was her?' she echoed. 'How? I mean, *why*?'

'I doubt if I could *ever* adequately explain why from Kasma's point of view. She introduced herself to me as Ariadne. She certainly knew who I was,' he delivered with perceptible bitterness. 'I was in Paris on a stopover between flights and she was staying in the same hotel. I've never believed that was a coincidence. I believe I was set up. I was alone. I was bored. She targeted me and I fell for it...and you could not begin to understand how deeply I regret taking the bait.'

Tabby was studying him with confused eyes. 'The bait?'

'I had a tacky one-night stand with her,' Acheron ground out grudgingly, dark colour accentuating his spectacular cheekbones, his jaw line clenching hard on the admission. 'A couple of stolen hours from a busy schedule of work and travel. I'm being honest here—it meant nothing more to me. Although I treated her with respect I never pretended at any stage that I wanted to see her again.'

Tabby averted her eyes, reflecting that respectful treatment would not have compensated Kasma for his ultimate rejection, when presumably she had persuaded herself that she could expect a much keener and less fleeting response.

'She picked me up in the hotel restaurant. Afterwards she started acting as though she knew me really well. To be frank, it was a freaky experience and I made my excuses and returned to my own room.'

Tabby was swallowing hard at a level of honesty she had not expected to receive from him. 'But if she already knew who you were, why did she lie about her own identity?'

Acheron shrugged a broad shoulder. 'Obviously because I would never have touched her had I known she was my father's precious little girl.'

'His precious little girl?' Tabby queried.

'Her mother was widowed when Kasma was only a baby. My father raised Kasma from the age of three. She was the apple of his eye, his favourite child, and he couldn't see any fault in her,' Acheron advanced tautly, his lips compressing. 'When I walked into the family dinner the week after the hotel encounter I was appalled to realise that Kasma was my father's stepchild and furious that she had lied to me and put me in that position, but that wasn't all I had to worry about. Before I could even decide how to behave, she stood up and announced that she had been saving a little surprise for everyone. And that surprise—according to her—was that she and I were *dating*.'

'Oh, my word…' Tabby was as stunned as he must've been by that development. 'And that one…er…episode at the hotel was really the extent of your relationship with her?'

'It was, but not according to Kasma. She had a very fertile imagination and over the months that followed she began acting like a stalker, flying round the world, turning up wherever I was,' he explained, lines of strain bracketing his mouth as he recalled that period. 'She tried to force her way into my life while telling my father a pack of lies about me. She told him I'd cheated on her, she told him I'd got her pregnant and then she told him she'd had a miscarriage. He fell for every one of her tales and nothing I could say would persuade him that my relationship with his stepdaughter was a fantasy she had made up. And having made that first mistake by getting involved with her that night at the hotel, I felt I had brought the whole nightmare down on my own head.'

'I don't think so—'

'It was casual sex but there was nothing casual about it,' Acheron opined grimly. 'I went to bed with a woman who was a stranger and maybe I deserved what I got.'

'Not when she set out to deliberately deceive you and then tried to trap you into a relationship,' Tabby declared stoutly. 'I don't agree with the way you behaved with her but she was obviously a disturbed personality.'

'She assaulted a woman I spent time with last year, which was why I was so concerned about your safety and Amber's.'

'What did she do?'

'She forced her way into my apartment and punched the woman while ranting about how I belonged to her.' He grimaced at the recollection. 'My father begged me to use my influence and prevent it from going to court but I was at the end of my rope. Kasma was dangerous and she needed treatment but as long as her family turned a blind eye and I swallowed what she was dishing out, she was free to do as she liked. The court accepted that she was lying and had never had a relationship with me and therefore had no excuse whatsoever for attacking the woman in my apartment and calling it a domestic dispute.'

'Didn't that convince your father that you were telling him the truth?'

'No, Kasma managed to convince him that I must've bribed someone and she had been stitched up by me to protect my own reputation,' he proffered with unconcealed regret. 'The sole saving grace was that after that court case I was able to take out a restraining order against her and at least that kept her out of my hair while I was on Greek soil.'

Tabby slowly shook her head, which was reeling with his revelations. 'Why didn't you tell me about her? Why wouldn't you explain?'

His bold bronzed profile clenched hard. 'I was ashamed of the whole business and I didn't want to frighten you either. My wealth didn't protect me from the fact that Kasma could still get to me almost everywhere I went. You have no idea how powerless I felt when she even managed to gatecrash the wedding because I didn't want to make a scene with my father's family present,' he confessed grittily. 'I didn't want to publicise my problems with her while my father was still alive either. She caused him enough grief with her wild stories about how badly I'd treated her.'

'So why on earth did he want you to marry her?' Tabby queried, struggling to understand that angle.

'He believed she loved me and he genuinely thought I owed her a wedding ring. He blamed me for her increasingly hysterical outbursts and strange behaviour.'

'That was probably easier for him than dealing with

the real problem, which was *her*. He would've had more faith in you if he had ever had the chance to get to know you properly,' Tabby opined, resting a soothing hand down on his. 'Kasma had the advantage and he trusted her and that gave her the power to put you through an awful ordeal.'

'It's over now,' Acheron reminded her flatly. 'Her brother, Simeon, believed me and tried to persuade her to see a therapist. Perhaps if she had listened she might not have died today.'

'It's not your fault though,' Tabby countered steadily. 'You weren't capable of fixing whatever was broken in her.'

Acheron groaned out loud. 'It's so *not* sexy that you feel sorry for me now.'

'I don't feel sorry for you. I just think you've been put through the mill a bit,' Tabby paraphrased awkwardly. 'No wonder you don't like clingy, needy women after that experience.'

'I wouldn't mind if you clung occasionally,' Acheron admitted.

Tabby rolled her eyes at him. 'Stop being such a smoothie…it's wasted on me.'

'What do you mean?' Acheron asked harshly as the limo drew up outside the beach house.

'It's not necessary to charm me. We both had good reasons to get married and that's the only fulfilment either of us require from our agreement. You got a wife and, hopefully, I will eventually be able to adopt Amber,' Tabby spelt out as she slid out of the car and walked into the house.

'That's not how I feel,' Acheron informed her stubbornly.

'We're not twin souls and nor are we required to be,'

Tabby flipped back, walking through to the lounge, which stood with doors wide open to the terrace and the view of the cove, draperies fluttering softly in the slight breeze that never seemed to leave the coast. 'I think we're overdue a little plain speaking here.'

Outside, she leant up against the rail bordering the terrace and folded her arms in a defensive position. She knew what she needed to say. She was more than halfway to getting her heart broken by the stupid, dangerous pretence that she was on a *real* honeymoon with a *real* husband! How had she let that happen? How had she let herself fall in love with a male who was simply doing what he had to do to give the appearance of being a newly married man?

'Meaning?' Acheron prompted, stilling in the doorway, six feet plus inches of stunning male beauty and charisma.

Tabby looked him over with carefully blank eyes. He was gorgeous; he had always been gorgeous from the crown of his slightly curly black head to the soles of his equally perfect feet. He focused sizzling dark golden eyes on her with interrogative intensity.

'Tabby?' he prompted afresh.

'Unlike you I call a spade a spade. I don't wrap it up.'

'I appreciate that about you...that what you say you mean,' he countered steadily.

Tabby threw her slight shoulders back, violet eyes wide and appealing. 'Look, let's just bring the whole charade to an end here and now,' she urged. 'Melinda was spying on us and she's gone. We've done all the newly happily married stuff for weeks and now surely we can both go back to normal?'

'Normal?'

Tabby was wondering what the matter with him was,

for it was not like him to take a back seat in any argument. Furthermore, he looked strained, having lost colour while his spectacular strong bone structure had set rigid below his bronzed skin. 'We were strangers with a legal agreement, Ash,' she reminded him painfully. 'We've met the terms, put on the show and now surely we can return to being ourselves again behind closed doors at least?'

'Is that what you want?' he pressed curtly, lean brown hands closing into fists by his side. 'Don't you think this is a decision best shelved for a less traumatic day?'

Tabby lifted her chin, her heart squeezing tight inside her chest, pain like a sharp little arrow twisting inside her because, of course, it was not what she wanted. She wanted him; she was in love with him but she had to protect herself, had to force herself to accept that what they had shared was only a pretence. 'No.'

'You want to go back to where we started out?' Acheron demanded starkly.

Tabby dropped her shoulders, her eyes veiling. 'No, I just want us to be honest and not faking anything.'

Acheron breathed in very slow and deep, dark golden eyes glittering like fireworks below the shield of his luxuriant black lashes. 'I *haven't* been faking anything...'

Tabby's dazed mind ran over all the romancing, the sexing, the hand-holding, the fun, and she blinked in bemusement. 'But *of course* you were faking.'

'It may have started out that way, but it ended up real, *yineka mou*.' Acheron surveyed her steadily but she knew he was putting up a front because he was really, really tense.

'How...*real*?' Tabby questioned, her heart thumping like mad.

Acheron lifted his arms and spread his hands in an oddly defenceless gesture. 'I fell in love with you...'

Tabby almost fell over in shock, her brain refusing to accept that he could have said that he loved her. 'I don't believe you. You're just scared that I'm about to walk out on our marriage agreement and you'll lose your company—but you don't *need* to be scared of that happening because I wouldn't do that to you. I'm still as determined to adopt Amber as I ever was, so I couldn't do that even if I wanted to,' she pointed out honestly.

'When I try to say, "I love you" for the first time in my life to a woman, you could at least listen to what I'm saying and stop talking a lot of rubbish!' Acheron shot back at her with scorching effect.

Tabby was struck dumb by that little speech. He was serious? He wasn't joking, faking, trying to manipulate her in some nefarious way? She stared back at him fixedly.

'And it was bloody hard to say too!' Acheron added in angry complaint at her response.

'I'm in shock,' Tabby mumbled shakily. 'I didn't think you had any feelings for me.'

'I tried very hard not to. I fought it every step of the way,' Acheron admitted ruefully. 'But in the end you got to me and you got to me so hard I ran away from it.'

'Ran away?' Tabby almost whispered in growing disbelief.

'I was feeling strange and that's why I took off on business…to give myself a little breathing space,' Acheron qualified tautly. 'But the minute I got away I realised I only wanted to come back and be with you.'

Tabby blinked slowly, struggling to react to that explanation when all her crazy head was full of was a single statement: that he loved her. *He loves me.* She tasted the idea, savoured it, very nearly careened across the terrace and flattened him to the tiles in gratitude, but mercifully retained enough restraint to stay where she was. 'You got cold feet, didn't you?' she guessed.

Acheron nodded. 'It was a little overwhelming when I realised what was wrong with me.'

Tabby moved closer. 'No, it wasn't anything wrong with you. It was a good thing, a wonderful thing...you love me. I love you.'

'If you feel the same way I do, why the hell are you putting me through this torture?' Acheron demanded rawly.

Tabby almost laughed, a sense of intoxication gripping her as she searched his darkly handsome features and the masculine bewilderment etched there. 'Talking about love is torture?'

Acheron rested his arms down on her slim shoulders and breathed, 'I thought once I said it, that would be that, but I was scared you wouldn't feel the same way and that you wanted it all to be fake.'

Tabby closed her arms round him and snuggled close. 'No, real is much better than fake. So, does this mean we're really and truly married?'

'Absolutely,' Acheron confirmed, and bent to lift her up into his arms. 'It also means we're going to be adoptive parents together because I sort of developed a fondness for Amber as well. Seems this love business is contagious...'

'Wow...' Tabby framed as he carried her upstairs to their bedroom and Teresa, with the baby in her arms, retreated back into the nursery with a warm smile. 'But how did it happen?'

Acheron arranged her on the bed with the care of a man setting up an art installation and stared down at her for what felt like ages. 'I think it started when I realised I was with a woman who was willing to sacrifice her home and her business to look after her sick best friend and child. I respect that level of loyalty and unselfishness. I respect what you were willing to do to retain custody of Amber even though I was pretty rough and crude about everything at the time. You stuck it out... you stood up to me...'

'And out of that came love?' Tabby whispered in shock.

'Out of those experiences came a woman I couldn't live without,' traded Acheron with a tender look in his lustrous dark eyes that she had never seen before. '*Thee mou*...if you had still wanted the fake marriage and the divorce I don't know what I would've done.'

'I don't want a divorce...I don't ever want to let go of you,' Tabby confided against his shirtfront.

'That desire is just about to come in very handy, *agape mou*,' Acheron murmured thickly, claiming her ripe mouth with his own, sending a thrill of heat and anticipation travelling through her relaxed body.

About an hour later, Acheron leapt naked out of bed to retrieve his trousers and dig into a pocket to produce a jewellers' box, which he pressed into her hand. 'I know it's not your birthday for another twenty-four hours but this is burning a hole in my pocket,' he admitted ruefully.

Tabby opened the box to find an unusual ring in the shape of a rose with a ruby at the centre.

'What do you think?' Acheron demanded anxiously. 'I wanted you to know that it was made in the image of your tattoo because it will always remind me what made you the special woman you are.'

'It's...gorgeous!' Tabby carolled as he removed his late mother's engagement ring from her wedding finger and replaced it with the new ring. The diamonds on the rose petals caught the sunlight and cast a rainbow of little sparkling reflections across the white bedding. 'But why on earth do you think I am so special when I'm so ordinary?'

'You're special because in spite of all the bad things that happened to you, you still have an open heart and a loving spirit. You love Amber, you love me—'

'So much,' Tabby emphasised feelingly as she smiled up at him. 'Although you might feel you love me a little less when you see what I spent on my credit card.'

'Never,' Acheron contradicted. 'You're the least extravagant person I know.'

'You might change your mind on that score,' she warned him, hoping he at least appreciated the gift of the pen on his birthday in three days' time.

'I love you,' he breathed softly, his attention locked on her smiling face.

He had fallen in love with her, he had genuinely fallen in love with her, Tabby savoured finally, and she allowed the happiness to well up inside her along with a sense of release from all anxiety. Somehow, by the most mysterious process of love known to mankind, two people who had loathed each other on sight because of their misconceptions had found love and formed a happy home and family and she was delirious with the joy of that miracle.

Tabby sucked in her tummy and studied the mirror. No, it was pointless: she was pregnant and there was no escaping that pregnant apple shape, no matter how well cut her maternity clothing was. With a wry smile at the foolishness of her vanity, Tabby went downstairs to check the last-minute arrangements for Amber's fourth birthday party.

The party was a catered affair, everything set up to entertain a whole posse of Amber's nursery-school friends.

There was a bouncy castle in the garden of their London town house, purchased after the birth of their first child, Andreus, who was already a rumbustious noisy toddler. Closely pursued by his nanny, Teresa, who had become as much a part of the family as the children, Andreus hurtled across the hall to throw his arms up to be lifted by his mother.

Tabby tried not to wince at the weight of her son, but, at eight months along in her second pregnancy, lifting a child who was already outstripping his peers in size was becoming quite a challenge. He hugged her tight, black curls like his father's silky against her throat, her own big blue eyes bright in his little smiling face. Sometimes, Tabby was still afraid that if she blinked her happy family life would disappear and she would discover she had been trapped in an inordinately convincing and wonderful daydream. And then she would look at Acheron and the children and she would be soothed by the closeness of their bonds.

Admittedly she would never have picked Acheron out as a keen father figure when she first met him, but exposure to Amber's charms had soon raised a desire in Acheron to have a child of his own. By the time the legalities of Amber's adoption had been settled and she had officially become their daughter, Tabby had been expecting Andreus. The little girl whom Tabby was currently carrying had been more of an accidental conception, thanks to a little spur-of-the-moment lovemaking on the beach in Sardinia where they had first found love, and which of all Acheron's properties they visited the most, although they had quickly extended the house to add on more bedroom capacity.

His father's widow, Ianthe, and her two surviving children had stayed with them there to attend Kasma's funeral. It had been a sad and sobering occasion but it had also done much to build a bridge between Ash and his father's former family. Ianthe had admitted to having been seriously worried about her daughter's mental health but Ash's late father, Angelos, had refused to face up to that reality. Kasma's brother, Simeon, and his family also had young children and the two couples had become close friends since that last sad encounter.

The front door opened and Andreus scrambled down from his mother's arms to hurl himself violently at Acheron, shouting, 'Dad!' at the top of his voice.

Tabby watched Acheron scoop his son up, and a warm smile curved her generous mouth because she never loved Acheron more than when she saw him with the children. He was kind, affectionate and patient, all the things that they had both so badly lacked when they were kids themselves. 'I thought you wouldn't make it back in time.'

'Where's the birthday girl?' Acheron enquired.

Amber came racing downstairs, a vivid little figure clad in a flouncy new party dress, and flung herself at her father with very little more circumspection than her toddler brother. 'You're here!' she carolled. 'You're here for my party.'

'Of course, I am,' Acheron said in the act of producing a present from behind his back, only to laugh as the housekeeper opened the door to let Amber's best friend and her mother enter and the two little girls went running off together. 'So much for being flavour of the month there!' he teased.

'But you're always my favourite flavour,' Tabby rushed to assure him in an undertone before she went to greet the arriving guests.

Acheron watched her acting hostess with quiet admiration. *His* Tabby, the best and luckiest find he had ever made, always warm, sunny and bright and still the most loving creature he had ever met. It didn't surprise him in the slightest that he loved her more with every passing year.

* * * * *

SEDUCING HIS SECRET WIFE

ROBIN COVINGTON

To Melissa Dark. You were there at the beginning.
Ten years ago we started this dream together and
I know that I wouldn't be here without you.
Thank you so much. Xoxo

One

Las Vegas, Nevada

There wasn't much in the world that could lure Justin Ling away from a poker table.

He loved the game. The strategy and the psychology and the emotion evoked with every hand that was dealt. It didn't hurt that he'd won far more than he'd ever lost. But he didn't need the money; he was a billionaire from the success of his company, Redhawk/Ling, so winning was a lucrative but empty victory. The upside was that he'd won enough to score invites to some of the largest private games and several of the popular public tournaments. Justin loved the game and when he earmarked weekends to devote to it there was almost nothing that was going to distract him from the cards in his hand.

That's why he couldn't explain why he was sitting down next to the sexy raven-haired beauty at the bar.

She was tall, slim and the kind of sexy that came from a confidence that ran deeper than the superficial trappings of a pair of high heels and makeup. This woman was the kind who made you work for it.

On a break from his current game, he'd seen her walk past the private rooms and head toward the lobby of the casino. And she'd seen him, too. It was a lightning strike of a moment when their eyes locked for several seconds, and the recognition of a reciprocal spark of sexual hunger was enough to find him cashing out and following her into this sad little bar.

"Can I buy you a drink?" He wasted no time getting to the point. Justin always went for what he wanted and this woman had captivated him.

She glanced over at him, giving him a thorough perusal from his toes to his four-hundred-dollar haircut. Her gaze lingered on his face and he thought he saw another flicker of interest in her espresso-colored eyes, but her expression gave nothing away before she turned to watch the football game on the TV at the back of the bar.

"I can buy my own drink." She picked up one of the three shots in front of her and downed it in one quick swallow.

"I'm sure you can," he answered, mirroring her position on his bar stool with his eyes mostly on the game. He eyed her in his peripheral vision, noting the way she tensed but also noting that she didn't make a move to leave or to tell him to get lost. It gave him encouragement. "In fact, I think *you* should buy *me* a drink."

A few beats of time passed, ratcheting his heart rate up a notch or two when the silence stretched out a little longer than comfortable. He wondered if he'd miscalculated the edge of challenge he'd glimpsed in the way she walked, the strength he'd seen flash in her eyes. If he'd been a betting man, and he was, he'd have all his money on her taking the bait.

And then she laughed.

It wasn't a giggle or a belly laugh. Her lips curved in a sexy twist and the low, husky rumble in her chest made him immediately think of Kathleen Turner, the finest aged whiskey, and secrets whispered in the dark and lost in the folds of tumbled sheets. He turned to face her, unable to resist the need to see her, to witness how the light played across her features and the glossy strands of her hair.

"Are you laughing at me?" he asked, feigning offense as he joined her in chuckling. "I could be offering to use my last twenty to buy you a beverage."

She snorted then and threw in an eye roll for good measure before reaching out and tapping his watch. "This is a Rolex Cosmograph Daytona 40mm. You can afford to buy this bar, so I'm not worried about cleaning out your bank account with an on-tap special."

Damn. His mystery lady had taken the bait, but the only one on the hook was him.

"How do you know so much about watches? Are you a jeweler?" Justin leaned on the bar to move in a little close and didn't even try to keep the impressed tone out of his voice.

She waved a hand in dismissal. "Paul Newman had one just like that and he wore it when he raced cars. I don't know jack about watches but I know cars."

Okay. This woman just got better and better and he had no choice but to keep wading into the deep end even though it looked like she wasn't going to throw him a life raft.

"I'm Justin—"

She shook her head. "I don't do last names."

Fine. If that was how she wanted it. It was how he usually liked it, too. He stuck his hand out.

"Okay, then. I'm just Justin."

She eyed his hand for a minute, an eyebrow raised with a mocking skepticism that took him back to high school and his ill-fated attempts to get the attention of Brandilynn Post, the head cheerleader. Obviously a crash and burn he'd not forgotten, but there'd been a million head cheerleaders in his bed since then and he wasn't scared off by a woman making him earn her attention. With all the women who normally threw themselves at him, this was an exciting change and one that had him hot and intrigued. He knew that if this night ended with her under him, she'd be magnificent.

"I'm Harley." She grasped his hand but instead of lingering on the handshake her long fingers traced along his palm to blatantly examine his ring finger. Now it was his turn to raise his eyebrow in question. She released his hand and shrugged. "Just checking. I'm not into married guys."

"You're assuming that I'm *into* you."

"We both know you are..." she said, taking a sip from her beer before giving him a lingering, hot look that had him shifting even closer. Close enough to feel the silk of her ink-black hair as it brushed against his face. Close enough to see a tiny scar that cut through the outer part of her perfectly arched left eyebrow. He took it as a good sign when she didn't move away and knew it for a fact when she continued, "...and for the moment, *you interest me*."

Bingo. Justin barely repressed the grin that plucked

at the corners of his mouth. He shifted on his bar stool with a pool of fire settling in his groin and making him hard. But while she was currently into him, everything about Harley screamed that she was an untamed filly, ready to bolt at the whisper of anything she didn't like. He wanted to lean over and kiss her but he glanced down at the bar in between them to resist the urge, deciding to circle back to the beginning of this adventure.

"Okay then, can I buy you a drink *now*?"

She picked up the second shot and drank it down. "I'll buy. You need to catch up."

She signaled to the bartender for three shots and motioned for them to be placed in front of him.

Justin picked up the first one, pausing before he put it to his lips. "Are we celebrating something?"

Harley cocked her head to the side, considering the question for a long moment before picking up her remaining shot and tapping it lightly against his own. "Freedom. New beginnings."

"Whoever he is, he's an idiot." Because the man who'd let this woman slip through his fingers had to be the dumbest man on the planet. Well, the second dumbest… Justin wasn't going to keep her, either. He wasn't deluding himself that what was happening here was a love match or anything.

The vodka burned as it went down; it wasn't as smooth as the brand he normally bought but any criticism disappeared with the chaser of the second shot. He shook his head a little, eyes watering as the alcohol took the first hit at his system and created a slow burn under his skin.

When his vision cleared, Harley was staring at him, her own gaze filled with a different kind of heat, a spark of something. She licked her lips, the universal symbol that she liked what she saw. He found himself back on familiar ground but he braced himself for the moment when she'd knock him off his feet. It wasn't a position he was used to being in with women, but he enjoyed the push and pull with Harley. It was different...more alive and more real than the usual games he played before taking a woman to bed.

"So, who's the guy?" Justin surprised himself with the question. What did he care about the dumb guy who'd let her go? He wasn't interested in the past or the future, just the right now. And unless the loser who'd lost Harley was walking into the bar at this minute to get her back, he didn't care.

But he didn't take back the question, either. Justin wanted to know everything.

Harley cut him a sly look, clearly amused by his curiosity. "His name was Sam. He wanted a commitment that I wasn't ready to make."

Well, that sounded familiar.

"Not ready to commit to him? Or anyone?"

"I think that settling down with someone for the long term is extremely overrated." Justin didn't hide his surprise at her words and so she continued with a tease and tug at the lapel of his jacket. "Whoa. Did I just morph into your dream girl?" She slid her fingertips over his jacket, tugging him closer as she ticked off her list. "No commitments. Can hold her liquor. Likes cars."

Justin grasped her hand and got even closer, murmuring against her ear. She shivered a little and he smiled at the reaction. "If you tell me that sex is your favorite indoor activity, I might just have to marry you."

Harley froze for a moment and he felt the jump and

stutter of her pulse under his lips. But in a flash she pushed him away and picked up her beer, taking a drink before leveling him with a glare that had more sizzle in it than censure.

"And you had to go and ruin it with the *M* word." She gestured toward his last glass. "Take your penalty shot."

He did as he was told, hooking his foot under the rung of her bar stool and easing her closer as he swallowed the liquid fire. "Is Harley your real name?"

She rested her right elbow on the bar, angling her body into the curve of his own. It was intimate, a mirror of his own posture, and he wondered if she knew she was doing it.

"It's a nickname. I like to restore old cars and bikes. I ride a 1975 Harley."

That was an answer he wasn't expecting. "You're a mechanic?"

"I'm between jobs right now. Taking some time to see this part of the world before I make any plans." Her vague nonanswer was delivered with enough finality that he knew it was nonstarter. But she intrigued him and he wanted to know more about her, so he decided to change tack.

"What's the last song you listened to on your phone?"

The change in topic threw her for a minute but she recovered quickly. "'Jolene' by Ray LaMontagne."

"Nice. Moody and soulful but also very sexy. It suits you," he commented, signaling for another round from the bartender after Harley gave a nod of agreement.

"Okay, now you. Last song," she prompted, as they both tipped back a shot.

Justin hesitated, remembering what he'd been listening to when he'd pulled into valet parking. Oh hell. This is what he got for letting his nephew program playlists into his account. "'Cool' by the Jonas Brothers."

"I don't even want to know what that song says about you." She grimaced and eased a shot glass closer to him. "I think you need to drink to make up for that terrible musical choice."

He paid his penalty, wiping his mouth with comic exaggeration that made her laugh. Damn, but he loved that sound and it made him wonder how her husky tone would wrap around a moan of pleasure. Justin reached down and tangled his fingers with hers, giving them a squeeze of encouragement. "Your turn."

Harley pondered a moment and then said, "Okay, beach or the mountains?"

"That's easy. I'm a California boy. Beaches." He held up his hand to stop her from answering and then reached out to skim the hair off her face and let the silky strands cool his skin, savoring the slow burn this woman stoked in him. "Let me guess for you."

"Take your best shot."

Justin's fingertips lightly stroked the smooth golden line of her cheekbone and down along her jawline until his hand curled behind her neck and pulled her closer. Harley eased into him, one leg sliding in between his own and her hand resting on his thigh. She was close enough for him to count her long lashes and to feel the fluttering beat of her pulse point. To hear the catch of her breath and the stifled moan of her desire.

Or was that his own?

He leaned in close, his lips brushing against her ear and body pressed against the length of her. Somehow they had ended up in alignment, mirrors of each other except for the brushes of knees, hands and feet. He was hard, every part of him yearning, aching to strip her down and discover all of her secrets. Not just the curve of her body, not just the places that made her want and need—he wanted to know it all.

But he'd start with her in his bed. Under him. Around him.

"Mountains."

"Lucky guess."

Harley shifted, moving just enough to look him in the eye, her mouth only a moment of bravery away from his own. Her eyes were dark, pupils blown with her desire and burning into his with focus flecked with flickers of doubt. Justin wondered what side would win, knowing with every fiber of his being that this had to be her choice. It was her move to make and he was helpless to do anything but wait and see if she would fold or bet it all on one night.

"Ask me what you really want to know," she whispered, biting her lower lip and then running her tongue over the plumpness left behind.

"Will you let me kiss you?"

Her answer was unexpected and exactly what he wanted. Her mouth on his own, soft but not tentative. It told him what he needed to know—that she wanted this, too. That she wanted him. Justin wove his fingers into her hair, anchoring her in place when he increased the pressure, his tongue against the seam of her lips, begging permission to enter and taste her secrets.

Harley's fingers curled around his lapel as she took over the kiss, slanting her mouth over his and opening to entice him inside. They both groaned and he took what he wanted, took what he needed, but it wasn't enough to quench the craving she'd ignited in him.

He pulled her into his lap, balancing both their weights as she straddled him on the stool. Justin's hands shifted, lifting her under her ass cheeks and pressing her against his achingly hard shaft through his pants. She wrapped her arms around his neck, her own desperate need to be closer evidenced by the scrape of her nails against his skin. The pain was good, just enough to ignite his lust to where it was flash point along his veins.

Harley broke away for air and he took the moment to get the answer he needed before they went any further.

Justin couldn't bear to break the connection, so he murmured his question against her mouth, their eyes locked and focused on each other. "Tell me what you want."

"I want you."

It wasn't the first time Justin had woken up in a strange hotel room.

He loved to travel, for business or pleasure, so it wasn't uncommon for him to awaken in a room and have to take a moment to recall the facts, the details of what VIP suite he was in in what VIP city. It also wasn't uncommon for him to wake up with a woman in his bed whom he desperately wanted to leave as soon as possible. But he couldn't remember a time when he'd woken up alone and regretted that a woman left in the middle of night.

Well, there was a first time for everything.

Harley was gone. Like a figment of his imagination or the silky remnant of a dream that he desperately tried to hold on to but couldn't solidify into a memory. Justin knew she had been real. The ache of his body and the scent of her, of them, of sex, lingered on his skin and on the tangle of sheets bunched around his waist.

He eased out of bed, grabbing his discarded pants and slipping them on as he navigated the detritus of their amazing night together flung all over the space of the penthouse suite: empty glasses and bottles on the floor alongside the remnants of an early-morning room service order of celebratory steak and lobster.

And...her wedding veil.

Justin leaned over, his throbbing head immediately signaling to him that it was the worst idea he'd ever had, and his stomach rumbled in ominous, queasy agreement. The veil was one of those cheap ones sold by every wedding chapel on the Strip. Harley had taken her time choosing it, laughing as she attempted to find one that matched her black leather pants and gray T-shirt. When she'd slipped it on, the combination of sex-on-wheels and virginal sacrifice had decimated what had been left of his very iffy mind and he'd marched down the aisle and said two words he'd never planned on saying in his life: "I do."

What had he been thinking? Nothing. That much was clear. He wasn't reckless but he was a risk-taker, never one to shy away from something just because the payoff wasn't guaranteed. It had served him well in business; he could run numbers better than anyone and he'd made himself and a lot of other people a metric ton of money. But nothing was a sure thing and he made people nervous, people who only liked to play it safe, people who hesitated to work with Redhawk/Ling because they couldn't pin him down.

People like the investor group currently considering

partnering with the company and giving them the ability to branch out even bigger than they thought possible.

The people who would have a coronary if they heard what he'd done here last night.

He'd gone to Vegas for a poker game and married a complete stranger.

A stranger who had left in the middle of the night.

Justin knew what he had to do. He needed to find this woman and get this marriage dissolved before the press found out and filled every news outlet with another story about his wild and reckless ways. Adam, his best friend and partner in Redhawk/Ling, was going to be pissed. Just last week he'd pleaded with Justin to lie low, to keep his profile more on the respectable side until they'd secured this investment deal and solidified their financial status in the eyes of potential partners. Justin had agreed and he'd kept his end of the bargain.

Until Harley.

And now he had to do damage control, find his wife and keep it out of the press.

He was a gambling man, and he didn't like his odds.

Two

One week later

This had been a mistake.

Sarina Redhawk stood on the deck of her older brother's house counting down the seconds until she could leave and head back to her hotel. In front of her, a crowd of people she didn't know ate barbecue and kept the bartenders occupied pouring fruity drinks while the guests placed their vote in either the blue box with a big bow on top or the pink box with a big bow on top. She'd dropped her ticket in the blue box under the incredibly insistent watch and instruction of someone called Nana Orla.

Adam's house was nice, not Kardashian massive but large enough to ensure that everyone knew that he was one of the top tech billionaires in Silicon Valley.

It had been professionally decorated, that was obvious, in bachelor-chic style but personal photographs, quirky artwork and splashes of color against the neutral sofas and such testified to the entrance of the fiery redhead into her brother's life. Tess wasn't timid, she stood tall next to her brother, and Sarina liked her for it. Adam had chosen well, that much was clear.

Just behind her the canyon spread out beneath the deck and dipped into deep purple shadows that reminded her of faraway places she'd served in the army, places that gave her memories that would always follow her no matter how many oceans and miles she put between them. But those memories had taken a back seat lately to the ones she'd been too young to remember, the ones re-created for her and contained in the package her brother Adam had given her and her twin, Roan, when he'd found them again.

Twenty-five years, seven crappy foster homes, one shitty adoptive home, one GED, one enlistment and two tours in the Middle East later and she was here: at the gender reveal party for her older brother Adam and his fiancée, Tess.

And completely out of her comfort zone.

She'd agreed to come to the party tonight because she felt bad about storming out of here the last time, repaying Adam and Tess's hospitality with hostility and painful words. She hadn't meant to hurt him but playing "happy family" with two brothers who were essentially strangers had been beyond her ability at the time.

She'd left that night, hopped on her Harley-Davidson and headed straight out of California, needing to put as much distance as she could between her guilty conscience and Adam and Roan's pleas for her to give them all a chance. She'd ignored Adam's voice mails and dodged Roan's FaceTime requests for a couple of months, taking her bike to every small-town, forgotten, one-stoplight spot on the map, enjoying the freedom of choosing her own path for the first time in her life.

She'd been a military policeman in the army and had liked her job but she'd hit the time when she'd had to get out or stay in until retirement. And she'd opted to get out, explore and figure out who the hell Sarina Redhawk was supposed to be when she grew up. She'd thought it would be scary but it had been amazing. Freedom. Time to think. Space to figure some crap out.

Sarina had camped in Tonopah, hung out with Area 51 enthusiasts in Rachel and explored caves in the Great Basin National Park. In the pretty town of Austin, Nevada, she'd found a stray dog outside her hotel and adopted the little Chihuahua, naming her Wilma, and then headed for Las Vegas. She wasn't much of a gambler but she'd picked up some work from an old army buddy for some extra cash while she figured out if she was ever going to answer her brother's phone calls and what she was going to do with the rest of her life.

Las. Fucking. Vegas.

Bright lights. The Blue Man Group. Five ninety-nine steak buffets. The scene of the best night and worst morning after in her life. Sarina had met a man so sexy in the casino bar that she'd violated her newly established rules to not hook up with guys she met in bars. But his smile had been intriguing, his focus unrelenting and their chemistry so explosive that she'd woken up the next morning naked, hungover and very much married. She'd taken one look at the sleeping man in the bed and the simple gold band on her finger and thrown on her clothes faster than tourists snapped up tickets to see the Britney Spears show.

Then she'd done what she did best: she ran. Right back to California to figure how to track down her husband and fix that colossal mistake. And to make amends with Adam and Roan.

And that was why she was at this party. Saying she was sorry for walking out on them before. Trying. It wasn't easy for her to open up to new people, and despite their shared DNA, they were strangers to each other.

Sarina watched Adam and Roan from across the room as they laughed together with Tess. Both men were slender and tall, but Adam was broader in the shoulders and Roan wore his hair long and halfway down his back. If you watched them closely, they had some of the same mannerisms and expressions, the proof that DNA did not lie.

Roan was a successful artist, his star on the rise. He was often in the tabloids, either due to his breakout talent or his revolving bedroom door that admitted both women and men. He was charismatic and outgoing, and drew everyone to him like he invented gravity. Adam was as successful but leaned into the strong, broody and silent vibe to command a room. It didn't surprise anyone that he'd been on the most eligible billionaire tech wiz list for the last decade.

And here Sarina was. Strong and capable—give her a firearm or a mountain to climb and she was the girl. But she was always an outsider; her superpower was knowing when to leave. The hard part was figuring out how to stay.

And figuring out how to ask for help.

Now that the panic had worn off, she had no idea how to find the husband she'd left behind in Vegas. So, she was going to toast her brother's new family tonight and tomorrow she was going to take him up on his offer to help her get her new life started. How surprised was he going to be to find that the first thing she needed was to locate a husband she had no intention on keeping?

Fun times.

"Everybody make sure to cast your vote for the gender of the baby," Nana Orla admonished the crowd in her delightful Irish accent. She was small and smiling but clearly a force of nature because nobody ignored her. Sarina smiled in spite of herself; the army had master sergeants who wished they had the command that she had. "Come in closer, everyone! Move in closer for the big moment!"

Sarina moved with the swell of the crowd, keeping to the outer edge of the mass of bodies but close enough to see the secret smiles and laughter Adam and Tess shared as they moved into place. Always touching in some way, there was no doubt about how much they loved each other. Sarina had been excited to hear about their engagement. She'd liked Tess from the first time they'd met when her future sister-in-law had tracked her down for Adam. She was a straight shooter, strong and smart. The perfect partner for Adam.

And now they were going to be parents and she was going to be an aunt.

Things were changing, and she had no idea where she belonged.

But it was time to figure it out.

Nana Orla summoned everyone closer for the long-awaited moment. People jostled against one another to get in closer to the happy couple and Sarina was suddenly thrust forward into the middle of the group, mumbling her apologies for the elbows jabbed into people's sides and drinks sloshed to the point of spilling. No one seemed to mind—it was a party and they were ready to forgive. She tried to squeeze in between a laughing couple and had to sidestep into a hard, tall body to avoid an elbow to the face. Another shuffle to keep her balance and she stepped onto the foot that belonged to the hard, tall body as did the hands that grasped her hips to keep her upright.

"I'm sorry."

"I've got you," the man said, his voice deep and smooth and interwoven with a thread of humor that had her lips curving into an involuntary smile.

She chuckled, memories of a night full of laughter and passion coming back with the impact of muscle memory. Her reaction was visceral, immediately sending warmth and heat along her skin. How many times had she shivered from the sizzle of just the memory of that night, craved the touch of the stranger she'd left in that bed?

It wasn't new.

Wait.

The voice wasn't new.

The man wasn't a stranger.

Sarina twisted away from the man, braced herself for what she knew was coming and looked up into the face of her husband.

The ground beneath her feet shifted, the room suddenly becoming too hot and the crowd unbearably close. She braced herself for impact, her body knowing full well what was coming even if her brain wasn't there yet.

"What the hell are you doing here?" she demanded, noticing the curious looks of the people immediately around them.

"Me? What about you?" the man replied in a hushed tone, his eyes scouring her face with eager curiosity and hunger that she knew all too well. It had been like this from the first, some unexplainable heat that sparked between them like electricity trying to complete the arc.

Justin. He'd said his name was Justin.

"Justin, right? What the hell? This doesn't make sense," she sputtered, chasing her erratic thoughts around like a dropped bag of marbles. "What are you doing in my brother's house?"

"Your what…brother?" Justin said, shaking his head as if to dislodge whatever was stuck in there. "The name on the marriage license is Sarah Moore…"

"It's my adopted name," she answered, holding her hand up to stop him from asking new questions before she got answers to her own. "Are you going to tell me why you're in Adam's house?"

"He's my best friend, my business partner. I'm Justin Ling." He gestured with his hands between himself and Adam standing a few feet away. "I'm the Ling part of Redhawk/Ling." He scrubbed a hand over his face, gazing up at the ceiling in disbelief with what looked a lot like disgust. "Not only did I marry a stranger, she turns out to be my best friend's little sister."

Sarina opened her mouth to tell him to keep his voice down but she was interrupted by a loud countdown from the crowd, and both she and Justin turned to watch as Adam and Tess pulled the string on the box in front of them. A huge bouquet of blue balloons sprang out of the box and shot to the ceiling.

"It's a boy!"
"Congrats!"

Applause rang out around them, loud and disorienting, as everyone around her toasted the new parents, completely oblivious to the shitstorm she had created with the man standing by her side. Life had a way of messing with you and right now she knew she was solidly in its crosshairs.

"It's a boy!" rose up again from somewhere behind her as she raised her eyes to the handsome face of the stranger she'd married.

She almost laughed at the ridiculousness of this moment, but it wasn't that funny. While Adam and Tess were celebrating the imminent arrival of their bouncing baby boy, she'd just been handed a sexy-as-hell, six-foot-something bundle of holy-shit-I-married-a-stranger-in-Vegas.

It was a boy all right.

What was she going to do with him?

Three

Adam was going to kill him.

Justin glanced over to where his best friend and business partner was kissing his fiancée and accepting the congratulations from the crowd assembled here to celebrate the biggest event of his life.

Well, the biggest event if you didn't count the recent discovery of Adam's long-lost siblings.

So, the fact that Justin had gone to Vegas, gotten ridiculously drunk with an incredibly captivating stranger and married her was bad enough. But the fact that the mesmerizing, mind-blowing, amazing woman turned out to be Adam's baby sister?

Justin. Was. A. Dead. Man.

He raked his eyes around the space for somewhere he could grab a minute of privacy with his newly surfaced wife. They had a lot to talk about.

Like why the hell she'd left that morning and where the hell she'd been.

"Come with me." Justin took Sarina's hand and guided her through the crowd, headed straight for Adam's office. He knew this house as well as he knew his own, and that room would be safe from curious partygoers.

"Where are we going?" Sarina asked behind him, her voice steely with warning that she was going to give him a little bit of rope and then she'd string him up with it if he didn't get to the point.

In spite of the absolute insanity of this moment, he caught himself smiling. It was her backbone, her direct promise to call him on his bullshit that had intrigued Justin back in that Vegas bar. People didn't call him on much—either because of his money or his family's position in society—and he liked that she didn't care.

The Lings were big money, and had even bigger social prominence in this part of California, his father a self-made man in real estate and his mother the queen of the fundraising committees. Justin, even with a billion-dollar company with his name on the door, was the runt of the over-achieving Ling litter. His siblings were upstanding members of the community while Justin gambled and had a revolving bedroom door and refused to even play Putt-Putt at the country club.

He bet that Sarina played a mean game of miniature golf.

"Hello? Where are we going?" she insisted, balking at being dragged across the room with no explanation.

"To Adam's office. We can get some privacy in there," he answered, feeling the acquiescence in her grip on his hand as they navigated the bodies in the crowd.

Once he reached the large double doors, he opened them and drew her inside. The immediate impact of blocking out the swell of voices was enough to disorient him for a few seconds.

Or maybe it was the woman standing before him.

She was tall, only a few inches shorter than his six feet two inches, muscular, slim, with straight hair the color of black licorice down to her shoulders. Her eyes were the deepest brown with flecks of bronze and her face was cut glass, angles etched in amber.

Sarina was stunning.

And he was staring and holding her hand like a kid who'd just figured out that girls were hot.

The only consolation was that she was staring right back at him, heat answering heat. The pull from that night was back, leaving no question about how they'd ended up in this mess.

Hormones. Chemistry. It was as simple and hard and confusing and amazing as that.

Justin let go of her hand, his body singing in protest at the break in the connection. He stalked around the room, needing the activity to think this through. There were so many moving parts to this catastrophe but he could figure it out. He'd bashed through other barriers, done stuff that nobody thought he could accomplish. He was the kid that nobody thought would make it and he'd figured out how to fight to make sense of stuff that came so easy to other people. He'd become an expert at solving problems. This was just another puzzle to solve, right?

"So, you're Adam's business partner?" Sarina asked, her expression dark with a healthy dose of confused thrown into the mix. She wasn't any happier about this than he was. "Does he know about…"

"About our getting hitched? Nope. I just got back to town a couple of days ago and I was trying to figure out how to deal with it without getting him involved." Justin paused, recollecting one pertinent fact that might be the solution to their problem. "Wait. You married me under a fake name. That must mean that our marriage is invalid."

She shook her head, her hand slashing across the air between them. "Not fake. *Adopted.* I'm in the middle of getting my name officially changed back to Sarina Redhawk but Sarah Moore is my name…for now."

"They didn't let you keep any part of your given name? Adam's adoptive parents let him keep his name," he said, realizing too late that he was probably not telling her anything she didn't know.

"Well, that was mighty nice of them, wasn't it? I guess it made them feel better about taking a kid from a perfectly happy family and erasing every piece of his heritage from his life. I'll make sure they get a prize."

Sarina did nothing to cloak the bitterness in her words and it was so potent that even he tasted the acrid taste of the betrayal. Justin had sat through many long talks with Adam over the years, wishing he could do something to help him, and this moment with Sarina was no different. He didn't know the details of her life—they weren't Adam's to tell—but Justin knew that Adam's younger siblings hadn't had easy lives.

Unfairly taken from their family by the state when Adam was six years old and the twins, Sarina and Roan, were three, they'd been shipped off to families in separate parts of the country. Adam had hired Tess to find them as soon as he had the means, a search that had resulted in their reunion several months earlier. It wasn't the happy event that Adam had envisioned, and Justin had ached for his friend. A quintessential first-born, Adam wanted to take care of everyone and it killed him that the pain of his siblings' lives wasn't something he could just fix with a wave of his hand.

Adam and Roan were making progress in their relationship but Adam had relayed that his sister had been angry, unwilling to even give it a try. She'd been through too much... They'd all been through too much.

"Yeah, Adam's family isn't great," Justin said, knowing that it was the worst of understatements but it also wasn't the point right this minute. Any minute now they could be interrupted, and they needed to figure some stuff out first. "But right now we have more pressing matters to worry about. No matter what your name is legally, we've got to figure out a way to end this marriage as quickly and as quietly as possible."

"Agreed. How do we do that?" Sarina asked, one hand on her hip, the other making the speed-it-up motion in the air.

Justin bit back a laugh. She was snarky and prickly but he thought it was sexy as hell. He was pretty sure that telling her that right now would end in his death, so he kept his mouth shut.

"What the hell is going on? What marriage?"

Justin and Sarina both jumped at the sound of Adam's voice, pivoting to take in the figures of Adam and Tess standing in the open office doorway. Sounds from the party drifted into the space, disguising Justin's muttered "oh, shit" as he motioned them inside the room.

So much for breaking it to Adam at the right time and place, and forget not telling him at all.

He looked at Sarina, knowing her irritated but resigned expression was echoed by his own. Finally, she lifted a shoulder in a shrug that said it all: it was what it was. It wasn't going to get any better. They needed to just get it over with.

Justin took a deep breath and faced his best friend, unconsciously moving closer to his wife as he broke the news. Maybe they weren't destined for a ruby wedding, but they were in this together for now.

"This isn't how we wanted to tell you…"

"I didn't want to tell you at all," murmured Sarina.

"That, too." Justin's lips twitched in a smile in spite of the seriousness of the situation. Sarina was a badass with a really twisted, dark sense of humor. He liked her. A lot. "When I went to Vegas last week I met Sarina at the casino…"

"You were at that high-roller poker game last week," Adam interrupted, his brow creased in confusion. "How…?"

"They don't tie us to the tables, man," Justin said, rushing into the next part. "I met Sarina and we hung out and got married."

It was overly simplistic and left out a shit ton of details, but did it really matter?

Apparently it did.

"How the hell do you go to Vegas and end up married to my sister?" Adam asked, not quite yelling but pretty damn close.

Justin really didn't want to go into the how and why of the entire night. Not when he couldn't remember all of it. But Sarina had no qualms about it. The brutal honesty he'd admired a few moments earlier was less appealing at the moment.

"Adam, it's not that hard to figure out," she said, her expression daring him to call her on any of this. "We met in a bar, got drunk, and woke up the next morning covered in glitter and in possession of a marriage license. I had no idea who he was."

"I've only ever seen pictures of her as a child, Adam. I had no idea she had a different name." Justin filled in his part of the story, hurrying to explain the insanity.

Adam's mouth fell open and Tess grabbed on to his arm in an attempt to calm him down. Justin wasn't worried—Adam wasn't the kind of guy who punched first and asked questions later. But Justin had never married his sister before, so there was always room for error.

"Justin, did you *sleep* with my sister?"

"Adam." Tess groaned at the question, flashing Sarina an apologetic look and Justin a lift of the eyebrows as if to say *really*.

Sarina wasn't having any part of it, either. "Nope. We're not going there. I wasn't some innocent virgin lured over to the dark side. I was a fully participating *adult* in all activities including the marriage part and the *sex* part…which was great, by the way."

"Agreed," Justin couldn't resist adding at the look of horror on Adam's face. It really wasn't funny but the alternative was facing up to the fact that he'd fucked up again and was living up to his reckless reputation. Adam was too shocked to be pissed right now but his anger when it came would be well deserved. Justin had one job and he'd messed up big time.

"No. No," Adam spat out, his hands shooting up in

a gesture meant to ward off all mention of his sister's sex life.

Tess jumped in, stifling a laugh as she steered the conversation back to the heart of the matter. "So what are you two going to do about the marriage? Are you going to stay together or what?"

"No," they both replied in unison, their gazes pulled together in a search for confirmation. The impact of the moment shook Justin again, as he felt the same connection, the same spark, the same flood of memories of smooth naked skin and hot, sweet kisses traded in the midst of tangled sheets.

His mind knew that he needed to end this marriage. His body said that he needed to get her back in his bed and indulge until he was ready to move on like he always did. His gut said that he'd be hard-pressed to find someone it was so easy to laugh with and talk to. Sarina had gotten him from the first moment.

Damn.

Sarina's cheeks pinkened and she blinked hard, breaking the connection with a sharp turn of her body away from him and several steps in the opposite direction. Justin fought the urge to go over to her but they didn't need to complicate this, especially since she'd still be in his life after this marriage was over because she was Adam's sister. Damn, this was tricky.

"Justin, I don't need to tell you how bad this would be if it got out in the press," Adam continued, oblivious to the undercurrent pulsing between the two of them. "We have the chance to partner with Aerospace Link. This is huge."

Sarina turned to face them with a confused expression, and Justin filled her in. "Aerospace Link is the largest satellite company in the world and it's still a family business. They are pretty old-school and have expressed hesitation at some of my lifestyle choices."

Sarina shook her head in confusion. "Your private life isn't part of the deal. One is business and one isn't."

"When you're asking people who've invested billions in a joint venture to trust a company that's a relative infant in the tech industry to deliver what we promise, the behavior of the guy who runs the financial end of the business is part of the deal," Justin explained. "If they can't trust me, they can't trust Redhawk/Ling."

"They act like he's the poster child for *Billionaires Gone Wild* and aren't thrilled that the CFO of our company spends a lot of time on the front page of tabloids," Adam added, his tone protective of Justin. It was a familiar theme of their friendship; Justin had been the black sheep of his family and Adam was his biggest cheerleader.

Justin appreciated it but he couldn't let Adam downplay the truth of the headlines. "I like women and parties and high-stakes poker games," he explained with unapologetic honesty. "But I don't gamble with company money and I'm a damn good CFO. Numbers are the easiest thing in the world to me and I can sniff out a turn in the market faster than anyone else. I'm not interested in letting them dictate my personal life, but I have to agree that getting married while drunk in Vegas isn't a great thing to put on my résumé and is a legitimate reason for them to question the stability of Redhawk/Ling."

"So dissolving this marriage needs to stay off the front page," Sarina stated, her expression reading more exasperated than confused.

"It needs to stay off *any* page, or Aerospace Link will back out and other partners and investors will wonder why. Big business leaders talk to each other and we'll be loath to find anyone who'll want to do business with Redhawk/Ling. This could be a long-term disaster for us," Justin said, flashing a look of regret at Adam. Once again he was a disappointment to the people in his life. "I'm sorry, Adam."

His best friend waved off his apology, his expression kind as usual. They'd been through a lot together, supported each other through the worst and celebrated each other through the best. It would take more than this to make Adam Redhawk turn his back on him, but sometimes Justin wondered where the line was and when he would cross it.

"Justin, you didn't do this by yourself." Sarina's voice was firm and clear across the room. She walked over, stopping to stand shoulder to shoulder with him to face her brother. "And I don't want to be part of the reason Redhawk/Ling suffers."

She didn't reach out to touch him but there was no doubt that she was in this with him, that she was here for the long haul. Justin recalled that she had been in the army and her body language was the definition of loyalty born from a shared experience in the trenches. This situation wasn't ideal but it would be easier if they weren't at each other's throats.

Justin smiled at her, hoping she read the high level of thanks in the expression before turning back to Adam and Tess. "I'll contact our attorneys to get this wrapped up as quickly and quietly as we can."

Sarina nodded at each of them as she backed away and headed for the door. "So let's recap—we get divorced but keep it off TMZ. Adam and Tess, congratulations on the baby boy. I'm tapped out on family time for now, so I'm going to go."

And just like that morning in Vegas, she was gone.

Justin watched the door shut behind her, admiring her style. It was why they hooked up in the first place and why he couldn't take his eyes off her. Sarina was direct, no-holds-barred and a challenge. Hell, he never could resist a challenge. And Sarina Redhawk was a walking, talking invitation for him to keep making bad choices.

Adam stepped into his field of vision, arms crossed as he glared at him. "Don't think I forgot that you *slept* with my sister."

Justin grinned. What else could he do? "But I married her first. That should be a consolation."

Four

The Valley Hotel was a shithole.

Okay, maybe that was a little bit harsh, but Justin felt like it was one double murder in the parking lot away from being in the category of hotel that was featured prominently on cable television shows with titles that included "unsolved" and "most wanted" and played in constant cycles of syndication. The faux-Spanish, single-story hacienda-style building was old and decaying and had given up a long time ago.

A Silicon Valley landmark it wasn't. He wasn't even sure it passed the fire code. He shuddered when he thought about what a black light would reveal if it was aimed at any surface in this place.

Justin navigated a discarded bag of fast food on the asphalt, narrowly missing stepping in a puddle of spilled milkshake and half a joint. He pulled his phone out of his pocket and tapped the screen to call Adam.

"Adam, do you know where Sarina is staying?" he asked, disgust coating every one of his words. "Why isn't she staying with you?"

A big sigh wafted over the connection and he could picture Adam sitting at his desk, hands reaching for the ever-present drumsticks to tap out his frustration. His buddy was secretly in a band that played at a local dive bar once a month. The members were a group of engineers from Stanford so it wasn't going to hit MTV anytime soon but they were pretty decent and had a rabid following. "Yeah, I do. It's a shithole. She won't stay with me and insists on paying her own bill. I'm not arguing with her about it anymore. It's exhausting."

"You can't let her stay here, Adam. This place is disgusting and very likely dangerous," Justin said as he scanned the room numbers for the correct one. He spied it across the lot and headed over, determined to find Sarina and get her out of here.

"Well, she's *your* wife, Justin. So good luck with that." Adam drawled, his tone more you're-an-idiot and less I'm-going-to-kill-you than it had been since they'd revealed the Vegas wedding to him. It was an improvement. Justin expected him to hang up so the chuckle over the line surprised him. "She was in the military, Justin. Trained in firearms. Be careful that she doesn't shoot you."

The call ended and Justin jammed the phone into his pocket and cursed out his best friend/brother-in-law. Sarina's staying at this place wasn't funny at all. It wasn't safe and she *was* his wife. He wouldn't sleep at night knowing that she was here. He had enough money to buy this hotel about thirty times over and he could pay for her to stay anywhere else. This was unacceptable.

He headed across the lot, growing more determined with each step to get to Sarina's room and get her out of here. Justin stopped at the door to room 18 and knocked, listening for any sign that she was inside. He glanced around the lot, looking for her motorcycle, but it was nowhere in sight. Sarina loved that bike—that was something she'd made clear that first night in Vegas—so its absence didn't bode well.

He heard someone approach the door and he knew that he was being observed through the peephole. He smiled and pointed at the doorknob.

"Let me in. I need to talk to you," he said, relieved when he heard the lock slide inside. The door opened enough for him to see Sarina scowling at him. Her hair was pulled back into a ponytail and she wore no makeup, but he'd never seen a more beautiful woman.

She didn't need any of that stuff his mom and sisters spent hours applying and hundreds of dollars stocking in their larger-than-life bathrooms. Her skin was flawless, a honey-caramel color, black lashes thick and heavy as they lined her deep, expressive brown eyes. Her lips were full even when they pulled tight in a frown, even when her smile only hinted at the plump, sexy pout.

Justin swallowed hard; his first instinct was to lean in, kiss her and claim that mouth just like he had that night in Vegas. He knew how to get that mouth to soften, knew how to coax her into opening to him and letting him take deep, drugging kisses that left them both shaking. Damn, he'd wanted her so much and they'd been combustible in bed. She'd been responsive and demanding and insatiable and completely into him. He'd had a lot of women under him over the years but none of them had left him aching and wanting more like her. It was the best time he'd ever had inside and out of the bedroom.

Sarina had been his match but he'd been too caught up in the maelstrom of passion that night and he'd had no time to overthink it. And the next morning when he'd woken up to her gone he'd experienced a level of disappointment he wasn't accustomed to. There wasn't much in life that Justin wanted that he didn't get. He'd grown up in a wealthy family and now he had his own money, a fortune that put his family's bank account to shame.

"Why are you here, Justin?" Sarina asked, noticeably not inviting him inside. He wasn't surprised; there was nothing easy about her.

"Can I come in? I need to talk to you about the divorce proceedings," he said as he cast a disgusted glance around the hotel. "And we need to talk about your current accommodations."

Her eyebrows shot up at the last part, and then her eyes narrowed into be-careful-what-you-say slits. "Did Adam send you?"

"Nope. In fact, he told me not to waste my time."

"So my brother is smarter than you are. Good to know who the brains and the beauty are in your relationship," she observed, stepping back to let him in the room.

It was as bad as he thought it would be. Shabby carpet and curtains in colors that were muted from sun exposure and many washings. The bed was unmade and there was an overwhelming smell of bleach wafting up from the linens, which made him feel better about the cleanliness of the place. None of it changed his mind about her staying here.

"At least you still think I'm pretty," he joked, scrambling for something to say now that they were alone and face-to-face in this odd place.

Sarina paused in her hurried effort to pick up a jacket thrown over the arm of the only chair in the room. She looked him over, nice and slow, not hiding the heated approval that slid across her expression. "Justin, my thinking you're pretty is how we got in this mess."

And there it was. He moved in closer, so they were standing chest-to-chest, close enough for him to see the flash of humor that battled with the attraction in her eyes.

Close enough to hear her growl.

"Did you just growl at me?" he asked, taking a step back just in case it really was her.

The bedcovers next to him moved and he jumped back, not sure what the hell was going on. The growling got louder as the thing under the covers crept closer and closer to the edge of the bedspread. Then, after much wiggling and growling, a small white fur-covered face appeared in the opening. With teeth bared and long pointy ears projected from each side of its head, it looked like something from a science fiction movie.

"Did you pick up Baby Yoda in Vegas?"

Sarina scoffed, lifting the creature in her arms and cradling it against her chest. It was a little white dog, a Chihuahua with big buggy eyes and wearing a tiny black T-shirt with Lady Gaga on it.

"This is Wilma Mankiller," she said, pressing a kiss to the little head and snuggling her closer. "I found her in a little town in Nevada. She bites."

Justin pulled back his hand, taking Sarina at her word. "That's quite a name. Has she actually killed a man?"

"Not yet," Sarina said, setting her down on the floor and watching as she headed over to a bowl of water. "But she's named after the first woman chief of the Cherokee nation. My Wilma is a badass. She was fighting off a really fat feral cat behind a dumpster at a diner. I had to take her."

"Does this place allow pets?" Justin asked, cringing at the worst segue in history. But he needed to get back to the subject of why she was staying in a dump like this.

Sarina plopped down in the chair. "It does and I can afford it. If you're here to tell me it's not the Ritz-Carlton, I know."

"Sarina, you can't stay here. I can afford to put you up in a much nicer place."

"I don't want your money, Justin. If I won't take Adam's money, why do you think I would take it from you?" Sarina crossed her arms across her chest, signaling that this was going to be a lot harder than he'd predicted. "This place is fine. I shouldn't be here that long. Once we put the marriage in the rearview mirror, I'll be back on the road."

"I heard back from the lawyers this morning and it's going to take six weeks for us to get the marriage dissolved. They think they can get it annulled."

"Six weeks?" Sarina scrunched up her nose in distaste. "I didn't think it took that long."

"Apparently, a quickie wedding doesn't equate to a quickie divorce." He sat down on the edge of the dresser, doling out the less-than-exciting news he'd received this morning. "The lawyers are drawing up the papers and they are contacting the Las Vegas officials to do what they can to keep it quiet. The six-week time frame should coincide perfectly with closing of the Aerospace Link deal so if we can keep it on the down low, it won't impact Redhawk/Ling."

"Well, damn." Sarina shook her head in frustration. "My money is going to run out before that happens." She glanced at Justin. "My bike needs work I can't do myself and I'm bleeding cash on that bill. I'm going to need to find a job to fund the repair and my next road trip. I still haven't made it to the Grand Canyon."

"I can give you the money," Justin said. "It's the least I can do." He knew the minute he said it and her arms crossed her chest that the answer to that offer had not changed. Time to try another option. "Okay, okay. I've got a job for you."

"Sure you do." Sarina scoffed, motioning toward him in a give-it-to-me waggle of her fingers. "Do I look like I was born yesterday?"

"It's a real job, Sarina. I swear." Justin lifted his hand in the Boy Scout pledge, chuckling when Sarina laughed and shook her head in disbelief. "Adam and I started a foundation called Rise Up to offer outreach to kids in the foster system. We provide sports, crafts, music, language lessons, all kinds of things for them. We're still looking for a new full-time director but we need someone to coordinate stuff in the meantime. I figure with your army background, you could do this in your sleep. I know you perfected organization and dealing with people in the service. All I need you to do is organize some activities for the older kids, be a presence at the center, show up for them. This will be a walk in the park."

"Foster kids? Still in the system?" Sarina was interested and he knew enough from her background that she had a lot in common with them. "Private home placement or group home?"

"Both. And these kids are getting ready to age out so we're helping them prepare for it. We offer them some support after they age out, but we can't do it forever."

"It's a hard thing for a kid to face." Sarina considered the offer, reaching down to pick up Wilma and put her on her lap. Her tone remained skeptical but he took it as a good sign that she was still asking questions. "It pays?"

"Enough to get your bike fixed and for you to put some money away for your road trip."

"And this is a real job? Not something made up to just give me a handout?" Sarina was suspicious and direct. "I don't take handouts, Justin. I'm not afraid of hard work but I want to earn what I have."

"Look, while I have enough money to fill your hands and about a million other people's, I respect your need to carry your own weight. *Believe me*, I get it. I wouldn't insult you by making up a job that didn't exist." And he really did get it. Being the black sheep in a family of overachievers wasn't the worst position in the world but it had made him determined to make it on his own. It also made him incredibly stubborn. Justin stood, not ready to take no for an answer. "But I have one condition on the job."

"And what is that?"

He looked around the room and shuddered. "You can't stay at the No-Tell Motel."

"It's fine."

"It's cheap," Justin countered, refusing to leave her here for one more minute. He cast another glance around the room and shuddered. "And terrifying."

Sarina rolled her eyes. "Well, I'm not staying with you."

Justin shook his head. He'd anticipated this. If she wouldn't stay with Adam, she wasn't going to shack up with him. "No. You're going to stay with Nana Orla."

Five

Sarina didn't like to owe anyone.

Justin had helped her pack her few belongings, then bundled her and Wilma into his Porsche 911 Turbo and peeled out of the parking lot so fast she expected to see a zombie horde chasing them in the rearview mirror. She'd debated fighting him on the move but the bottom line was that she couldn't afford to stay at that hotel for six weeks and pay for the repairs on her bike. She had some savings after leaving the army but she'd spent a lot of money on her road trip, and the truth of the matter was that it was flowing out faster than it was flowing in.

She'd spent the morning scouring the want ads for jobs she could walk to or get to by bus. It didn't matter what the job was; she'd done every kind of work there was to put money in her pocket and food on her table. Honest work was honest work. She wasn't too proud to clean a toilet but she was independent.

And while she was currently married to one billionaire and was the younger sister of another, she wasn't ready to lean on them for her livelihood. She'd spent most of her life trying not to owe people anything.

Owing people gave them power over you and while it was a given that everybody had to work for somebody, she wanted to choose who had any control over her life. But she also knew when she had to take what was on offer in order to get back to where she was in control of her life again.

So this job was a lucky break and she'd earn her keep and some cash. She didn't like the condition of accepting a free room but she really didn't have a choice. Justin had been 100 percent correct when he'd said that she'd never get her bike fixed if she had to pay for a room for that long.

This was practical and smart, but she didn't have to like it.

But there was something she needed to clear up first.

"Who is Nana Orla and why is she going to let me stay at her house?"

Justin chuckled, giving her a side-eye glance as he changed lanes. "She's my grandmother on my mother's side. She came over from Ireland when I was five or six years old to live with us. You couldn't have missed her at the party. She's loud and bossy and takes no shit from anyone." He winked at her. "Sound like anyone else I know?"

Sarina ignored him, refusing to be drawn in by his amusing sex appeal. "And why would she let me live with her?"

"Because I'm her favorite."

"Uh-huh."

"True story."

Sarina sneaked a peek at the man she'd married as they drove toward Nana Orla's house. He focused on the road, tapping the steering wheel to the beat of the Red Hot Chili Peppers song pouring out of the speakers, so she took the opportunity to take a longer look.

Justin was still ridiculously hot. Tall and slim, with dark hair and tanned skin, he moved like a man who was in complete control of his life. She'd known he was rich the first minute she'd laid eyes on him. He walked like someone who owned the world around him and could buy several others. Charming and charismatic, his sparkling eyes and contagious smile were the things that drew her to him from jump. Justin was like the pied piper—his sex appeal the only flute he'd needed to entice her to follow him into that wedding chapel.

Yeah, they'd been drunk but she'd married him because he'd made her feel like she was all he needed. And that was something she hadn't felt in her life. Ever.

And that night in the hotel room had been like nothing she'd ever experienced before. Sarina had never felt so wanted or needed or desired. Sex had always been good. She liked it a lot and never felt ashamed of taking what she wanted. But sex with Justin had been...earth-shattering. So gravity-shifting that she'd felt compelled to run as fast as she could the next morning. And now that she'd found him again it was terrifying that the last thing she wanted to do was run. She wanted to stay. To get to know him better. To satisfy her curiosity and figure out why this man intrigued her.

Which was why she was going to keep as much distance between them as she could until they were no longer bound for better or for worse...richer and poorer wasn't an issue. His bank account testified that money was never a problem for him.

Justin glanced over, catching her in mid-ogle. He lifted his lips in a smirk, his eyes dancing with mischief. "To be honest, I thought you'd fight me more on this."

She chuckled, turning to face the window and watching the scenery change from the Amanda Jones side of the tracks to the Cher Horowitz suburbs. "I'm self-sufficient, not stupid. I need to get my bike fixed."

"And that place was disgusting. Zero stars."

She rolled her eyes. "Justin, I was in the army. Two tours in Afghanistan. I can stay anywhere. I've stayed in places with no heat or running water. My biggest worry was wondering what would have crawled into my clothes during the night."

"Yeah, well," he said, shifting in his seat and clearing his throat. "You don't have to do that anymore."

"Why? Because my brother is rich?" She snorted out a laugh. "Because I married you?"

"Well...yeah." He sounded perplexed, like he didn't understand why she didn't just rush out and buy a Rolex or apply for an American Express Centurion card.

Not gonna happen.

She leaned back in the seat, turning to look at Justin as they navigated the road up into the hills. "Justin, that's not my money. Never has been and never will be. I'm not trying to be mean but that's just the only way this is ever going to be."

"I know you didn't have it easy growing up. I know Adam would like to help you," Justin said.

"What did he tell you about my life?" Sarina asked, her voice harsh with the anger that suddenly erupted in her gut. She sat up, the seat belt pressing against her chest with the sudden movement and slapping her back against the leather seats. "What do you *think* you know?"

Justin jumped in. "Whoa. Adam told me nothing, but I'm his best friend. It didn't take much for me to figure out that wherever you ended up after you guys were taken wasn't great. It upset him. In case you hadn't figured it out, your brother has a huge white knight complex going on. He takes that shit on like it's all his fault. I put two and two together." He cast a meaningful glance in her direction, a mix of confusion and disapproval. He didn't like her thinking poorly of her brother—and his best friend. That was clear. It made her feel good knowing that her brother had this guy in his corner. "Adam would *never* betray you like that. He's the best man I know."

Sarina let that sink in, recalling a similar observation from Adam. "That's funny. He said the same thing about you."

Justin huffed out a laugh. "Was that before or after he found out about Vegas?"

"Both." Sarina shifted the sleeping Wilma on her lap, smiling at the snuffling snores that racked her little body. "Back at the hotel you said you got that I needed to carry my own weight."

"Is there a question in there?" Justin asked, his voice guarded and his body shifting away from her. It was a subtle move but she was hyper-focused on him and didn't miss it. It was a touchy subject for him, so she'd tread carefully.

"Just the obvious one. You grew up rich—"

"And that means I've never had to work for anything? I was handed everything on a silver platter?"

She sighed, realizing that she'd stepped in it. "I'm sorry, that's not what I meant. I'm genuinely curious. I want to know what you meant."

A long silence stretched out between them. Anthony Kiedis sang about a bridge and she settled back in her seat, totally okay with passing the rest of the ride without talking. She'd learned to live in the quiet spaces and the army had exposed her to every kind of person. She didn't take everything personally; just because someone didn't want to share the intimate details of their life with her, it wasn't the end of the world. Justin didn't owe her anything. Especially not an explanation of his life.

If they kept this arm's length, that would be better anyway. Neither of them needed to form an attachment.

"Let's just say that my path to success wasn't the one my parents expected me to take. Compared to my brothers and sisters, I was the intellectual runt of the litter," Justin said, his voice flat with the effort to try not to sound like it mattered. But it was obvious that it mattered…a lot.

"You did okay, *more* than okay," Sarina said, stating the obvious when they were sitting in a car that cost over one hundred thousand dollars.

"I proved what I needed to prove," Justin answered, turning into a driveway framed by a pair of elaborate metal gates. He rolled down the window, keying in a code that opened the gates and let them onto the property. "I never had to prove anything to Nana Orla. She accepted me just the way I was." He flashed her a grin, but Sarina didn't miss the genuine affection in his eyes when he talked about his grandmother. "I *told* you I'm her favorite."

Sarina sat up straighter, the large estate spreading

out as far as she could see. Landscaped grounds spilled into water features and orchards that opened up to a majestic Spanish-style manor house that sat nestled into the shelter of the rising hills. She leaned forward, jaw dropping at the sheer mass of the mansion. It looked like something featured on one of the reality TV shows that had nothing to do with actual reality. Instead of pulling up into the circular driveway, Justin followed the road around the mansion, heading past an elaborate garden and pool area straight toward a smaller home set in the middle of a grove of orange trees.

The house was built in the same style of the mansion, but it was much smaller. Large enough to hold a few bedrooms, it was bigger than any house she'd ever lived in. With pots of flowers on each side of the front walk and a hand-painted welcome sign on the door, it was inviting. Staying here would be…nice.

A smaller pool and patio with a firepit and barbecue were nestled next to the house, just beyond the two-car garage. Justin pulled to a stop in front of it, turning off the car and waking up a grumbling Wilma, who growled at the disruption to her nineteen-hour-per-day nap routine. Sarina shushed her, stroking the silky soft fur between her ears and getting a doggy kiss reward.

The interior of the car was quiet but not uncomfortable as they both stared forward. For her part, Sarina was processing all that had happened in the last few days to get her in this spot with this man. She didn't know Justin well enough to know what he was thinking but she could probably guess.

He shifted in his seat to face her and she mirrored his movements. Sarina held her breath, trying to still the flutter of butterflies in her stomach and the race of heat-induced goose bumps on her skin. He smiled, the slow, I-know-how-to-flip-your-world-on-its-head grin that had kept her glued to that bar stool in Vegas and then following him down the path to the altar. It was hard to believe that this man ever had to prove anything to anyone and harder to believe that he might not have measured up.

She wasn't the only one feeling something. Justin swallowed hard, his gaze hot and heavy on her. His focus drifted from her mouth, down to where her breasts pushed against her tank top with the ridiculously fast beat of her heart, and then lifted again to her eyes. Everything from the taut lines of his muscles under his shirt, to the fierce grip of his fingers on his thighs, to his heavy breathing that mirrored her own proved he was right here in this craziness with her. And it scared her to death.

"Sarina..." Justin reached out, his hand sliding over her own, the rough brush of his fingers sparking all of her nerve endings. He leaned in closer, his breath drifting across her cheek, his gaze drifting down to her mouth and back up to her eyes. He wanted to kiss her. She *wanted* him to kiss her. It was a bad idea and she didn't care. "You are trouble."

"I think you *like* a little trouble."

His grin turned sultry and he nodded, leaning in even closer. All she had to do was move forward an inch and she'd be able to taste him again.

A knock on the passenger-side window made them both jump and Wilma barked in warning as she scrambled to lunge at the window. Justin peered over her shoulder, rolling his eyes as he recognized the woman gesturing at them through the glass.

Justin reached over to hit the button to lower the window. "Brace yourself. Nana Orla is one-of-a-kind and we are all thankful for that."

The older woman quickly assessed the situation, the eyebrows raised in disapproval and the hands on her hips testifying that she wasn't going to put up with any nonsense. She spoke in a flurry of words that left Sarina blinking in astonishment.

"Justin, what are you doing sitting in my driveway with a girl? Weren't you raised to bring her inside the house? Where are your manners? It's like that boy that used to pull up and honk for your sister on dates. Disgusting." Nana Orla turned her attention to Sarina, her grin a matching twin to Justin's. "I apologize, love. Raised by wolves, I swear."

Her accent was amazing, full Irish and the kind that made getting chewed out a pure pleasure.

"Here, give me the wee dog." Before Sarina could warn her, Nana Orla reached in and picked up Wilma, tucking the dog close to her chest as she opened the door to the car.

"Be careful, Nana. Wilma bites," Justin warned, alarm wiping the smile from his face.

"I doubt that," Nana Orla responded, waving off the warning and placing a kiss on Wilma's little head. "Get out of the car and explain why you're the one bringing Adam's baby sister over instead of him? He's not been here for weeks and we have baby plans to make. And wedding plans, too. I don't want him to think he's getting away with not having a wedding."

Sarina got out of the car, squinting against the sunlight as she watched Justin fold the tiny woman into a hug, cutting it short when Wilma growled from her place tucked against Nana Orla's generous chest. Justin's grandmother was miniature, no more than five feet tall, her silver hair cut in a short angular bob that framed her face. Her eyes were a gray-blue and she wore little makeup except for the bright pink lipstick that matched the linen tunic and flowy pants she wore.

There was only a little physical resemblance between Justin and his Nana, but they had the same energy and his grin was definitely due to her genetic contribution. In fact, the more Sarina observed them both together, the more she saw the similarity in their smiles and the mischievous gleam in their eyes.

There might be two of her but Justin was the heir apparent of her brand of trouble. Sarina smiled in spite of herself, their obvious love and happiness at seeing each other was infectious.

"Nana Orla, Adam asked me to bring Sarina over here. I'm just helping out my best friend," Justin explained, sticking to the joint decision to let as few people as possible know about the marriage.

Nana Orla's gaze ping-ponged between them like she was at Wimbledon, her expression skeptical. "Don't give me the shite, Justin Ling. I saw the two of you having some sort of altercation at the baby gender reveal party and then the two of you skittered off to Adam's office and you were in there an awfully long time with Tess and Adam for me to buy that crackpot explanation." She narrowed her gaze, her eyes lighting up as she looked Sarina up and down. "Are you pregnant, Sarina? Am I finally going to get a great-grandchild?"

Sarina scooted backward, putting as much distance between her body and that insane idea as she could. "Uh, no. I'm not pregnant."

"That's a shame," Nana Orla said.

"You already have five great-grandchildren, Nana Orla. You can drop the Princess Leia impression because I am not your only hope," Justin said, acting like there was nothing weird about this conversation. "I'm just helping out a friend. *We* are just helping out a friend."

Nana Orla considered him for a moment and then she swiveled, turning all of her intense focus on Sarina. "Are you going to live under my roof and tell me that pack of lies, too? Justin is used to sweet-talking everybody and getting away with it but I'm not so easily fooled. I watched him fine-tune those skills from the crib." She cocked her head to the side. "Spill it, Sarina. I know something's going on. What mess has my grandson dragged you into?"

Sarina glanced at Justin and he let out a long sigh. It was more resigned than frustrated so she took that as permission to come clean with Nana Orla…her new roomie.

"I'm his wife." Sarina rushed in to cut off the woman when she looked far too happy at this news. She didn't want to see the fallout of raising her hopes and then being the one to let her down but it couldn't be avoided. "Only temporarily. We're getting it annulled."

Nana Orla eyeballed Justin, her expression disapproving. "I'm guessing one of your trips to Vegas was involved." She shifted over and poked him in the chest. Her voice was chastising but her words were coated in the love and affection they clearly had flowing between them. Sarina looked away, pushing down the pang of longing that threatened to rise up in her chest. She turned back just in time to see Nana Orla flick him upside the head and then pat him on the cheek. "I've got you, Justin. I want to throttle you but I've got you."

"Geez. Warn a guy next time," Justin grumbled, rubbing the spot on the back of his head with exaggerated care.

The older lady shifted to include Sarina in her appraisal. Nana Orla scanned her up and down, her gaze assessing and thoroughly unnerving. It was like she could see right through her. "You look like a smart girl. How did you end up in this mess?"

Sarina ran through the events of that night, discarding all the things she was never going to tell someone's grandmother. She settled for the truth, minus a few details. "Justin is charming."

"He is," she said, nodding. "I just can't believe it worked on you."

"Hey!" Justin protested. "I'm right here."

Nana Orla waved him off. "I still love you anyway."

"Thank you, Nana Orla. One more thing. Don't tell my folks about the marriage."

She rolled her eyes, poking him one last time and wagging a finger of warning in his face. "Now you need me to lie for you, too? Jesus, Mary and Joseph. I'm not doing this in the driveway, let's go inside and get Sarina settled."

Justin leaned in to kiss Nana Orla's cheek and Wilma bared her teeth, growls rumbling up from the little body cradled in his grandmother's arms.

"Well, at least Wilma's got sense to stay away from you and your 'charm.'"

Six

"How was the pajama party?" Justin asked.

He grinned over at Sarina in the passenger seat of his car, trying to gauge how she'd fared her first night with Nana Orla. His wife was a blank slate, her expression neutral as she gazed out the window as they cruised down the highway toward the Rise Up Center. She looked over at him, one eyebrow raised and a smirk tugging at her lips.

"Nana Orla stole my dog," she said, her tone telling him that she wasn't upset about this theft. "She bribed Wilma with lunch meat and tummy rubs so I slept alone."

Justin bit back the first thing that came to his lips: the offer to personally make sure she wasn't alone in the king-size bed in the guest suite of his nana's house. He had his own place, a sterile professionally decorated penthouse in the nicest retail/living town center in Silicon Valley. It was a place to sleep and grab a shower but he didn't consider it a home. He'd taken women there and ushered them out the next morning with a cup of coffee and an apology that he didn't have any food in the fridge. No, it wasn't a home and he didn't want to take Sarina there.

If he had a home, it was at Nana Orla's house. He'd crashed there before, usually when he just couldn't stomach so much family time with his parents in the main house. It was why he'd immediately thought of moving Sarina there; that house was a safe place, a place where a person could weather storms with support and love. Tough love—Nana Orla was always going to call you on your crap—but you never doubted you were loved.

"Don't worry, I'll make sure you get her back before you leave," he said, turning off the scenic highway, navigating busy streets and the typical glut of morning traffic. He glanced over at Sarina, surprised to find her still examining him. He maintained eye contact as long as he safely could, regretting that he hadn't ordered a driver today. Sarina intrigued him and he couldn't take his eyes off of her. "Although I'm not surprised Wilma gets along with Nana Orla."

"Me either," Sarina mused, her voice resigned but amused. "It kept her from asking too many questions so I'm not complaining." She laughed. "But I'm pretty sure that it was a reprieve, not a cease-fire, from the interrogation that is coming."

"You're probably right," he said, pausing before he asked a question he knew Sarina wasn't going to answer. "So, what don't you want to tell her?"

Sarina turned, her gaze locked on his face, and he

could just feel the mind-your-own-business death ray aimed at him.

He shrugged. "What? I want to know more about my wife."

"You know what you need to know."

Justin knew he shouldn't poke at her but he couldn't stop himself. He wanted to know more about Sarina. If he was honest, he wanted to know everything. She fascinated him, and his desire for her had been immediate and visceral. He was a risk-taker, but that didn't include making foolish, drunken mistakes. His risks were calculated and thoughtful and while they looked reckless, they weren't stupid. Sarina had been…undeniable.

He pushed. Because he was Justin Ling. "Why'd you leave the army?"

She pushed back. Because she was Sarina Redhawk. "Why are you avoiding your parents?"

Okay, score a point for Team Redhawk. He hadn't said he was avoiding his parents but he'd shared the fact that he didn't fit into his family and he hadn't taken her to the mansion, he'd hidden her away at Nana Orla's with strict instructions not to tell his folks.

She was right. But that didn't mean he was talking.

"You first," he said, winking at her.

The pause was longer than usual, no doubt giving him time to retract the question. She had read him wrong. He was fine with awkward silences. He could do this all day long.

"I had been in the army almost ten years and it was time for me to either sign up for the long haul toward retirement or to get out. The people I served with were all making the same decision, moving on with their families…it was time for me figure out my own path."

"And have you? Figured out your own path?"

She shook her head. "I answered. Your turn."

That was the deal. "My parents don't approve of my life choices. They think I could be better, could have done better. They think I don't act like a Ling."

Sarina turned fully in her seat, the expression on her face incredulous. "Wait. A billion-dollar company isn't good enough?"

Justin turned into the entrance to the center, pulling his car into one of the reserved spots at the front. He unfastened his seat belt and turned to face Sarina. "Look, I don't want to sound like a poor little rich kid, so don't take it that way." He paused, waiting until she nodded before he continued. Sarina's expression was placid, no indication of where she was falling on this. "I wasn't the high achiever like my brothers and sisters in the things that counted—school, grades, tests, appropriate behavior. I dropped out of Stanford after squeaking in because of my math ability, the one thing that made sense to me. I was dyslexic and a smart-ass and not the obedient son. They think my success is a fluke and that it will be gone in a minute." He mimicked his father's severe tone. *"It's not a stable undertaking."*

Sarina scoffed at that. "That's nuts. You're a mega success. Most parents would kill to have a son who's done as well as you have."

Justin shrugged it off. It wasn't what he hadn't thought a million times before. "My dad grew up in mainland China and broke all ties with his family, refusing an arranged marriage to be with my mom. They met when he was studying in England and she was there working at the university. They fell in love but his very traditional Chinese family disowned him when he ran off to the United States with her and got married. The marriage they were pushing on him had been a business arrangement and his refusal embarrassed them in the eyes of their friends and colleagues. Luckily my father had other family, also exiled, living here in California, and they took them in, helped him to build his business."

"So your parents were badass rebels who chose love. Sounds like they would totally embrace your way of life." She patted the dashboard of the expensive car they were sitting in. "And it looks like it worked out okay, at least from the monetary point of view."

"Yeah, yeah. But my parents went old-school when it came to raising their kids. They went super-traditional and conservative, in a way, to make up for their rebellion. They loved us, I never doubted that, but their expectations didn't leave room for a kid with a learning disability who had a gift for numbers and finance but who also likes to gamble and have no-string affairs with women." He shook his head, still stumped by his folks. "We were expected to do the private school to college to good job in a respected field of work that pays well and marriage with a suitable woman. My parents are the poster children for social status. If it involves doing the 'right' thing and supporting the 'right' charities and all that rot, they are on it. It would be funny if it wasn't so exhausting. It has put a strain on our relationship, to put it mildly."

Sarina considered this, nodding her head in understanding. "And your brothers and sisters went along with it?"

"Two doctors, a lawyer, and one taking over my dad's real estate business. I'm the black sheep."

Silence settled between them. Sarina looked at him, shrugging in answer. "I don't know what to say about that. Family is weird."

"It is." Justin didn't know what else to say about that, either. He'd just shared more with Sarina than he did with anyone and he needed to let it sit for a while. He needed to think about why it had been so easy to tell Sarina, why he'd *wanted* to tell Sarina. Time to change the subject. "This is the Rise Up Center."

He gestured at the building in front of them, opening his car door and motioning for Sarina to get out. He squinted against the bright sun. The sky was clear and the rising heat promised that today was going to be a scorcher. He clicked the lock on his key fob, joining his wife on the sidewalk. She was soaking it all in and he would be a liar to say that he wasn't a little bit proud of the admiration on her face.

"So, Nana Orla picked the name for the center. She's a *Hamilton* fan, so...we went with it."

"Like you were going to tell Nana Orla no."

"Yeah, that's never going to happen," he agreed with a grin. "This center is something that Adam and I thought up on one of our many all-nighters in college. We made a pledge that when we made a shit ton of money, we'd create a center for kids who were in the foster system, specifically targeting the older kids who have a smaller chance for adoption or who are close to aging out. This place is for those kids."

Sarina smiled, her face lit up with approval and interest. "This is amazing. You have *got* to show me around."

Justin grinned, opening the door and waving her inside. "That is exactly what I was hoping you'd say."

* * *

The center was incredible.

Sarina was completely blown away with what her brother and her husband had created. Taking over a large, abandoned community center and athletic facility in a poorer neighborhood, they'd gutted the building and created an indoor gymnasium, studios for dance and yoga classes, tutoring and group therapy rooms, and space for arts, crafts and music lessons. Outside they'd added all-new soccer fields, baseball diamond, tracks and a swimming pool. Kids from all over the Valley came here, using transportation provided by the center, and when they aged out, Rise Up provided a year of post-support and classes geared toward helping them start their new life.

It was ridiculously amazing.

"Justin, this is incredible," Sarina said, grabbing his arm in her excitement. "I cannot believe what you're doing here. This is life-changing."

"That means a lot, coming from you." Justin shifted their bodies, grabbing her hand and weaving their fingers together. She wanted to touch him, needed to feel that connection, and she just went with it. It didn't make sense but nothing with Justin did. "We knew we wanted to do something good with the millions we'd make." He waggled his eyebrows, completely owning his cockiness. Considering that they'd made billions, it was well-deserved. She'd give him a pass. "We knew that we wanted to give back to the community. Adam always wondered about where you and Roan had ended up. He didn't know if it was in care or with a family. He worked with kids when we were in college, foster kids…this was his idea, really."

"And you just went along for the ride?" She knew that Justin's role was bigger than he let on. Everyone in the center, staff and kids alike, knew him by name and he knew personal details about them. It was clear that he spent a lot of time here. Not just writing checks or giving tours to big donors; nope, he was here all the time.

"Something like that," he said with a wink, leading her by the hand to the gymnasium where a dozen or so kids were playing basketball. She should have dropped his hand, broken the connection, but it felt good. It felt kind of right.

The group stopped the game and all turned when the doors clanged shut behind them. Within seconds their skeptical expressions morphed into wide grins and excited chatter erupted and bounced off the high ceilings.

"Justin!"

"Hey, man!"

The kids were ecstatic to see him, most of them swooping in to give him a hug or a back slap. He had a connection with these kids. He loved them and they loved him right back. She was starting to think that resisting the charisma of Justin Ling was easier said than done.

Justin turned and led her over, still holding her hand as he introduced his fan club. "That's Mike, Sarah, Ruben, Marcus, Big Pete, Little Pete, Katie, Teresa and Jose."

Each kid saluted her in turn, their smiles genuine even if a little shy. All of their gazes drifted down to where her hand joined with Justin's. She didn't miss the looks they gave each other. Sarina let go of Justin before anyone got the wrong idea, extending it to shake each of their hands.

"I'm Sarina Redhawk. Nice to meet you."

The impact of her name was immediate. Their grins got even wider, their excitement almost palpable.

"What? You're Adam's sister?"

"That is so cool."

"Does Adam know you're hitting on his sister, man?" The last question came from Little Pete, a tall kid who reached to at least six and half feet. Big Pete was closer to seven feet, so the name was appropriate. "He's gonna kill you."

"Adam knows, you goofball." Justin lightly punched the boy in the arm. "And he doesn't scare me."

"Uh-huh," Little Pete mused, his expression saying that he didn't believe any of it. He tossed the basketball at Justin, who caught it easily. "You got time for a game?"

Justin tossed the ball back, shaking his head. "No man, I've got to get back to the office. We're working a big deal but I'll come back in a couple of days, I promise."

"I can stay." Sarina didn't realize she'd said it until everyone turned to face her. She twisted to look at Justin. "I've got nowhere to be and this is where I'm going to be working for the next few weeks. Why not start now?" She reached over and popped the ball out of Little Pete's hand, dribbling past him to make the shot. The ball swooshed through the net and all the kids whooped and hollered. "I'm a little rusty but I think I can remember how to play."

"All right," Katie said, throwing an exaggerated wave at Justin, motioning for him to exit the gym. "You can go. We've got Sarina."

Justin grabbed his chest in mock dismay, stumbling back from the group. "Whoa, you guys suck."

The kids erupted in laughter, piling on Justin to offer him hugs of apology.

"Okay, okay." Justin held his hands up in surrender. "I'd love to leave Sarina here but I'm her ride, guys. She's got to go."

"I can get a ride back to the house," Sarina said. It couldn't be that hard to order an Uber or to get Adam to come get her. "I'm a grown person. If I could figure out how to get around Afghanistan, I can get home."

"You were over there?" Katie asked, her voice a little awestruck.

Sarina grinned at her. "Yeah. Two tours." She looked around at the group of kids. They would be spending a lot of time together the next few weeks. If they were going to trust her, she needed to let them know she trusted them. "I joined the army when I aged out of care."

"So, you weren't adopted like Adam?" This time the question came from Marcus. He was shy, speaking out from behind Mike's back, but his smile was genuine if tentative.

"I was..." She faltered at this part. Her past was complicated and hadn't been pleasant to live through, and talking about it wasn't easy, either. Justin was watching her, his eyes inquisitive but his expression kind. He inclined his head, letting her know that it was up to her. She took a breath and dived in. "I was adopted but it didn't work out."

"They gave you back?" Teresa was disgusted, her hand on her hip in indication.

"No. CPS came in, took me out and put me back in the system." She debated about how to tell the next part, going for a middle-of-the-road answer. "My adoptive parents weren't great people and they didn't treat me so well. Care wasn't great but was better than what I had."

Silence fell on the group and she watched as each of the kids processed her story.

"That really sucks, Sarina," Marcus said, nodding along with the other kids. "It's a good thing that you're here. You've been in the system so that makes you a center kid. You belong here with us."

And just like that, she was one of them. It felt good. Right. As easy as it was with Justin.

Sarina nodded at each of them in thanks, letting a grin take over her face. It was time to lift the mood in this joint. "Well, then it won't hurt so much when I kick all of your butts."

Catcalls and trash talk filled the room as the kids moved into their positions on the court. Justin came up beside her, one arm looping around her waist as he drew her in closer. He was warm, body as firm and taut as she remembered, and he still smelled so damn good. Sarina leaned into him involuntarily, giving in to the pull of attraction that always pulsed between them.

"You're pretty amazing, Sarina Redhawk Ling," he murmured low so that only she could hear. She ignored the little flip her heart did when she heard her name joined with his. "It took me months to get these kids to accept me like that."

"Well, I'm a center kid. You heard Marcus." Sarina was more pleased with the approval in Justin's eyes and voice than she wanted to admit. Knowing that he didn't pity her or pepper her with a million questions meant a lot. He was giving her the time and space she needed to share, or not. It was seductive.

And she didn't mind the use of her married name. Not at all.

That was...interesting.

Justin gauged her mood accurately and let it drop. Instead he pulled out his key fob and dangled it in front of her. "I'll call a car to come get me and take me to the office. I'll leave the Porsche for you."

"What? You're going to leave me your one-hundred-thousand-dollar sports car? Are you high?"

"California is a community property state so technically, the car is half yours," Justin answered, jangling the key fob so that it made a metallic clinking sound. His grin slid into seductive, a little dirty. "Come on, you know you want to drive it. If I recall, you prefer a wild ride."

Sarina flushed, her skin hot and goose bumps racing down her arms. She remembered this Justin.

This Justin had kept her up all night.

She let her gaze drift down to his mouth, her heart racing when his lips curved into a smile that told her he knew exactly where her thoughts had gone. He leaned in, so close she almost tasted his kiss.

"Are we going to play ball or are you two going to kiss it out?"

Sarina had no idea which kid said it but it broke the tension immediately. Justin's grin got wider and he rolled his eyes, releasing her from his hold.

Sarina snatched the key fob out of Justin's hand, her grin wide and her heart light for the first time in a long time. "Get out of here. I'm going to play some ball."

Seven

"Your car handles like a dream, Justin."

Sarina stretched out her hand, dangling the key fob over the open palm of the car's owner. Justin was kicked back on a lounge chair by the pool at Nana Orla's house, his grin as warm as the lingering sunshine. The beer in his other hand looked as cool as the water spilling out of the fountain water feature. At the last minute she yanked back her hand.

"Nope." She smiled at his shocked expression. "No beer, no expensive car keys."

"Are you holding my car hostage until I get you a beer?"

Sarina glanced over at Nana Orla, winking at the older woman. "He's cute *and* smart. If *only* he was rich."

Nana Orla cracked up, a belly laugh that had her doubled over on her lounger. "Justin, if you let this girl go I will disown you."

"*Really*, Nana? I thought I was your favorite!" Justin said, fishing an ice-cold bottle out of the outdoor fridge, popping it open and heading back over to Sarina.

"I don't have any favorites, Justin. I love all of my grandkids equally," Nana Orla assured him. "But if you don't keep this girl, you won't be my favorite anymore."

"You wound me, Nana. I'm gutted." Justin handed the beer to Sarina.

She took it and slid into his vacant lounger with a grin on her face, effectively stealing his seat. "Sorry. You're too slow."

Justin paused, his head cocked at her, his smile big but confused. "What's gotten into you?" He held his hands up in the universal gesture for surrender. "Don't get me wrong. This is the Sarina I met in Vegas and I like her a lot. I'm just wondering where the grumpy, prickly one went and is she coming back?"

Nana Orla snorted. "If that's your best pickup line it's no wonder you're single."

"Ignore him." Sarina waved him off. She was riding high and nothing was going to knock her off this mountain. "I had a great day with the kids at the center. They're so smart and brave and the center is extraordinary. I think I can do some good with them in the next few weeks. You and Adam have created something really special there."

Justin sat down, straddling the lounger to face her. He reached out to take her hand and she let him, leaning into the moment. His smile was bright and contagious and only for her.

"You had a good day, yeah?" Justin asked, his thumb rubbing softly against her wrist. It was mesmerizing, sucking her into his orbit once again. She knew it was a bad idea but she couldn't bring herself to stop it.

"Yeah, I did." She leaned forward; it was impossible to wipe the smile off her face. "Those kids are so great. Thank you for taking me there."

"I knew you'd love it."

"Oh, Ma, I didn't know you had company."

Sarina jumped at the female, Irish-tinged voice, shifting quickly to look over her shoulder at the couple standing on the patio. Justin stilled beside her, his fingers tightening on her own, his body tense. The couple were in their early 60s, tan and fit and dressed for a cocktail event in clothes that reeked of money and status. They were both tall, the man broad-shouldered with dark hair sprinkled heavily with silver. The woman was also willowy, but athletic and fit, with dark hair pulled up into a sleek updo. But what stood out to Sarina most was the fact that the woman had Justin's smile and the man moved like him, quick but controlled and smooth.

It didn't take a genius to figure out that they were Justin's parents, Mr. and Mrs. Ling.

It also didn't take a Mensa member to realize that they were not thrilled that she was sitting here holding their son's hand.

Nana Orla put her drink down on the little side table before rising from her lounger and greeting the newcomers with open arms.

"Come here, you two. Give someone a heart attack sneaking up on somebody like that." She pulled them both in, fussing over them as she kept talking. "Where are you going all dressed up? It's Wednesday. What could possibly be happening on a Wednesday?"

"It's a cocktail party to meet the new director of the

arts coalition, Mother. I thought I told you," Saoirse Ling responded, her gaze settled intently on Sarina, so focused it was almost like a physical touch. "Who is your guest, Ma?"

Her accent wasn't as intense as Nana Orla's, softened by either years spent in the United States or purposefully polished down to the point where it hinted at time spent abroad in places more glamorous than California. But her gaze was 100 percent her mother's, inquisitive and not missing a thing.

Justin's father was just as intense but more quiet and removed. Sarina got the impression that he didn't have much to say but that he missed nothing, especially where his children were concerned.

Either way Sarina had met them before; they were echoes of the countless parents of potential friends she'd met through the years who'd been thrilled that little Molly/Susie/Amanda had a new buddy until they'd realized it was a kid in foster care. Especially a kid in foster care who had a folder of failures and problems as she moved from home to home. She couldn't blame them for protecting their kids, but she couldn't forgive them, either.

Mr. and Mrs. Ling weren't thrilled at the stray Justin had brought home this time if their reactions were any indicator. She allowed herself a small huff of laughter when she thought about how they'd react if they knew she was their daughter-in-law.

"My new friend is Sarina Redhawk," Nana Orla answered, turning to grin down at her, letting everyone know that she was very welcome here. It was a kind gesture, protective, and it set Sarina on alert. "She's staying with me for a few weeks while she assists Justin at the Rise Up Center." Nana Orla gestured to the newcomers. "You've probably guessed that these are Justin's parents, Allan and Saoirse."

"Redhawk?" Allan Ling, looking at her more closely. Man, his razor-sharp, dark-eyed gaze reminded her so much of Justin. "Adam's sister? The one who recently left the army?"

Sarina stood, noting that Justin rose with her and let go of her hand but kept a protective hand at her back. She held out her hand, falling back on her military training to handle this awkward situation. "Yes, sir. It's nice to meet you."

He took her hand, shaking it and nodding in greeting. "Thank you for your service, Sarina. Adam speaks highly of you."

"I think Adam is a good brother, sir." She shot a glance at Nana Orla. "I'm grateful to Nana Orla for letting me stay here while I have my motorcycle fixed. She's a wonderful lady."

"Yes, well, Ma can't resist a stray in need." Saoirse interjected, her smile an attempt to dull the edges of her blade. She didn't want to kill, only wound and warn. Sarina appreciated the transparency in the rules of engagement. "Justin gets that from her."

"Well, if that's true, then they've found the right project in the Rise Up Center," Sarina replied, taking pains to keep her words and tone respectful, but making sure her position was clear. She didn't want to make trouble for Justin or Nana Orla but she wasn't going to let anyone put down their incredible hearts. "They are doing incredible things with those kids… I guess you'd call them 'strays.'"

Justin's hand on her back slid around her waist, drawing her ever so slightly closer to him. It wasn't a big move but it made his point and both of his parents noticed. Both tensed, standing taller and straighter in their fancy clothes.

"Mom and Dad, Sarina has agreed to fill in at the center for the next few weeks while we look for a new director." He looked at her, his gaze full of admiration and his smile only for her. "We are lucky to have her. She's already bonded with some of the kids."

There was a long pause but nobody rushed to fill it. *Awkward* was the appropriate word but it didn't even come close to describing the width and breadth of all the things unsaid. Mrs. Ling finally broke the impasse and it was like someone had let the air out of an explosive-filled balloon.

"Well, that's nice, although it will be a shame when you have to go. But we all understand, and appreciate your work for these few weeks." She reached out to give a half hug to her mother as they prepared to leave. Then she let the other shoe drop so casually that it almost didn't make an impact. "Justin, Heather Scarborough will be at this party. I'll make sure to tell her you said hello."

Justin cleared his throat. "Sure, Mom. Tell her I said hello."

Sarina didn't have to be a genius to read between the lines here. Saoirse didn't like whatever she sensed was going on between her and Justin and she made sure that Sarina knew that her presence in his life had a shelf life. *Check*. She was also reminded that Justin had other options, more suitable options who attended Wednesday-night charity parties and got along with his mother. *Check*. Message received.

They watched as the Lings made their exit, heading toward their Mercedes and leaving behind a lingering scent of expensive perfume, aftershave and money. They had killed the mood for the evening, ushering in a chill that mimicked the one brought on by the setting of the sun.

Justin let out a heavy sigh, his hand tightening on her waist as he looked into her eyes. "Well, you met your in-laws."

It wasn't funny but it let loose the tension in her shoulders, stress from the last few moments expelled in a laugh that sounded off to her ears. Holy hell, why was a short-term marriage suddenly so complicated? It didn't take a rocket scientist to figure that out. It was complicated because she cared for Justin and so it mattered that his parents thought she was trash.

And if she was honest, they were just the latest in the long line of parents who didn't think she was good enough for their kids, their lives. Some things never changed.

She couldn't stop how she felt. But she could stop her feelings for Justin from growing any bigger.

Sarina moved to go inside. She'd take a shower, grab something to eat and hide in her room watching Netflix. She needed time to process, to construct stronger barriers around her feelings when it came to Justin Ling. She needed to remember that they did have a shelf life, that there was a pending divorce looming between them.

"Sarina, come with me. I want to show you something."

It was his voice. Soft, intimate, a tone and cadence she knew was one he only used with her. All he had to do was say her name and all her reservations vanished.

She'd waited her whole life to have someone look at her the way he did, speak to her the way he did.

Even if it was just for now, she couldn't walk away from it.

Justin took her hand and scooped up two beers, saying a quick goodbye to Nana Orla. He led her across the lawn toward the grove of trees filling the space between the house and rising hills. It was quiet and serene here, a million miles away from the bustle of the Silicon Valley just beyond the perimeter of the property. Here, it was just the two of them; no parents, no long-lost brothers, no lawyers or investors.

They entered the copse of trees, the waning sunlight now just dapples of light on the ground all around them. It was like nature's version of those fairy lights people draped all over the place at the holidays. The temperature dropped in the shade of the trees, causing goosebumps to erupt on her skin. Or it could have just been anticipation that had her alert and aware of every breath and brush of skin as they walked side by side.

It took her a moment to adjust to the shadows and then she saw it. A small house, nestled in the crook of the limbs of a huge old tree. It was made of wood, so expertly interwoven with the trees around it that it looked like it had been there forever. A staircase curved along the tree trunk, and led to the structure now rising up directly over their heads.

Justin flashed her a smile that took over his face, lighting his eyes up with childish delight. She smiled back, unable to resist his undiluted joy or the tug of his hand as he led her up the stairs.

If she thought the approach was amazing, the inside of the structure took her breath away. Exposed hardwood, maybe oak or pecan, formed the one-room tree house, the ceiling tall enough for them to stand easily, glass skylights and a wall of windows giving them a full view of their surroundings and the sky. From this vantage point, everything disappeared except for the treetops and the stars filling up the darkening sky.

"Oh my God," Sarina breathed out, her eyes darting from one detail to the next. Shelves built into the walls held books, candles, a fallen bird's nest, the mementos of exploration and indulgence. Colorful quilts were piled on an oversize daybed stationed in the middle of the room, an inviting place to take a nap, read a book or gaze at the stars.

Justin let go of her hand, placing the bottles on the small table next to the daybed before walking over to the windows and unlatching them in several places before he pushed them to the side, effectively joining this space with the great outdoors.

"Justin, I have never seen anything like this in my life."

"It's awesome, isn't it?" His smile was now full of pride; he was clearly pleased that she liked his show-and-tell surprise. It made her blood warm, knowing that her opinion mattered so much to him. "Nana Orla didn't want us to forget what it was like to just be kids, so she had this built for us when I was little. It was just a simple tree fort back then but I had it renovated a couple of years ago, had an architect shore up the structure, add the windows and electricity that can run a small fridge and add a powder room at the back. It's one of my favorite places in the world."

"This is incredible. I cannot believe it. It's like something in a fairy tale."

Justin's grin got wider as he opened the two bottles, settling down on the daybed and stretching his long legs out in front of him. He nodded toward the spot next to him. "Sit down. Check out the stars."

She knew that this was dangerous territory. This man, the stars, a tree house. Everything was tailor-made for her to do something foolish. She did it anyway.

The bed was comfortable, perfectly situated to give them the best view of the stars that were taking over the darkening sky. The birds were settling down for the night, adding their own muted sounds to the show.

Justin's arm stretched out on the daybed behind her, his movement shifting the cushions between them and easing their bodies together so that they touched from shoulder to knee, their body warmth mingling and causing Sarina to shiver with the contrast of the cooler night air.

"You know what was the worst thing about waking up in Vegas and realizing you were gone?" Justin asked, his voice low, as if he thought he'd spook her.

She shook her head. She had her suspicions, but really she didn't know. She only knew how she'd felt when she'd realized that she had to leave.

"It wasn't that I was horrified or embarrassed about waking up married. It was the thought that I'd made up the way we connected, the way I felt when I was with you." He swallowed hard, taking a sip from his beer before continuing. "I wanted that to be as real as I thought it was. I still do, even if I know we can't stay together."

She could go two ways with this: she could lie and tell him that it was just the shots at the bar, or she could tell him the truth and assure him that she'd felt it, too. But she knew she couldn't lie because she understood completely what he was saying, because it was the reason she'd left.

"It was real, Justin," she whispered, taking a deep breath to steady the frantic beat of her heart. "It was why I had to leave."

Justin placed his beer bottle on the table and turned to her, his free hand sliding over her jaw, fingers winding into her hair. She lifted her face to his, shutting her eyes to the intensity of his gaze at the same time his mouth pressed against her own. Soft lips, quick breaths, and then groans and mouths opening to each other, tongues tangling and the kiss deepening to the point where she didn't know where she ended and he began.

Sarina wrapped her arms around his neck, hungry to be as close to him as she could get, her body craving what it remembered was so good. Justin's hands roamed over her body, coasting over her back, her hip, back into her hair. Everywhere he touched her was liquid heat, nerve endings responding to him and sending messages to her brain that defied logic and drove out any rational thought.

It was need and connection and pheromones and hunger.

Justin groaned, lifting her onto his lap. She straddled him, the tender, aroused center of her body pressed against his hard dick under his jeans. Sarina gasped, releasing his mouth as she threw her head back, eyes open, with nothing but the stars above and Justin's hard, sexy body beneath.

"Damn, Sarina," Justin moaned out beneath her as his body bucked up to meet every one of her downward thrusts. His fingers went to the neckline of her V-neck T-shirt, tugging it and the soft cup of her bra down to expose a nipple. She looked down just in time to see his mouth close over the tight peak and then she felt the tug of his wet, hot mouth on her nipple. She was close, so close.

It was so primal, something she hadn't indulged in since a teenager, the not-so-innocent humping of two bodies together as they pursued one of life's best gifts. But she couldn't get naked with Justin, not now. It was too much. Her body wanted him but she couldn't be that vulnerable. Not when she knew she had to leave.

But she would be selfish and take what she could. Because she needed him.

She bore down on his hard length, pleased when he released her breast on a moan that was half pain and half pleasure. Their eyes locked, mouths swollen and lips wet as they ground their bodies together, both needing the same thing.

One minute she was on the edge and the next she was arching into him, crying out loudly as her orgasm hit her like a bolt of lightning. Hot, intense, sharp-edged with pleasure that tightened every muscle in her body, it was drawn out by the sound of Justin moaning underneath her, his hips and cock pulsing against her body as he came.

Sarina collapsed against him, trying to catch her breath and glad for his arms around her as she tried to wrap her brain around what had just happened.

It had been real in Vegas. It was real in the here and now.

But it didn't change anything.

Eight

Sarina was avoiding him.

The mind-blowing orgasm in the tree house had been unbelievably hot. They'd needed to talk about it but in true Justin and Sarina avoidance protocol, they'd cleaned themselves up, headed back to the house and then retreated to their corners to process what had just happened.

And two days had gone by with no contact and it was driving him nuts.

He'd gone to the office, burying himself in the financials he was working up to accompany the deal they were executing with the investors at Aerospace Link. This wasn't a typical deal for Redhawk/Ling but it was exciting. In the past, they'd been the ones seeking people to assist them, doing the work to prove that they were a good investment. Now they were one of the frontrunners in app and cloud-based technology and

Aerospace Link was a leader in satellites. And this new venture would put them both in the position of leading the next wave of technological innovation.

This was a collaboration that would lead to opportunities that Redhawk/Ling wanted and needed to be a part of in order to solidify their lead in the market, so nothing could jeopardize it. They had made the money and the money had gotten them a spot at the table but Justin and Adam wanted to be at the head of the table and this deal would put them there. Which was why it was so important to keep the marriage to Sarina a secret.

Adam wasn't wrong when he said that Justin's reputation wasn't always an asset to the company. People admired his ability to crunch numbers and project trends in finance, to think outside of the box and make people a shit ton of money. There was a reason why the upstart companies who had nothing to lose were the ones that shook things up and pushed the boundaries. Once people got rich they got scared and they played it safe.

So they didn't like that he loved poker, high-stakes poker with players who could match his skill. Outsiders saw his participation as an indication that he lacked control and that he had a problem. But he wasn't an addict, he was a puzzle solver, a human calculator. It wasn't risky, it was statistics and probabilities. Poker was numbers and numbers always made sense to Justin; it wasn't risky for him because it was just math.

But the only thing that they mistrusted more than the poker was the women. No matter how trend-setting the men and women of Silicon Valley were supposed to be they were pure 1950s when it came to sex. Stability was going home to the same partner every night for dinner, and investors preferred to trust people who were *stable* with their bank accounts.

Justin was never going to apologize for enjoying sex with a variety of partners. His parents would love for him to settle down but the women he picked weren't there for *him*. They showed up for his money and they stayed for the orgasms and the good times. Everybody was an adult and everybody knew the rules. Nobody got attached and nobody got hurt.

But Sarina was different. He wasn't in love with her but they had *something*. A connection. She made him feel good, like he was doing it right by doing it his way.

Which is why he was walking into the Rise Up Center in the middle of the day to see her when he should have been at the office. Estelle, the assistant extraordinaire he shared with Adam, had given him a sly smile and amused side-eye when he'd told her that he'd be taking the rest of the day. He didn't even stop to wonder how she knew what he was up to; Estelle knew everything.

After a quick exchange with Kori at the center's front desk, he headed to the rock climbing room, following the excited voices.

He entered the space, familiar to him since he'd designed it. He'd wanted it to be a place for the kids to push themselves, to try something new and different. The result was a room surrounded by climbing walls from floor to ceiling with every level from beginner to advanced. The kids loved it.

The sight of it made him a little queasy.

Teresa spotted him first, hanging from a rope halfway up the wall. "Hey, Justin! You here to join us? Get your climb on?"

"Holy crap, Teresa, pay attention to what you're doing!" Justin shouted, his unease impossible to hide. Didn't she see how far up she was? And with nothing beneath her but air. He shuddered a little.

"Green ain't your color, man!" Big Pete joked, inspecting his equipment on one of the benches that ran along the center of the room.

Justin waved them off, eyes searching for the person he came here to see. He scanned the room, heart jumping in his chest when he spotted a familiar figure, wearing black form-fitting clothes and hovering forty feet above the ground. Sarina was stunning, her body strong and in perfect control as she strained to climb higher, muscles tense with the effort.

His fingers flexed, memories of touching her body, gliding along her smooth skin as she responded so sweetly to the passion that flared between the two of them. The other evening in the tree house it had been combustible, something he'd known was coming and he'd done nothing to stop. The next few weeks were going to be agony if he stayed around her and couldn't touch her.

But he knew that staying away was going to be impossible.

His current location was proof of that.

He held his breath as she reached the top, grinning down at the kids who yelled out their congratulations to her. Their eyes locked and it was a moment of recognition, a spark, and he saw delight in her gaze. It made his stomach flip and he grinned up at her unabashedly, not caring who saw. His excitement didn't even dim when she checked her equipment, glanced behind her and then descended at a rate of speed that made the floor move under his feet.

Damn it. Why had he built this rock climbing gym?

Sarina landed with sure-footed confidence, turning to high-five the kids who swarmed around her to offer their congratulations. She laughed, her usual placid expression replaced with the enthusiastic affection she already had for the kids. He gave himself an inner high five for taking the chance that she would be the right fit for this group. They were older kids, pasts full of disappointment and with few adults to look up to, but he'd known that they'd find what they needed in Sarina.

"Don't you have a job?" Sarina's question broke into his thoughts. She walked over to him, hand on her hip and head cocked to the side. "Don't you have a bunch of tech billionaire things to do?"

He laughed, moving in closer just to catch a little bit of the citrus scent that clung to her hair and skin. His first impulse was to lean in and kiss her but he knew they had an audience. A young, impressionable audience.

An audience that would rat them out to Adam.

"I do, but I wanted to invite myself over tonight. I've got a present."

"For me?" she asked, her nose scrunched up in confusion. "For what?"

He shook his head, knowing she'd never accept a gift from him. "No way. It's for Wilma."

"Ah," she replied, giving him a dubious side-eye. "You know that she can't be bribed."

"A man has to try."

"Good luck with that." Sarina unhooked the equipment from around her waist, offering it up to him. "You want to climb?"

He couldn't back up fast enough. "Oh no."

"He's afraid of heights, Sarina," Katie offered. "We can't get him up there for love or money."

"Really?" Sarina looked really confused now. "What about the tree house? You know it's up in the air, right? Off the ground?"

"Yeah, but it has a floor. I'm okay with things that have floors. I just can't have the vast expanse of nothing below me."

Sarina moved into him, her fingers brushing against his midriff. She meant it to be teasing, comforting, but it made him ache for her. "So I guess you wouldn't walk the Grand Canyon Skywalk with me?"

He reached down and took her hand, his thumb rubbing over her knuckles. "Not if it doesn't have a floor."

"Oh no. It's a glass bridge that extends seventy feet out beyond the rim of the Grand Canyon and four thousand feet above the bottom of the canyon. My old master sergeant said that if you stand on it you can look down and see your future."

"Is that before or after you puke?" he asked, horrified by the image that popped into his mind.

"Ha! Before, I would guess." Sarina winked at him, turning and pointing at Marcus. "You ready?"

The boy nodded, his expression tentative as he shifted his big eyes between Sarina and the wall.

"Don't worry. We'll do this together," she assured him, giving his arm a squeeze of encouragement.

Justin moved back, keeping his eye focused on his wife and the young man she gently guided through the steps of preparing to climb. Marcus was nervous but Sarina was calm, telling him that he could do it and running him the through the steps until he could repeat it back to her verbatim.

They positioned themselves along the wall, both making the final preparation to ascend. Sarina looked around at the kids standing around. "Come on, join us. Marcus needs the support and he's *sidanelv*—that's Cherokee for *family*. We don't let our family do it alone, right?"

Big Pete, Katie and Teresa all stepped up and prepared to climb with their friend. And they did it—together. Marcus stumbled at times and he was scared, but the other kids and Sarina kept him going, cheering him on and giving him helpful pointers when necessary. Forty-five minutes later Marcus was standing on the ground again, smiling proudly as his buddies all piled on with hugs and high fives.

Hair mussed and cheeks pink with her efforts, her grin contagious, Sarina moved over to Justin. "So, when am I going to get you up on that wall?"

"I think you need to reconcile yourself to disappointment," Justin said, helping her as she divested herself of her equipment again. He sneaked a peek at her, turning over in his head something he'd wondered about since meeting Sarina. "You were really good with him. I could see your military training working so well and it makes me wonder why you left the army when you were obviously made for it."

Sarina messed with the stuff in her hands, taking so long that he wasn't sure she was going to answer him. When she did, it was in a quiet tone, edged with regret and little wistfulness. "The army works because we all have the same purpose but also because we become a family for one another. My people had moved on to the next duty station, left the service, gotten married and had babies. It was time for me to find my own life, my own future."

Justin debated asking her the question on his mind. The obvious question. He did it anyway. He wasn't good with waiting. "How is that working out for you?"

She flashed him a half smile, shaking her hair out of her eyes. "I'm working on it."

And while he knew he shouldn't, he wanted her plans to include him.

Nine

"Permission to come aboard?"

Sarina popped her head out the window of the tree house and looked down at the man standing at the bottom of the steps. Justin was so sexy, wearing a black T-shirt and shorts, a pair of flip-flops on his long feet. He had his sunglasses pushed up on top of his head and he was holding a bag with a local sandwich shop name on the side in one hand and a six-pack of beer in the other.

It had only been a couple of hours since she'd seen him at the center and he was still hot. Still making her stomach flip with the jolt of heated sensual recognition.

"Justin, that's for boats, not tree houses," she chastised him with a laugh. "And this is *your* tree house."

"Nope. I think I've lost ownership of the tree house while you and Wilma are in residence. That's what Nana

Orla says," he answered, nodding toward his uplifted hands. "I come bearing food and drink."

"Well, in that case, come on up."

Sarina retreated into the tree house, pulling the scrunchie off her hair and fluffing it up. She caught her reflection in the small mirror over the bookcase on the wall; her cheeks were flushed even without a stitch of makeup. She'd seen the photos online of Justin with women and they were all beauty queens with perfect hair, clothes and makeup. Sarina had never worried about it before and now was too late with her messy hair and old cotton sundress.

She couldn't do anything about it in the next five seconds She was who she was.

And why was she thinking about this at all? This was never going to be anything. Her husband wouldn't be her husband in a few short weeks. She needed to stop acting like every encounter with him was a first date. It wasn't anything like that.

So why did it feel like that's exactly what it was?

"You look gorgeous."

Sarina spun, surprised to see Justin standing behind her so soon. He must have raced up the steps and here he was, his expression telling her that he liked what he saw. She blushed, heat spreading over her skin like the breeze whispering through the windows of the tree house.

Wilma growled from her little nest of blankets on the daybed. She was buried underneath the covers; the only visible part of her little body was her nose and two big dark eyes.

"Oh wait, I forgot to offer my tribute to the lady of the manor," Justin said, dumping the food and the beer on the side table. He fished a little gift bag covered in a design of various cartoon dogs out of his pocket, the paper crumpled from being shoved in there. "I noticed that our grumpy Wilma needed a new collar and tag. I took the liberty of getting her one that's fit for the badass she is."

Sarina took the bag from him, opened it and pulled out the little collar. It was black leather with three rows of shiny silver studs and a metal piece that had "Wilma" engraved on it. From it dangled a motorcycle-shaped silver tag with Sarina's name and cell phone number. It was perfect.

"I figured she'd love the motorcycle babe theme. You know, for when you get your bike back and you two start your road trip up all over again." Justin dipped his head, his demeanor unsure and shy.

"I love it. She'll love it." Sarina wavered, not sure of what she should do and finally sitting down next to Wilma, drawing the little dog onto her lap. She removed the old collar, easing the new one around her neck and fastening it securely. It looked great on her. "She looks like a little badass."

"She does."

"Thank you, Justin," Sarina said, nodding her head when Justin reached out to pet the dog's head. Wilma growled at first, dipping her head in submission when Justin stroked the silky spot between her ears. She hid her face in the crook of Sarina's arm, peeking out to look up at Justin with sweet, sad eyes. "Wilma says thank you, too."

"She didn't bite me. I'll take that as a win."

Sarina put down the little dog and they both watched as she crossed the room, curling up in a ball on a floor cushion. Wilma burrowed into the fabric, huffing out a long sigh before she closed her eyes and ignored the humans.

"Here, I'll thank you properly," Sarina said, rising to her feet and pulling Justin to her in a soft, sweet kiss. Just barely a brush of the lips; she meant it to be brief, a throwaway, but she felt it down to her toes.

His arms slid around her waist and she gripped them, drawing him closer to her body. They didn't deepen the kiss; it was enough to be wrapped around each other, sinking into the sweetness of the moment.

"Sarina," Justin breathed, his fingertips ghosting over her face, tracing her lips and cheekbones. "I want you all the time."

"I want you, too," she sighed, kissing his palm, her breath catching in her chest. "This is such a bad idea."

"The worst," he agreed, tightening his hold when she tried to pull away. "The best." He groaned, kissing her mouth, his tongue dipping inside, teasing her. Driving her crazy. "I think we should keep doing it."

"Of course you do." Sarina smiled against his lips. She should be putting an end to this but she just couldn't. It was beyond her power. "You *are* a gambler, right?"

"Hear me out," Justin said, pulling back enough to look her in the eye. "We have this connection, attraction, that has been there from the first. But neither of us is looking for anything serious or permanent, right?"

"If we were, we'd stay married."

"Exactly." Justin ran his thumb across her bottom lip, visibly holding back a moan when she licked it. "But I'm here and you're here for the next few weeks. We want each other. We know we're good together. So why not indulge? All we're going to do is give in over and over and then beat ourselves up for it." He pulled her closer and she could feel the heat of him, the hardness of his cock pressed against her body. "I want to be inside you again. I want to make you fall apart all over me. That's what I want, Sarina."

Sarina considered him; there were a million reasons why she should say no to this and push him away. She wasn't classy enough to fit in his life. She didn't know how to be with someone in a relationship. They weren't headed for a happily ever after. Their divorce papers were in the works.

But the bottom line was that she didn't want to. She was lonely, or at least tired of being alone in her bed, and she knew that Justin wouldn't try to stop her when it was time for her to leave.

And she wanted him. She liked the way he looked at her, as if she was important to him, as if she had a power over him that she'd never had with anyone else. The power to linger, to be remembered, to be yearned for.

But she'd never tell him that. It wasn't necessary for their current arrangement.

"Yes. I want you inside me again. Please, Justin."

"Thank God," he breathed and she was suddenly surrounded by him. His hard, muscled arms wrapped around her and his mouth possessed hers. The kiss was intense, hungry, and so was his touch as it roamed all over her body, tracing heat over her bare skin.

She clutched at him, finding it frustrating to be unable to get close enough. To feel enough. Sarina tugged him back, sitting down on the mattress of the daybed and pulling him down on top of her. She needed to feel his weight on her, to have something to strain against, something to hold on to when he drove her out of her mind.

"Justin, please." She reached down, snagging the hem of his T-shirt and dragging it over his head. Sarina sighed, some of the tension in her gut easing when she touched him, skimmed her fingertips over the warm expanse of his skin. It was as if her body had been waiting for this moment, the moment when she could feel him again, connect with him again. "I remember this."

Sarina traced a finger down his chest, over the tensing muscles of his abdomen to the edge of his waistband. She watched his face, the way he bit his lip in pleasure, the soft flutter of his eyelashes as he fought the urge to close his eyes and just sink into the anticipation of her touch.

"Do you remember this?" she asked as she unfastened the button on his shorts and eased down the zipper. His cock was hard, straining upward behind his boxer briefs, and she wasted no time in easing down the fabric and holding him, hot and heavy in her hand.

"Damn, Sarina. Touch me, please." Justin panted above her, his words deep and guttural.

She was never going to tell him no, never going to deny him. Not this. Not when she wanted to taste him again so very badly.

Sarina shoved him over onto his back, using the movement to push down his shorts and boxer briefs to his thighs and then slide them down his legs. Justin sprawled out beneath her, his long, hard body so gorgeous in the sunlight that filtered through the windows of the tree house.

"You don't have to," he whispered, his fingers tangled in her hair.

"But I want to. I need to taste you."

Sarina leaned over and took him in her mouth, tentatively at first as she got used to the width and length of him. He smelled of heat and salt and sweat and the sand-and-sun fragrance that was Justin to her. He reached down and wrapped his long fingers around his dick as he offered it to her like a present.

Sarina moaned at the invitation, taking more of him in her mouth as his hips rocked forward in an invitation too good to pass up. She opened her mouth wider and slid him in, indulging in the weight of him on her tongue. His taste was intoxicating, seductive and familiar as she sucked and teased him in turn.

Justin moved beneath her; with each stroke of her tongue he grunted and gasped, his fingers digging into her hair, pulling and leaving a shock of tingling pleasure on her scalp. He grew harder, skin tighter, his moans of pleasure louder in the silence of the treetops and Sarina reveled in her power to make him feel all these things. Giving him pleasure made her wet, the ache in her breasts, her belly, her sex building with each thrust and suck. If this was only temporary, she was going to make sure she had amazing memories to take with her.

"Sarina, stop, baby." Justin pulled away from her, his expression half pain and half feral as he reversed their positions and flipped her underneath him.

He dipped his head, taking her mouth in a kiss that was meant to calm him—or her, she wasn't sure. She wove her fingers in his hair, opening her mouth to him, spreading her legs in a sexual invitation. Justin ground against her, the friction delicious but not enough with her clothing still between them. She whimpered in frustration and he broke off the kiss, pulling back enough to be able to look down at her.

"Sarina, I'm going to take this dress off you and then

I'm not going to stop until you come." He swallowed hard, his eyes intent on her face. "If you don't want it, tell me to stop."

Sarina pushed against his chest, urging him to sit back on his knees. He complied immediately, trying hard to mask the disappointment that slid back into heated desire when she lifted the hem of her sundress and slipped it over her head.

"Does that answer your question?"

Sarina was the answer to all of his questions.

Justin knew this as sure as he knew that he would die if he didn't get inside her soon. But first he needed to explore her, taste her, make her feel a tenth of what he was experiencing right now. Sarina was usually an island unto herself, insulated from the world, and he understood why. But she let him in and now he wouldn't be satisfied until he had it all.

He inched backward off the daybed, reaching down to slip off her panties on the way down her body. He paused over her abdomen, placing soft, searching kisses along her flesh, loving the heavy inhales and exhales. Justin peered up at her, finding her eyes locked on his, intense and dark with her desire.

Sarina licked her lips and reached out to touch him but pulled back at the last moment, her swollen lips curved into a hint of a smile. He watched, riveted, as she let her fingers coast across her collarbone and in between her full breasts. She took her time, killing him slowly but he had no power to look away when she lifted a finger to her mouth, sucked on it and then used it to slowly caress a dark, hard nipple.

"Oh, you asked for this," he groaned, dragging her

to the edge of the couch and spreading her wide with the breadth of his shoulders.

Justin locked his eyes on her face, soaking in every flutter of her lashes, every bite of her teeth into her lower lip, every moan that escaped her mouth. The first glancing touch of his fingertips against her clit had her moaning and biting her lip.

"No way," he murmured. "Don't hold back. I want to hear you, Sarina. You've been haunting my dreams for weeks and now I want the real thing."

The next pass of his fingertip against her clit had her throwing her head back, exposing her throat to him as her moan washed over his skin and carried across the treetops.

"Look at me, baby. Watch." Justin was patient, waiting until Sarina returned her gaze to his before he lowered his head and licked her, letting her taste explode across his tongue. His mouth watered and her hips thrust upward in an invitation he fully intended to accept. Justin was going to dive in and take his fill, try to satisfy his cravings for this woman.

There was no rush. He'd cleared his calendar for the evening and he had nowhere to be, so he took his time, in spite of the voice in his head urging him to take her now, to bury himself inside her and come. Sarina hadn't been taken care of enough in her life; she hadn't been made a priority enough. He couldn't give her forever but he could give her this now.

Sarina writhed against his mouth, pressed into the deep thrusts of his tongue, moaned and clutched his hair in a painful twist when he lavished her with sucking strokes of his tongue that ended circling her clit. She was wet and he was hard as a rock. Her legs shook with pleasure and her body shifted under him, her muscles taut and straining as she came against his mouth and shouted out her pleasure.

"Justin, fuck me," she panted out between attempts to catch her breath. "Do you have protection?"

"Yes." Justin had never been a Boy Scout but he was glad that he'd slipped a strip of condoms in his pocket before he'd come over. He hadn't been sure that anything would happen but he'd known he was at his limit of restraint with Sarina, and he'd come prepared.

He fished them out of his pocket and ripped one off, opening the wrapper with shaking fingers. He slid the condom over his length, took himself in hand and stroked the tip of his penis against the slick flesh of her sex. Sarina gasped, arching against him and trying to press down on his cock. He let her push down and watched as he entered her body; her sweet, searing heat made his eyes cross. Then he retreated, gathering up his strength to make this last.

Justin pressed in deeper, bearing down and into her, letting gravity and desire take him to the place he'd dreamed about since that night in Vegas. Sarina wrapped her arms around his neck and pulled him tighter against her body, her nails scraping the flesh of his back in long, nerve-tingling strokes. He claimed her mouth in a kiss, opening her lips with his tongue and greedily taking what he wanted, what he needed. Sarina gave as good as she got, nipping his bottom lip with her teeth as she thrust up against him, driving him deeper and deeper.

Sarina clung to him, a strangled sound of protest erupting from her when he pulled back as he started a slow, deep glide in and out of her body.

"Look at us, baby." Justin adjusted the angle to give them the perfect view of the way they moved together. He was hard and she was soft and it was agony and heaven to watch him enter and retreat, empty and fill. He needed to slow down; he needed to look away because the combination of her body and scent and the sounds of their lovemaking was driving him toward his orgasm too fast. And he wanted this to last.

But looking at her didn't work any better. Their gazes locked. Her face flushed with her passion, lips swollen with kisses, was a whole new kind of hell, the good kind. Justin leaned down, covering her body with his as she wrapped her legs around his waist, hooking her ankles together behind his back. The movement tensed her body and her sex clenched around him as he entered her again and again.

Justin slammed over and over into her heat. Deep, primal, possessive groans he could not stop erupted with each thrust as his entire world narrowed to the woman in his arms. He wanted her to come, needed her to come. He needed to be the man who brought her to the point where she let down all of the walls that kept her heart safe, that kept everyone at arm's length. Justin needed to be the only man she let in.

Her orgasm hit and he reveled in the way that she screamed his name, dug her nails into his skin, wrapped herself tighter around him. Justin sped up his thrusts, holding her even tighter as he gave in to his own orgasm, coming with a roar buried in her hair and against her sweat-damp skin.

He held her close, shifting their bodies into a tangled mess of arms and legs and tousled blankets as they both settled back into their retreat in the trees. Sarina was quiet, her eyes shut as her fingers traced sweet circles on the skin of his chest. He could feel her withdrawing from him, her brain reconstructing the walls that she'd needed to survive.

Justin didn't want her to shut him out. He knew that eventually it would happen when they both went their separate ways but he couldn't face it today. Not after what had just happened.

"Don't run, Sarina," he whispered.

"I'm right here."

"You're running away, in here." He lightly tapped a finger against her temple. "Just don't. Not tonight."

The silence dragged out between them and he waited for her to sit up and get dressed, to hurry back to her room at the house. But she didn't do any of those things. She stayed, wrapped in his arms as the stars popped up in the sky above them.

But when she did speak, it wasn't what he wanted to hear.

"I won't run tonight but it's what I do, Justin. It's what I do."

And he accepted it—for now.

Ten

"And this deal is done."

Justin pushed back from his desk, setting down his pen as his eyes scanned the three huge monitors sitting on the large surface. The screens were filled with spreadsheets, charts and computations. A few feet behind them on the wall, large TV screens featured the major news stations on mute, covering the domestic and foreign markets. The screen to the far right had a running Twitch feed of one of his favorite gamers taking down alternative civilizations in a CGI environment.

But the stuff that mattered, the stuff that he and Adam had busted their asses to make happen, was going to work. The deal with Aerospace Link was going to solidify their leadership in the future of cloud-based technology.

And it was going to make them even more ridiculously rich than they already were.

More importantly, it was going to allow them to fund and mentor other scrappy kids who dropped out of school with nothing but Red Bull-fueled dreams and a couple of laptop computers.

"Are you sure?" Adam paced across the floor in front of Justin's desk, his brows scrunched together in an intense expression. Adam was the worrier and he wasn't great with numbers, so Justin walked him through it one more time.

Numbers were as basic as breathing for Justin. When words twisted up on him and made things that came so easily to everyone else so hard for him, so hurtful, numbers had been his solace. So he gladly walked Adam through all of it and showed him exactly how their dreams were still coming true.

"And this is solid. A sure thing?" Adam asked, gesturing toward the multicolored pie chart on one screen.

"Well, nothing is guaranteed but our part is solid. Worst case—we make millions. Best case—we make levels of fuck-you money that will enable our great-great-great-great-great-great-great-grandkids to tell people to fuck off." Justin went over to his fridge and pulled out two bottles of beer, popping the tops and handing one off to his best friend. They clinked bottles and both took a long drink. "Now, normally we don't drink on the job but this is a celebration and we are done for the day."

Employees walked by just outside the glass walls of Justin's office. His space was on the same floor as Adam's but at the opposite corner. They both had windows that looked out over the lush green campus of

Redhawk/Ling and he loved to watch their employees come and go from the building, enjoying lunch or coffee in the sunshine on the patios, or exercising on the trails. Standing here, shoulder to shoulder with his best friend, it was a little...incredible.

"I can't believe we're doing this," Justin said, nudging Adam with his elbow.

"I can't believe we *did* this," Adam replied, his smile huge as he waved his hand around like a sovereign viewing his subjects from the balcony of the palace. "I wouldn't have wanted to do it with anyone else."

"Me either," Justin said, his voice tight with emotion. He wasn't going to start bawling or anything but he loved the man standing next to him. He was more of a brother to him than his own blood and one day he'd tell him. Just not here in the middle of their business. He had a professional reputation to try to uphold. "Hey, Nana Orla and I want you, Tess and Roan to come over for a cookout tonight. You don't need to bring anything, we've got it covered."

"What's the occasion? Other than the obvious?" Adam asked.

Justin shrugged. "Nana Orla and I thought that Sarina would love to see you. Get a little family time." He walked over to his desk, moving aside piles of papers to find the documents he'd pulled about the center for Sarina. "She's doing so great with the kids at Rise Up, Adam. Your sister is an incredible woman. What she has done with those kids is insane. I don't know how we are ever going to find anyone to replace her." He found the folder, placing it in his briefcase so that he wouldn't forget it. When he straightened up, Adam was staring at him, a strange expression on his face. "What?"

"Are you sleeping with my sister?" Adam's voice was even, raising Justin's hackles. He couldn't tell if Adam was going to hit him or welcome him to the family. They'd never really talked about his quickie-Vegas-temporary marriage to Sarina.

It looked like it was happening now.

"Yes. I am." Justin wasn't going to lie about it. Hell, Adam would see the two of them together tonight and with one look know that they were involved. "She's my wife."

Justin closed his eyes the minute the words had left his mouth. They were true but not the ones to say.

"Not for long." Adam leveled his gaze at him, placing his beer bottle down on the table by the window. "Unless the plan to get a divorce has changed?"

"No, that plan hasn't changed."

"Then what the fuck are you doing, Justin? Sarina isn't one of the many women you cycle through your life like food that's about to expire. She's been disposable her whole life, Justin. So I'm going to ask you again— what the hell are you doing with Sarina?"

I'm falling for her.

Shit. Where did that come from? Justin rolled it around in his head, over his tongue, let it settle in the vicinity of his heart.

Nope. It wasn't romance. It wasn't feelings that lead to forever and golden wedding anniversaries. It was just a sex-induced crush on a woman he admired and respected.

Justin didn't do love and he didn't do permanent. All the women in his life prior to Sarina had known this and Sarina knew it now. This was just a longer-term hookup and he had no business confusing it with anything more than that.

But that wasn't what you told the brother of the woman you were hooking up with. Not if you wanted to live. "I care for her. She cares for me. We're friends," Justin replied, not encouraged by the tightening of Adam's jaw. "We're working it out, Adam. There's been something there since the night we met. We have…a connection. I don't know where it's going to end up but I swear to you that I'm not going to hurt her."

"You can't promise that, Justin. The only way to do that is to not get involved with her."

Justin sighed, holding his hands up in surrender. "I don't think anybody is going to get hurt. We're two adults and we both know the score."

The silence that followed was awkward. Not only because it stretched out but because Justin couldn't breathe. His chest hurt like he'd taken a stray kick in the ring at the gym.

Finally, Adam huffed out his answer, his voice equal parts pity and warning. "I don't know which one of you is the bigger fool."

Eleven

"Did you tell Adam we're sleeping together?"

Sarina pulled Justin aside, hissing the question into his ear as everyone filed down the buffet line and piled their plates with food. She'd arrived home from a day at the center and found her brothers, Nana Orla and Tess all on the patio with cold beverages and the boys fighting over who got to control the grill.

Tess had won the argument, and now she was Sarina's vote to always run the barbecue. The food was delicious.

"Adam is giving me these weird sad eyes and Roan and Tess are giving him the cut-that-out eyes and then looking at me so I can only assume that you spilled the beans with my brother-slash-your best friend," she whispered, looking over her shoulder to find Adam staring at them both, only to be nudged out of stalking mode by a poke from Tess. "What did you tell him?"

"The truth, when he asked me point-blank. I didn't think it would do anybody any good to lie about it." Justin moved over to the buffet table, grabbing a plate and adding a piece of steak and some shrimp to it. He stopped, sneaking a look over his shoulder toward her brothers and then back to her face.

Justin paused to consider something and then put down his plate, reaching for her and pulling her into a kiss. It wasn't porn-level but it was deep, intense, wet, and left no doubt that they were more than friends. Spouses with benefits?

And everyone was staring. Not that she had eyes in the back of her head but everything had gone silent around them. Even the birds had stopped chirping.

They parted and Justin rubbed his thumb against her bottom lip, pressing another quick kiss to it before picking up an empty plate and placing it in her hands.

"Eat up, baby." Justin grinned, then continued to load his plate up with grilled veggies and potatoes.

Sarina glanced over to where her family was seated, shaking her head at their reactions. Roan and Tess had their thumbs up, Adam acted like he hadn't seen anything, and Nana Orla was fanning herself with her napkin and pretending to faint on the lounger.

Sarina shook her head. "Family is weird."

When they finished filling their plates and took seats nearby, everyone decided to act like nothing had happened. She was okay with that. One hundred percent.

They ate their food, trading small talk while the sun set behind the hills and the solar lights cast a warm glow over the patio. This house was beautiful, the setting stunning, and tonight the company was perfect. Sarina soaked it in, pushing aside the somber thoughts about what they could have had if she and her brothers had grown up together instead of being separated. Would they have spent summer evenings eating hamburgers off the grill and trading inside family jokes? Would Adam and Roan have given her boyfriends the stink eye when they came to pick her up?

Would she have been braver? More willing to take a chance on what was happening between her and Justin?

Woulda. Coulda. Shoulda.

"So, Sarina, how do you like working at the center?" Tess asked, her plate balanced on her belly like a pregnancy party trick. "Adam says you're doing great."

"I love it. The kids are wonderful and so supportive of one another." She flashed appreciative glances at Adam and Justin. "You guys did an amazing thing by giving those kids that place. Giving them each other. It's something to be proud of. I hope you know that."

"I knew you'd get it," Justin answered, reaching over to cover her hand with his own. "And the kids. I knew you'd get them." He turned and winked at Adam. "We don't even rate anymore, buddy. I stopped by the other day and the first thing out of Little Pete's mouth was, 'Where's Sarina?'"

"All I got was, 'You're so lucky to have Sarina as a sister.'" Adam mimicked the big guy's booming, puberty-cracking voice. He turned his gaze toward Sarina, his smile tender and sweet enough to bring tears to her eyes. "But I have to agree with him. I'm really lucky to have you as a sister, Sarina."

She cleared her throat, trying to pull herself together. There were things she needed to say, but this wasn't the time. But she could set one thing straight. "I think I'm the lucky one." She looked between her two brothers. "I'm lucky to have both of you."

And she was lucky. Their family had been broken, torn apart by people in the system who decided that the three kids would be better off with families who could give them "a better life." They weren't the only Native kids who were taken from their parents and adopted by non-Native families, but having company didn't make the pain it had caused any easier.

But Adam had found her and Roan and now they had a chance to be a family again.

Adam and Roan exchanged a look and she wondered what was going on. Roan got up and walked over to where he'd placed his messenger bag next to the back door. He opened the flap and pulled out a small package, handing it to her when he came back to the group.

"Adam and I had some things from our folks, things we managed to keep when they split us up. I don't know how I got any of it when I was so young but it followed me around and I just stashed it away." Roan pushed a long chunk of hair behind his ear, giving her a shy smile as he handed it over. "We wanted you to have it."

She took the package, placing it on the table in front of her, squeezing her hands to stop the shaking. Justin scooted closer to her, his hand at her back, soothing and supporting. Sarina looked at him and he smiled, nodding in encouragement.

"Baby, go ahead," he whispered, nudging the package closer.

"Okay. Okay," she replied, voice shaky and thready to her own ears. With a deep breath she opened the package, sliding back the zipper and upending the bag to let all the contents slide out.

Photographs. Two of her parents. They looked happy, her mother sitting in her father's lap. One of Adam, holding a football in a Pop Warner uniform. One of two fat babies—clearly her and Roan.

Sarina covered her mouth with her hand, choking back emotion. Tears slid over her cheeks but she didn't wipe them away as she sorted through the remainder of the items.

A Christmas card signed by people whose names she didn't recognize. A beaded woven bracelet with red and black beads on a leather strap.

And a CD. Linda Ronstadt's *Living in the USA*.

"This was my mother's." She glanced up at Adam and Roan, surprised to see the tears on their faces. "This was our mother's CD. The only thing I have from our home is a copy of Linda Ronstadt's *Heart Like a Wheel*. I know it was hers because she put her name on it. I listen to it all the time." She wiped away the tears and let Justin take her hand. "My only memory is her singing to me."

"'Different Drum,'" Adam said, nodding his head in agreement. "She used to sing 'Different Drum' to us when she was trying to get us to sleep."

Sarina laughed. Really it was more of a snort joined with a weepy half sob but it was as good as it was going to get tonight. This was…a lot. Good *a lot* but…a lot.

Roan started humming the tune and Adam joined in. They were awful, tone-deaf, and any minute now Wilma was going to start barking.

Her brothers were awful but they were hers and now that she had them back, she was never going to let them go.

But she might temporarily lose them if they kept making the terrible noises they thought was music.

"If either of you start singing, I'll punch you in the face."

Justin buried deep inside her was the best part of her day.

"Deeper. Harder. Please." Sarina pulled him closer, her arms and legs wrapped around his sweat-slick body as he drove into her. It wasn't enough. She could never get enough.

It had been a long, incredible day. First, the kids at the center and the way they'd pulled together at the rock climbing wall and then the amazing dinner with her brothers, Tess and Nana Orla. The package of items from her parents had been overwhelming; she still hadn't processed all the memories that it had dredged up.

It really had been one of the best days of her life.

They'd wrapped up dinner and all she could think of was getting Justin in her room, stripping off all their clothes and making each other feel good all night long.

But it wasn't enough. Sarina strained, moaned, clutched him closer, and she needed more. Wanted more.

"Hold on, baby." Justin flipped them both over, lifting his arms and resting them over his head as he stared up at her.

It was dark in the room but his body was illuminated by a swath of moonlight pouring through the window. He was smiling at her, his eyes roaming over her face and body, his fingers flexing with his obvious desire to reach out and touch her. Take control. But he knew what she needed.

She didn't want to think about how that made her feel or what that meant.

"Baby, you take what you need."

"Justin."

"Sarina, take what you need. Use me." He reached a hand up and touched her lower lip with his fingertips. "Whatever you need, baby. I'm here for it."

She nodded, placing her hands on his chest as she began a slow glide up and down his cock. He was deep, hitting all the spots where she needed him the most. And she was in control of this, in control of her pleasure and his, when she wasn't in control of anything in her life right now.

So she took control. Riding him, taking him inside her body, clenching around him until he writhed beneath her. He kept his hands above his head, his moans and upward thrusts adding to her pleasure, the fire growing in her belly and racing along her skin. This was what she needed.

Justin. Sex. Power. Control.

The way he looked at her like she was the only person in his world.

Sarina leaned over him, joining their fingers at the same time she joined their mouths in a kiss. His tongue tangled with hers as they moved together, faster and harder and deeper. She came, crying out her pleasure against his neck, inhaling his scent and ignoring the tears that stung her eyes.

Justin froze underneath her, his cock stiffening inside her as he shattered, crying out her name.

A million heartbeats later he shifted them over on their sides, facing the moon. She was the little spoon to his big spoon and there was nowhere she wanted to be other than wrapped up in his arms.

"Big night. The stuff Roan and Adam gave you was pretty amazing." Justin whispered against her hair, his lips brushing against her temple. "You okay?"

"I don't know." Sarina reached back to stroke his hair, laughing when he pressed a kiss against her palm. "I think I will be."

"What was the word you used with the kids at the rock climbing wall? It started with an *S*."

She thought back to that day, finally realizing what he was referring to. *"Sidanelv?"*

"Yep. *Sidanelv*." He hugged her tight. "You've got a good *sidanelv*."

She giggled at his butchering of the word but loved that he tried. "I do. Adam and Roan are great."

The house settled around them, the evening slipping into deeper night as they held each other. Sarina closed her eyes, drifting in that place between sleep and wakefulness, the place where she had it all figured out.

But she didn't have anything figured out. Not even close. And the more time she spent with Justin the easier it was to forget that this was temporary. They had a committee of lawyers making sure they never got to their first anniversary and while she and Justin were having fun with the "honeymoon" part of the marriage, the rules had not changed. Justin liked her and he liked sex with her even more but that wasn't a love match and it never would be.

Justin interrupted her thoughts, his voice scratchy with sleep. "I want to take you somewhere. As a surprise."

Sarina shook her head. "I don't like surprises."

"You'll like this one."

Twelve

"How long have you been able to fly a helicopter?"

Justin glanced over to where Sarina sat in the passenger seat of the Redhawk/Ling helicopter. Her cheeks were flushed, her eyes lit up from within with excitement. She hadn't balked at all, jumping into the passenger seat immediately and soaking in every bit of the scenery outside the front window during the flight. They weren't even at their destination and his plan was already a success, worth all the hassle he'd had to navigate to get a couple of days off.

"I learned to fly when I was twenty-three and we bought the bird last year. It's easier to get to meetings when we have our own helicopter."

"And you love it," Sarina said, her grin wide and knowing.

"I love it," he agreed. He pointed out a few dolphins

swimming in the ocean below them as they headed up the coast. "You really can't beat the view."

"I have to say I'm surprised that you enjoy flying with your fear of heights. Doesn't this freak you out?" Sarina asked, watching him closely.

"Shockingly, no. I think it's because I'm in control of the machine. I'm so focused on flying that I just don't worry about it." Justin scanned the gauges, expanding on a topic he'd thought about often. "I'm dyslexic—reading is so tough for me but I can unravel numbers and math problems in my sleep. Brains are so strange, such a mystery, and mine is not the same as other people's. So how much weirder is it that I can't climb a wall but I can fly over the ocean?"

"I think your brain is pretty amazing."

Justin bit back a grin, the warmth in his belly caused by her words threatening to spill over in a laugh. "And I thought you wanted me for my body."

"Well, your ass *is* mighty fine," she teased, her voice coming through the headset as she turned away from him to look out the window. "But I think I'm more interested in your helicopter."

"Keep it up, baby. I'll just turn around and you'll never know where we're going."

She whipped back around, her face full of horror, prompting him to laugh out loud. "You wouldn't."

"Try me," Justin replied, looking over his shoulder and easing the helicopter into a turn back toward Silicon Valley. "It will be no problem to just head on back home. Wilma will be thrilled to see us."

"You don't scare me." Her lips pressed together in a frown but her voice and her side-eye glance were full of mischief.

"Well, that's good because we'll be landing in five minutes."

In spite of his ridiculous level of excitement, Justin carefully went through all of the maneuvers to get them safely on the ground. He settled it all with the staff at the heliport, turning over the keys to the helicopter and making arrangements for it to be ready in two days for their return home. The whole time he watched Sarina out of the corner of his eye, soaking in her excitement and barely contained curiosity.

Finally, he grabbed their bags and headed over to the car he'd ordered. She slid into the passenger seat and he couldn't wait another minute to end the suspense—whether for his own benefit or hers, he wasn't sure. All he knew was that he wanted to give this weekend to Sarina because she deserved it and more.

And he was beginning to realize that he wanted to give her more than a romantic weekend away; he wanted to give her the world. He wanted to give her a part of himself that he was pretty sure she'd already stolen.

It wasn't pity that drove him to want to take care of her, to make her life easier. Sarina was a survivor and had made a great life for herself. And when you got past her walls, she was generous and supportive and totally in your corner. When she told him that she believed in him he believed her. When she looked at him like he was enough and perfect just the way he was? He believed her.

That was something he'd never gotten from anyone else in his life and so Sarina deserved all the best things because she'd given the best thing to him.

But she was skittish, only comfortable in the construct of their having an end date, and she was poised to run.

And he needed more time to figure himself out. Because of one thing he was certain: he never wanted to be part of the long line of people who let Sarina Redhawk down. He just didn't know if he could be the man to break through her defenses.

Their divorce papers would arrive any day now, so the clock was ticking on his time to figure it out.

But today it was all about giving Sarina a weekend she'd never forget and a memory to last a lifetime.

"Are you going to tell me where we are? Where are we going?" Sarina asked, fastening her seat belt. "I don't like surprises."

"Really? I haven't heard that before."

Justin leaned over the middle console, tipping up her face to kiss her. She opened to him, humming into the kiss as he drew it out, relishing the taste of her. Reluctantly, he broke it off, his excitement at getting to their final destination greater than his desire to keep kissing her.

"So, we're in Malibu," Justin revealed as he ended the kiss.

"Malibu? What's in Malibu?"

"The ocean." He started the car and pulled out of the heliport.

"Funny."

"Let me spoil you, baby. You deserve it." Justin dropped his voice lower, shamelessly using all his tools of seduction to get her to let him do this for her. Sarina's cheeks flushed, the bashful shake of her head telling him that she didn't believe she deserved it. But he knew she did; that was enough.

"Fine," she huffed out on a pout that didn't look real. He knew she was enjoying this but she'd never admit it.

They drove down the highway a few miles. Sarina focused on the scenery that whizzed past the windows: gorgeous homes, green hills, and on the one side the Pacific Ocean spreading out as far as the eye could see. He saw his landmark mile marker and pulled his next-to-last surprise out of his pocket and handed it to Sarina. She took it, shaking it out and staring at it and then Justin with a raised eyebrow.

"A blindfold?" Sarina tossed it back in his lap. "I'm not into that stuff, Justin."

"That's an interesting place you went there, Little Miss Kinky, but that's not what the blindfold is for. I want you to be completely surprised. So put it on, please." He tossed it back at her, slowing the car down as if he was going to pull over to the side of the road. "Don't make me stop the car."

"Fine," she sighed heavily and put the blindfold on over her eyes.

"You can't see anything?"

"No, Justin, I can't see anything."

"Okay, grumpy, we'll be there in five minutes." Justin navigated the traffic, turning into the Colony enclave. He rolled down the window and showed the gate guard his ID, mentioning that their final destination was a surprise for his wife. The guard winked at him and pointed to the direction he needed to drive. The directions were perfect and before he knew it they were on the right street and slowing down for the house number.

The houses were similar, many built in the 1920s and then greatly expanded in the successive decades as oceanfront property became the hottest topic in California. These houses were passed down from generation to generation, only rarely hitting the open market. The one he was looking for wasn't usually available for rent but he knew a guy who knew a guy and he asked him to help make a dream come true for his girl.

Being a billionaire absolutely had its perks.

He saw the house he was looking for and turned into the driveway, shutting off the engine and undoing his seat belt with shaking fingers. Justin couldn't believe how nervous he was; he desperately hoped that Sarina would love it. He just wanted to make her happy. It was quickly becoming the most important part of his life: making her smile and living for ways to keep her smiling.

This weekend would be big for the both of them. The divorce papers were on the way and he wasn't so sure he wanted to sign them anymore.

He had no idea how he'd arrived at this point but he knew he had to face up to the feelings he had for Sarina. Justin was scared shitless; he loved his commitment-free life and just a few short weeks ago he'd have bet all his chips that it was never going to change. And now he was more worried about Sarina signing those papers and leaving than he was about giving up his freedom.

He had no idea how Sarina felt about him but this weekend he'd find out. It was the emotional equivalent of walking out on that crazy Grand Canyon glass bridge but he was going to do it.

And he really hoped the glass didn't shatter underneath his feet.

"Stay here. I'll come around and get you," he said, leaving their bags for later. He opened the door, taking her hand and easing her out of the vehicle. She was unsteady, her fingers gripping tightly on his arm as she found her balance. She was scowling, and so cute that he couldn't resist leaning forward and stealing a kiss. He'd meant for it to be quick, light, but he couldn't resist Sarina when she was this close. He deepened the connection, lingering, tasting and exploring. "You are addictive."

She hummed out her reaction, licking her lips and leaning toward him for more. Justin loved this part of the surprise but he missed seeing her look at him like he was the answer to all of her questions. Sarina's approval drowned out a lifetime of missing the mark on his parents' expectations and he wanted to give her everything in return. He'd start with the next couple of days and then see if they could have forever.

"Okay, hold on to me. I'll lead you inside, don't worry. I won't let you fall."

The scents in the air were already different, salty and warmed by the sunshine with a hint of sunscreen and outdoor cooking. Sarina lifted her face to the sun, head cocked to pick up nearby sounds as he guided her toward the front of the house.

He unlocked the front door and she paused, stopping briefly as the first wave of air-conditioning hit their bodies. "Okay, two more steps and then I need you to stand still while I close the door and pull back the blinds. Just wait here."

"Okay," she said. Sarina stood in place, her body adjusting to follow the sounds of his progress around the room.

He watched her closely, the anticipation building inside him like Christmas and his birthday all rolled up into one moment. Justin made his way back to her, placing his hand on her cheek, sighing when she leaned into his touch, her hands reaching out to seek him, her fingers snagging and tangling with the cotton of his T-shirt.

"Are you ready?" When she nodded, he eased around her, stopping when he stood behind her and she leaned back against his chest. Justin reached up, fingers hovering over the ties to the blindfold. "I really hope you like this. I'm going feel like an idiot if you don't."

She laughed. "Justin, you do realize that the longer you drag this out the bigger this gets and then the chances of you looking like an idiot increase?"

"Well, when you put it that way…" he huffed out in mock indignation, pulling the ties loose. "But I really do hope that you love this, baby."

The blindfold slid off and he stepped to the side so that he could watch her as she took it all in. She blinked a few times, letting her eyes adjust to the light, brushing her hair back from her eyes. Her face scrunched up in confusion and he could see the cogs of her brain working as every synapse fired in an attempt to put two and two together. She moved forward, stepping down into the sunken den that led to the wall of windows that framed the patio, the deck, and the Pacific Ocean beyond.

"Justin, this is beautiful," she said, peering at a line of black-and-white photographs on the wall. He watched as she froze, moving closer to get a better look, reaching out to trace a finger over an image. She put her face a little closer, squinting as if she didn't believe what she was looking at, and then she turned to look at him. "This is not…"

"Number thirty-eight Malibu Colony was the home

of Linda Ronstadt from 1975 to 1980. She moved here just after she released *Heart Like a Wheel* and this is where they filmed her in the *Wonderland* documentary." Justin stopped, not sure how to continue. "That's all I know about her but I thought…" He faltered, feeling like an idiot now that they were here and this surprise that had felt like such a big deal in his head sounded really dumb as he was saying it out loud. "…I don't know, Sarina. I know she's one of your favorites and your mom…damn, I just thought you might like it."

Sarina was all big eyes and open mouth and looking at him like he'd lost his damn mind one minute and then she was in his arms, kissing him, and his whole world was right again.

"You *are* an idiot," she said between kisses and laughter. "But you are the sweetest idiot I know and I don't know why you're so good to me."

"Because you deserve to get all the good things, Sarina. I don't know what's more wrong, the fact that you don't think you deserve it or that someone hasn't made it their business to ensure you always have the best of everything." Justin said it without thinking, knowing that he was revealing more than he probably should.

Sarina placed her palm on his cheek, her eyes searching his for something she needed to know. But Sarina was direct, so she just asked him.

"Do you think you're that person?"

He paused for only a minute, feeling like he was at the top of the rock wall, getting ready to take a plunge with no net beneath him. "I think I might be that person."

They stared at each other for several long minutes,

both waiting for the other to say something, to do something. He took the coward's way out.

"I'm going to get the bags while you go explore."

They had a great day in Linda Ronstadt's house.

The four-bedroom beach bungalow sat right on the ocean, with only an expanse of outdoor space and large rocks to buffer it from the waves that lapped right up to the edge of the wooden deck when the tide was at its highest. Right now there was a wide swath of sand, full of people running, children playing and neighbors enjoying the gorgeous California sunshine. A private beach, it wasn't crowded, and Sarina was easy to find once he'd moved the luggage into the gorgeous master bedroom on the second floor.

Swimming. A long walk on the sand. It was a perfect day that led to a perfect dinner. Shrimp and lobster, grilled to perfection with vegetables and the perfect bottle of wine on the deck, under the stars. Now they were full, skin warm from hours in the sun, and just the two of them talking about nothing and everything.

Except the one thing he couldn't get the nerve to ask her because if the answer was that she still wanted to leave, he didn't want to hear it. Not today. They had all the time in the world to mess this up, to walk away from something that was really great.

"Top three things you love to eat," Justin said, refilling her wineglass.

"What? Are we playing some weird version of twenty questions?" Sarina leaned back in her chair, long bare legs extended with her feet in his lap.

"Yes, we are. It is my incredibly transparent attempt to get you to tell me more about yourself," Justin replied, running his hand up her calf, admiring the way her mini sundress fell off her shoulder. She was so damn sexy and didn't even know it. He knew a dozen women in LA who spent the price of a small car to look the way that Sarina did without even trying. "Would you divulge all of your secrets if I just asked you flat out?"

"Probably not."

"So indulge me. I don't think there has ever been a husband in the history of husbands who knew so little about his wife."

She stared at him over the rim of her wineglass, shaking her head at him and trying to hide a smile. "Okay, fine. Top three favorite foods…a rare steak, cotton candy and MRE beef Stroganoff."

He cocked his head at her. "MRE? Like a military meal that you shake and heat up?"

"Yep. Most of them were awful but I really loved that one." Sarina pointed to him. "Your turn."

"So, easy. Nana Orla's corned beef, my father's *youtiao* and shrimp scampi."

"What's *youtiao*?"

"It's like a fried breakfast doughnut except that it's a stick, two sticks connected, not a ring. He made them on our birthday and holidays." He chuckled. "I think it was one of the only times that fried foods were allowed in the house."

"You need to make that for me."

"Only for your birthday. When *is* your birthday?" He sat up, realizing that he had no idea.

"September second." Sarina raised an eyebrow in question. "Yours?"

"March twenty-first." He stood, holding his hand out to her. "Do you want to dance?"

She shook her head, taking his hand and standing, looking him right in the eye. "No."

"No?"

"Let's go to bed," she said, leaning forward to kiss him. Her lips were soft, tasting of the wine and the intoxicating flavor of Sarina. "I think I know everything I need to know."

Justin knew only one thing: that he needed Sarina Redhawk like he needed his next breath. He pulled her close, taking her mouth in a kiss that was full of everything he was feeling, everything she made him want and need. He didn't want it from just anyone, he wanted it from her and only her.

She tasted like secrets and risk and the forbidden, but she felt like home and the future in his arms. She was perfect for him and she was his. Now he just needed to figure out how to keep her.

Justin ran his hand over the bare skin of her shoulder, catching the thin little strap of her sundress and lowering it slowly, only stopping when her breast was bare to him. He leaned down, taking her nipple in his mouth, sucking on it with a moan, circling the puckered tip with his tongue. Sarina's hands wove into his hair, gasping as she kept his mouth exactly where they both wanted it to be.

"Take me upstairs, Justin. I want you naked, now. I need you. Please."

She would never have to ask him twice.

Justin leaned over, picking Sarina up and carrying her over his shoulder. She gasped, laughing out loud as the snagged the bottle of wine on their way to the stairs.

"You're going to drop me," Sarina protested, her fingers squeezing his ass cheeks as he mounted the stairs.

"If you keep playing with my ass I can guarantee that I'm going to drop you on yours," he half joked as he arrived on the second floor, entered the bedroom and placed her on the floor.

Sarina took the wine from his hand and put it on the side table, turning to give him a sexy, lingering once-over. When she straightened, she took one finger and hooked it under a sundress strap and lowered it, then did the same on the other side.

The tiny little sundress slithered down her body and pooled on the floor at her feet. She was naked, skin glowing in the low lights of the room, her body long and lean and mouthwateringly beautiful.

Justin let out a wolf whistle. "You are the most gorgeous woman I've ever seen."

Sarina moved forward, stopping right in front of him, and began unfastening his shorts. Her eyes were dark with her desire, her smile full of challenge. "Prove it."

Thirteen

Issuing Justin Ling a challenge was the best idea she'd ever had.

Her husband was kind, mischievous, challenging, outspoken, dedicated, romantic and sexy. She still couldn't believe that he was still available, that a woman hadn't snatched him up and put a ring on it before now.

But she wasn't any different from any of the women who'd cycled in and out of his bed before. She hadn't put a ring on it—at least she hadn't put one on again after ditching him the morning after their wedding.

And now she needed to decide if she wanted to see that ring back on her finger for good.

She'd worry about that later. After about a dozen orgasms.

Because what crazy woman would get bogged down thinking deep thoughts when Justin was standing in front of her completely naked?

"I love your body," she said, taking her time checking him out. He was so fit, his muscles under skin so smooth and tan from days spent in the California sun that all she wanted to do was taste him all over.

So she did.

Sarina slowly dropped to her knees, tracing a path down his body with her lips, pressing openmouthed kisses across his collarbone, just under his heart, on his stomach, and landing at the top of his dark treasure trail. She looked up at him, placing her hands on his thighs and offering herself to him.

"You're going to kill me," Justin murmured, taking his cock in his hand and offering it to her.

Sarina took him in her mouth, tongue caressing the long length of him, closing her eyes and savoring the pleasure it brought her to draw out his moans of desire and gasps of surrender. She opened her eyes and found him gazing down at her, his eyes dark with his passion but lit with the feelings she knew he had for her. Unspoken but there nonetheless.

She recognized it because she also felt it, knew it to be true in her heart, deeper in her soul.

It was something she'd never had before. It was precious, fragile, but also stronger than she would have thought possible with her brokenness.

He groaned above her, his thighs trembling under her hands as he struggled for control, and suddenly she wanted nothing more than to be under his control, under his body.

She released him, standing on knees liquid with her own desire. Justin took her face in his hands, the calluses on his palms abrasive against her skin, igniting sparks of need in her blood, making her wet and hot and heavy for him. He kissed her slowly, deeply, tenderly—in total contrast to the slide of their bodies, the sweat-slick friction of hard body against soft skin, smooth flesh against coarse hair.

"Lie down on the bed," Justin ordered, his tone fierce with need.

Sarina walked backward, maintaining eye contact as she complied with the gentle command. The sheets were cool on her heated skin, silky against the back of her knees, her thighs.

Justin covered her with his body, kissing her mouth and then traveling lower to press kisses along her jaw, down her neck, into the shallow between her collarbones, lower still to the valley between her aching breasts. He layered them with kisses, the merest whisper of lips along the swell of each, until she writhed beneath him, her fingers clutching his back with long scrapes of her nails.

Justin finally claimed her nipples, licking, sucking, swirling them with his tongue until she was wet and needy between her thighs. He shifted on top of her, his fingertips trailing along the tender, sensitive skin of her thighs upward until he stroked her wet folds, finding her clit and rubbing it in small, firm circles.

"Oh, yes. Please." Sarina opened her legs wider, arm thrown over her eyes, lower lip bitten as she fought the sensation he drew out of her, as she gave in to the sensations he created inside her.

"I can do better than that," Justin murmured, releasing her breast and easing down her body with single-minded determination. "So much better."

She watched as he lowered his head between her legs, his broad shoulders opening her even wider. Justin kissed her wet folds, his tongue swirling around her clit, inside her heat, his attention's sole purpose to bring her pleasure. Justin was on his knees, but he was in control and she was completely subject to his power.

She writhed under him, thrusting herself against his face, riding his tongue, his mouth, straining for the orgasm teasing along the edges of her electrified nerve endings. Every time she got close, Justin changed his angle, pressure, intensity. He kept her on the edge, so close that when it hit, she cried out in surprise and relief. The pleasure hit her with its expected ferocity and she lurched forward, draping herself over the broad expanse of his back as she pulsed and shook with pleasure.

Sarina collapsed against the mattress, gasping for air and clutching at him when he moved over her, his body covering her as he took her mouth in a sex-flavored kiss. He stared down at her, his eyes dark and hot, molten pools of whiskey-colored lava that she could not ignore, could not break away from.

Justin broke contact only long enough to put on a condom, easing it down the length of him with sure strokes.

"Sarina, I want you so much." His chest heaved with each of his labored breaths, body taut with desire. "I'm going to fuck you until you come again because I can't get enough of it. I can't get enough of you."

"Please, Justin. I need you inside me. Please." She knew she was begging and she didn't care. She held so much of herself back from everyone but she couldn't do that here, not in this bed. They might not know what the future held for them but when they were together like this, they were infinite. They were complete; just the two of them were perfection. She didn't want to ruin that, didn't want reality to intrude.

Justin groaned at her words, and his fingers dug painfully into her hips as he dragged her forward and positioned her over his hard cock. He trembled and she thrilled at the power that she had over this man. But his words shook her control.

"Sarina, I want you to come for me. Getting you off, feeling your body grip me so tight, hearing the whimpers and sounds you make for me, just for me, keeps me up at night. I can't stop thinking about you. I want you all the time and I need to know that I'm not alone in this." Justin reached down between them and grabbed his dick, pushing inside her and joining them in the best way possible. She moaned, bucking up with a flare of pleasure when he began a slow, deliberate circle of the pad of his thumb over her clit. "Don't leave me alone in this, Sarina. Show me that you're here with me. Show me that you feel what I feel."

She couldn't have denied him even if she wanted to. Justin was so open, so vulnerable in this moment, so raw and naked. Not just in the physical sense. They were both stripped bare and even if she wanted to deny him, she couldn't. If she tried to hold it in she'd explode with the intensity, come apart in a way she was afraid would leave nothing of her remaining. So she opened herself to him; her body, her heart. She let him have all of her.

Justin drove into her, his cock moving in deep as she pushed back against him, struggling and straining to get even closer. She was playing with fire, she knew, and she wasn't the risk-taker. Nothing was settled between them and the voice telling her to run was getting louder and louder in her head. She knew that if she left, Justin would move on and fill his life and his bed with someone who was better suited for him. She just wanted this for tonight.

"Sarina, I need you," Justin moaned on a deep thrust, his body covering hers as he took her hands and lifted them over her head. Their fingers tangled together, bodies moving in the same rhythm, their heartbeats and the thrust and retreat of their bodies in perfect synchronicity.

Sarina looked up at him, letting him take over as her orgasm built tighter and hotter in her belly. Justin thrust deeper, harder, groaning his desire out between clenched teeth. Their skin was slick with sweat as they pressed against each other and his hardness rubbed against her clit with every stroke.

"Sarina, please."

She tightened her legs around him. The orgasm was building inside her, up from the base of her spine, making her legs shake and grow weak with the effort. It was terrifying, this all-consuming need, and she fought the urge to disengage her body, her heart, to run from this man.

Justin leaned down, his lips brushing her, his tongue exploring her mouth. He ended the kiss, whispering, "Don't run."

Sarina gasped out loud, her arms breaking free from his grip to wrap around his neck and hold him against her as she came. Justin's cock drove inside her one last time and his muscles shook with the impact of his orgasm. His fingers wove into her hair, clutching and releasing as his body came down.

Justin moved to shift off her, complaining quietly that he was hurting her, but she shook her head. She wrapped herself tighter around him, wanting to draw this moment out as long as she possibly could.

Justin wanted more, that message was coming through loud and clear. And she wanted it too. But she was afraid. Terrified.

She'd been wanted by people before and they'd rejected her in the end, sending her back into the system. She'd learned to not need anyone, to reject them before they pushed her to the side. She ran—it was what she did—and now she had to decide if she was willing to stay and see if the risk was worth the reward.

They were spooning again. This was quickly becoming one of her favorite ways to spend the hours of quiet between the busyness of the day and stillness of the night. The stars outside the open French doors of the bedroom were better than anything on TV and Justin was warm, strong and surrounding her as if he wanted to protect her from the world. She wanted to let him.

"Thank you for this, Justin." The words weren't enough but they were all she had.

"I wanted to do something for you." He kissed her shoulder, spanning his hand across her body in a gesture that made her chest tighten and warm with emotion. "It was risky. I wasn't sure if you would like it or not."

She rushed in to reassure him; the vulnerability in his tone wasn't something he allowed to come through very often. "I loved it. This has been the best day." Sarina peeked over her shoulder at him, taking his hand and weaving their fingers together. "You're good with risks. You take them. It's better than not taking any at all."

"Being cautious isn't a character flaw," he said, his breath stirring her hair, warming the back of her neck. "I know people wish I was more careful."

"Sometimes being cautious feels a little like being the walking dead. It's like standing on the edge of the game but never going in."

"You're braver than you realize."

"If I were brave, I'd say that we need to talk about it…about us. My bike is fixed. The divorce papers have arrived."

His fingers tightened on her hand and his heartbeat started a hammer against her back. "Are we going to talk about it?"

She rolled his question over in her mind, letting the sound of the waves as they eased in and out on the sand and the rocks below soothe her fear. They needed to talk, needed to get things settled between them. Now was the time.

But she didn't want to lose this, lose this moment. She'd learned over the years to take each moment as it came. She didn't give the bad ones the power to take more of her than the time she had to endure them, and the good ones were places she could be fully in the moment.

And this moment, this weekend, was the best of her life and she was too scared to end it too soon.

She didn't want anything to spoil it.

She wasn't so brave after all.

"Not tonight," she murmured, drawing him closer. "Not tonight."

Fourteen

The Mountain Winery was the perfect place to hold a celebration gala.

The historic location in the mountains of Saratoga, California, was part of the Paul Masson company. It hosted weddings, corporate events, concerts and wine tastings. Redhawk/Ling had rented the entire place for the party to celebrate signing the deal with Aerospace Link. Tonight, not only Redhawk/Ling employees but also the staffs of their new business partners would mix and mingle to live music and multiple open bars.

It was not a cheap evening but Adam and Justin weren't guys who skimped on the good times when their employees busted their asses.

Sarina walked into the massive space with Nana Orla, Tess and Roan and realized that finding their hosts was going to be the great mission of the evening. Sarina was anxious to see Justin; the week since they had returned from Malibu had been hectic for him as he finalized this deal and he'd slid into bed late every night. She missed him. So much.

But it had given her a lot of time to think about them and tonight was the night she was going to tell him that she was ready to take a chance on them. She didn't want to sign the divorce papers. Sarina was ready to stop running.

She was scared but he was worth the risk.

"This place is huge," Sarina said, hanging on tight to Nana Orla. The crowd was bustling and although she was a tough lady, Sarina didn't want her trampled on her watch. "I'm going to text Justin and see where the hell they are."

"I just sent a text to Adam," Tess replied, waving her phone in the air. "Nothing yet. I'm sure they're both busy wining and dining their new best friends at Aerospace Link. We won't see them until they are dancing on top of some wine barrels or something."

"No way," Roan said, looking the women over and punctuating his appraisal with a definite thumbs-up. "You girls are smokin' and there is no way that Adam and Justin are going to let you just wander around a party with a bunch of drunk idiots hitting on you."

"What about me?" Nana Orla asked, a hand placed on her hip while she made the what-am-I-chopped-liver gesture with her free hand. "I didn't spend three hours at the salon today to get ignored by all the hot guys at this party."

"Since you're my date tonight," Roan replied, looping her arm through his, "all these guys better just back off."

"That's fine but if I give you the signal to go away, do it. I don't want you to ruin my game," Nana Orla teased.

"Your wish is my command."

"Excuse me, Ms. Redhawk? Miss Lynch?" A young guy with glasses and an earpiece carrying a clipboard approached them and gestured toward a waiting golf cart. "I'm Evan. Mr. Redhawk and Mr. Ling arranged for transportation to take all of you to the VIP section on the Vista Deck."

"You don't have to ask me twice," Nana Orla said, making her way to the empty cart. "Take me to the open bar, young man."

"Yes, ma'am." Evan smiled, waiting until they were all settled before starting the machine and slowly navigating the crowds of people wandering around in all kinds of party clothes.

Sarina took in the entire property, comparing the reality with the photos she'd viewed on the internet. It really was a large place and she was glad she didn't have to walk all this way in the ridiculously high heels she'd chosen for the evening. They were sexy as hell but they weren't walking shoes.

They passed several terraces and open-air spaces, strewn with fairy lights and dotted with tables groaning with food and bartenders making every cocktail known to man. People were dancing, laughing, enjoying their success after having worked so hard the previous months. If this didn't make them all loyal employees, Sarina wasn't sure what would do the trick.

They passed the large amphitheater-style concert venue, with its Spanish-inspired decor lit up with colored lights. A local band with a huge following was playing a live show and the seats were packed with bodies swaying back and forth to the tunes. Sarina would have to convince Justin to come back here later and catch some of the show.

The golf cart turned a corner and directly in front of them, the area marked as the Vista Deck, was an area cordoned off by a velvet rope and monitored by a really big guy holding a clipboard.

Evan stopped the cart and they all piled out, offering him smiles and waves as Roan slipped him a business card with his cell phone written on the back.

"Did you just hit on Evan?" Sarina asked, turning her head to catch the guy still checking out her brother.

"He was adorable. Why not?" Roan shrugged, approaching the bouncer with the clipboard and giving their names.

They passed the test with flying colors and were all admitted into the exclusive area of the party. There were lots of people here as well, but they were better dressed and the waiters came to you for your food and drink orders, no waiting in lines.

Sarina checked out the women in the section, noting the sexy, sparkly dresses they were wearing. These women were glamorous, dressed like movie stars, and she was thankful she'd gone with Nana Orla and Tess to the salon and had her hair and makeup done. Even with the best that money could buy in beauty preparation, she was no match for these women.

"There they are." Tess pointed to an area just to the right where Adam and Justin were standing and talking to a number of people whose clothes and jewelry proclaimed that they were definitely rich and maybe famous.

Adam was dressed all in black, his resemblance to

Roan so pronounced at this angle. Sarina's breath caught at the way they both resembled their father, the dark hair and high cheekbones making them ridiculously handsome.

And then she saw Justin, in dark pants and a white button-down shirt with the sleeves rolled up. He was the epitome of everything she thought was sexy. Strong, masculine, confident, charming—he made her smile and her chest tighten with an emotion she'd never really felt before.

In Malibu she'd asked him to wait to talk about their future, fear making her put off accepting what she wanted. But standing here, watching him and feeling the pull of her body and soul toward him, she knew what she wanted.

Justin.

A future together.

She wanted to remain Mrs. Ling.

And then he looked over and did an honest-to-God double take as their eyes met and she knew that he wanted the same thing. No words could have convinced her, but that look, that absolute and immediate connection between the two of them, told her what an entire dictionary full of words would never be able to tell her: Justin wanted her, too.

She started walking, grinning like an idiot with every step she took across the stone pavers to meet Justin halfway. He was smiling, too, giving his lips a sexy curve as he perused her body with eyes full of desire. And just like that, she knew she'd chosen the right thing to wear.

"You're beautiful," he breathed as soon as they were close enough not to be overheard.

They'd decided not to publicize their involvement tonight. The journalists would latch onto any whisper of a new woman in Justin's life and with nothing settled between them, she'd been wary of any attention. It had been the right decision. She was already nervous about this event and didn't need the extra pressure.

But it was damn hard not to kiss him, not to touch him.

"This old thing?" she replied, looking down at the black jumpsuit with its plunging neckline and almost nonexistent back.

"I can't wait to take it off you later," he replied, his fingers lightly brushing against the inside of her wrist, sending lightning up her arm and racing across her skin. She shivered with the impact of his touch. "Are you cold?"

She didn't get to answer, interrupted by the approach of one of the most beautiful women she'd ever seen. This woman was stunning, tall and willowy with her blond hair in loose curls falling around her tan shoulders. She wore very little makeup, her skin dewy and fresh, lashes long, and lips stained with a red gloss. This woman was the epitome of a California girl, the kind of woman men dreamed about and boys had on posters in their rooms.

"Justin, your parents want you to meet their friends from the hospital board," the woman said, her hand grasping his so easily that Sarina knew it wasn't the first time. Her eyes got wide when she saw Sarina standing there, her expression immediately apologetic. "I'm so sorry, I interrupted you. Forgive me."

Great. And she was nice, too. Sarina was good at

reading people and nothing about this woman rang false.

Justin gestured between the two women, deftly removing his hand from the other woman's grasp. "Sarina Redhawk, this is Heather Scarborough."

"It's nice to meet you," they replied at the same time, causing them both to stutter and smile awkwardly.

"Oh, good. You found him." Mrs. Ling appeared over Justin's other shoulder as if she'd been conjured out of Sarina's most awkward nightmares, and the older woman's smile faltered when her gaze landed on Sarina. "Hello, Sarina. It's nice to see you here." She turned to Justin and gestured over to the other side of the space. "Justin, I need you to come and meet some people from the hospital board."

"Mom, I was just going to dance with Sarina. I'll meet them later," Justin answered, his tone tired. He held his hand out to her, his smile apologetic. "Come on."

Sarina placed her hand in his, relieved to have a few more moments alone with him, but they were stopped by the arrival of a man at their side. She didn't recognize him and by the look on Justin's face, he didn't know him either.

"Mr. Ling, Tim Gilbert from *Celebrity News*. I'm writing an article and I was hoping to get a quote." The man punctuated his question by shoving a digital recorder in their faces.

The *Celebrity News* was a trashy tabloid specializing in gossip and half-truths that barely kept on the right side of slander. This was not a good thing and the tension in Justin's body told her that he knew it.

"I'm sorry, Mr. Gilbert, but we'll be answering questions about the new deal at the press conference in a couple of days. I'll be happy to talk to you then. If you'll excuse me, we're off to dance." Justin nodded at the man with a smile and moved to go around him but the guy fell back and blocked their path.

"I'm not interested in the new deal, Mr. Ling. I was hoping you could talk to me about your secret marriage to Sarina Redhawk."

Fifteen

"Justin, what is this man talking about?" his mother demanded, her raised voice drawing the attention of nearby VIPs.

Justin closed his eyes, knowing that he should have seen this coming. He'd been congratulating himself that they'd pulled it off, that they would be able to sneak off for a couple more days and plan their future together and then announce it to the world on their terms. And now they were exactly where he didn't want to be at the worst possible time.

So close and yet not even in the damn zip code.

"Mr. Ling, I'd like to give you and Ms. Redhawk… Mrs. Ling—" the reporter turned to smile at Sarina "—the chance to tell your story."

"I'm not going to talk to you about this here," Justin replied, pointing toward the exit and the bouncer. "Call my office and we'll schedule an interview at a better time."

"It's not going to work like that, Mr. Ling. I'm sorry. I'm going to run with this story tomorrow, with or without your comment."

Justin looked around them. They were starting to draw the attention of the crowd in the VIP area and his mother continuing to ask what was going on was not helping. His father approached, closely followed by Adam and three of the investors. He had to do damage control and he had to do it fast.

"Justin, what is he talking about?" his mother repeated, her voice filling in the silence that developed whenever people sensed a scandal looming on the horizon. "Tell him that you are *not* married to Sarina!"

"I can't do that, Ma."

The reporter smiled, the triumphant grin of a man who had a solid story that he'd file by midnight.

"So, can you confirm that you two were married in a Vegas quickie wedding? Witnesses say that you were drunk and that you both stated that you had only met a few hours before. Is that correct, Mr. Ling? Ms. Redhawk? Did you guys get married when you were total strangers and drunk? What do you plan on doing about it? We heard that you've hired divorce lawyers to end the marriage on the down low. Keep it out of the press. Although nobody would be surprised about it with your reputation, right, Mr. Ling?"

If possible, their audience got even quieter as they all processed that information. Justin couldn't blame them; this was good stuff. Better than reality TV. Did they have a popcorn station at this party? They should.

Justin motioned for the bouncer to take care of this problem. "Get this guy out of here, now."

The reporter went quietly if not entirely willingly,

his expression smug. He didn't need their statement and so he wasn't going to make a fuss to stick around until he got it. His removal did little to dissolve the crowd although Roan and Adam tried to get people to give Sarina and Justin some privacy. In the end he still had his parents and several investors standing by and waiting for answers.

This time it was his father's turn to ask the million-dollar question. "Justin, is any of this true?"

The question was echoed by two of Aerospace Link's highest executives, their frowns telling him exactly what they expected his answer to be.

Justin looked at Sarina, unable to gauge where she was with this. Her face was blank, the old Sarina back in place. The one who gave away nothing and had walls that nobody could climb.

He wished that they'd had their talk because he didn't know where she was on all of this. The last time they'd talked about it they were getting divorced and she'd avoided any discussion about a change in status since then. Justin knew she cared about him, and he knew that she enjoyed sex with him, and he knew that she still planned to get on her bike and leave him behind once the ink was dry on the divorce papers.

And he knew that a couple thousand people were here celebrating a deal that would guarantee that employees still had jobs and Redhawk/Ling could survive any downturn in the tech sector. He knew this deal was security for many people and he knew he couldn't kill it at the eleventh hour.

What he didn't know was if his wife loved him enough to stay.

He couldn't make a grand statement that they were

in love and staying married when he didn't know if Sarina was willing to play along with that story. Because that couldn't be a short-term thing. It would have to be a long-haul commitment to convince everyone that it was the truth and as far as he knew, she was still going to sign those divorce papers.

So, he really had no choice. He didn't have a winning hand and it was time to fold.

Sarina would understand. He'd make her understand. It was time for him to do some damage control.

"Look, I'm married...we're married...but it was a mistake and we are in the process of having the marriage dissolved." He reached for Sarina's hand and she let him take it, but it was cold and her body was stiff. "We are committed to staying friends and remaining in each other's lives in the future. We are both part of the Redhawk/Ling family and that is how it will remain even though we will no longer be married."

"Excuse me, I think you've got this. I'm leaving." Sarina ripped her hand away from him and turned, pushing her way through the crowd and heading toward the exit.

Roan and Tess followed in her wake, their withering looks of disappointment unmistakable. Adam stayed behind but he was pissed, anger setting his jaw in a hard line and his eyes almost black with his emotion. Justin looked behind him one more time, watching Sarina's retreat, and suddenly he didn't care—he had to talk to her.

"Sarina, wait!"

His father's grip on his arm, firm and strong, stopped him in his tracks. His tone was brittle, voice deep and loud enough for only Justin to hear, but it sounded like a gunshot going off in his brain. "Justin, where are you going? Let her go. Don't throw this away right now, son. You need to keep your priorities straight and at this moment your priority *has* to be your company."

His father cast a meaningful glance at the investors, who were talking quietly together in a group, throwing the occasional skeptical glance in his direction. Nothing about their demeanor said that they were holding him or Redhawk/Ling in high regard. Everything about them said that he'd fucked up and needed to fix it—now.

His father continued. "Justin, you're always trying to tell me that I don't understand or respect your business and your accomplishments. You're wrong. I do respect your work ethic, but I think your personal life leaves a lot to be desired. You're reckless but I wouldn't care if it just impacted your personal life. You do what you want and then get offended when your poor choices jeopardize your business." His father gestured around, his movement meant to encompass all of the guests enjoying themselves at the party. "You have a lot of people who depend on you to do the right thing, to be the right thing. And I'm presuming that your new partners have insisted on the standard morality clauses?" He didn't wait for Justin to confirm it; a businessman in his own right, he already knew the answer. "So be the man these people can depend on and fix this. You are the only one who can fix this."

Justin looked in the direction where Sarina had disappeared, wishing he could do what he wanted but knowing he had to do the right thing. He'd created this mess and his father was right: he was the only one who could fix it.

He'd make this right and then he'd find Sarina and fix their forever.

Sixteen

Sarina was used to packing light and fast.

Years of moving from foster care situation to foster care situation with nothing but a few things thrown in a plastic trash bag had prepared her for the military. The army had perfected her ability to move quickly and disappear when she wanted to be gone.

She'd left the party after that humiliating fiasco and ordered the car to take her back to Nana Orla's as fast as it could without getting pulled over by the police. She'd barely set foot in the house before Wilma was growling at her. And not fifteen minutes after that, Sarina heard a car pull up outside the house and Nana Orla burst through the door on full alert, wanting to know if everything was okay.

But Sarina couldn't answer her. How could she talk about the moment when she'd been humiliated in front of the press and all of Justin and Adam's rich friends? She'd known that going to the party was a bad idea but she'd been fooled by Justin, blinded by what she felt for him.

Stupid, stupid girl.

Sarina wiped at her eyes, refusing to let the tears fall. It had been years since she'd cried over something as stupid as a guy or having her feelings hurt. She'd cried over dead men and women in the desert, so far from home and family. She'd cried as a child, missing her mom and dad and her brothers, confused by being surrounded by strangers.

She wasn't going to cry over Justin Ling.

Sarina stripped off her jumpsuit, throwing it over the chair in the room. She wouldn't need it where she was going and it would take up space in her backpack. She was back to being Sarina, finally awakened from the spell that she belonged in a world of money and power and privilege. She didn't belong in that world. She didn't belong with Justin. She'd just forgotten that for a while.

Wilma paced the floor, sensing her agitation and whining with her own anxiety. Sarina scooped her up, speaking soothingly to the dog as she showed her that she was going with her.

"Don't worry, baby." Sarina pressed a kiss to the dog's head, nuzzling against her when Wilma pressed into her body. "Look, I'm putting your toys in the bag. You're going with me. You always go with me."

"I'm going to miss the wee dog. She's mean as a snake but I love her anyway."

Sarina turned to find Nana Orla standing in the doorway. She'd changed into her nightclothes; her robe was teal tonight, embroidered with flowers and edged with multicolored pom-pom trim. It was eye-wateringly bright, but suited her with its loud and cheerful colors and design. Sarina was going to miss Nana Orla's outfits; they were a never-ending source of curiosity for her.

"You two get along because you're both little and you both bite," Sarina said, her smile hopefully conveying how much she cared for this woman. She approached Nana Orla and handed her the little dog, who went with copious wiggles and kisses. Man, leaving this time was going to hurt. Not only leaving Justin but saying goodbye to Nana Orla and Adam and Tess…these people were going to be hard to let go.

But it wasn't letting go. Not really. Her brothers would understand that she had to go and they'd support her. Their bond was new but it was strong and she knew they'd give her time to figure out her future because they were destined to be a part of it.

"Well, that's true enough, I guess." Orla entered the room, eyeing the half-packed bag and the chaos of clothing strewn all over the floor. "You can leave your things here if they don't fit in your bags. I'll keep them for you until you come back home."

Home.

Oh hell. Sarina turned from her, biting the inside of her cheek to stop the tears that threatened to spill over onto her cheeks.

"That's really sweet but I don't think I'll be back." She cut off the words *anytime soon* because they sat on the edge of her tongue, poised to add a caveat and hedge on the decision she knew she had to make. This needed to be the last time she came here, at least until she could get over the ache in her chest that throbbed every time she thought of Justin.

Home. Justin had become that place for her. She couldn't pinpoint the exact moment it had happened, but she couldn't deny it and now she had to figure out her exit plan. Time and distance would help her get over him.

"This is your home, girl." Nana Orla's voice was soft but firm, the Irish brogue wrapping around Sarina like a warm blanket. The older woman moved in close, locking eyes with Sarina before she spoke. "You know better than anyone that family is not just blood and DNA, it's the people you choose. What Justin did, it doesn't change the fact that you and I are family and always will be." The older woman reached out and placed a hand on Sarina's cheek. Her touch was warm but the surge of emotion, of love, that Sarina felt for her was enough to loosen the tears and important enough that she didn't care. "I choose you, Sarina. You and I will always be family."

"She's right, Sarina."

They both turned to find Adam standing in the doorway. He was still dressed in his tux, a tense expression on his face. He smiled apologetically at Nana Orla.

"I used the key you gave me," he explained, his gaze drifting back to Sarina. "How are you doing?"

She could feel the big-brother protectiveness rolling off him in waves and for once it didn't piss her off. It made her feel wanted, included. When he walked over to her and pulled her into a tight hug, she didn't fight him but hugged him back. Tighter. Harder. She was going to be gone for a while and she needed to make this one count, make it one she would remember.

"I'm doing better now," she admitted, surprising the both of them with her honesty. Adam went still for a moment and then he pulled her in tighter, pressing a kiss to her hair. "But I've got to go, Adam. I'm sorry."

He released her, looking down at her, clearly gauging how successful he would be if he tried to change her mind. She shook her head, wishing that this could be different. "Adam, you know I can't stay. This thing with Justin, it got complicated and so real, so fast. I have to go to get my head straight, to figure things out."

"You can't outrun these feelings, Sarina. You love him. That isn't just going to go away just because you have a few states in between the two of you."

"I know, Adam. But I need time to put this behind me. I need to find a place where I can land and stay, build a life." Sarina glanced at Nana Orla, wishing that this could be different. "I thought it might be here but I was wrong. This way I can move on and so can Justin."

"Justin is being an ass," Nana Orla said, setting Wilma on the bed. "I still can't believe what he said to that reporter."

"Look, he told them the truth," Sarina broke in, needing to make sure that they all understood exactly what had gone down between her and Justin. "Justin and I never changed our plans. He didn't betray me with what he said tonight because he was absolutely correct. I just made the mistake of thinking that things were going to be different without saying or hearing the words. The only thing we're guilty of is getting caught up in our feelings, in the emotions of the moment."

"I know what I know, Sarina," Nana Orla insisted. "I know that you love Justin and he loves you."

Sarina didn't deny it. She wouldn't disrespect what

had happened between them. It was real and it was powerful. It just wasn't forever.

"But that doesn't change the truth of the matter. His parents are right—I'm not the girl for Justin. It's that simple."

"You can't just give up, Sarina," Adam said, his voice pleading. "Don't give up on Justin. Don't give up on us."

Oh no. She couldn't let him think that this had anything to do with them. "Adam, no, we're good." She swallowed hard, realizing that there were things she needed to say this man, the brother who had loved her enough to never stop looking for her. "You're my family, my brother. My *agido*. And I have never thanked you for finding me. I have never thanked you for looking for me and not giving up. All I ever wanted was to be the person who mattered to someone, a person worth remembering. A person worth missing. You gave me that. I'm prickly and stubborn but I love you, Adam. Nothing will ever change that, not ever again."

"Damn, Sarina, it took you long enough. I love you, too," Adam said, tears streaming down his face as he pulled her to him again for a longer and tighter hug. She was going to miss this. She was going to miss her brother.

She considered staying and just dodging Justin but she couldn't face that prospect. It would take longer to get over him if she stayed, and she *needed* to get over him. Distance and time would give her the strength to watch him forget about her and move on to the next woman. It wasn't brave but it was reality. Running wasn't always a bad thing. Sometimes the best defense was an organized retreat.

And this wasn't going to get any easier the longer

she dragged it out. Sarina needed to go and she needed to go now.

But there was one thing she needed to do first. Sarina pushed on Adam's chest, laughing softly when he refused to let her go. After a long moment, he finally did, grumbling in protest. She walked over to the desk in the corner of the room and picked up a manila envelope, sliding out the papers and flipping to the one with the "sign here" sticky note on it. She didn't need to read the document. She'd read it a million times; the words never changed.

Those words put an end to the first time she ever dared to believe she could have the happily-ever-after. The first time in a long time she'd allowed herself to think that she could be someone's everything, the person they couldn't leave behind.

Sarina picked up a pen from the desk and weighed it in her hand. Then she signed her name.

It was that simple. A few strokes of black ink and she broke her own heart.

Sarina gathered the papers and stuffed them back in the envelope, hesitating for one moment before she took a piece of notepaper and scribbled a few words on it and shoved it in with her divorce papers. Knowing she was doing the right thing gave her the strength to turn and hand over the package to Adam.

"Can you give these to Justin for me?"

The tic in his jaw was the only sign that Adam wanted to argue with her. In the end he nodded, taking the papers from her with a grimace. "You matter to Justin. He loves you and he will remember you. He'll miss you. These papers won't change that."

She laughed, wiping the tears away as she reached

for her bag and the keys to her bike. He was right. The stuff in his hand was just paper and ink, words that did nothing to change the pain settled in her chest. "Those papers aren't meant to help Justin get over me, they're what I need to get over him."

Seventeen

Sarina had just vanished.

Justin stood in the doorway to the room she'd made her own the last few weeks. He stared at the bed where they'd made love and he'd given his heart away without even realizing it. They'd been happy together.

And for the first time in his life he'd been good enough just as he was.

And now she was gone with her motorcycle and her dog and all the ways she'd made his life complete.

All because he was a coward.

He'd been stuck at the party until the early-morning hours, making sure Aerospace Link wasn't going to jump ship and bail. Adam had disappeared and it had been impossible for Justin to leave.

The investors hadn't been happy with the news of his quickie Vegas marriage, most of them giving him disapproving looks that rivaled ones he'd received from his father over the years. At first he'd downplayed the whole night in Vegas, omitting the parts about the alcohol that fueled their matrimonial bravado and emphasizing the instant connection with Sarina.

He'd found himself telling them about how amazing his wife was. They'd heard about her separation from Adam and Roan and while he didn't get into the details of her life, he'd relayed how she'd grown up in foster care and then joined the army and served her country with bravery and loyalty.

And then he'd found himself telling them about her work with the kids at the center, how she loved his Nana Orla, and even how she'd found a dog behind a dumpster in some tiny little town in Nevada and now spoiled it rotten with love and cuddles. And he'd told them about how she loved Linda Ronstadt and that the best moment in his life was seeing her smile on the beach in Malibu while an old beat-up CD of *Heart Like a Wheel* played in a constant loop on the stereo system.

And that was when he'd known that he had just made the biggest mistake of his life.

Justin would never forget the shocked looks on their faces when he'd stood up from where they were all seated and announced that he was going to find his wife and tell her that he loved her and beg her not to sign the divorce papers. He'd made it clear that if the deal was off, he understood, but he didn't care.

They'd blown his mind when they'd shoved him towards one of the property golf carts and told him to go get her. The deal was solid. Now was the time to save his marriage.

And so he'd raced home, not surprised when all of his calls to her had gone straight to voicemail. He'd pleaded with her to just wait for him, that he didn't want to finalize the divorce. He'd not told her that he loved her. Justin wanted the first time he said it to be in person, with her in his arms and agreeing to forever with him.

But he'd been too late.

Now, with the sun rising over the hills, Justin walked over to the large bay window and looked over the expanse of landscaped gardens and lawns, seeing Sarina everywhere. On the patio by the pool. Walking in the orchard with Nana Orla or playing with Wilma on the grass. If he focused he could see the tree house just on the edge of the horizon, the place she'd turned into magic. He reached up and rubbed the palm of his hand over his chest, trying to massage out an ache that he knew had nothing to do with the physical. It was marrow-deep. Painful. Permanent.

"Justin."

He turned quickly, almost falling off balance with surprise. Adam was standing in the doorway, his face taut with anger and eyes soaked in disappointment. Everything about his posture, ramrod straight and muscles tense, radiated how much effort it took for him to maintain his control. Adam had never raised a hand to him but Justin braced himself for the blow. He deserved it.

"Adam." Justin motioned around the empty room, everything about Sarina gone except the lingering trace of the citrus-sweet scent from her shampoo. She was on the run. Again. "She's just gone."

His voice cracked on the last word and he didn't even try to cover it up. He'd spent his life hiding how he was really feeling, protecting himself with a quick smile and the pretense that nothing touched him. This was killing him and he had nothing, no joke or defense or mask. His hand was exposed for all to see and he'd gone all in and lost.

Adam cocked his head to one side, his eyes narrowing into laser-focused slits as he examined Justin like he was a specimen at the zoo.

Heartbroken Homo sapiens. Genus Dumbass.

"Jesus, Justin."

He could see the anger leach out of Adam's body, replaced with sympathy and pity. He'd thought Adam being pissed at him was the worst but he'd been wrong—this was worse.

"Adam, if you have any idea where she's gone, please tell me. I have to get her to talk to me. I have to explain and tell her I'm sorry." He approached his best friend, the man who was like a brother to him, raking his hands through his hair in frustration and rising panic. "I know you're pissed at me and I deserve it but you've got to help me find her." His voice wavered again, his emotions spilling over the dam after a lifetime of keeping them bottled up. "I don't know how you did this, man. When Tess walked away, how did you breathe?"

"Justin, I—" Adam broke off, his gaze drifting to the window and then back to his face. "Sarina asked me to bring these to you."

Adam held out a manila envelope to him. Justin's name was scrawled across the front in Sarina's sharp, dark handwriting and he knew immediately that he didn't want whatever was in that envelope. He took a step back and shook his head.

"Justin, take it. I saw her before she left town. I tried to get her to stay with us but she was determined to leave as soon as possible. She made me promise to give this to you."

"Adam, why didn't you keep her here? I know I fucked up and you want to kill me but you should have thought of some excuse to hold her up and called me."

"Yeah, right. Like I had any chance of keeping Sarina here when she was determined to go." Anger was back in his tone as Adam thrust the papers at him. "You did fuck up, Justin. I'm not going to force her to stay so that you can shit on her again. I wasn't thrilled when I heard about your marriage but I've watched you two together the last few weeks and it was good, man. You were good for her and she was good for you. You were amazing together." Adam's voice dropped lower, and he shook his head with obvious disappointment. "I love you like a brother, Justin, but I saw Sarina's face when you denied all of that last night and I don't know if I ever want to give you the chance to make her feel like that again."

"Adam, I'm so sorry." He had some apologizing to do and it needed to start with Adam. "Look, I made the wrong move tonight. I panicked when the reporter showed up and brought my biggest fear to life right in front of the Aerospace Link partners. Sarina and I hadn't talked about our next steps. We both kept putting it off because we didn't want to ruin how good it was, so I defaulted to a conversation we had weeks ago and ignored everything that had happened between us." He ran his hands through his hair, sitting down on the bed to get off legs suddenly too wobbly to hold him up. The adrenaline was wearing off and all that was left behind was bone-deep weariness. "I should have told the reporter 'no comment' and talked to Sarina but I didn't. All I could think about was the deal and the people who depended on us and I didn't want to be the reason we let them down. I couldn't be the fuckup again."

Adam settled beside him with a deep sigh, his voice scratchy and gruff with the fatigue of the last twenty-four hours. "Justin, you're not a fuckup. You're bold and energetic and you do things that nobody else can do because you're willing to take the risks necessary to make it happen." He nudged him with his elbow, pausing until Justin turned to look at him. "It's why we work so well together. I'm cautious but you push me and our company to be innovative and that has made all the difference in our success. You're not reckless, you're brave. If something gets fucked up then we fuck it up together just like we've done since college. I wouldn't do this with anyone but you. We're in this together. That's how it works."

Justin nodded, wondering how he'd lost sight of the way things were between them. He'd let the voices of his parents and all the crap they'd piled on him over the years drown out the fact that Adam believed in him and always had.

"Thanks, Adam. I came clean with the Aerospace Link people, told them that I didn't want to divorce Sarina. They were fine with it, practically drove me here themselves."

"Good. I knew you'd fix it," Adam said, his jaw tense with the frown that returned with the mention of the situation with Sarina. "Business is business. But the bigger issue is, you hurt my sister. Why should I trust you not to do it again?"

Justin deserved that. He struggled with the words to make Adam believe that he was sorry, that he was the guy he could trust with Sarina's heart. There was only the truth. It was the only thing that had any chance to set him free.

"I love her, Adam," Justin said, his words loud in the empty room. "I *love* her. With everything I am."

Adam observed him, letting the revelation settle between them. A new truth between old friends. Finally, he sighed, reaching out to pull Justin into a hug. They stood that way for several long moments before Adam spoke.

"I'm sorry, man."

Justin pulled back, finally taking the envelope from him, turning it over and over in his hands. His gut told him that he knew what was inside. He glanced up at Adam, huffing out a heavy breath as he peeled back the sealed flap of the envelope and pulled the papers out.

Their divorce papers. Sarina's signature stood out, decisive and final in bold strokes of black ink.

Damn.

"She put a note in there, I think," Adam said, gesturing toward the envelope. "She wrote one. I saw her."

Justin riffled through the papers, heart sinking when he didn't find a note. He tipped the envelope over, shaking it. Something that felt like relief coursed through him when a half sheet of paper slid into his hand. He turned it over, eyes skimming over what she'd written.

Justin—I'm going back on the road to find my future. Thank you for the place to land even if it was only temporary. You're good enough. More than enough. Sarina.

"What did she say?" Adam asked, concern etched over his features. "It's good that she wrote a note, yeah?"

Justin turned it over in his mind. Was it a good thing that she wrote a note? All she had to do was sign the papers. The note had to mean something, didn't it?

"I think it has to be a good sign, Adam, but it doesn't matter. I'm going to find her anyway." Justin motioned toward the door. He was going now. He wasn't wasting any more time reading papers that he was never going to file. "I've got to go."

Justin headed toward the door, his mind going over every conversation he'd had with Sarina searching for a clue about where he could find her. He knew her and if he could just focus for a minute he'd figure this out. But time was flying by and with every minute she was on her bike and putting distance between the two of them.

Adam was right on his heels, pulling his phone out of his pocket. "Let me call Tess. She'll know how to search for Sarina. She found her once. She can do it again."

Justin entered the family room, looking for Nana Orla. He would say a quick goodbye and then hit the road. Only she wasn't alone.

"Mom. Dad. I didn't know you were here," he said, walking over to where his nana sat to give her a hug goodbye. "I can't stay. I've got to go and find Sarina."

"That's why we're here, Justin," his father said, tone firm with the conviction that whatever he was going to say was correct. "We need to talk about your marriage to Sarina."

"Dad, I know what you're going to say, so I can save you the time. She's not right for me and I need to just get divorced and marry someone like Heather." He held his hands out in a how-am-I-doing? gesture that he knew would piss off his parents. The only difference was that today he didn't care. Not anymore. "That's never going to happen. I love Sarina and I'm going to go find her, beg her to forgive me, and come back and build a life together."

"Justin, think about this. She's not the wife you need by your side." His mom looked beyond him to where Adam stood, her smile apologetic and expression sincere. "Adam, we mean no offense to your family. Sarina is a wonderful girl, I'm sure. She's just not what Justin needs. He needs someone who is more polished and familiar with the social circles you both have to navigate now. Justin needs a cool head, someone who will protect him from his worst impulses. I'm sure you agree."

Adam scoffed, shaking his head as he walked farther into the room. "No, Mrs. Ling, I don't agree. Sarina and Justin brought out the best in each other. I couldn't have asked for a better man for my sister and I think he's lucky to have her."

"We're not here to disparage your family, Adam. That's not the point," Allan Ling interjected in obvious frustration. His face was flushing red as he stood up from where he sat on the sofa. He focused his stare on Justin. "It is time for you to understand and accept your responsibility to this family, Justin. What you do reflects on all of us and it is time for you to stop putting yourself first and think of others. It is already all over town that you ended up in this drunken sham of a marriage. How am I supposed to do business with these people when they read your exploits in the tabloids? Why should your brothers and sisters have to hope that your behavior doesn't negatively impact their livelihoods? The circles we run in are small and memories are long. Your honor and reputation are all you have in the end, it's what keeps you on top."

Justin was done. The things he needed to say were long overdue. "Mom and Dad, I've spent my whole life worrying about reflecting poorly on the family and

I'm done. I work hard and it's not good enough. I build a successful business with Adam and we land on the front page of *Forbes* and it's not good enough. I help kids who have nobody in their corner and it's not good enough." He held his hand up when his father moved to interrupt him. "No, I'm not finished. I understand that you want the best for me and I know that you sincerely think you know what that is, but you don't. You think the best thing for me is playing it safe, traditional, the road trampled by the million others on the same path, but you're wrong. I'm never going to do it the way everyone else does. I'm different. I've had to find my own path and I'm so damn proud of what I've accomplished, what Adam and I are doing." He took a deep breath, getting to the heart of it, and he could almost hear Sarina whispering in his ear. "I work every day to leave this world a little better than I've found it. I'm a good man, friend, boss, and God willing, I'll be a good husband. I don't know what the future holds for me because I'm open to any possibility but I do know that I can't—won't—do it without Sarina. I love her. She looks at me and I know I'm good enough because I have her love. If that's not good enough for you, then you need to live with the fact that you won't be a part of our lives."

"Justin," his mother sniffled, her cheeks wet with her tears and her voice choked with emotion. "We just don't want you to make a mistake."

He walked over and sat down next to her on the couch, pulling her against him in a hug. "Dad's parents thought you were a mistake and look at how wrong they were. You two came to the United States because you weren't accepted by his family but you loved each other too much to walk away. You proved them all wrong. I would think that you would understand."

"It wasn't always easy, son," his dad said, staring down at the woman he'd defied his family to love. "We want it to be easier for you, Justin."

"I don't need it to be easier. I just need it to be with her," he answered. "A hard day with Sarina is better than easy with anyone else. I think you both know that I'm right. It's what you lived every day right in front of me. I just want a chance to have what you have." He smiled at his parents, hoping that they were really listening to him. "I don't want to do it without you, but I will."

He let that sit in the air between them. He'd said his piece and his parents knew where he stood. He loved them but he also loved Sarina. If he had to choose, it wouldn't be an easy choice but it would be a clear one.

"Allan. Saoirse." Nana Orla spoke out from across the room and they turned to look at her. Her usually cheerful expression was gone, replaced with equal parts censure and compassion. She spoke slowly, her words clearly chosen with care and love. "I don't know if you know how proud I am of you both. I watched you struggle with loving each other and knowing that you'd have to give up so much to be together. You taught your children, you taught me, how important love is and that it's worth fighting for. You've raised a son who knows the value of love, the real kind of love that makes you want to be better. The kind that makes you stronger. I've watched Justin and Sarina together for weeks and they remind me of the two of you. If you don't see that, you're blind. If you don't give them your blessing, then you've been living a lie."

His parents looked at each other, several decades of marriage and love allowing them to communicate without words. He'd seen this a million times over his lifetime, finding it fascinating and terrifying at the same time. Whatever passed between them was settled with a nod from his father and another round of sniffles from his mother.

"Justin, do you have any idea where Sarina could be?" his father asked, his question settling it all between them.

He shook his head, memories of his wife ping-ponging around in his head as he searched for the answer. She had her bike and Wilma; she could be going anywhere. He picked up the note, reading it over again, letting the words sink in.

"She said she was going to find her future…"

And suddenly it was crystal clear.

"I know where she's going." Justin stood, scooping up the papers and calculating how much of a lead she had on him and how fast he could get there. If he hurried he could intercept her and beg her to come home with him. It was worth a shot. Sarina was worth everything. "I need to hurry and I need a helicopter."

Adam grinned from across the room, pulling out his phone to make the call. "Luckily, we have one."

Eighteen

Justin Ling had ruined the Grand Canyon for her.

Sarina stood on the Skywalk, the glass bridge cantilevered seventy feet beyond the west rim, and glanced down at the view beneath her feet. Only air came between her and the valley of the canyon four thousand feet below. This place had been on her bucket list, one of the most anticipated stops on her road trip and she'd headed straight here after leaving California a couple of days ago, but she couldn't get beyond the tumult of thoughts banging around in her mind to register the beauty. A perfect combination of man-made genius and creator-formed nature, this Skywalk should have taken her breath away.

But she couldn't breathe around the pain ripping through her chest.

Dramatic? Yes.

Inaccurate? Damn, she wished.

The sound of a helicopter approaching from behind the visitor center caused the crowd to turn from the natural beauty to gape at the sleek black vehicle coming closer and closer and then lowering itself down to the ground. From where she stood, it looked like the bird had landed in the parking lot. Unmarked by any National Park Service logo, it had to be a private ride bringing someone here to the Grand Canyon for a VIP tour of the area.

Sarina couldn't help but remember the incredible weekend in Malibu with Justin. He'd orchestrated every move to make sure that she'd had the type of weekend only featured in celebrity magazines. The luxuries had been sweet but the way he'd looked at her, touched her, made love to her—those were the things she would never forget.

But she had to forget them. She had to put them behind her and move forward toward a life she could build for herself. For a minute she'd imagined that maybe she'd found a place where she could stop running, stop searching and put down roots. It had been a mistake.

That much Justin had gotten right.

A family walked past her, the young boy noticing Wilma with an excited tug at his mom's hand and a pointing finger. Wilma wagged her tail in excitement, standing on her hind legs and pawing at the air in the direction of her new friend.

"You can pet her if you want. She's friendly with kids," Sarina offered, watching closely as Wilma worked her magic and claimed another willing admirer.

Not for the first time did she wish she knew how Wilma still had this boundless joy for life and trust in people, even after she'd been abandoned and disappointed by an owner who should have done better by her. Once she would have scoffed at such optimism, counted it as the ultimate in stupidity to keep leaving yourself open for more heartbreak. But now Sarina knew that it wasn't foolishness—it was courage.

And even though she'd faced moments that teetered on the edge of life and death, risking heartbreak was scarier.

The little boy leaned over and hugged Wilma, pressing a loud, smacking kiss on her head before being led away by his mom. Wilma wagged her entire body at the kid, tugging at the leash to follow her new friend.

"Good girl." Sarina gave Wilma a scratch behind the ear, making a mental note to give her an extra treat when they got back to the bike. She glanced at her watch and realized that it was time to leave and get back on the road. If she was going to make Kingman, Arizona, before sundown she needed to go. She'd hang out there a couple of days and then she'd figure out where to head next. Anywhere was fair game. As long as she kept moving.

She needed to put miles between her and Justin. At some point she would stop feeling the pull to return to him and the tree house and Nana Orla.

She didn't belong there. No matter how much she wanted it to be the place where she belonged. She'd learned a long time ago that wishing didn't make anything true.

Sarina stood and turned to head back to the visitor center, squinting into the bright Arizona sun as she scanned the growing crowds of tourists. It was time to get back to the bike, grab some water for her and Willa, and hit Route 66.

"Sarina?"

The sound of her name stopped her in her tracks. Wilma tugged on the leash, whining in confusion at the sudden halt in forward momentum.

"Sarina."

She scanned the crowd, finally seeing the face that belonged to the voice when a family of four with "Brecken Family Reunion" T-shirts parted like the Red Sea and Sarina glimpsed the man who'd somehow become her promised land.

"Justin?"

Wilma whined louder and tugged even harder on the leash, the whines erupting into low growls as she fully recognized the man standing a short distance away. Sarina let Wilma pull her closer to Justin and unlocked the retractable leash so the dog could cover the last bit of distance between them. Justin loosened his white-knuckle grip on the Skywalk railing but didn't let go as he leaned over and patted Wilma on her head.

"Hey, girl, did you miss me?" Justin scratched behind her ears, huffing out a chuckle as she growled at him but leaned into the touch at the same time. "Well, that's progress, I guess." He pulled back his hand when Wilma bared her teeth and retreated to hide behind Sarina. "Or maybe not."

Justin straightened and moved closer to Sarina, his right hand wrapped around the railing as he shuffled closer to her one inch at a time. He was pale under the tan of his skin, every part of his body stiff with the fear she knew was coursing through him. For a guy who had a fear of heights, this had to be his worst nightmare on steroids.

"You had to pick a glass bridge four thousand feet over the fucking Grand Canyon, didn't you?" Justin complained, shooting an apologetic look at an elderly couple standing nearby. "Sorry, I don't like heights."

"No apology needed, son," the older man said, his expression entirely sympathetic. He glanced down at the silver-haired lady standing next to him, snaking an arm around her waist, then looked back at Justin and winked. "We do what we have to do for the women we love."

"Yeah, we do." Justin sneaked a glance at the glass floor under his feet and shuddered. Taking a deep breath, he turned and faced Sarina, moving to close the gap between them even more. He stopped when he was within arm's length of her. "I'm here to do what I need to do for the woman I love."

"Justin." She shook her head, refusing to let the hesitant bubble of elation in her belly cut loose. She'd been here before and nothing like this had ever worked for her. Sarina had opened herself up and hoped to be loved but it never worked out for her. She'd been that kid who'd allowed herself to hope that the next place she was sent would be the place where she was loved. But too many rejections in too many foster homes and the failure of her adoption had taught her that this wasn't for her. Not everyone got their happiness and that would have to be okay. So she couldn't let Justin's arrival raise her hopes again. She couldn't fall for it now. "What are you doing here? Didn't Adam give you the papers?"

Justin nodded, reaching into his back pocket and pulling out the mangled and folded envelope. He waved it in her face, his grin breaking through his panic over being on the Skywalk. "Got them."

"So what are you doing here? File them. Be done with it." Sarina shook her head, getting a little pissed off that they were even having this conversation. What had they been doing all these weeks if he was just going to walk around with the damn divorce papers in his pocket? "Justin, I don't know what's going on."

"I'm here to do this," he said, extracting the papers from the envelope and ripping them in half, and then in half again. He waved them at her and smiled. "I don't want a divorce."

Sarina shook her head, letting her anger break the surface and coat her words with the hurt and betrayal she'd carried with her since walking away from Justin at the winery.

"Well, I remember you saying something very different at the party. In fact, I think I remember you calling us *'a mistake.'*" She leveled a gaze at him intended to make sure that he would think twice about coming any closer. Tugging on Wilma's leash, she turned away from him and moved to exit the Skywalk. "This is your mistake walking away. Don't follow me. Don't contact me. Find a way to file those papers. Let me know when I'm cut loose from your ass. Have a nice life."

"Sarina, wait."

She kept walking. There was nothing Justin had to say to her that she wanted to hear.

"Sarina," Justin shouted, causing people to stop and turn to see the real-life drama playing out before them. Forget the Kardashians. The Redhawks and Lings were giving everybody a free show. "Sarina Redhawk, I want you to marry me."

Justin's voice carried, amplified by the slight echo created by the canyon. If anyone hadn't noticed their little scene yet, they were all riveted now. Conversations around them had dwindled down to murmured directions to be quiet and shushing sounds. She didn't want to marry him but she wanted to strangle him. Was that an option?

Sarina turned to face down her husband, who now stood only two feet away from her.

"What the hell are you talking about, Justin? Thanks to you ripping up the divorce papers, *we are still married*."

"I know. I know," Justin said in a calming voice, his hand extended in a gesture calculated to soothe but producing the opposite result. She was so tired of the games and drama.

"No, you don't know anything," she said through gritted teeth. "We made a mistake and now we can fix it. You don't want me, you just don't like losing. You don't like the fact that your family was right about us. Let it go, Justin. Let me go." She swallowed hard, stifling the emotions that pressed against her chest bone and shot pain up and down her body. "I need to go. I stayed too long."

"No. Sarina. You need to stay. With me." Justin reduced the distance between them a little more; now he was close enough for her to see the deep brown of his eyes, smell the smoky citrus of his cologne. "I told my family everything. I told them that I don't want a divorce and that marrying you was the best thing I'd ever done in my life. I told them that I love you and that you are my life. They are warming up to the idea and they'll get there eventually. Or not." He shrugged. "But you have to know, Sarina, I would have walked away from all of them and straight to you if they had refused to accept us. I choose you. Every time."

"What about Aerospace Link and the tabloid story?"

"I told the Aerospace Link people everything. They are completely on board and they won't care about the story because they know the truth. But even if they didn't, it wouldn't matter. I choose you, Sarina. Every. Single. Time."

Oh damn. He was close enough for her to reach out to him. If she did that he'd pull her into his arms and kiss her and make her feel like she was finally in a place where she belonged. A place where she was wanted. A place where she was the chosen one.

If she kept listening, he'd convince her to stay.

But she couldn't stay. Staying meant giving other people the option to tell her she didn't belong or to move on without her. She needed to go. Now.

So why couldn't she move?

Justin took her hesitation as all the permission he needed to continue. "Sarina, baby, marry me. Again. For real this time. Marry me with our eyes wide open. Marry me knowing all of my faults. Marry me in spite of my fear of heights, my meddling grandmother and my love of poker." Justin took two steps forward, lifting his hand to cover his heart. "Marry me because you make me feel like I'm good enough for the first time in my life. Marry me because you make me want to be a better person. Marry me and let me love you. Marry me and be my family and I swear I will always be yours."

Sarina closed her eyes, trying to erase the echo of his words in her brain and the bubbling joy running though her veins. She just needed to go. She needed to grab Wilma and get on her bike and keep moving until she was free again.

"Justin," she said, opening her eyes and looking at him head-on. She cringed at the wobble in her voice, clearing her throat quickly in an attempt to cover up just how hard this was for her. She loved him. She just couldn't stay. "I have to go. You know that."

"You want to keep running, Sarina?" Justin asked, his eyes searching her face.

Okay. Truth time. "I don't know how to stop, Justin. If I stop…"

She searched for the words to explain the panic and fear that washed over her. Justin closed the distance between them completely, raising his hands to cup her face. His eyes were focused on hers and then he smiled. That ridiculously wolfish grin that lit up his whole face and made her feel like she was the center of his world. That grin promised excitement and joy and laughter and acceptance.

Justin saw her. Fears and all. Prickly defense mechanisms and all. Scars and all.

"Sarina, baby, I'm not asking you to stop running. I'm just asking that you run to me." He leaned in and brushed a kiss across her mouth. "I love you, Sarina. Run to me. I promise you I'll always be here."

Sarina reached for him, her arms wrapping around his waist as she leaned up into his kiss. Justin hesitated for the briefest moment and then he slanted his mouth over hers, deepening the kiss with a groan. His hands slid from her face into her hair and the tug to give him better access was possessive and hot. Justin tasted like sin and safety, danger and homecoming.

He was her home. She'd found it in his arms and she'd never let him go.

Justin broke off the kiss and smiled at her as he released her. She protested the separation but her frustration turned to confusion as he dug around in his pocket, withdrew a small box and then dropped to one knee at her feet. Around them the crowd stirred into a wave of murmurs and gasps of surprise, and more than one cell phone was lifted and pointed in their direction. Sarina didn't care; she was laser-focused on Justin.

And he was focused on her.

"We didn't get to do this the traditional way the first time. I won't say that we did it wrong because it brought us together. So it was perfect. But I want to leave no doubt in anyone's mind that you are the one that I choose and the one I love." Justin opened the box and removed the ring, a square-cut sapphire surrounded by diamonds, reached out and took her hand and placed it on her finger. It was heavy but in all the best ways possible. "Sarina Redhawk, will you marry me?"

She was scared, terrified. But for the first time in her life she was more afraid of letting someone go without a fight. One word was all that was needed to take the leap and have a shot at the dreams she'd given up on a long time ago. This man was worth the risk. His love was worth the risk.

"Yes."

"Thank you." Justin rose to his feet and pulled her back in his arms, the kiss passionate and filled with laughter. He nodded at the crowd surrounding them, waving to those who held their phones up to film the proposal. Wilma barked and jumped around at their feet, wagging her tail in excitement. "I love you, Sarina Redhawk."

"It's Sarina Redhawk *Ling*," she answered, pressing a kiss to his lips. "I love you, too."

"Let's go home," Justin said, holding her hand as they navigated the crowd on the Skywalk. It was slow going, with everyone congratulating them and bending over to pet Wilma. "Fair warning. Nana Orla wants a wedding. She said that we couldn't come home if we didn't agree to have another wedding."

Sarina laughed, looking forward to a life with Justin. It would never be boring. "I can do a wedding. But not in Vegas. This time we do it right."

Epilogue

One month later

He'd marry her a million times over. Anywhere she wanted.

Sarina had looked beyond stunning when she'd walked down the aisle toward him just a few hours earlier. Wearing a white jumpsuit with full legs, a halter-style top with a plunging neckline, and a transparent, filmy train attached to the waist, she was the most beautiful woman he'd ever seen. He couldn't say that she was breathtaking because his every inhale and exhale, every heartbeat—they were for Sarina. Hell, the reason he got up every morning and hurried home each night was because of her. His wife.

Nana Orla had taken over the planning of the wedding, running everyone and everything in her orbit with a precision that rivaled the military. Now Adam wanted to hire her to head up their project management division at Redhawk/Ling. Justin was all for it if it would stop her from making a plea for another great-grandchild at every opportunity. He wanted a family with Sarina, wanted to build with her a life where their children knew they were loved and were always enough. But they had time. A lifetime together to make those dreams come true.

And today they were surrounded by two hundred of their friends and family, on the grounds of his family home.

"Nana Orla sure knows how to throw a party. This is amazing," Adam said, easing up beside him and handing him a beer. It was pretty epic and the hottest invitation of the year. Justin's only requirement was that the wedding not be held in a stuffy hotel, so their two hundred guests were gathered under several tents, with the entire lawn and pool area covered in white roses and lilies. The best catering in Silicon Valley and a live band at the reception ensured that everybody on the guest list was having a good time. Socialites and business colleagues mixed and mingled with a few of the kids from the Rise Up Center and some of Sarina's army buddies. Even Wilma was dressed to the doggy nines in a Chihuahua-sized tux jacket and rhinestone collar.

Roan eased up next to the two of them, saluting them both with his drink. "I need to hire Nana Orla to handle my next gallery show. She's incredible."

"We couldn't have done this without her. And I was determined to make it official again with your sister as soon as I could." Justin turned and tapped his beer bottle against the one held by both his best friend and brother-in-law. They were family now. For real. "Thanks for pulling double duty today, brother."

"You bet," Adam laughed, wearing the light gray linen suit Justin had chosen for the wedding. "How many times has the best man also given away the bride?"

"It meant a lot to Sarina that you two were here to walk her down the aisle," Justin shared, knowing that it was a significant step for the Redhawk family to take together. Everything wasn't settled between them but they were all trying to replace the hard memories and the loss with new ones of love, and fun, and being together. Justin threw an arm around Adam's shoulders. "The next big event will be when your son makes an appearance. I can't believe you're going to be a daddy."

"I know, man. But I'm ready." Adam flashed the smile of a man who was happy and content as he looked over at where the bride stood with Tess. She was radiant in a gray silk dress, cut to highlight her pregnant belly. Sarina had been anxious to have Tess stand up with her at the wedding, given that there were just a few weeks left before her due date. All in all, it had been a family affair. "Are you two ready to be godfathers?"

Justin snorted out a laugh and shook his head, humbled by the request. "I hope you know that Sarina is the adult in this equation. I'm on tap to take him to get his first tattoo and pick up girls."

"Or boys," Roan added, winking at the two of them. "Why should he have to choose?"

"Truer words have never been spoken," Justin agreed, and Adam nodded his head in assent.

"I have to go to Washington, DC, next week but I'll be back in time to meet the newest Redhawk," Roan said, his smile definitely the one worn by the cat that ate the canary. "I've been summoned to the White House by President Irons to paint the official portrait of his daughter."

"Whoa. That's huge, little brother," Adam crowed, drawing the attention of several nearby guests. "How did you score that job?"

"How did you ever get cleared by the Secret Service?" Justin asked, acknowledging the raised middle finger of his brother-in-law with the salute of his beer bottle.

"President Irons is the first Native American president and he's determined to represent," Roan explained, flashing a shit-eating grin that made them all laugh. "*And* he picked the best of the bunch."

"And that's you?" Justin teased, unable to resist.

"Yeah, that's me," Roan answered, giving them both a big wink.

"Well done, Roan." Justin placed his beer bottle on a nearby table and patted both of the men on the back. "Gentlemen, I'm going to dance with my wife."

He waved off their teasing farewells, making a short detour to the band and putting in a request before sauntering over to where Sarina chatted with Nana Orla and Tess. He eased up behind her and looped his right arm around her waist, placing a kiss on the soft skin of her shoulder. She leaned back into him, her fingers linking with his as they molded their bodies together. It was like he could only take a full breath when he was with her, like he only stood as a complete man when she was by his side. How had he thought he was living all those years before Sarina?

"Nana Orla, can I steal my wife for a dance?" he

asked, smiling down at the woman who'd given a home to Sarina when she needed it the most. If he hadn't already loved his grandmother beyond reason, that would have sealed the deal.

Orla nodded, smiling at both of them as she reached up and placed a hand on his cheek. "Of course, my love. Go and dance with your best girl."

He shook his head. "Sarina and I agreed—she's the love of my life but *you'll* always be my best girl."

"Flatterer."

"It's not flattery if it's true." He pressed a kiss to her cheek and reached a hand out to his wife, still in awe that she was really his. "Sarina, dance with me?"

She smiled, an expression that lit up her entire face and made her dark eyes shine like onyx. Her raven-black hair was pulled back in a sleek ponytail, diamond earrings sparkling in her ears. A gift from his parents, they were a peace offering. It wasn't a perfect fix but it was a start.

"Forever," she murmured, stepping into his arms as the band started the slow-dance version of "Just One Look." The recognition of the song fueled joy on her face. They'd collaborated on a playlist but he'd secretly added all of her favorite Linda Ronstadt songs as a surprise. "Thank you for this."

"I wanted your mom—both of your parents—to be here with you today." Justin leaned in to press a kiss to the end of her nose, pretending not to see the sheen of tears in her eyes. "I know you wish they could be here."

"They're here, Justin," Sarina said, conviction in her voice. "I've felt them with me all day. How could they not be here when I'm so happy?"

"I promise you that I will spend the rest of my life

making sure you're this happy every day," Justin said, soaking in her smile. "I love you, Sarina."

"I love you too, Justin." Sarina kissed him, long and sweet, the smile on her mouth a promise of forever. "Thank you for loving me, for being my family."

* * * * *

WED FOR THE SPANIARD'S REDEMPTION

CHANTELLE SHAW

For Adrian,

being a writer's husband is no easy job!

love you

CHAPTER ONE

*Spanish Stud's Sex Romp with
Cabinet Minister's Wife!*

RAFAEL MENDOZA-CASILLAS SCOWLED as he sifted through the pile of newspapers on his desk. All the tabloids bore similar headlines, and even the broadsheets had deemed that it was in the public interest to report his affair with Michelle Urquhart.

The story wasn't only in the UK. All across Europe people were eating their breakfast while studying a front-page photograph of the heir to Spain's biggest retail company entering a top London hotel late at night accompanied by the voluptuous Mrs Urquhart. A second photo showed him and Michelle leaving the hotel by a back door the next morning.

One can only speculate on how Europe's most prolific playboy and the Minister's wife spent the intervening hours!

That was one journalist, writing in a particularly tacky tabloid.

'It is one scandal too many, Rafael.'

Hector Casillas's strident voice shook with anger and Rafael held his phone away from his ear.

'On the very day that the company's top-selling Rozita fashion line launches a new bridal collection *your* affair with a married woman is headline news. You have made the Casillas Group a laughing stock.'

'I was not aware that Michelle is married,' Rafael said laconically when his grandfather paused to draw a breath.

Not that her marital status interested him particularly. He was not responsible for other people's morals—especially as his own morality was questionable. But if he'd known that Michelle's husband was a public figure he would not have slept with her. Even though she had made it clear that she was available within minutes of him meeting her in a nightclub. Rafael never had a problem finding women to occupy his bed and, frankly, Michelle had not been worth this fallout.

He leaned back in his chair and watched the rain lash the windows of his office at the Casillas Group's UK headquarters in London's Canary Wharf. The Casillas Group was one of the world's largest clothing retailers, and as well as Rozita the company owned several other top fashion brands.

Rafael visualised his grandfather sitting behind his desk in the study of the opulent Casillas family mansion in Valencia. There had been many occasions in the past when he had been summoned to that study so that Hector could lecture him on his failings and remind him—as if Rafael needed to be reminded—that he was part *gitano*. The English word for *gitano* was gypsy, and in other areas of Europe the term was *Roma*. But the meaning was the same—Rafael was an outsider.

'Yet again you have brought shame on the family

and, even worse, on the company,' Hector said coldly. 'Your mother warned me that you had inherited many of your father's faults. When I rescued you from the slums and brought you into the family I intended that you would succeed me as head of the Casillas Group. You are my grandson, after all. But sadly there is too much of your father's blood in you, and tacking Casillas on to your name does not change who you are.'

Rafael's jaw clenched and he told himself he should have expected this dig. His grandfather never missed an opportunity to remind him that he did not have the blue blood of Spanish nobility running through his veins. His father had been a low-life drug dealer, and his mother's relationship with him, a rebellion against the Casillas family's centuries-old aristocratic heritage, had ended when she'd fled from Ivan Mendoza, leaving behind Rafael and his baby sister in a notorious slum on the outskirts of Madrid.

'The situation cannot continue. I have decided that you must marry—and quickly.'

For a moment Rafael assumed that he had misheard Hector. 'Abuelo...' he said in a placating tone.

'The board want me to name Francisco as my successor.'

A lead weight dropped into the pit of Rafael's stomach. 'You would put a *boy* in charge? The Casillas Group is a global company with a multi-billion-dollar annual turnover. Frankie would be out of his depth.'

'Your half-brother is twenty and in a year he will finish studying at university. More importantly he keeps his pants on.'

Bile burned a bitter path down Rafael's throat. 'Has my mother put you up to this? She has never made it a secret that she thinks her second son is a true Casillas and should be the heir to the company.'

'No one has put me up to anything. I make my own decisions,' Hector snapped. 'But I share the concerns of the board members and the shareholders that your notoriety and frequent appearances in the gutter press do not reflect well on the company. Our CEO should be a man of high principles and an advocate of family values. I am prepared to give you one more chance, Rafael. Bring your wife to my eightieth birthday celebrations at the beginning of May and I will retire from my position as Chairman and CEO and appoint you as my successor.'

'I have no desire to marry,' Rafael gritted, barely able to control his anger.

'In that case I will appoint your half-brother as my heir on my eightieth birthday.'

'*Dios!* Your birthday is six weeks from now. It will be impossible for me to find a bride and marry her in such a short time.'

'Nothing is impossible,' Hector said smoothly. 'Over the last eighteen months you have been introduced to several high-born Spanish women and any one of them would be a suitable wife for you. If you want to be my heir badly enough you will present your bride to me and we will have a double celebration to mark my landmark birthday and your marriage.'

Hector ended the call and Rafael swore as he threw his phone down on the desk. The old man was crazy. It was tempting to think his grandfather had lost his marbles, but Rafael knew that Hector Casillas was a shrewd businessman. The CEO-ship had been passed down to the next generation's firstborn male since Rafael's great-great-great-grandfather had established the company, one hundred and fifty years ago.

Hector Casillas's only offspring had been a daughter so Rafael, the oldest grandson, was next in line. But he knew that many on the board of directors and many of his relatives were not in favour of an outsider—which was how they regarded him—being handed the reins of power.

Hector's words taunted him. *'If you want to be my heir badly enough...'* Rafael bared his teeth in a mirthless smile. Becoming CEO of the company was the *only* thing he wanted. Being named as his grandfather's successor had been his dream, his obsession, since he was a skinny twelve-year-old kid who had been taken from poverty into the unimaginably wealthy lifestyle of his aristocratic family.

He was determined to prove that he was worthy of the role to his detractors, of whom there were many—including his mother and her second husband. Alberto Casillas was his mother Delfina's second cousin, which meant that their son Francisco was a Casillas to his core. Like that of many aristocratic families, the Casillas gene pool was very exclusive, and the majority of Rafael's relatives wanted it to stay that way.

But the retail industry was going through big changes, with increasing focus on internet sales, and Rafael understood better than most of the board members that the Casillas Group must use innovation and new technology so that it could continue to be a market leader. His grandfather had been a great CEO but now new blood was needed.

But not a gitano's blood, taunted a voice inside him. Once he had begged for food like a stray dog on the filthy streets of a slum. And, like a dog, he had learned to run fast to avoid his father's fists.

Rafael shut off the dark memories of his childhood and turned his thoughts to the potential brides his grandfather had mentioned. He'd guessed there must be an ulterior motive when his mother had invited the daughters of various elite Spanish families to dinner parties and insisted that Rafael should attend. But he hadn't taken the bait which had been dangled in front of him and he had no intention of doing so—despite Hector's ultimatum.

He would have to marry, but he would choose his own bride. And it would *not* be a love match, he thought cynically.

A psychologist would probably suggest that Rafael's trust issues and avoidance of commitment stemmed from his being abandoned by his mother when he was seven. The truth was that he could forgive her for deserting *him*, but not for leaving his sister, who had been a baby of not even two years old. Sofia's distress had been harder for him to bear than his father's indifference, or the sting of Ivan Mendoza's belt across the back of Rafael's legs.

His determination to gain acceptance by the Casillas family was as much for his sister as for himself. He *would* be CEO and he was prepared to offer a financial incentive to any woman who would agree to be his temporary wife.

Once he had achieved his goal there would be no reason to continue with his unwanted marriage, Rafael brooded as he grabbed his briefcase and car keys and strode out of his office.

His PA looked up when he stopped by her desk. 'I'm going to my ten o'clock meeting and I should be back around lunchtime,' he told her. 'If my grandfather calls again tell him that I am unavailable for the rest of the day.' He paused on his way out of the door. 'Oh, and, Philippa—get rid of those damned newspapers from my office.'

The day couldn't get any worse, surely?

Juliet chucked her phone onto the passenger seat of the van and slid the key into the ignition. She wouldn't cry, she told herself. After she had lost her parents in the car accident which had also ended her dancing career she'd decided that nothing could ever be so terrible that it would warrant her tears.

But today had started disastrously, when she'd read a letter from an Australian law firm informing her that Bryan intended to seek custody of Poppy. A knot of fear tightened in her stomach. She couldn't lose her daughter. Poppy was her reason for living, and even though her life as a single mum was a struggle she would fight with the last breath in her body to keep her little girl rather than hand her over to her father, who had never shown any interest in her until now.

A phone conversation with her business partner Mel a few minutes ago had been the final straw on this day from hell. *Her life was falling apart!*

Juliet watched the rain streaming down the windscreen and blinked back her tears. There was no point sitting here in the car park behind the Casillas Group's plush offices in Canary Wharf. She still had sandwich deliveries to make to other offices in the area. Her business, Lunch To Go, might be facing ruin, but her customers had paid for their sandwiches and wraps and they were expecting her to turn up.

She sniffed as she started the engine and pulled her

seat belt across her lap before putting the van into gear and pressing her foot down on the accelerator pedal. But instead of moving forward the van lurched backwards, and there was a loud bang followed by the tinkling sound of broken glass.

For a split second Juliet couldn't think what had happened. But when she looked in her rear-view mirror it was obvious that she had reversed into the car which had swung into the parking bay behind her.

And not just any car, she realised with mounting horror. The sleek gunmetal-grey Lamborghini was one of the most expensive cars in production—so Danny, the parking attendant who allowed her to park her van in this car park, which was reserved exclusively for Casillas Group executives, had told her.

The day had just got a whole lot worse.

She watched the owner of the Lamborghini climb out of his car and stoop down to inspect the front bumper. Rafael Mendoza-Casillas: managing director of the Casillas Group UK, international playboy and sex god—if the stories about his love-life which regularly appeared in a certain type of newspaper were to be believed.

Juliet's heart collided with her ribs when he straightened up and strode towards her van. The thunderous expression on his handsome face galvanised her into action and she released her seat belt and opened the driver's door. God, she hoped the damage to his car wasn't too bad or too expensive to repair. A claim on her vehicle insurance would bump up her premium next year.

'*Idiota!* Why did you try to reverse out of your parking space? If you'd had the sense to use your mirror you would have seen that I had parked behind you.'

His gravelly voice with its distinct Mediterranean

accent was clipped with anger. But it was the sexiest voice Juliet had ever heard and her skin prickled with awareness of the man who towered over her.

She was five feet four—the minimum height for dancers in the *corps de ballet*—and she had to tilt her head so that she could look at him. His eyes were an unusual olive-green, glinting furiously in his tanned face. And what a face. Juliet had caught sight of him occasionally at the Casillas Group offices, when she'd been delivering sandwiches, but he hadn't so much as glanced at her whenever she'd walked past him in a corridor. One time she'd entered the lift as he had stepped out of it and the sleeve of his jacket had brushed against her arm. The spicy scent of his aftershave had stayed with her for the rest of the day, and now her stomach muscles contracted when she inhaled his exotic fragrance.

'I'm not an idiot,' she muttered, stung by his superior tone and dismayed by her unbidden reaction to his potent masculinity.

The torrential rain was flattening his thick black hair to his skull, but nothing could detract from his film star looks. With chiselled features, razor-edged cheekbones and a square jaw shaded with dark stubble, he was utterly gorgeous. Beneath her apron, which was part of her uniform, Juliet felt her nipples tighten.

Heavy black brows winged upwards, as if he was surprised that she had answered him back. 'The evidence suggests otherwise,' he drawled. 'I hope your vehicle insurance will cover you for an accident on private land. This car park has a notice which clearly states that it is for the Casillas Group's senior staff's use only. You are trespassing, and if your insurance is not valid you can look forward to receiving a hefty repair bill for the damage you have caused to my car.'

Of course she would be covered by her insurance—wouldn't she? Doubt crept into Juliet's mind and her shoulders sagged. 'I'm sorry. It was an accident, as you said. I didn't mean to reverse into your car.' Panic swept through her. 'I don't have the money to pay for your repairs.'

The rain had soaked through her shirt and was dripping off her peaked cap. She remembered how excited she and Mel had been when they had ordered the red caps and aprons with their company logo on. They'd had such high hopes for their sandwich business when they'd started up a year ago, but the two bombshells Juliet had received today made it likely that now Lunch To Go would fold.

To make matters even worse, the most handsome man she'd ever set eyes on was now glaring at her as if she was something unpleasant that he'd scraped off the bottom of his shoe.

Misery welled up inside her and the tears that she'd managed to hold back until now ran down her cheeks, mingling with the rain. 'The truth is that I don't even have enough money to buy my daughter a new pair of shoes,' she said in a choked voice.

She'd felt so guilty when Poppy had said yesterday that her shoes made her toes hurt. And now there was a pain in Juliet's chest as if the oxygen was being squeezed out of her lungs. She couldn't breathe. She felt as if a dam inside her had burst, releasing the emotions she had held back for so long.

'I certainly can't afford to pay for work on your fancy car. What will happen if my insurance company refuses to pay for the damage? I can't take out a bank loan because I already have debts...'

Her logical thought processes had given way to near

hysteria. Ever since her parents had been killed in that horrific accident she had subconsciously been waiting for another disaster.

'Could I be sent to prison? Who would look after my daughter? If I'm deemed to be a bad mother Bryan will be allowed to take Poppy to Australia and I'll hardly ever see her.'

It was Juliet's worst fear and she covered her face with her hands and wept.

'Calm yourself,' Rafael Mendoza-Casillas commanded. 'Of course you won't go to prison,' he said impatiently as her shoulders shook with the force of her sobs. 'I am sure your insurance will cover the cost of the repairs to my car, and if it doesn't I will not demand money from you.'

Juliet's relief at his assurance was temporary. Her other problems still seemed insurmountable and she couldn't stop crying.

Rafael swore. 'We need to get out of this rain before we drown,' he muttered as he took hold of her arm and led her towards his car. He opened the passenger door. 'Get in and take a few minutes to bring yourself under control.' Moments later he slid into the driver's seat and raked a hand through his wet hair. He opened the glove box and thrust some tissues into her lap. 'Here. Dry your tears.'

'Thank you.' She mopped her eyes and took a deep breath. In the confines of the car she was conscious of his closeness. She smelled rain, and the cologne he wore. Another indefinable scent which was uniquely male teased her senses.

'I'm making your car wet,' she mumbled when she was able to speak. She was conscious that her rain-soaked clothes were dripping onto the car's cream leather upholstery. 'I really am sorry about damaging your car, Mr Mendoza-Casillas.'

'You can call me Rafael. My surname is a mouthful, don't you think?' There was an oddly bitter note in his voice. 'What is your name?'

'Juliet Lacey.' She supposed he needed to know her name and other details for the insurance claim.

Her eyes were drawn to his hard-boned profile and a sizzle of heat ran through her, counteracting the cold that was seeping into her skin from her wet clothes. He glanced at her and she quickly looked away from him. She could not bear to think what she must look like, wet and bedraggled, with her face blotchy and her eyes red-rimmed from crying.

'I apologise for losing my temper. I did not mean to frighten or upset you,' he said curtly. 'You said that you have a child?'

'Yes, a three-year-old daughter.'

'*Dios*, you can only be—what?—nineteen?—and you have a three-year-old?' He sounded faintly appalled. 'I assume that as you are not wearing a wedding ring you're not married.'

'I'm twenty-four,' she corrected him stiffly, 'and, no, I'm not married. Poppy's father didn't want anything to do with either of us when she was born.'

'Who is this Bryan you mentioned?'

'He's Poppy's father. He has now decided that he wants custody of her. Under Australian law both parents are responsible for their child, even if they have never married or been a couple. Bryan can afford the best lawyers and if he wins the court case he intends to take Poppy to live in Australia with him.'

More tears filled Juliet's eyes and she scrubbed them away with a tissue.

'It's so unfair,' she blurted out. 'Bryan saw Poppy once when she was a baby. He told me he might have been more interested if she'd been a boy. But it's my word against his that he rejected his daughter. His lawyers are twisting everything to make it seem as though I refused to allow him to see his child. But I only brought Poppy back to England because Bryan insisted he wanted nothing to do with her.'

Juliet had no idea why she was confiding in Rafael when she didn't know him, and she was sure he wouldn't be interested in her problems. But there was something strangely reassuring about his size and obvious strength, the air of power that surrounded him. Words had tumbled from her lips before she could stop them.

'I've heard through my cousin, who lives in Sydney, that Bryan is dating the daughter of a billionaire and he wants to marry her. Apparently his girlfriend can't have children of her own because of a medical condition, but she desperately wants a child. My guess is that Bryan hopes to persuade his heiress to marry him if he can present her with a cute little daughter.'

Juliet bit her lip. 'Eighteen months ago Poppy spent a few weeks in temporary foster care when I had to go into hospital. She was very happy staying with the lovely family who looked after her. But somehow Bryan has found out that Poppy was fostered and he's using it as proof that I can't give her a secure upbringing and she'll be better off living with him.'

'Couldn't someone in your family have looked after your daughter while you were in hospital?'

The anger had gone from Rafael's voice and the sexy huskiness of his accent sent a little tremor through Juliet.

'My parents are dead and my only other relatives live in Australia. My aunt and uncle were kind to me when I stayed with them after my parents died, but they have busy lives and I try to manage on my own.'

'Why are you short of money?' Rafael turned his head towards her and Juliet felt his gaze sweep over her cap and apron. 'I take it that you have a job? What do the initials LTG stand for?'

'Lunch To Go is my sandwich business, which I co-own with my business partner. We've only been running for a year and our profit margins have been low while we have been getting established.' She gave another sniff and crumpled the soggy tissue in her hand. 'Things are finally looking up. But today I was called in by your HR manager and told that the contract we have to supply sandwiches to the Casillas Group's staff will finish at the end of the week because a new staff canteen is to open.'

Rafael nodded. 'When I established the London headquarters of the company it was always my plan to open a restaurant and a gym in the basement of the building for staff to use in their lunch break. The construction work took longer than anticipated and I asked HR to make a temporary alternative arrangement for staff to be able to buy their lunch from an outside source but still be subsidised by the company.'

'I didn't know about the staff restaurant,' Juliet said dully.

She'd never been down to the basement level—although she had overheard a couple of secretaries talking about the new staff gym. Her contract with the Casillas Group only required her to be given a week's notice.

'Will losing the contract have an impact on your business?'

'It will halve our profits,' she admitted heavily. 'I thought we could advertise for new customers at other offices—although a number of other food delivery companies have started up in this area, and the competition is high. And then I spoke to my business partner after my meeting and Mel told me she's going to sell the bakery shop where we're based. Her decision is for personal reasons—she and her husband want to move out of London. Mel owns the shop, and I can't afford to buy it or rent a new premises.'

'If your business closes what will you do?'

She shrugged. 'I'll have to look for another job, but I don't have any qualifications, or training in a career, and it will be almost impossible to earn enough to cover childcare for Poppy.'

Juliet thought of the home study business degree she had started but had had to abandon because she hadn't been able to afford the fees for the second year. That degree would have enabled her to find a better-paid job, or at least given her knowledge of the business strategies which would have been useful to develop Lunch To Go. But without Mel she simply could not manage, either financially or practically, to run the sandwich business.

Rafael was drumming his fingers on the steering wheel and seemed to be deep in thought. He had beautiful hands. Juliet imagined his tanned hands sliding over her naked body, those long fingers curving around her breasts and caressing the sensitive peaks of her nipples. Heat swept through her and she was startled by her wayward thoughts.

Bryan had broken her heart when he'd dumped her the morning after she'd given her virginity to him. A month later, when she'd tearfully told him that she was pregnant with his baby, his cruel rejection of her and her unborn child had forced her to grow up fast. She had felt a fool for falling for his easy charm and had vowed never to be so trusting again.

Being a single mother had left her little time to meet men, and it was a shock to discover that she could still feel sexual awareness and desire. Perhaps she was attracted to Rafael because he was so far out of her league that there was no chance that anything would come of it—a bit like a teenager with a crush on a pop star they were never likely to meet in real life, Juliet thought ruefully.

'I may be able to help you,' Rafael said, jolting her out of her reverie.

Her heart leapt. If he agreed to allow her to continue selling sandwiches to his office staff her business might just survive.

'Help me how?'

'I have an idea that would resolve your financial worries and also be advantageous to me.'

Juliet stiffened. 'What do you mean by "advantageous"?'

Was he suggesting what she thought he was? She knew that some of the women on the housing estate where she lived worked as prostitutes. Most of them were single mothers like her, struggling to feed their children on minimum wages. She didn't judge them, but it wasn't something she could ever imagine doing herself.

She put her hand on the door handle, ready to jump out of the car. 'I won't have sex with you for money,' she said bluntly.

For a few seconds he looked stunned—and then he laughed. The rich sound filled the car and made Juliet think of golden sunshine. She felt as if it had been rain-ing in her heart since her parents had died and she'd been left alone. How wonderful it would be to have someone to laugh with, be happy with.

With a jolt she realised that Rafael was speaking.

'I don't want to have sex with you.'

His slight emphasis on the word *you* made Juliet squirm with embarrassment, which intensified when he skimmed his gaze over her. His dismissive expression said quite clearly that he found her unattractive.

'I have never had to pay for sex with any woman,' he drawled. 'What I am suggesting is a business proposition—albeit an unusual one.'

'I make sandwiches for a living,' she said flatly, wishing the ground would open up and swallow her. 'I can't think what kind of business we could do together.'

'I want you to be my wife. If you agree to marry me I will pay you five million pounds.'

CHAPTER TWO

'Very funny,' Juliet muttered, disappointment thickening her voice. 'I'm not in the mood for jokes, Mr Mendoza-Casillas.'

'Rafael,' he corrected her. 'And it's not a joke. I need a wife. A temporary wife—in name only,' he added, evidently reading the crucial question that had leapt into her mind. He stared at her broodingly. 'You have admitted that being a single parent is a financial burden. What if, instead of struggling, you could live a comfortable life with your daughter without having to work?'

'Some hope,' she said ruefully. 'I'd have to win the lottery to be able to do that.'

'Consider me your winning ticket, *chiquita*.'

His sudden smile softened his chiselled features and stole Juliet's breath. When he smiled he went from handsome to impossibly gorgeous. He reminded her of the male models on those TV adverts for expensive aftershaves—only Rafael was much more rugged and masculine.

She tore her eyes from him, conscious that her heart was beating at twice its normal rate. 'You're crazy,' she told him flatly.

And so was she, to be still sitting in his car. Five million pounds! He couldn't be serious. Or if he was serious there must be a catch. She felt hot, remembering his amused reaction to her suggestion that he was offering to pay her for sex. God, what had made her say that? Many of today's newspapers had a photo on the front page of Rafael and a beautiful blonde woman with an eye-catching cleavage. Juliet glanced down at her shapeless figure. She looked like a stick insect compared to Rafael's latest love interest.

'If you need a wife why don't you marry your girlfriend, whose picture is all over the front pages of the papers?'

'For one thing, Michelle is already married—but even if she were free to marry me she would not be suitable. All of my lovers, past and current, would expect me to fall in love with them,' he said drily.

He was so arrogant! She wanted to come back with a clever comment but she was mesmerised by the perfect symmetry of his angular features, which were softened a little by his blatantly sensual mouth.

'But you're not worried that *I* might fall in love with you?' She'd intended to sound sarcastic, but instead her voice was annoyingly breathless.

'I don't recommend that you do,' he said in a hard voice. 'I do not believe in love,—or marriage, for that matter. I'm not crazy,' he insisted. 'I have a genuine reason for needing to be married.'

He swore when his phone rang, and then took his mobile out of his jacket pocket and cut the call.

'We can't talk now. I'll meet you this evening and we can discuss my proposition.'

She shook her head. 'I'm not interested.'

'Not interested in earning yourself five million pounds for being my wife for a couple of months?' He reached across her and put his hand over hers to prevent her from opening the car door. 'At least give me a chance to explain, and then you can make up your mind whether I'm crazy or not. Although, frankly, you would be foolish to miss out on the chance to earn a life-changing amount of money. Think what you could do with five million pounds. You would never have to worry about the cost of buying your little girl a pair of shoes ever again.'

'All right.' Juliet released a shaky breath. He was relentlessly persuasive. She couldn't think properly when his face was so close to hers that as he leaned across her body she was able to count his thick black eyelashes. 'I'll meet you to discuss your proposition, but I'm not saying that I'll agree to it.'

She pressed herself into the leather seat, hoping he would not notice the pulse at the base of her throat that she could feel thudding erratically. It would add to her humiliation if he guessed that she was attracted to him—especially as he quite obviously did not feel the same way about her.

'It will have to be after nine,' she told him. 'I work the evening shift as a cleaner at a shopping centre close to where I live.'

Juliet felt a mixture of relief and disappointment when Rafael straightened up and moved away from her.

He handed her a business card. 'Here is my phone number. Text me your address and I'll collect you from your home at nine-fifteen.' He frowned. 'What about your daughter? Does someone look after her while you are at work in the evenings?'

'Of course I have childcare for Poppy. I certainly wouldn't leave her on her own,' she said indignantly, stung by his implication that she might be an irresponsible mother.

It was the accusation that Bryan's lawyer had levelled against her, and remembering the custody battle she was facing over her daughter evoked a heavy sense of dread in the pit of her stomach.

Five million pounds would enable her to hire her own top lawyer to fight Bryan's claim on Poppy, Juliet thought as she climbed out of Rafael's car and ran through the rain back to her van. But she would be nuts even to consider the idea.

Rafael parked his Lamborghini outside a grim-looking tower block and his conviction that it had been a mistake to suggest to a woman he had never met before today that she should marry him grew stronger. He visualised Juliet Lacey, who had resembled a drowned rat when he'd shoved her into his car out of the rain. Her voluminous apron had covered her figure, but from what he'd been able to see she was skinny rather than curvaceous. Her face had been mostly hidden behind by the peak of a baseball cap that was surely the most unfeminine and unflattering headwear.

In Rafael's opinion women should be elegant, decorative and sexy, but the waif-like sandwich-seller failed on all counts. His fury that she had damaged his beloved Lamborghini had turned to impatience when she'd burst into tears. He was well aware of how easily women could turn on the waterworks when it suited them. But as he'd watched Juliet literally fall apart in front of him he'd felt a flicker of sympathy.

He had heard a woman sob brokenly only once before, in the slum where he had spent the first twelve years of his life. Maria Gonzales had been a neighbour, a kind woman who had often given food to him and his sister. But Maria's teenage son had been drawn into one of the many drug gangs who'd operated in the slum and Pedro had been stabbed in a fight. Rafael had never forgotten the sound of Maria's raw grief as she'd wept over the body of her boy.

When Juliet had told him of her financial problems and her fear that she might lose custody of her young daughter the idea had formed in his mind that she would make him an ideal wife. The money he was prepared to pay her would change her life, and more importantly she would have no expectations that their marriage would be anything other than a business deal.

Maybe he *was* crazy, Rafael thought as he climbed out of his car and glanced around the notoriously rough housing estate—a concrete jungle where the walls were covered in graffiti. A gang of surly-looking youths were staring at his car, and they watched him suspiciously when he walked past them on his way into the tower block. He guessed that the older male in the group, who was wearing a thick gold chain around his neck, was a drug dealer.

Rafael had grown up in a shanty town on the outskirts of Madrid, where dire poverty was a breeding ground for crime and lawless gangs ruled the street. His father had been involved in the criminal underworld, and as a boy Rafael had seen things that no child should see.

His jaw tightened as he took the lift up to the eleventh floor and strode along a poorly lit walkway strewn with litter. The tower block was not a slum but a sense of poverty and deprivation pervaded the air, as well as a pungent smell of urine. It was not a good place to bring up a child.

Juliet and her young daughter were not his responsibility, he reminded himself. But it was hard to see how she would turn down five million pounds and the chance to move away from this dump.

He knocked on the door of her flat and it opened almost immediately. Rafael guessed from the unbecoming nylon overall Juliet was wearing that she must have returned from her cleaning job only minutes before he'd arrived. Without the baseball cap hiding her face he saw that she had delicate features, and might even have been reasonably pretty if she hadn't been so pale and drawn. Her hair was a nondescript brownish colour, scraped back from her face and tied in a long braid. Only her light blue eyes, the colour of the sky on an English spring day, were at all remarkable. But the dark shadows beneath them emphasised her waif-like appearance.

A suspicion slid into Rafael's mind, and when Juliet took off her overall to reveal a baggy grey T-shirt that looked fit for the rag bag he studied her arms. There were none of the tell-tale track marks associated with drug addiction.

He flicked his gaze over cheap, badly fitting jeans tucked into scuffed black boots and thought of glamorous Camila Martinez, the daughter of the Duque de Feria and his grandfather's favoured contender to be Rafael's bride.

The difference between aristocratic Camila, who could trace her family's noble lineage back centuries, and Juliet, who looked as if she had stepped from the pages of *Oliver Twist*, was painfully obvious. It would show his grandfather that he was not a puppet willing to dance to the old man's tune if he turned up at Hector's birthday party and announced that he had married this drab sparrow instead of a golden peacock,

Rafael mused, feeling a flicker of amusement as the scene played out in his imagination.

'I told you to call me when you arrived and I would meet you outside the flats,' Juliet greeted him. 'If you've left your car on the estate there's a good chance it will be vandalised. There's a big problem with gangs around here.'

Rafael shuddered inwardly at the thought of his Lamborghini being damaged. 'This area is not a safe place for you to be out alone at night,' he said gruffly, thinking that she must have to walk through the estate in the dark every evening when she'd finished her cleaning shift.

He looked along the narrow hallway as a door opened and a small child darted out.

'Mummy, where are you going?'

The little girl had the same slight build and pale complexion as her mother. She stared at Rafael warily and he was struck by how vulnerable she was—how vulnerable they *both* were.

Juliet lifted her daughter into her arms. 'Poppy, I've told you I'm going out for a little while with a…a friend and Agata is going to look after you.'

An elderly woman emerged from the small sitting room and gave Rafael a curious look. 'Come back to bed, *kotek*. I will read to you and it will help you to fall back to sleep.' She took the child from Juliet. 'The baby will be happy with me. Go and have the nice dinner with your friend.'

'Who is looking after your daughter?' Rafael asked when Juliet followed him out of the flat and shut the front door behind her. She had pulled on a black fake leather jacket that looked as cheaply made as the rest of her outfit.

For a moment he wondered what the hell he was doing. Could he *really* marry this insipid girl who looked much younger than mid-twenties?

But her air of innocence had to be an illusion, he reminded himself, thinking of her illegitimate child. And besides, he did not care what she looked like. All he was interested in was putting a wedding ring on her finger. Once he had fulfilled his grandfather's outrageous marriage ultimatum he would be CEO of the Casillas Group. He did not anticipate that he would spend much time with his wife and would seek to end the marriage as soon as possible.

'Agata is a neighbour,' Juliet said. 'She's Polish and very kind. I couldn't do my cleaning job if she hadn't agreed to babysit every evening. Poppy doesn't have any grandparents but she loves Agata.'

'What happened to your parents?'

'They were killed in a car accident six years ago.'

Her tone was matter-of-fact, but Rafael sensed that she kept a tight hold on her emotions and her breakdown earlier in the day had been unusual.

'I believe you said that you have no other family apart from some relatives in Australia?'

She nodded. 'Aunt Vivian is my mum's sister. I stayed with her and my uncle and three cousins, but they only have a small house and it was a squeeze—especially after I had Poppy.'

So Juliet did not have any family in England who might question her sudden marriage, Rafael mused as they stepped into the lift. Once again he imagined his ultra-conservative grandfather's reaction if he introduced an unmarried mother who sold sandwiches for a living as his bride. It would teach Hector not to try to interfere in his life, Rafael thought grimly.

The lift doors opened on the ground floor and he took hold of Juliet's arm as they passed the gang of youths, who were now loitering in the entrance hall and passing a joint between them.

'Why do you live in this hellhole?' he demanded as he hurried her outside to his car. 'It can't be a good place to bring up a child.'

'I don't live here out of choice,' she said wryly. 'When Poppy was a baby we lived in a lovely little house with a garden. Kate was my mum's best friend, and the reason why I left Australia and came back to England was because she invited me and Poppy to move in with her. She was a widow, and I think she enjoyed the company. But Kate died after a short illness and her son sold the house. I only had a few weeks to find somewhere else to live. I had already started my sandwich business and needed to live in London, but I couldn't afford to rent privately. I was lucky that the local authority offered me social housing. Living on this estate isn't ideal, but it's better than being homeless.'

She ran her hand over the bonnet of the Lamborghini. 'You are a multi-millionaire—you can have no idea about the real world outside of your ivory tower.'

You think?

Inexplicably Rafael was tempted to tell her that he understood exactly what it was like to live in poverty—wondering where the next meal was coming from and struggling to survive in an often hostile environment. But there was no reason why he should explain to Juliet about his background. He dismissed the odd sense of connection he felt with her because they both knew what hardship felt like. His childhood had given him a single-minded determination to get what he wanted, and Juliet was merely a pawn in the game of wills with his grandfather.

He opened the car door and waited for her to climb inside before he walked round to the driver's side and slid behind the wheel.

'I know that five million pounds could transform your situation and allow you to provide your little girl with a safe home and a very comfortable lifestyle free from financial worries.' He gunned the Lamborghini away from the grim estate and glanced across at her. 'I'm offering you an incredible opportunity and for your daughter's sake you should give it serious consideration.'

It occurred to Juliet as she sank into the soft leather seat of the sports car that this might all be a dream and in a minute she would wake up. Things like this did not happen in real life. A stunningly handsome man offering her five million pounds to be his wife was the stuff of fantasy and fairy tales.

She darted a glance at Rafael's chiselled profile and felt a restless longing stir deep inside her. It was a long time since she had been kissed by a man, and she'd never felt such an intense awareness of one before.

Bryan had been her first and only sexual experience. She'd spent her teenage years at a boarding ballet school, and although she'd known boys, and danced with them, she had been entirely focused on her goal of becoming a prima ballerina and hadn't had time for boyfriends.

The scholarship she had been awarded had paid the school's fees, but there had been numerous other costs and her parents had scrimped and saved so that she could follow her dream. She'd always felt that she owed it to her mum and dad to succeed in her chosen career.

But the car accident which had taken her parents' lives had left Juliet with serious injuries—including a shattered thigh bone. The months she'd spent in hospital had intensified her sense of isolation and loneliness.

She had been painfully naïve when she'd met Bryan Westfield, soon after she'd moved out to Australia to stay with her aunt Vivian and uncle Carlos. She'd been looking for someone to fill the hole in her heart left by her parents' deaths, and blonde good-looking Bryan had seemed like 'the one'—until she'd realised he had only wanted sex.

'You're not the first young woman to have your heart broken and be left with a baby and you won't be the last,' Aunt Vivian had said briskly when Juliet had admitted that she was pregnant.

Her aunt had meant well but Juliet had felt stupid, as well as bitterly hurt by Bryan's rejection, and she'd vowed never to lay herself open to that level of pain again. It made her reaction to Rafael's undeniable sexual magnetism all the more confusing.

The look of distaste that had flickered over his face when she'd opened the door to him wearing her cleaning overalls had made her shrivel inside. She knew from photographs of him in gossip magazines—invariably with a blonde glamour model or actress hanging on to him—that she was as far from his ideal woman as the earth was from Mars. But his lack of interest in her made it easier to consider his proposition.

'You said I would be your wife in name only? Does that mean the marriage would not be...' she hesitated '...consummated?'

She was thankful that her scarlet cheeks were hidden

in the dark interior of the car. If he laughed she would die of mortification.

'Physical intimacy between us will not be necessary,' he said coolly.

He did not actually state that he wouldn't touch her with a barge pole but the message was clear. Juliet swallowed, feeling ashamed that the gorgeous man beside her found her repellent. They were both wearing jeans, but his were undoubtedly a designer brand, and she'd noted when he had walked around to his side of the car how the denim clung to his lean hips. His tan leather jacket looked as if it had cost the earth, while her clothes came from a discount store and her boots had seen three winters.

With a sigh, she turned her head and stared out of the window.

'We're here.'

Rafael's voice pulled Juliet from her thoughts and she discovered that he had turned the car onto the driveway in front of a large and very beautiful house.

'Where is "here"?' she asked when he switched off the engine.

'My home in England—Ferndown House. It's too dark to see now, but the house backs on to Hampstead Heath.'

Juliet looked down at the rip in her jeans. 'I suppose you don't want to be seen with me in public when I look like this,' she said flatly.

He turned his head towards her but she could not bring herself to look at him and see his disdainful expression.

After a moment he sighed. 'I brought you to my home because we will be assured of privacy while we talk, which we would not be in a bar or restaurant. There is no shame in being poor. It is obvious that you work hard to provide for your daughter, but I can help you. We can help each other. Now, come inside and meet my housekeeper. Alice has prepared dinner for us.'

If Juliet could have designed her dream home Ferndown House would have been perfect in every way. From the outside it was a gothic-style Victorian property, but inside it had been cleverly remodelled and refurbished into a sophisticated modern house which still managed to retain many original period features.

She caught her breath when Rafael showed her one huge room, with a stunning parquet floor and floor-to-ceiling mirrors on one wall.

'The previous owners enjoyed hosting parties in here, but I don't entertain very often and the room is not used much,' he told her.

The room would be an ideal dance studio, Juliet thought. It was her dream to one day own a ballet school, and she visualised ballet *barres* along the walls and a box of the powdered chalk called rosin on the floor, for dancers to rub onto their pointe shoes to help stop them slipping.

She followed Rafael along the hall and looked into another reception room, a study, and a library that overlooked the garden. Outside lighting revealed a large, pretty space with wide lawns, where Poppy would love to play. Juliet gave a faint sigh, thinking of the couple of rusty swings in the playground on the housing estate where she sometimes took her daughter.

Upstairs on the second floor they walked past what she guessed was the master bedroom, with a four-poster bed. Juliet carefully avoided Rafael's gaze as she wondered how many women had spent the night with him in that enormous bed.

'There is a nursery along here,' he said, leading the way along the corridor. He opened a door into a large room with painted murals of fairies on the walls and laughed at her startled expression. 'I'm not planning to fill the nursery with my own children, but my sister has four-year-old twin girls who sometimes come to stay here.'

They went back downstairs to the dining room, where a cheery fire burned in the hearth and velvet curtains were drawn across the windows.

'You have a beautiful home,' Juliet murmured when Rafael drew out a chair at the table and waited for her to sit down before he took his place opposite her.

He was silent while Alice served a first course of gooey baked brie with warm pears. Then the housekeeper left the main course on a heated trolley for them to serve themselves and Rafael poured wine.

'If you agree to my proposition Ferndown House will be yours and your daughter's home for the duration of our marriage. When, after a few months, the marriage is dissolved, five million pounds will be transferred into your bank account and you will be able to buy a property of your own. Have you any ideas about where you would like to live?'

'Somewhere on the coast,' she said instantly. 'When I was a child my parents took me on holiday to Cornwall a few times. We stayed in a caravan next to the beach.' Memories of a happy childhood full of love and laughter tugged on her heart. 'I've always thought how wonderful it would be for Poppy to grow up by the sea.'

'Agree to my deal and you can make your dreams reality,' Rafael said in a softly persuasive tone.

Excitement fizzed inside Juliet, overriding the voice of caution in her head. With the money that Rafael was offering she could buy a little cottage with a garden and a sea view. She didn't want a mansion—just a place that she and Poppy could call home. But what Rafael was asking was *wrong*, her conscience whispered. Marriage should be a life-long commitment. Her parents had enjoyed a happy marriage and, although Juliet had learned a harsh lesson with Bryan, she still hoped that one day she would fall in love with someone special who would love her in return.

She took a small sip of her wine, determined to keep her wits about her. 'I'm curious to know why you need a wife so badly that you're prepared to fork out five million pounds for one.'

'My grandfather has demanded that I marry before he steps down as head of the Casillas Group and appoints me as CEO of the company and Chairman of the board of directors,' Rafael said curtly. 'The dual roles have been passed down to the eldest son for generations. My mother does not have any siblings, which means that I am the next firstborn male and I should be Hector's successor. *Dios*, it is my *birthright*.'

He slapped his hand down on the table and Juliet flinched.

'Why does your grandfather want you to marry?'

'He disapproves of my lifestyle.'

She nodded. 'You do have a reputation as a playboy, and your affair with the wife of a prominent politician was reported in most of today's newspapers.'

'I spent one night with Michelle two months ago. The paparazzi must have seen us leave the nightclub together and go to a hotel, but those pictures did not appear in the papers the next day.' Rafael's jaw hardened. 'My guess is that someone paid the photographer to delay offering the pictures to the tabloids until the day the Casillas Group's biggest-selling retail line Rozita launched a new bridal collection.'

Juliet stared at him. 'Why would anyone do that?'

'It could have been a competitor, hoping to damage the company's reputation, or more likely someone who wanted to blacken my name and convince my grandfather that I would not be a responsible CEO.'

'Do you have any idea who?'

'In all probability it was someone on the Casillas Group's board who does not support my claim to be Hector's successor, or one of my relatives for the same reason.'

'How awful that someone in your own family might have betrayed you,' Juliet murmured. 'Families are supposed to support one another.'

Rafael stared at her broodingly. 'The pursuit of power is a ruthless game, with no place for weakness or emotions,' he said harshly.

While he served their main course of chicken cooked in a creamy sauce Juliet played his words over in her mind and felt a little shiver run through her. She had no doubt that Rafael was ruthless, and he must be utterly determined to become CEO if he was prepared to pay such an incredible amount of money for a wife.

Could she do it? His proposition had seemed crazy at first, but now she understood that his grandfather was forcing Rafael to marry. What he was suggesting was a business deal, she told herself.

The chicken was delicious, and a welcome change from the cheap, microwavable ready meals she tended to live on because fresh, good-quality produce was so expensive. She concentrated on eating her dinner, glad of the distraction.

Rafael got up to throw another log on the fire. The

flames crackled and an evocative scent of applewood filled the room. The wine, the food and the general ambience of the room was helping Juliet to relax, and she gave a soft sigh.

'Can you honestly tell me that you're not tempted?'

Rafael's seductive voice curled around her. She took another sip of her wine.

'Of course I'm tempted. To be honest I can't even *imagine* having five million pounds. It's an unbelievable sum of money and it would certainly transform my life. But I have to consider what is best for Poppy. I'm worried that she might become attached to you while we're married and be upset when we divorce and you're no longer around.'

Rafael frowned. 'I think that scenario is extremely unlikely. Immediately after our marriage you and Poppy will accompany me to Spain to attend my grandfather's eightieth birthday party. I will present you as my new wife to Hector and he will announce me as his successor. The transition of power will take a little while—maybe a month or two—and we will need to attend a few social engagements together to show the Casillas board members and shareholders that I have reformed my playboy lifestyle since my marriage,' he said sardonically. 'After a suitable period of time you and your daughter will be able to return here to Ferndown House—we'll make the excuse that you prefer her to attend a nursery school in England. It will be necessary for me to spend much of my time at the Casillas Group's headquarters in Valencia, and the truth is that I won't come to England very often.'

'How romantic.'

Juliet told herself it was stupid to feel disappointed

that Rafael had made it clear he would avoid her as much as possible.

'I am not offering you romance,' he said in a hard voice. 'I want you to be my wife for no other reason than to fulfil my grandfather's command that I must marry before he will make me CEO.'

He stood up and walked over to the sideboard, returning to lay some papers on the table.

'We are required to give twenty-eight days' notice of our intention to marry at the register office. My lawyers have prepared a contract stating that five million pounds will be transferred into your bank account when I succeed my grandfather as head of the Casillas Group. All you have to do is sign your name. I will take care of all the arrangements for our wedding, and for you and your daughter to move from your current home into Ferndown House.'

Juliet stared at the document in front of her and imagined Poppy running around the garden and playing with the dolls' house in the nursery.

She swallowed. 'It seems too easy.'

'It *is* easy. Everything will be as I have explained to you. There are no catches.'

Rafael's voice was like warm honey sliding over her. Tempting her. She wished her dad was around so that she could ask his advice—although she knew in her heart that he would advise her against marrying for money.

But five million pounds! Her heart was thudding so hard she was surprised it wasn't audible in the silent room. If she accepted Rafael's proposition her money worries would be over, but would she be selling her soul to the devil?

'I need time to think about it,' she whispered.

'I don't have the luxury of time. I have to be married by my grandfather's eightieth birthday, which is six weeks from now, or he will appoint my half-brother as his successor.' Rafael picked up a pen from the table and held it out to her. 'I am offering you a chance to give your daughter a better life. If you walk away now you will have thrown away that chance. I won't make the offer again and I will find another bride.'

The clock on the wall ticked loudly.

Do it. Do it.

Juliet snatched the pen from Rafael and signed her name where he showed her. It was for Poppy, she tried to reassure herself. A better future for her daughter.

'Bueno!' Rafael did not try to disguise the satisfaction in his voice. He picked up their wine glasses and handed Juliet hers. 'Let us drink a toast, *chiquita*, to the shortest marriage on record.'

CHAPTER THREE

A MONTH HAD never passed so quickly—or so it seemed to Juliet.

For the first couple of weeks after she had agreed to Rafael's marriage proposition she had been busy winding down her sandwich business. Mel had found a buyer for the bakery shop and it had been an emotional moment as they'd closed the door for the last time.

'I'm intrigued to know more about your new business opportunity in Spain,' Mel had said. 'Why are you being so secretive?'

'I'll tell you more if it happens.'

Juliet hadn't revealed to her friend the true reason why she would be going to Spain. She was sure Mel would think she was mad if she explained that she had agreed to marry a man she did not know for money.

As the date of the wedding had drawn closer her doubts had multiplied. But Rafael had promised that there was no catch to their business deal.

Deciding what to tell Agata had been more difficult. Juliet was fond of the Polish woman who had helped her and Poppy so much, and after some soul-searching she'd told Agata the white lie that she was marrying Rafael after a whirlwind courtship.

Today, packing her's and Poppy's belongings hadn't

taken long, and a member of Rafael's staff had come and taken the few cardboard boxes down to an SUV.

Juliet strapped Poppy into the child seat and as the car drove away from the estate on its way to Ferndown House she felt a mixture of relief, apprehension and excitement that refused to be quashed at the prospect of seeing Rafael again.

She had spoken to him once on the phone, when he'd called her to check some details he needed in order to complete the paperwork for their wedding. His gravelly voice with its sexy accent had made her feel hot all over, and she'd closed her eyes and pictured his devastatingly handsome face.

Remembering his disdainful expression when he'd seen her wearing her cleaning overalls, she had taken a bit of time over her appearance today. The pink jumper that Agata had given her at Christmas lent some colour to her washed-out complexion, and the old tube of mascara she'd found at the back of the bathroom cabinet had still had enough in it to darken her pale eyelashes.

But when they arrived at Ferndown House Alice the housekeeper greeted Juliet and explained that Rafael had left the previous day for a business trip to America.

'He is not sure when he will be back but he asked me to give you his PA's phone number. Miss Foxton will answer any queries you might have.' Alice smiled at Poppy. 'I've made some cookies. Would you like one?'

Juliet tried to shrug off her disappointment at Rafael's absence. There was no reason for them to spend any time together. Their marriage would be a formality which would allow Rafael to become CEO of his family's company and he was paying her an astounding amount of money to be his temporary wife, she reminded herself.

And sitting alone in the elegant dining room at Ferndown House, enjoying one of the delicious meals that the housekeeper had prepared, was a lot nicer than sitting in her flat with a microwaveable meal after Poppy had gone to bed—although she felt just as lonely.

Rafael finally phoned her the evening before they were due to marry the following day. 'My plane has just touched down in London and I'm going straight to the office,' he told her.

His gravelly voice had its usual effect of bringing Juliet's skin out in goosebumps.

'I don't know what time I'll get back to the house. Make sure you're ready to leave for the register office at ten-thirty tomorrow morning.'

On her way up to bed she wondered if he really was going to the office so late, or if he planned to spend the night with a mistress. Perhaps he wanted to enjoy his last night as a bachelor before he was forced into a marriage that he patently didn't want.

It was none of her business what he did, Juliet reminded herself.

There was no logical explanation for her dismal mood. In a few months' time she would have five million pounds in the bank—more than enough to buy a cottage by the sea and for her to establish her own dance school.

It was after midnight when she heard a car pull up outside the house, and when she hopped out of bed and ran across to the window her heart skipped a beat as she saw Rafael's tall frame unfold from his Lamborghini. The moonlight danced across his face, highlighting his chiselled jaw and sharp cheekbones.

Tomorrow he would be her husband.

Butterflies leapt in her stomach—nerves, she supposed. But around dawn she woke feeling horribly sick. Frequent trips to the bathroom followed, and the severe bouts of vomiting left her feeling drained.

She certainly did not look like a blushing bride, Juliet thought as she stared at her ashen face and lank hair in the mirror. It was ten o'clock and she needed to hurry up and get ready.

Choosing what to wear did not take her long. She lived in jeans or a denim skirt, and the only vaguely smart item of clothing she owned was a mustard-coloured dress she'd bought in a sale years ago when she had first moved to Australia and needed something to wear to job interviews. The colour hadn't looked so bad in the Australian sunshine, but on a grey spring day in England it made her pale skin look sallow.

She would have liked to buy something pretty to wear on her wedding day, but since her sandwich business had closed down and she'd given up her cleaning job she hadn't had an income. Living at Ferndown House meant that she hadn't had to pay for food, but she'd spent the last of her money on new shoes for Poppy.

Juliet had no time to worry about her appearance when another bout of sickness sent her rushing into the bathroom, and she emerged feeling shivery and hot at the same time. Then she spent ten minutes searching for Poppy's favourite teddy, knowing that her daughter would not sleep at night without Mr Bear. Finally they were ready.

Was she doing the right thing?

It was too late for second thoughts now, she told herself. She had already given up her flat and her job. If she did not marry Rafael she would be homeless.

As Juliet walked down the stairs a wave of dizziness

swept over her. She clung to the banister rail with one hand and held on to Poppy with the other.

Rafael strolled into the hall and an expression of horror flickered across his face as he studied her appearance, before he quickly schooled his features and gave her a cool smile. He looked utterly gorgeous in a grey three-piece suit that emphasised his broad shoulders and athletic build. His black hair was swept back from his brow and the designer stubble on his jaw gave him an edgy sex appeal that was irresistible.

'I couldn't afford to buy a new outfit for the wedding,' Juliet told him stiffly.

She wished the ground would open up beneath her feet when she caught sight of herself in the hall mirror. She hadn't had the energy to do anything fancy with her hair and it hung in a heavy braid down her back.

'You look fine,' Rafael assured her smoothly.

It was a blatant lie, she thought.

She wished she wasn't so agonisingly aware of him. Her breath snagged in her throat when he lifted his hand and lightly touched her face.

'Although I'm guessing from the dark circles beneath your eyes that you did not sleep well last night,' he murmured. 'You will do very well,' he added, in a satisfied tone that puzzled her.

But then he hurried her out to the car and she was too busy strapping Poppy into the child seat to think about Rafael's odd statement.

From then on everything about the day had an air of unreality. The wedding ceremony took place in an unremarkable room at the council offices, and the two witnesses were Rafael's PA and his chauffeur.

Juliet had asked Agata to come to the register office to look after Poppy during the ceremony, and Poppy's joy when she saw Agata brought tears to Juliet's eyes. Her parents would have loved their little granddaughter as much as Poppy would have loved to have grandparents.

Rafael had told her that he had a large extended family and that several of his relatives, including his mother, lived at the Casillas family mansion in Valencia. Perhaps his mother would enjoy having a child around and would make a fuss of Poppy? Juliet hoped so.

She must have made all the right responses to the registrar, and even managed to smile—although she felt numb and her voice sounded strangely disembodied. Rafael slid a gold band onto her finger and she tensed when he lowered his face towards hers. She realised with a jolt of shock that he was going to kiss her. She had secretly longed to feel his lips on hers, but not like this—not to seal their farce of a marriage.

His mouth was centimetres from hers, and she quickly turned her head so that he kissed her cheek. He frowned, and she guessed that no woman had ever rejected him before. But then the registrar was presenting them with the marriage certificate and Juliet felt as brittle as glass as she stepped into the corridor, hardly able to believe that she was now Mrs Mendoza-Casillas.

'I hope you know what you are doing,' Agata said when Juliet hugged her outside the register office. 'You told me that you fell in love with your husband at the first sight, but I do not see love between you.'

Somehow Juliet dredged up a smile. 'I'm very happy.' She tried to sound convincing. 'I'll bring Poppy to visit you soon.'

Rafael was uncommunicative in the limousine that took them to the airport, and once they had boarded his private jet he opened his laptop, saying that he needed to work.

Juliet devoted herself to keeping Poppy entertained during the flight, and by the time the plane had landed in Valencia and they were in a car on the way to his family home she had a thumping headache—although thankfully the sickness seemed to be over. Poppy was tired and fretful, and Juliet felt frazzled, and she was relieved when the car turned onto a long driveway.

'You didn't tell me you lived in a palace,' she said to Rafael in an awed voice as the Casillas mansion came into view.

Built over four storeys, the villa had white walls and tall windows gleaming in the bright afternoon sunshine. The car drove past manicured lawns and a huge ornamental pool and fountain before coming to a halt by the imposing front entrance which was framed by elegant colonnades.

Juliet knew, of course, that Rafael was wealthy, but travelling on his private jet and seeing his family's palatial home had made her realise that she'd entered a world of incredible luxury and opulence which was a million miles away from her tower block in one of London's most deprived boroughs, and from her life as a single mother.

They climbed out of the car and her tension escalated as she lifted Poppy out of the child seat and attempted to set her down on her feet. Tears ensued until she picked the little girl up again.

'Poppy is tired from travelling,' she told a grim-faced Rafael. 'I'd like to get her settled and give her something to eat.'

'You will be able to do that soon, but first I will introduce you to my family. My grandfather has arranged a reception to celebrate our marriage.'

Was it her imagination or did Rafael sound as tense as she felt?

She bit her lip as he strode up the steps leading to the front door of the villa, leaving her to trail behind him with Poppy balanced on her hip.

On the top step, he turned to her and frowned. 'Let me take the child. She is too heavy for you to carry.'

Juliet felt beads of sweat running down her face—which was strange, because she was shivering even though the sun was warm. Poppy clung to her like a limpet and shrank away from Rafael when he tried to take her into his arms.

A man whom she guessed was the butler opened the door and ushered them into the villa. Juliet's stunned gaze took in a vast entrance hall with pink marble walls and floor. Rafael placed his hand between her shoulder blades and propelled her forward as the butler flung open a set of double doors into another enormous room that seemed to be filled with people.

The hum of voices became quiet and silence pressed on Juliet's ears. An elderly man stepped out of the crowd and came to greet them—but the smile of welcome on his face faded and his eyes narrowed.

'Rafael, I understood that you would be bringing your new wife with you.' The man spoke in Spanish and his harsh tone sent a shiver through Juliet.

'Abuelo...' Rafael drawled. 'I would like you to meet my bride.'

There was a collective gasp from the people in the room and the old man swore. He flicked his sharp black eyes over Poppy before he spoke to Juliet in English. 'Were you a widow before you married my grandson?'

Confused by the question, she shook her head. 'No. I've never been married before.'

His implication suddenly became clear, and a terrible certainty slid into her mind when the man whom she realised was Hector Casillas glared at Rafael.

'Tu esposa y su bastarda son de la cuneta!' he hissed in a venomous voice.

He was white-lipped with anger, but his grandson laughed.

'What is the matter, Abuelo?' Rafael drawled. 'You demanded that I marry and I have done what you asked.'

'There is something you should know.'

Juliet's teeth were chattering so hard that she could barely get the words out. Anger burned like a white-hot flame inside her, but she was determined to control her temper in front of Poppy, who was running around in the little courtyard behind the kitchen. Her daughter had been subjected to enough ugly emotions from Rafael's grandfather.

Rafael. *Judas*.

'What should I know?' he said indifferently.

'I understand Spanish. I learned to speak the language when I lived with my aunt Vivian and her husband Carlos, who is Spanish by birth.'

His brows lifted. 'Ah...'

'Is that all you can say?' she choked.

She wanted to scream at him. Worse than her rage was her sense of hurt, which felt like an iron band wrapped around her chest that was squeezing the breath from her lungs.

'Your grandfather said that I am from the gutter and he called Poppy a bastard.' Juliet swallowed hard. 'Technically, I suppose it's true. Poppy's father did not offer to marry me when I fell pregnant, and he refused to have any involvement with his daughter when she was born. But I don't regret for one second having my little girl, and I will not allow your grandfather or anyone else to upset her.'

'My grandfather has very old-fashioned views.' Rafael gave a shrug. 'He is disappointed because he hoped I would marry the daughter of a duke. Hector sets great store on aristocratic titles,' he said drily.

'You threw me to the lions deliberately. Your grandfather said those awful things about me and you didn't defend me.'

It was not just raw emotion that was making it hard for Juliet to swallow. Her throat was sore and she recognised that the shivery feeling and her jelly-like legs were signs of a flu-like virus, the start of which must have been the sickness she'd experienced that morning.

'Mummy, can I give some yoghurt to the cat?'

She forced a smile for Poppy. 'I don't think cats eat yoghurt, darling. And I want you to sit down and finish your tea.'

Juliet lifted her daughter onto a chair at the wooden table in the shade of a pergola. Although Poppy could not have understood the things that had been said by Rafael's grandfather, she had sensed the tension in the room and burst into tears. Rafael had brought them to the kitchen and asked the cook to find some food for the little girl.

Luckily Poppy had been distracted when she'd seen a tabby cat in a pretty courtyard where terracotta pots were filled with a profusion of herbs.

While Poppy tucked into a bowl of fresh fruit and yoghurt, Juliet said in a low tone to Rafael, 'I don't understand why you chose me to be your wife if you knew that your grandfather would not approve of me.'

She stared at him and saw a ruthlessness in his hard-boned face that sent a shiver through her.

'That was the point, wasn't it?' she whispered. 'You were angry that your grandfather had insisted on you being married before he would make you CEO, so to pay him back you married a woman you knew he would despise—a single mother from the gutter.'

She was mortified to think of the vision she must have presented to Rafael's family, looking like Little Orphan Annie in her horrible dress and scuffed boots, with a child on her hip.

'You are not from the gutter.' Rafael sounded impatient rather than penitent.

'I come from a run-down council estate where the police have given up trying to arrest the drug dealers because there are too many of them,' she said flatly.

Juliet wasn't ashamed of her background. Her parents had worked hard in low-paid jobs to give her the chance to pursue her dream of being a ballerina. And most of the families living in that tower block were good people who struggled to make ends meet.

None of them had judged her for being a single mother—like Rafael's grandfather had and perhaps Rafael himself did. One thing was certain—she did not belong in the Casillas mansion with Rafael's sophisticated relatives.

'I can't stay here knowing that your family despise me,' she told him. 'More importantly, I don't want Poppy to meet your grandfather again. I'll book us onto the next available flight to England.'

She kept a credit card for extreme emergencies and her current situation definitely qualified as an emergency. Poppy had been terrified when Rafael's grandfather had shouted at them. But Juliet had no idea how she would pay the credit card bill, or where she would go when she reached London. Perhaps Agata would allow her and Poppy to stay at her flat for a few days.

'My grandfather will calm down,' Rafael told her. 'Even if he doesn't, you are my wife and there is nothing Hector can do about it.'

'You can't use me and especially not my three-year-old child as pawns in your row with your grandfather. I don't understand why such bitterness exists between the two of you. There is poison here in paradise and I want no part in an ugly war of wills between two men who have more money than people like me—people from the *gutter*,' she flung at him, 'can only dream of.'

She could tell from the way his dark brows slashed together like a scar across his brow that he hadn't expected her to stand up to him.

It was about time she grew a backbone, Juliet told herself grimly. But even though she had discovered the unedifying reason why Rafael had married her she still could not control the heat that coiled low in her pelvis when he pushed himself away from the wall that he had been lounging against and crossed the small courtyard to stand in front of her.

Too close, she thought, lifting her hand up to her throat to try and hide the betraying leap of her pulse.

'You became part of this when you signed our marriage agreement and it is too bad if you don't like it,' he said curtly. 'Let us not forget that your motives were hardly altruistic, *chiquita*. You sold yourself to me for five million pounds.'

'I see now that I sold my soul to the devil.' She put her hand on his arm and felt the iron strength of sinew and muscle beneath his olive-gold skin. 'It's not too late to end this madness. We can have our marriage annulled.'

'And give up what should be mine?' Rafael gave a harsh laugh. 'I am afraid not. I will be CEO, whatever it takes. We are in this together.'

A violent shiver shook Juliet and she gripped the edge of the table as the ground beneath her feet lurched.

'What's the matter?' Rafael demanded. 'You're even paler than you were at the register office.'

'I've been feeling unwell all day,' she admitted.

She turned away from him and started to walk across the courtyard, but the ground tilted and she felt herself falling. From a long way off she heard Rafael call her name.

She mustn't faint because Poppy would be frightened, she thought before blackness blotted out everything.

When he was growing up Rafael had learned to run fast—to escape his father's temper, or shopkeepers who chased him for stealing food, or to avoid the dealers who forced the slum kids to deliver drugs.

As an adult he still ran to escape his demons. His favourite route took him through the Albufera Natural Park, where a huge freshwater lagoon was separated from the sea by a narrow strip of coastline. There he could run along the beach before heading into the sand dunes and the pine forest beyond.

The Casillas mansion overlooked the beach, and right now Rafael, gazing out of an upper-floor window, would have liked nothing better than to be pounding along the shoreline, with the sea breeze ruffling his hair and the sun on his back. Running gave him the head space to find solutions to his problems—but there was no easy solution to the situation he found himself in, with a marriage that he had been forced into against his will.

There had even been a chance of a reprieve. It might not have been necessary to go ahead with the wedding at all. He would have paid Juliet off and thought it a small price to pay for his freedom.

An opportunity had arisen to buy out a popular American fashion brand, and Rafael had spent the past month in California, determined to secure the deal which would give the Casillas Group a major stake in the US clothing retail market. The acquisition would, he hoped, prove to the board members and shareholders that he *should* be CEO.

But even his success had not been enough to persuade his grandfather to withdraw his marriage ultimatum.

'A wife will be good for you. Now that you are thirty-five it is time for you to settle down and think about the future,' Hector had said when Rafael had phoned to tell him that the Casillas Group now owned the US fashion brand Up Town Girl. 'I am an old man, and when I die I want to be certain that the next generation of my family will lead the company into the future.'

If Hector believed that having great-grandchildren would be ensured by forcing his eldest grandson to marry he was going to be disappointed, Rafael brooded. He had no burning desire to have children. His parents had hardly been ideal role models, and although he was fond of his nieces he was too driven by his ambition to believe that he could be a devoted parent like his sister, or like Juliet.

His wife.

Dios. He pictured the sickly waif who had occupied his bed for the past two nights while he slept on the sofa in his dressing room. He hadn't thought about what he would do with Juliet once he'd married her, and he resented his nagging conscience which insisted that he was now responsible for her and her child.

Damn his grandfather for issuing his ridiculous marriage ultimatum. Rafael's jaw clenched. Once his temper would have made him lash out and punch something—or someone. At fifteen he had been expelled from an exclusive private school for fighting with another pupil who had taunted him for his rough manners.

'You grew up in the gutter, Mendoza. You call yourself Casillas but everyone knows your father was a *gitano*.'

Rafael had wiped the grin off the other boy's face with his fists, but when he'd cooled off he'd felt ashamed of his behaviour. As a child he had often been on the receiving end of his father's violent outbursts, but he wanted to be a better man than Ivan Mendoza and prove to his grandfather that he deserved the name Casillas.

From then on he'd learned to control his emotions. *Don't get mad, get even* had become his mantra.

At a new school Rafael had ignored the boys who'd reminded him about his background. Instead of losing his temper he had focused his energy on his studies, determined to catch up on the education he'd missed while he'd lived in the slum.

That single-mindedness had seen him gain a master's degree from Harvard Business School before he had joined the Casillas Group in a junior role and worked his way up the company ladder.

He pulled his mind back to the present when a small hand slipped into his, and glanced down at Juliet's daughter. Poppy was an enchanting child, with a knack of disarming Rafael's defences which he would have sworn were impenetrable.

'Will you read me a story, Raf?'

He hunkered down in front of her. 'Go and find a book from the shelf. I'll read you a story and then we will go and see if your *mamà* is feeling better.'

Across the room Rafael caught his sister's amused expression.

'Raf?' Sofia murmured.

'My name is unfamiliar for the child, and hard to say, so she shortens it to Raf. I seem to have made a hit with her,' he said ruefully.

'"The child" has a name,' his sister reproved him. 'Poppy is younger than the twins and you are the only person she knows in a house full of strangers. It's hardly surprising that she wants to be with you while her mother—*your wife*—is too unwell to look after her.' Sofia sighed. 'What made you do it, Rafael?'

He did not pretend to misunderstand, or to try to convince his sister that his marriage was anything other than a calculated ploy which would give him what he wanted.

'Abuelo blackmailed me into choosing a wife by threatening to name Francisco as his successor if I did not marry. The CEO-ship should be *mine*—and not only by birthright. I don't feel a sense of entitlement,' he insisted. 'When I joined the company I started at the bottom—sweeping the floor in a warehouse. Hector did not want me to receive special favours just because I am his eldest grandson. I quickly rose through the managerial ranks because I worked harder than anyone else. I have *proved* my worth.'

Rafael's gaze met his sister's eyes, which were the same shade of olive-green as his own. Their unusual eye colour was a physical sign of the difference that set them apart from the rest of the Casillas family.

'You and I are still seen as outsiders. Especially me,' he muttered. 'You smile and say the right things, and you are not viewed as a threat to Madre's ambition to see her beloved Francisco—the true Casillas heir, in her opinion—made CEO.'

Sofia moved to break up a squabble between her two daughters. 'Ana, give the doll to Inez if she was playing with it first. Your uncle says he will read a story. Why don't you help Poppy choose a book?'

She turned her attention back to Rafael.

'I'm sorry I wasn't here two days ago, when you introduced your wife to the rest of the family. Madre says the girl you have married is so thin and pale perhaps she is a drug addict.'

'Dios!' Rafael growled, biting back a curse when he caught his sister's warning look to remind him that children were present. 'Juliet fell ill with a gastric virus shortly after we arrived.'

He was angered by his mother's unjust accusation. But his conscience pricked. When he had first met Juliet her hollow cheeks and extreme pallor had made *him* suspicious that she was a drug user. And her drab appearance was one reason he had picked her for his bride, he acknowledged, feeling a faint flicker of shame as he pictured her in the ghastly creased dress she'd been wearing when he had introduced her to his grandfather.

He hadn't realised that she was ill when they had arrived at the Casillas mansion. With another stab of discomfort Rafael admitted to himself that he'd been busy taking a vicious pleasure in Hector's fury when he'd announced that the waif clutching her illegitimate child in her arms was his wife.

Juliet was as far removed from any of the high-society daughters of Spanish aristocratic families whom

Hector had expected him to marry as chalk was from cheese. But her lack of sophistication did not warrant his family's scorn.

'Juliet is a devoted mother—which is more than can be said for *our* mother,' he said harshly. 'Delfina is embarrassed by us because we remind her that she was once married to a low-life drug dealer. Sometimes I think she would have preferred it if Hector *hadn't* found us and brought us into the family.'

Sofia looked at him closely. 'I hope you have not led your wife to believe that you are in love with her?'

'Juliet understands that we have a business deal and she will be well recompensed after she has served her purpose.'

'Oh, Rafael,' his sister murmured. 'I worry about where your ruthless ambition will lead you. When can I meet your bride?'

He shrugged. 'Perhaps later today. The doctor I called in to examine her has said that the virus hit her hard. But the nurse reported that Juliet's temperature was nearly back to normal this morning and she should be well enough to attend Hector's eightieth birthday party on Saturday evening.'

When *he* would be named as his grandfather's successor, Rafael thought with satisfaction. He had met the old man's stipulation for him to marry and now it was time for Hector to publicly recognise his firstborn grandson as the true Casillas heir.

There was a knock on the door and the butler entered the nursery. 'Yes, Alfredo, what is it?'

'Señor Casillas wishes to speak to you,' the butler told Rafael. 'He is waiting for you in his study.'

CHAPTER FOUR

Rafael looked down at Poppy, who was holding a book out to him, before he responded to the butler. 'Tell my grandfather that I am with my stepdaughter and I will be along in ten minutes.'

'Why do you have to antagonise Hector?' Sofia demanded when Alfredo had left.

'He needs to realise that I am not one of the yes-men he surrounds himself with,' Rafael muttered. 'I am sick of his attempts to manipulate me. Besides, I promised to read to Poppy.'

He had felt oddly protective of Juliet's daughter since the ugly scene with his grandfather when they had arrived at the house had upset the little girl.

'You and Abuelo are both too proud,' Sofia said impatiently. 'It's like a clash of bulls.'

She broke off as the nursery door was flung open.

Rafael glanced across the room and saw Juliet standing in the doorway. She was wearing a pair of baggy pyjamas that had faded to an indeterminate colour and her hair was scraped back from her white face.

'Where is my daughter?'

She gave a low cry when she saw Poppy, and flew across the room to scoop the little girl into her arms.

'Oh, munchkin, there you are. I was scared I'd lost

you.' Juliet's relief was palpable and tears spilled down her cheeks as she looked at Rafael. 'I thought you had taken Poppy away. I woke up and I didn't know where she was. I thought...' She shook her head and hugged her daughter to her. 'I hope that no one has upset her. Your grandfather...?'

'Hector has not met Poppy again since we arrived two days ago,' Rafael assured her gruffly.

He was not completely heartless, and Juliet looked pathetic in her rag-bag clothes that hung off her angular body, with her face blotchy and wet with tears.

'As you can see, Poppy is quite safe. I have been taking care of her.'

'You?'

The mistrust in her voice exasperated him, but he felt uncomfortable as he remembered how she had accused him—rightly—of failing to defend her and Poppy in front of his grandfather.

'I am not an ogre,' he said curtly. But the wounded expression in Juliet's eyes made him feel like the evil villain in a Victorian melodrama.

'I can't believe that we have been here for two days,' she said unsteadily. 'What happened to me?'

'You have been ill with a virulent virus which gave you a high fever. The doctor I called in gave you medication to bring your temperature down and it knocked you out.'

Rafael did not add that the doctor had voiced his concern that Juliet was underweight and most likely undernourished, which had lowered her immune system, allowing the virus to take a hold.

'I don't remember putting my pyjamas on.' She looked at him with something akin to horror in her eyes. 'Did you undress me?'

'The nurse I hired put you to bed.'

Dios, Rafael thought irritably. Juliet had sounded appalled at the idea of him taking her clothes off. It was not a response he'd ever had from a woman before.

He recalled that at their wedding, when the registrar had invited him to kiss his bride and for the sake of convention he had tried to brush his lips over Juliet's, she had turned her head away to prevent him from kissing her mouth. Her behaviour had been puzzling because he knew she was attracted to him. Rafael always knew.

Before he was twenty he had discovered that he could have any woman he wanted with minimum effort on his part. No doubt his wealth and the name Casillas were partly responsible for his popularity, but he indulged his high sex drive with countless affairs with women who understood that commitment was not a word in his vocabulary.

He wasn't interested in his poor, plain bride. Although those attributes were the reason he had married her, he acknowledged, feeling guilt snaking through him as he remembered the crushed look on her face when his grandfather had insulted her. How was he to have known that Juliet understood Spanish? Rafael asked himself irritably.

'Rafael, are you going to introduce me to your wife?' Sofia walked up to Juliet and held out her hand. 'I apologise for my brother's lapse in manners. You must be Juliet. I'm Sofia, and my daughters are Ana and Inez. The twins have had a wonderful time playing with Poppy. She really has been quite happy with Rafael and me and the nanny, Elvira.'

'I panicked when I woke up in a strange place and couldn't find her.' Juliet set Poppy on her feet and the fierce look of love on her face as she watched her daughter tugged on emotions buried deep inside Rafael.

He had long ago got over the fact that his mother did not love him and that his relatives—with the exception of his sister—resented his existence. He'd never felt that he belonged anywhere or with anyone, and he had assured himself that he did not care. No one had ever looked at him as though they would give their life for him...as if they loved him more than anything in the world.

'Rafael—quick!'

Sofia's urgent tone jolted him from his thoughts and he sprang forward and caught Juliet as her legs crumpled beneath her. She weighed next to nothing, he thought as he carried her over to the door.

'You are not fully recovered,' he said, ignoring her attempts to slide out of his arms. 'You should be in bed. I'll ask the nurse to check your temperature and bring you something to eat.'

'Poppy will be fine with me,' Sofia assured Juliet. 'I'll read the girls a story.'

'As soon as I'm better—which I'm sure I will be by tomorrow—I want to take Poppy home,' Juliet told Rafael when he'd carried her into the bedroom and sat her on the edge of the bed.

She was a slip of a thing, perched on the huge bed like a little sparrow, he mused. But as he straightened up he noticed that her eyes were really a quite remarkable bright blue. His gaze dropped to her mouth, which was pulled down at the corners in a sulky expression.

'Where is home, exactly?' he asked sardonically. 'I made it clear when you signed the marriage contract that you cannot return to Ferndown House until after we have attended my grandfather's eightieth birthday party and he has appointed me as CEO.'

'I wish I'd never signed the contract. You said there were no catches, but you didn't tell me that you had chosen me as your bride to punish your grandfather,' she said in choked voice. 'You certainly didn't think about my feelings when your family looked at me as though I had crawled out of the gutter.'

Rafael ignored the prick of his conscience. 'I'm paying you five million pounds,' he reminded her harshly. 'It is regrettable that my grandfather spoke to you the way he did, but I'm sure you'll get over it when the money is in your bank account and you can buy yourself nice clothes and jewellery—whatever you want.'

'All I want is security for Poppy,' she whispered. 'I'm not interested in jewellery and clothes.'

'That much I can believe,' he muttered, flicking his gaze over her revolting pyjamas before he stalked out of the room, away from the accusing expression in Juliet's eyes that made him feel ashamed of himself.

Dios, she should be grateful that she and her daughter would no longer have to live in poverty, Rafael brooded as he strode down the grand staircase.

His foul mood was not improved when he entered his grandfather's study and saw the company's senior lawyer, Lionel Silva, seated behind the desk next to Hector. Rafael strolled across the room and lowered himself into a chair facing the two men, resting his ankle across his opposite thigh. His appearance was relaxed but his instincts sensed trouble.

'Lionel, I am glad to see you,' he drawled. 'I presume my grandfather asked you here today to set in motion the transfer of the CEO-ship to me, now that I am married. It is what we agreed, did we not, Abuelo?'

His grandfather gave a snort. 'Once again you have disappointed me, Rafael. I cannot say that I am surprised, when you have so often proved to be a disappointment. But this time you have excelled yourself.'

Rafael felt a flare of irritation mixed with something raw that he assured himself wasn't hurt. He'd spent the past twenty-odd years trying to earn Hector's approval—hoping to win his grandfather's love—although he refused to admit as much even to himself. Now all he cared about was his right to be recognised as the Casillas heir.

'I trust you were not *disappointed* when I secured a deal to buy out the biggest clothing retail company on America's west coast?' he said drily. 'The acquisition puts Casillas Group among the top five largest apparel retailers in the world.'

'I do not dispute that your business acumen is impressive,' Hector barked. 'But, as I have said before, our CEO is the figurehead of the company—all the more so because the role is combined with that of Chairman. It is a position of great power and responsibility that requires a sense of humility—which you lack, Rafael.'

'I have met the condition you imposed on me and brought my wife to Spain in time for your eightieth birthday celebrations. How does that show a lack of humility?' Rafael said grittily.

'Do not insult my intelligence. You know that I expected you to make a good marriage, befitting the Casillas family's noble heritage, but you have deliberately sought to undermine me by marrying an unprepossessing girl. Your wife looks no more than a teenager and yet she already has one illegitimate child and no doubt lives off hand-outs from the state.'

'Juliet is in her mid-twenties and she has always worked to support her daughter.'

Fury simmered inside Rafael at his grandfather's

unfair description of Juliet. But his conscience prodded him that his reason for marrying her *had* been to infuriate Hector by introducing an untitled and unsophisticated bride.

The lawyer cleared his throat as he picked up a printed document. 'This is the agreement between you, Rafael, and your grandfather, stating Hector's intention to name you as his successor following your marriage.'

Rafael nodded. 'I have given you a copy of my marriage certificate.'

'Yes, it seems to be legitimate,' Lionel murmured, studying the other document in front of him. 'Nevertheless your grandfather has expressed his concern that your marriage to Miss Juliet Lacey is in fact a marriage of convenience which you have entered into for the purpose of gaining benefit or advantage arising from that status. In other words, your marriage to Miss Lacey is a sham, meant to deceive Hector and persuade him to name you as his heir and the next CEO of Casillas Group.'

'The marriage is perfectly legal.'

Rafael's grip on his temper broke and he jerked to his feet, slamming his hands down on the desk. He noted that the lawyer flinched but Hector remained absolutely still. A clash of bulls, his sister had once said, describing his battle of wills with his grandfather.

'I have kept to my side of our agreement and I expect you to honour your word, Abuelo.'

'What do *you* know of honour?' Hector snapped. 'It is my belief that you do not intend your marriage to be a permanent arrangement and that once you are CEO you will seek a divorce. But the wedding took place in England, and under UK law you cannot apply for a divorce until you have been married for one year.'

Rafael stiffened. 'So? Where is this leading?'

His grandfather gave a smug smile.

'On my eightieth birthday this Saturday I will announce that you are my successor, as we agreed, but I will not step down until the date of the first anniversary of your marriage—and only then if I am convinced that your marriage is genuine rather than an attempt to trick me.'

Hector gave Rafael a sly look.

'I am certain that there will be no need for me to try to prove or disprove the validity of your marriage A year will, I suspect, seem like a lifetime to a playboy such as you are, to maintain the pretence of a committed relationship with your unappealing bride.'

'You can't do that,' Rafael gritted. 'You agreed—'

'I can do whatever I think best protects the interests of the Casillas Group,' Hector interrupted. 'If I handed the company over to you and you divorced after only a few months of marriage it would suggest that you lack commitment. Instead I will appoint you CEO-in-waiting, and it will make sense that you should be based in Valencia in order for us to be in daily contact and ensure a smooth hand-over of leadership. I will expect you and your wife to spend the first year of your marriage living here at the Casillas mansion. If you return to your home in England it might lead to rumours of a rift between us, which would worry the board and our shareholders, who already have reservations about your suitability to head the company.'

The old man was as wily as a fox, Rafael thought furiously. 'I am certain that Juliet will not want to stay here after the vile way you spoke to her. Her daughter is settled at my home in London and it would not be good for the child to be brought to live in a different country.'

'Children are adaptable,' Hector said coolly. His black eyes bored into Rafael. 'Either you remain married for a year, or Lionel and his legal team will convince a court of law that your marriage is a fraudulent exercise intended to dupe me into appointing you as CEO.'

Rafael swore savagely. 'You cannot dictate where I choose to live or how I conduct my marriage.'

But he would not give his grandfather the satisfaction of seeing him lose his temper, and he swung round and strode out of the study. The truth was that the old man could do whatever he liked. Hector had won this round in their battle of wills, but he would not win the war. Whatever it took, he *would* claim his birthright, Rafael vowed.

An hour on the treadmill relieved some of his tension, but he was still in a black rage when he left the gym and returned to his private suite of rooms. He headed straight to the bar and took a beer from the fridge. He could do with something stronger, but spending the afternoon getting drunk on Orujo—a fiercely strong spirit sometimes referred to as Spanish firewater—would not be a good idea. Especially as he was expected to attend a family lunch later with his wife.

His wife.

Rafael swore under his breath as he stepped outside onto the balcony which ran along the entire length of his apartment at the back of the mansion and overlooked the extensive gardens. In the distance the swimming pool glinted in the sunshine, but he wasn't interested in the view. His attention was fixed on Juliet.

She was standing a little way along the balcony, leaning against the stone balustrade. He knew it must be her, but his brain could not believe what his eyes were seeing. Gone were the saggy grey pyjamas and instead she was wearing an ivory-coloured silk chemise that skimmed her slender body. Her hair was even more of a surprise. Freed from the tight braid she usually wore, it reached almost to her waist and was not a dull brown, as Rafael had thought, but red-gold, gleaming like silk in the sunshine.

She was unaware of him and he stood and stared at her, not daring to move in case she was an illusion that might disappear if he alerted her to his presence. He was stunned to realise that the unflattering clothes he had always seen her wearing had hidden a slender but definitely feminine figure, with graceful lines and delicate curves.

As Rafael watched Juliet tilted her face up to the sun and lifted her arms above her head, stretching like a sleepy kitten. The gentle breeze flattened the silk chemise against her body, drawing his gaze to her small, high breasts. He could see the faint outline of her nipples, and heat rushed to his groin as he imagined sliding the straps of the chemise down her arms and peeling the silky material away from her breasts.

He cursed silently when he felt his arousal press against the thin material of his running shorts. *What the hell was happening to him?* Discovering that his mousy little wife might be more appealing than his initial opinion of her had suggested was not something he had ever anticipated.

Nor had he anticipated that his grandfather would react the way he had, Rafael thought grimly. He'd guessed Hector would be annoyed that he had not chosen a bride from the Spanish aristocracy, but he'd never imagined that the old man would break their agreement and refuse to appoint him CEO.

Rafael did not know if Juliet had heard him sigh or if she'd sensed that she was no longer alone. She was still half turned away from him, but when she spun round he felt another jolt of shock when he saw how her features were softened by the hair now framing her face. Her high cheekbones and almond-shaped eyes gave her a fey prettiness.

Now that he was really looking at her—rather than flicking an uninterested gaze over her—he noticed that her mouth was a little too wide for her heart-shaped face and the sweet curve of her lips was unexpectedly sensual.

He walked across the balcony, and as he came nearer to her he saw the rosy flush on her face spread down her throat and across her décolletage. Her eyes widened, the pupils dilating. These subtle signals her body was sending out betrayed her awareness of him—which might work in his favour in light of the news he was about to break to her, he brooded.

Juliet watched Rafael saunter towards her and the wariness she felt for this stranger who was her husband was muddled with other confusing emotions that evoked a dragging sensation low in her pelvis.

It wasn't fair that he was so gorgeous, she thought ruefully. It had been difficult enough to keep her eyes off him when he'd been wearing a suit, or jeans and the navy polo shirt that he'd worn earlier when she had found him in the nursery with Poppy.

Now he must have come from the gym, and his black shorts and matching vest top revealed his powerfully muscular physique. His legs and arms were tanned a deep bronze, and she wondered if the sprinkling of black hair visible above his gym vest covered the whole of his chest.

She hated her reaction to his smouldering sensuality, very aware that he did not find her remotely attractive. But it was odd that he was staring at her intently, almost as if he had never seen her before. When she glanced down at the silk chemise she understood the reason for his scrutiny.

'Your sister lent me a nightdress because my pyjamas have been sent to the laundry,' she explained. 'I should have them back later today.'

'I do hope not,' Rafael said drily.

She grimaced, thinking of her pyjamas, which were as old and cheaply made as everything else she owned. After paying the bills and the monthly repayments on the money she'd borrowed from a loan company which charged a high interest rate, she used any spare cash to buy clothes for Poppy.

'It hardly matters to you that I have horrible pyjamas,' she said defensively. 'You won't see me wearing them. It's not as if we will have to spend any time together, or so you assured me.'

'I only meant that the temperature here in Valencia is much warmer than in England and you won't need to wear thick pyjamas to sleep in.'

'No, you didn't. You think I look terrible and so do your family—apart from your sister, who is very kind.'

Juliet was grateful to Sofia for taking Poppy to play in a summerhouse in the garden with her twin daughters. Sofia had explained that she was married to an Englishman—Marcus Davenport. Her husband worked for a bank in Valencia and the family lived at the Casillas mansion. The twins had been brought up to be bilingual and happily chatted away to Poppy in English.

'I don't care what you or your relatives think of me. I have never pretended to be anything other than a working class single mother—which is precisely why you chose me for your bride,' Juliet reminded Rafael sharply, desperate to hide the hurt she felt.

She was quite aware that he had married her because he needed a wife, but it was humiliating to realise that he'd picked the most disgusting woman he could find so that he could antagonise his grandfather.

He exhaled heavily. 'I'm sorry that I subjected you to my grandfather's temper. Hector is angry with me, not you, but I should have considered your feelings when I involved you in my conflict with him.'

She bit her lip. Rafael's apology had sounded genuine but it did not change the situation. 'I don't want to stay here when it is patently obvious that Poppy and I are not welcome. It don't suppose your grandfather will want me to attend his birthday party. You said that he would make you CEO if you were married by the time of his birthday, and presumably that will still happen. There is no reason for me to stick around and I'm sure you will be relieved when I go.'

'I'm afraid you won't be going anywhere for a while,' Rafael said smoothly. 'For a year, in fact.'

'What do you mean?'

A frisson of unease ran the length of Juliet's spine as she stared at his hard face. He was so beautiful that just looking at him made her insides melt. But she had already experienced his ruthlessness and she did not trust him.

'Hector is refusing to make me CEO because he believes that our marriage is not genuine.'

'Well, that's that, then. Your plan has backfired.'

'Not entirely. On Saturday my grandfather will name me as his successor, and in a year's time he will stand down as head of the company as long as I am still married.' While Juliet was digesting this information, he continued. 'All we have to do is prove that our marriage is the real thing for a year.'

'No way.' She shook her head. 'Our agreement was that we would separate after a couple of months and divorce as soon as legally possible.'

'The contract you signed states that you will receive your money when I become CEO,' he reminded her.

'Then I'll forfeit the money.' She should have known it was too good to be true. 'I should never have agreed to a fake marriage. I just want to take Poppy back to England and forget that I ever met you.'

Rafael's eyes narrowed. 'Five million pounds for a year of your life doesn't sound unreasonable. The deal will be the same, except that you will live here at the Casillas mansion rather than at Ferndown House.'

'With one major difference. You said you wouldn't visit your home in Hampstead very often, but you're asking me to share your family's home in Spain with you. Even though the mansion is huge, we won't be able to avoid each other completely.'

'That's the point,' he said, in that sardonic way of his which made Juliet feel small and insignificant in the grand scheme of his determination to be CEO of his family's business. 'We'll have to live together to show my grandfather that our marriage is real.'

'But it isn't...' she whispered.

An image flashed into her mind of her parents, who had celebrated their wedding anniversary a few weeks before they were killed. Her mum had baked a cake in the shape of a heart, and her dad had gone to his allotment before dawn and come back with a huge bunch of colourful, fragrant sweetpeas which he'd left on the kitchen table next to a card addressed to his darling wife.

Her parents hadn't needed money to make them happy. Their love for each other and for her had been more precious than gold, Juliet thought, blinking away her tears before Rafael saw them.

'It doesn't make sense that your grandfather is insisting on you staying married to me when he doesn't approve of me and knows that I am not the kind of woman you're attracted to,' she muttered.

Rafael's expression was inscrutable, but Juliet was mortified as the truth dawned on her.

'Hector thinks that you won't be able to bear being married to me for a whole year, doesn't he?'

'He is mistaken. I will do whatever I have to,' he said grimly.

'*You* might be willing to lie back and think...not of England, in this case, but of the CEO-ship that you'll gain from being married to the Bride of Frankenstein,' Juliet snapped, 'but I won't do it. You can't force me to stay.'

'You're being melodramatic.' Rafael sounded amused. 'I can't force you to remain in our marriage, it's true. But I suggest you think about what you stand to lose if you walk away now. You told me that your daughter's father wants custody of her and will try to prove that you are unfit to have Poppy living with you. It's hard to see how a judge would back your claim over your ex's if you were homeless or placed in a hostel by social services.'

Juliet swallowed hard, knowing that Rafael was right. 'However,' he continued, 'you are my wife, and Poppy is my stepdaughter, and I will ensure that you have the support of my best legal team. I think it is likely that a family court will look favourably on the fact that Poppy is living in a comfortable home in a secure family unit and she will be allowed to remain with her mother.'

She couldn't argue with Rafael's logical assessment of the situation, Juliet acknowledged despairingly. He had said he would do whatever it took to get what he wanted and she understood that, because she would walk over hot coals to keep Poppy.

'If your grandfather suspects that you've tried to trick him how can we convince him that our marriage is not fake? No one will believe that you fell for someone like me.' When his brows lifted, she said crossly, 'You've dated some of the most beautiful women in the world and you are frequently photographed by the paparazzi with a supermodel or a famous actress draped around you. I'm under no illusions about the way I look. I've always been thin, and I was clearly in the wrong queue when breasts were given out...'

He laughed, and it was so unexpected that Juliet stared at him, mesmerised by the way his lips curved upwards at the corners.

'You're funny,' he said, and there was faint surprise in his voice, as if he had discovered something unexpected about her. He stretched out his hand and touched her hair. 'I see now where your daughter gets her strawberry blonde hair from.'

Suddenly it was hard to speak because her mouth had gone dry. 'Poppy's hair is much fairer than mine,' she muttered.

'Your hair is the colour of amber. It suits you when you leave it loose.'

'After a shower I came to sit outside, so that my hair would dry in the sunshine. Usually I keep it tied up, because it gets in the way when I'm playing with Poppy...'

Juliet knew she was waffling, to distract herself from

suddenly finding that Rafael was much closer. How had he moved without her noticing?

He was so much taller than her and she found herself staring at the ridges of his impressive pectoral muscles visible through his tight-fitting sports vest. The scent of him—spicy cologne, sweat, *male*—assailed her senses. She tilted her head so that she could see his face and her heart missed a beat when she discovered that he was looking at her intently. The gleam in his olive-green eyes startled her, and she told herself she must be imagining the very male interest in gaze.

Rafael wasn't interested in her as a woman. To him she was merely a tool to help him get what he wanted, she reminded herself.

She backed away from him but found herself trapped between his partially clothed muscle-packed body and the wall of the balcony. He placed his hands flat on the top of the balustrade on either side of her and frowned when she shrank from him.

'We are going to have trouble convincing my grandfather that our marriage was made in heaven if you flinch every time I come near you,' he said impatiently. 'You did the same thing during our wedding.'

'You didn't warn me before the ceremony that you would kiss me, and I wasn't expecting it.'

He gave her a sardonic look, but slowly the expression in his eyes changed to something else—something hot that caused Juliet's heart-rate to quicken. 'In that case I'm giving you fair warning that it will be necessary for us to kiss whenever any of my relatives are around and we are on show, so to speak.'

Her tongue darted out to moisten her dry lips. 'You don't want to kiss me…' She would never forget his appalled expression when he had seen her in the mustard-coloured dress she had worn for their wedding.

'I'm coming round to the idea,' he drawled. 'And by the way, I don't think you look like the Bride of Frankenstein.'

'I'm flattered.' She tried to sound sarcastic but her voice was a thread of sound.

Her breath hitched in her throat when Rafael bent his head towards her so that he blotted out the sun. He was so gorgeous, and it would be so easy to fall under his magnetic spell, but it would be dangerous.

She turned her face away and felt his warm breath graze her cheek. 'I don't want you to kiss me.'

He captured her chin between his long fingers and exerted gentle pressure so that she was forced to look at him. 'How do you know until you've tried it? You might enjoy it.'

That was what she was afraid of.

She could not hide the tremor that ran through her when he dragged his thumb pad over her bottom lip.

'You are not my prisoner, and I am not doing anything to prevent you from going back inside the house,' Rafael murmured. 'But if you don't move in the next ten seconds I *am* going to kiss you.'

It was true that she could easily step past him. But her feet seemed to be cemented to the floor. Her instinct for self-protection urged her to run, but a stronger instinct that was deeply rooted in her womanhood held her there against the balustrade as Rafael's mouth came nearer.

Her heart was beating at three times its normal rate and he placed his finger over the pulse that was going crazy at the base of her throat. And then he brushed his lips across hers and the world tilted on its axis.

She had expected him to kiss her with the bold arrogance that was integral to him, but his mouth was gentle on hers, warm and seductive, disarming her defences so that her lips parted without her volition. Even then he kept it light, undemanding, tasting her with little sips that teased and tantalised so that she pressed her body closer to his and placed her hands flat on his chest.

Juliet felt the powerful thud of his heart beneath her fingertips and with a little sigh of capitulation kissed him back. Her eyelashes swept down and her senses became attuned to the taste of him on her lips, the warmth of his breath filling her mouth and the evocative masculine scent that wrapped around her as she melted, soft and pliant, against his whipcord body.

CHAPTER FIVE

'That wasn't so difficult, was it?'

Rafael's voice broke through the sensual haze that had wrapped around Juliet and she blinked at him, half blinded by the bright sunshine in her eyes as he lifted his head and she was no longer in his shadow. She wondered why he had stopped kissing her, but then reality hit and she remembered he had been demonstrating how they would have to act in public to convince his grandfather that their marriage was genuine.

And she had just demonstrated to Rafael that she couldn't resist him!

Following his gaze, she glanced down and a fresh wave of embarrassment swept over her when she saw the outline of her pebble-hard nipples beneath the silk chemise. She looked back at him, expecting to see mockery in his eyes, but he seemed unusually tense, and it was obvious that he couldn't wait to get away from her when he swung round and strode across the balcony.

He paused as he reached the bi-fold glass doors. 'The nurse said that your temperature has returned to normal and you are feeling much better?' When Juliet nodded, he continued, 'We are expected to attend a family lunch later, so that you can meet more of my relatives.'

She thought of the sea of faces that had stared at

her as if she had been beamed down from Mars when Rafael had brought her to the Casillas mansion. 'You mean there are *more*?'

'My grandfather is the oldest of seven siblings, and there are numerous uncles, aunts and cousins, many of whom work within the company and have an opinion on who they think should succeed Hector. Some of them support me—rather more of them don't,' he said sardonically.

It sounded like a family at war. Juliet bit her lip. 'I'd rather not be subjected to further humiliation and I don't want to risk Poppy being upset again. Can't you say that I am still unwell?'

'My grandfather will expect us to be at the lunch and it will be an opportunity to show him that we are a couple who are in love.'

Juliet wondered why his words evoked an ache in her heart. She had never been in love. Her crush on Bryan had ended abruptly when he'd brutally told her she had been a one-night stand. And Rafael had warned her not to fall in love with him. But now he was asking her to pretend that he was the man of her dreams.

'I'm not that good an actress,' she muttered.

'I thought your performance a few moments ago was very convincing—unless it wasn't an act and you actually *enjoyed* kissing me?' he said silkily.

While Juliet was searching her mind for a clever retort, he spoke again.

'Sofia's twins will have their lunch in the nursery with the nanny—Poppy might be happier staying with them.'

He had kissed Juliet to show her how they would have to act like happy newlyweds in front of his grandfather.

That was the *only* reason, Rafael assured himself. Although perhaps there had been an element of curiosity too, he conceded.

The realisation that he had been too hasty when he'd dismissed his wife as being plain and unattractive had stirred his interest. But he had been unprepared for his reaction to the feel of her soft lips beneath his. Quite simply he had been blown away by the sweet sensuality of Juliet's response, and his gut had clenched when she had kissed him with an intriguing mix of innocence and desire.

Dios, there had been a moment when his cool logic had almost been superseded by fiery passion, and he'd been on the verge of deepening the kiss and drawing her slender figure up close against his hard body. Fortunately he had remembered in time that it would be a mistake to become involved with her. Juliet was more vulnerable than he had thought when he'd suggested their marriage deal.

Face it, Rafael told himself grimly, you didn't think about *her* at all.

She was simply a means by which he could achieve his goal of becoming CEO, and nothing in that respect had changed—except that out there on the balcony it had fleetingly crossed his mind that he would like to have sex with her. But that would further complicate an already complicated situation, he brooded as he slid his arms into his suit jacket.

Rafael's private apartment in the mansion consisted of an open-plan lounge-cum-dining room, a kitchen and his study. There was also a large master bedroom, with his-and-hers dressing rooms and en suite bathrooms. He had asked the staff to put a single bed in Juliet's dressing room, so that Poppy could sleep near to her mother, and he had been sleeping on the sofa in his dressing room, leaving the bed for Juliet while she was ill.

There would have to be a change to the sleeping arrangements, he decided. He was six foot three, and he couldn't spend every night for the next year with his feet hanging off the end of a sofa.

Pushing open the bedroom door, he stifled a sigh when he saw Juliet. It had suited him that she looked like a drab waif when he'd wanted to annoy his grandfather with his unsuitable bride. Now there had been a change of plan, but unfortunately Juliet's dress sense had not improved.

Her outfit of a denim skirt with a frayed hem and a flamingo-pink jumper that clashed with her reddish hair was only marginally less unflattering than the abomination of a dress she had been wearing when he had introduced her to his family two days ago.

'I should have mentioned that lunch will be a formal affair,' he said.

At least she had made a bit of effort with her hair, and it was piled on top of her head in a neat bun. The style showed off the elegant line of her throat, but inexplicably Rafael wished she had left her hair loose so that he could run his fingers through it.

Her face was no longer unhealthily pale. Spending some time outside in the sunshine had put a pink flush on her cheeks. He would have to make sure that she wore sunscreen, he thought. Her English rose complexion would burn easily.

She shrugged. 'I don't own any designer clothes. There wasn't any need for them at my cleaning job,' she told him drily.

He strode into her dressing room and opened the wardrobe door, grimacing when it was immediately obvious that she had spoken the truth. 'You *must* own other footwear besides those things,' he muttered, looking at her scuffed winter boots.

Instead of replying she took a pair of tatty trainers out of the wardrobe and waved them in front of him. 'You married me precisely because my clothes look like they came from a jumble sale. Frankly, your plan to try and convince your grandfather that you've married your fantasy woman is just not going to work.'

'We both have a vested interest in *making* it work,' he reminded her. 'And we will have a better chance if you are a little less lippy.'

Against his will his gaze was drawn to her mouth, and he remembered how her lips had parted beneath his, so soft and moist and willing. He'd sensed her disappointment when he'd ended the kiss. Beneath her belligerent attitude she was attracted to him. But it would not be fair to lead her on or let her believe that he could fulfil any romantic notions she might have about him.

'I will arrange an appointment for you with a personal stylist who can advise you on what clothes will suit your figure instead of swamping you,' he said abruptly. He glanced at his watch. 'We had better go downstairs. Lunch is in ten minutes.'

He escorted Juliet out of his private suite, and as they descended the grand staircase and walked through the house he had to wait several times while she stopped to admire the artwork on the walls.

'Don't tell me that's an original Van Gogh?' she said, sounding amazed. 'And a Cezanne and a Renoir? It's an impressive art collection. Do the paintings belong to your grandfather?'

'Some of them are mine. I bought the Jackson Pollock at auction a year ago.'

He was curious about where a girl from a council estate who sold sandwiches and cleaned for a living had gained such an in-depth knowledge of art. Juliet intrigued him... Rafael frowned as he admitted to himself that she was the only woman ever to have done so.

She stood in front of the Pollock and studied the painting. 'It looks like the artist just threw paint at the canvas. I don't like it. Do you?'

He shrugged. 'I've never thought about whether I like it or not. I paid one hundred and twenty million dollars for the painting, which I bought as an investment.'

She tilted her head to one side and studied him thoughtfully, the same way she had looked at the painting. 'Fancy paying all that money for something that doesn't fill your heart with joy.'

'I will be paying a lot of money for *you*, but I am not feeling joy right now, *chiquita*. I'm feeling exasperated,' he growled. He glanced at her, clumping along next to him in her scuffed boots, and sighed. 'I had forgotten that you haven't had a chance to look around the house because your illness has confined you to bed. I'll give you a tour after lunch.'

He was about to open the dining room door but Juliet put her hand on his arm. 'Is it going to be as awful as last time?' she said in a low tone.

Why hadn't he thought that she would be nervous about meeting his family again—especially his grandfather? And who could blame her? Guilt snaked through Rafael at knowing he had put Juliet in this situation.

Her eyes were huge in her face and her small hand was cold when he wrapped his fingers around hers. 'I have explained that Hector is not angry with *you*.'

'He's disappointed with me because I'm not good enough to be your wife.'

He grimaced. 'No, *cariño*. My grandfather has always been disappointed with *me*. You have done nothing wrong and I won't allow him to insult you again.'

Despite Rafael's reassurance, Juliet felt sick with nerves when he ushered her into the dining room and led her over to the group of people who were gathered by the open French doors where pre-lunch drinks were being served.

He introduced her to his numerous relatives and she was conscious of the curious glances they gave her.

Worse were the unflattering comments she overheard his mother make about her clothes. Perhaps Rafael had not informed his family that she understood Spanish.

The tangible antagonism between him and his mother, the icily elegant Delfina Casillas, was another puzzle. She remembered that Rafael had mentioned he had a stepbrother, but he didn't seem to be at the lunch.

When they sat down for the meal she was relieved that Hector was seated at the far end of the table. He did not pay her any attention, but she was too on edge to enjoy the five courses, and she opted for water rather than wine so that she kept a clear head. She was toying with her dessert—a chocolate confection that at any other time she would have adored—when Hector spoke to her in English.

'Rafael tells me that you ran your own business in London. What type of business?'

Conversation around the table suddenly stopped and Juliet sensed that everyone was looking at her. She lifted her chin. 'I sold sandwiches and delivered them to office staff at lunchtimes.'

'You worked in catering?'

Hector's tone was as scathing as if she'd announced that she had worked as a stripper. Her temper simmered. She hated snobbery, and having been subjected to it at ballet school by some of the other pupils she had learned to stand up for herself.

'Yes. I also had a cleaning job in the evenings—pushing an industrial floor-polishing machine around a shopping centre.'

'Santa Madre! Ella es un domestico!' the old man muttered to Rafael's mother, who was sitting next to him.

Delfina's expression became even haughtier as she glanced along the table at Juliet.

'Abuelo, there is no need for you to be rude about my wife,' Rafael said curtly.

Juliet's heart lifted at his defence of her—until she remembered that he was determined to convince his grandfather he was in love with her.

She looked over at Hector. 'Presumably you are unaware that I speak Spanish and that I can understand the horrible things you have said about me? I am not from the gutter. My parents weren't wealthy but they were hard-working, and they taught me good manners—which you seem to lack.'

A gasp went around the table, and beside her she felt Rafael stiffen, but she was too angry to care.

'And there is no shame in doing domestic work. Without the staff who run this house you would have to clean your own floors.'

As quickly as her temper had flared it cooled again, and she wished she was anywhere but sitting at this table, with Hector Casillas looking at her disdainfully as if she were a piece of rubbish. What if he decided not to appoint Rafael CEO because she had allowed her pride to get the better of her? She did not dare glance at Rafael, certain that he must be furious with her, and she was startled when he gave a shout of laughter.

'Well said, *querida*.' He looked over at his grandfather. 'As you have just discovered, Abuelo, my wife is petite in stature but she is as fierce as a lioness.'

Juliet turned her head towards her husband and her heart lurched when he smiled at her, showing his even white teeth. She must have imagined that note of admiration in his voice, she told herself.

Following her outburst the atmosphere in the dining room among his relatives was strained and she could not wait for the meal to be over. It was Sofia who broke the awkward silence.

'Where did you learn to speak Spanish, Juliet?'

'My aunt is married to a Spaniard and Uncle Carlos insisted on speaking Spanish at home with Aunt Vivian and my cousins. I lived with them for a couple of years, and quickly picked up on how to speak the language, but I'm not confident at reading and writing in Spanish.'

It was for that reason she had been unable to find a better paid job as a translator, Juliet thought ruefully.

'Did you live in Spain with your aunt and uncle?' Sofia asked.

'No—Australia. They settled in Sydney twenty years ago, but my uncle wanted to feel a connection to his birth country.'

'What about your parents? Do they also live in Australia?'

She shook her head. 'Mum and Dad died before Poppy was born.'

'I'm so sorry,' Sofia said gently. 'I assume your parents were not very old. Did they lose their lives in an accident?'

'Their car broke down on a motorway and they were waiting for the rescue truck. It was a foggy night and a lorry ploughed into them. They were both killed instantly.'

'What a terrible tragedy. You must have been devastated.'

'Yes.'

Memories flooded Juliet's mind of the night that her life had been blown apart. She missed her parents so much and she felt very alone—an outsider in Rafael's family home, made to feel unwelcome by his relatives. Tears blurred her eyes and she stared down at the table while she struggled to bring her emotions under control. To her horror she felt a tear slide down her cheek and drip onto the tablecloth. The bead of moisture darkened the pristine white cloth as it soaked into the material.

Rafael made a low sound in his throat, almost like a groan, and placed his hand over hers, where she was resting it on the table. That human connection—the warmth of his skin as he threaded his fingers through hers—tugged on her heart.

For a few moments she allowed herself to daydream that he actually cared about her as he lifted her hand to his mouth and pressed his lips against her knuckles. Her eyes flew to his and he held her gaze, his expression softer than she had ever seen it. Time seemed to be suspended, and it was as if there were only the two of them floating in a private universe.

Juliet released a shaky breath—but when she glanced around the table she saw that Hector was watching them and understanding dawned. Rafael was acting in front of his grandfather and she was a fool for wishing that his concern was genuine.

When the lunch was over, and they stood up and

walked out of the dining room, she tried to snatch her hand out of his. 'Hector can't see us now, so you can stop pretending to be sympathetic,' she muttered.

'I wasn't pretending.' He stopped walking and stared down at her, tightening his fingers around her hand so that she could not pull free. 'I am not without compassion. You have been through a hell of a lot.'

She shook her head, refusing to allow herself to fall for the huskiness in his voice. 'Like you *care*, Rafael,' she said sarcastically. 'I realise that for the next year I will have to act like your loving wife in public, but I don't want your pseudo-sympathy or your fake kisses.'

Something indecipherable flared in his eyes. 'There was nothing fake about the chemistry we both felt this morning or the way you responded when I kissed you. Perhaps I should remind you?'

Without being aware of how she'd got there, Juliet found herself standing in a small alcove off the marble-lined entrance hall. Rafael ignored her renewed attempts to free her hand by the simple method of repositioning it behind her back.

He swore when she kicked his shin. 'Calm down, you little wildcat.'

She glared at him, her heart thudding unevenly as he lowered his head. 'I don't want you to kiss me.'

'We've been through that once.'

He sounded bored, but his eyes glittered with something that Juliet was stunned to realise was desire. For *her*. He lifted his other hand and pulled the pins out of her bun, so that her hair unravelled and spilled over her shoulders.

'No one is around to see us so why are you doing this?' she asked desperately.

'You need to practise kissing,' he told her.

His voice was deadpan, but there was a wicked gleam in his eyes that made her stomach swoop.

'It's my guess that you haven't had much experience.'

'I'm sorry if you were disappointed by my efforts earlier,' she choked. 'Do you take pleasure in humiliating me?'

'I find this much more pleasurable,' he murmured against her lips, his breath mingling with hers as he brought his mouth down and kissed her with a possessiveness that decimated her defences.

And Juliet surrendered. She suspected that she would hate herself later, but right now she was powerless to fight the restless longing that stirred low in her belly as Rafael deepened the kiss and explored the shape of her lips with his tongue before he dipped it into her mouth, demanding a response that she could not deny him.

She had never felt like this before—wild and hungry and aching with a passion that stung her nipples and tugged sharp and needy between her thighs. Rafael had been right to think that she hadn't had much experience of kissing or anything else.

She'd only been on a few dates with Bryan before he had suggested they spend the night together. Naively she'd believed that he was in love with her, as she had been with him, and so she had agreed.

Her first and only sexual experience had been uncomfortable and unsatisfactory—which he had assured her was *her* fault. Bryan had not wanted her for more than one night—and Rafael did not want her at all. Not really.

He had married her because she was unattractive and now he was stuck with her for a year. He couldn't resume his playboy lifestyle while he had to convince his grandfather that his marriage was genuine. Faced with a choice of celibacy or sex with his wife, perhaps he had decided that she was the better of the two options.

Shame doused the fire inside her and she jerked her mouth away from his. 'No.'

'No?' He sounded as dazed as she felt and he was breathing hard. 'I could very easily persuade you to retract that statement, *chiquita*...' he rasped.

'Why would you want to? We both know that I am the last woman you would desire. I am too thin and plain.' She bit her lip. 'I've seen pictures of the supermodels you take to bed.'

His eyes narrowed. 'You are not plain. You just need the right clothes for your shape.'

'My mother used to say that you can't make a silk purse out of a sow's ear. I know what I am, and more to the point I know my lack of looks and sophistication are the reasons you married me.'

It hurt more than it should, and she pushed past him, hating the idea that he might pity her.

She ran up the grand staircase and then hesitated on the landing when she realised that she had no idea where Rafael's suite of rooms were or, more importantly, the location of the nursery. Her arms ached to hold her daughter and feel the unconditional love that Poppy gave her and she returned a thousandfold.

'Are you lost?' Rafael's sister walked along the corridor towards her and laughed when Juliet nodded. 'The house is huge, isn't it? When Rafael and I first came to live here we couldn't get over how grand it is.'

'I assumed you were both born here. Where did you live before you moved into the mansion?'

Sofia gave her a thoughtful look. 'You should ask my brother. Here's the nursery.' She seemed relieved to change the subject. 'I promised to take the twins swimming this afternoon. Will you and Poppy join us?'

'Neither of us have swimwear. I've never taken Poppy swimming. The local pool where we lived in London was closed down by the council. There was a pool at a private gym but I couldn't afford the membership fees.' Juliet flushed and looked away from Rafael's elegant sister.

'I'm sure you have always done your best for your daughter,' Sofia said gently. 'But Poppy can use one of the swimsuits that the girls have grown out of, and I'll lend you a swimming costume.'

Juliet's conscience would not allow Poppy to miss out on her first experience of swimming, and the little girl's excitement when they arrived at the pool later that afternoon helped her to overcome her reluctance to slip off the towelling robe and reveal the sky-blue swimsuit that Sofia had lent her.

The twins were already in the water and Juliet noted that they were proficient swimmers. She felt guilty that her circumstances meant that Poppy had missed out on so many things—especially a father, she thought as she watched Sofia's husband playing with his daughters. He waded up the steps carrying Ana and Inez in each arm, and Sofia introduced him to Juliet.

'I was meant to arrive back in time for lunch but my flight was delayed,' Marcus Davenport explained. His pleasant face broke into a grin. 'I hear that you stood up to Hector? I wish I had been there to witness it.'

Sofia and Marcus were so friendly that Juliet started to relax as she played in the pool with Poppy, who was wearing armbands and bobbing about happily in the water.

'There's an indoor pool too, and Poppy will soon

learn to swim without water aids if you bring her every day,' Sofia said.

For the first time since Rafael had dropped the bombshell that they would have to remain married for a year and live at the Casillas mansion Juliet realised that there would be some benefits—especially for her daughter. Poppy was already picking up a few Spanish words from the twins, and she would have so much freedom to play in the gardens or at the beach, which had been visible when Juliet had stood on the balcony that morning.

Her stomach hollowed as she remembered what had happened when Rafael had found her on the balcony. He had kissed her, and it had been so much better than she'd imagined.

And she had imagined it often.

Her secret fantasies, in which he swept her into his arms and claimed her mouth with his, had not been disappointed by the sensual expertise of his kiss. Just thinking about it made her breasts tingle, and when she glanced down she was dismayed to see the hard points of her nipples outlined beneath her swimsuit.

The sound of a familiar gravelly voice with a sexy accent caused her to spin round, and she quickly ducked her shoulders under the water when she saw Rafael standing at the edge of the pool. A pair of navy blue swim shorts sat low on his hips, and Juliet's gaze skittered over his hair-roughened thighs before moving up to his flat abdomen and broad, tanned chest covered in silky black hair.

Oh, my! She edged into deeper water to hide her body's reaction to his rampant masculinity.

Poppy gave a squeal of delight when she saw Rafael. 'Raf—are you coming swimming?'

'Would you like me to, *conejita*?'

He swung himself down into the pool and dived below the surface before reappearing and raking his wet hair off his brow with his hands.

'Let me see you swim, little rabbit,' he said to Poppy, and she immediately kicked her feet the way Juliet had tried to persuade her to do for the past twenty minutes.

They stayed in the water for a while longer, until Poppy started to shiver, and then Rafael lifted her onto the poolside where Elvira was waiting with a towel. He turned back to Juliet and frowned when he saw her tense expression. 'What's the matter? We are meant to be playing happy families but you haven't stopped glaring at me.'

'That's just it. This is a game to you,' she said tautly. 'But while you are *"playing happy families"* to impress your grandfather, there is a danger that Poppy will become fond of you. When I agreed to our marriage deal it was only going to be for a couple of months, but now we have to stay together for a year and it will be harder on Poppy when I take her back to England.'

'Are you saying that I should *ignore* your daughter?' Rafael's frown deepened. 'I realise the situation has changed and I won't suddenly drop out of Poppy's life in a year's time.' He swore beneath his breath when Juliet gave him a disbelieving look. 'It is not my intention to upset Poppy. She is a delightful child and a credit to you,' he said gruffly.

'She likes you,' Juliet muttered. 'You are good with her and your nieces.'

The truth was that she'd felt a tug of jealousy when Poppy had wanted to play with Rafael rather than with her. She had been surprised that he was so patient with her daughter and his sister's little girls.

'You'll make a good father when you have children of your own.'

'That's never going to happen.' His tone dropped several degrees. 'I've no desire to have children.'

'What if your wife wants a family? I don't mean me,' she added hastily. 'But in the future you might meet the right woman and fall in love with her.'

'I told you when you agreed to be my wife that I do not believe in love.' He walked up the steps out of the pool and grabbed a towel from a nearby sunbed. 'Lust is an emotion I understand, but that doesn't last for ever. Unfortunately too many people only discover that after they have made a legal commitment to spend the rest of their lives together, and the only winners are the divorce lawyers.'

'Why are you so cynical? My parents were as much in love with each other when they died as they were on the day they married. They were happy together for more than twenty years.' She swallowed. 'It might sound odd, but I'm glad they were together when they were killed. I don't know how one would have survived without the other.'

Juliet followed Rafael out of the pool and stopped dead when she saw him staring at her leg. She had been so engrossed in their conversation that she'd forgotten about the scar that ran from the top of her thigh to just above her knee. The scar had faded over the years, but she was chilly after being in the pool and it was now a vivid purple welt on her pale skin.

Avoiding his gaze, she hurried over to where she had left her robe and wrapped it around her, thankful that it covered her leg. She had come to terms with the scar, or so she'd thought, but she wished Rafael hadn't seen it. No doubt now he thought she was ugly as well as plain.

'What happened to you?' he asked quietly.

'I was in my parents' car when the lorry crashed into the back of it.'

'Dios.' He dropped his towel and strode over to her, settling his hand on her shoulder. 'I didn't realise that you were with your parents when they died.'

'I don't remember much about the accident.' Juliet automatically turned her head to check on Poppy, and saw her playing in a sandpit with the twins. 'The car developed a problem while we were driving along the motorway and my dad pulled over onto the hard shoulder. It was winter and very foggy. I was sitting in the front passenger seat and Dad told me to stay there while he went to get my coat out of the boot. Mum got out with him, and that's when the lorry smashed into us.'

She was conscious of Rafael curling his fingers tighter around her shoulder. She had never really spoken about what had happened to anyone before, but now the words came tumbling out.

'All I remember is a loud noise like an explosion. I was in a coma for two weeks, and when I came round I was told that my femur had been shattered by the impact of the crash. At first the surgeon thought that my leg would have to be amputated, but he did everything he could and saved it. My thigh bone is held together with several metal pins.' She swallowed. 'My aunt had flown over from Australia and she broke the news about my parents when I came out of Intensive Care.'

'Dios!' Rafael repeated roughly. 'Has your leg healed fully?'

'It's fine now, but eighteen months ago I had to have some more surgery and I was in hospital for a few weeks. Aunt Viv couldn't come over from Australia then, because she was ill herself. There was no one to look after Poppy so she stayed with foster parents.'

Juliet felt a pang, remembering how desperately she had missed her daughter while they had been apart. She watched the sunlight glinting on the surface of the pool. It was so bright that it made her eyes sting. That was the reason for the tears that blurred her vision, she assured herself.

'Poppy is all I have,' she whispered. 'Bryan has never been interested in her but now he's threatening to take my baby away from me.' She spun away from Rafael and his hand fell from her shoulder. 'I won't let that happen,' she said fiercely. 'That's why I agreed to your marriage deal and why I am determined to see it through.'

She stared at his beautiful face, at the mouth that had wreaked such havoc on hers.

'I'm using you as much as you are using me. Let's hope that we both end up with what we want in a year's time.'

CHAPTER SIX

RAFAEL STROLLED THROUGH the marble and gold entrance hall in the Casillas mansion, clearly designed to impress, with a champagne flute in one hand and a smile on his lips that anyone who knew him well—which only his sister did—would realise was entirely fake. He stopped to speak to his uncle, but although he was fond of Tio Alvaro, who was one of his supporters, Rafael's attention was on the grand staircase where he expected to see Juliet appear.

Where the hell *was* his wife?

When he had knocked on the door of her dressing room before he'd come down to greet the guests who were arriving for his grandfather's birthday party Sofia had called out that Juliet would be ready in ten minutes. That had been a quarter of an hour ago, and Rafael was growing concerned that she did not want to leave her room because she was afraid of being subjected to another frosty reception from certain members of his family.

He had barely seen her for the past two days, while he had been at work at the Casillas Group's head office in Valencia. He'd arranged for her to go shopping with a personal stylist who would advise her on a new wardrobe, and Sofia had offered to look after Poppy.

However, Rafael had yet to see if the stylist had been successful in finding some clothes which suited Juliet's figure.

She had been fast asleep in his bed by the time he'd returned to the mansion late in the evenings, after long days of business meetings. And, aware that she had only recently recovered from the virus that had made her so unwell, he had been reluctant to disturb her and had slept on the sofa in his dressing room again.

But she had been on his mind a lot. Too much. Instead of concentrating on what was being said at the meetings he had found himself thinking of Juliet when they had been at the pool. He'd pictured her in that light blue swimsuit which matched the startling blue of her eyes. The clingy material had revealed her slender figure and small, round breasts. She was as fragile as a bird, and when he'd seen that scar on her leg, before she had quickly wrapped her robe around her to hide it from him, he'd been struck once again by her mix of vulnerability and incredible courage.

The realisation that Juliet might have died along with her parents in the car accident, and that he might never have met her, disturbed Rafael more than it should. After all, it was not as if she meant anything to him. He kept his affairs short and sweet, aware of the damage that the unstable mix of emotions and relationships could produce. His mother had followed her heart when she'd eloped with his father, and Rafael was the damaged product of his parents' messed-up lives.

'It is a big night for you tonight, eh?' said Tio Alvaro.

Rafael nodded his head, not entirely sure what his uncle meant.

'I have heard rumours that Hector is going to announce you as his successor. It is what you have wanted for a long time?'

'Ah, yes.'

Rafael did not explain that his grandfather's announcement would contain a caveat and that the handover of power would not happen immediately. To his astonishment he realised that he had not given Hector's announcement a thought. He had waited for years and fought hard to claim his birthright, but tonight his mind was on Juliet rather than the CEO-ship.

He raked a hand through his hair and asked himself why he was allowing a slip of a girl with an understated sensuality and eyes that he could drown in to affect him. Something caught his attention, and when he looked up towards the top of the staircase he felt the new experience of his heart colliding painfully with his ribs.

'Ah, querida...' he murmured beneath his breath.

He had already been surprised by Juliet—by her unexpected fiery nature and the sensual heat of her kiss that had made him ache for hours afterwards. But as he watched her begin to descend the grand marble staircase, one hand holding lightly onto the banister rail, he was quite simply awestruck.

She shimmered. There was no other way to describe her. The effect was created by the hundreds of gold sequins that covered her ball gown, but there was something else that made Juliet sparkle. It was self-confidence and pride, Rafael thought as he strode across the hall to the base of the staircase. It was also, he mused as he stood there, unable to take his eyes off her, her own realisation that she was beautiful. So very beautiful.

And she was certainly making an entrance. The eyes of every person in the hall were focused on his stunning, sexy wife as she walked down the stairs towards him.

How had he not seen before how utterly lovely she was? Well-fitting clothes helped, of course. The gown had been designed to mould her slender frame and emphasise the narrowness of her waist. The bodice was strapless and her small breasts were displayed like perfect round peaches above the low-cut neckline. The shimmering gold material followed the gentle contours of her hips before finally flaring out trumpet style to the floor.

She seemed to glide down the stairs, and Rafael caught a glimpse of gold stiletto heels beneath the hem of her dress. He lifted his gaze up to her hair, which had had three or four inches cut off its length and now fell to mid-way down her back, gleaming like polished amber beneath the bright lights of the chandeliers. A stylist had added some wispy layers to the front sections of her hair, which framed her face and drew attention to her high cheekbones and forget-me-not-blue eyes.

When she halted two steps above where he was waiting for her Rafael saw that her fair eyebrows and lashes had been darkened with make-up and her mouth was coated in a rose-coloured gloss. The finishing touch to her transformation was her perfume—floral notes mixed with an edgier, more sensual fragrance that assailed his senses and evoked a kick of heat in his groin.

As he studied her he saw a wariness in her expression that he instantly wanted to banish. *'Bella,'* he murmured, capturing her hand in his and lifting it to his mouth. 'I'm speechless, *chiquita*. I would never have believed...'

'That a sow's ear could be turned into something passably attractive?' she suggested.

'I never want to hear you use that terrible expression again. You are not and never have been a sow's ear.'

But he had been blind, Rafael acknowledged. Worse, he had been arrogant enough to believe that he could use Juliet to further his raging ambition. He had chosen her because of her downtrodden appearance. *Dios*, he had treated her as scornfully as his grandfather had. But Juliet's ethereal beauty hid an incredible strength of will. She was a survivor—as he was—and he knew how lonely that felt.

Shame ran through Rafael. Distaste for his presumption that Juliet's lack of money made her less worthy of his respect. He had spent the past twenty years fighting prejudice from his family because of his lowly background—part-*gitano*, born in the gutter to a drug-dealer father. But he had ruthlessly exploited Juliet's financial problems to persuade her to marry him without considering how humiliated she would feel to be despised by his rich relatives.

'You look exquisite,' he assured her. 'I take it that your shopping trip was a success?'

She caught her lower lip between her teeth, making him want to soothe the place with his tongue. 'The personal stylist insisted that I needed dozens of outfits to reflect my position as your wife. She spent a *fortune* on clothes. But I'll pay you back when—' She broke off and glanced around to check that they could not be overheard by anyone. 'When our marriage deal ends.'

Rafael laid his finger lightly across her lips, refusing to question why he did not want to think of the motive behind their marriage. 'I believe in living for the moment,' he said softly. 'And at this moment, *querida*, I will be honoured to escort my beautiful wife into the ballroom.'

Juliet smiled and her elfin beauty made his gut clench. He drew her arm through his and walked her into the ballroom, where most of the three hundred guests were now assembled and waiters were serving champagne and canapés. Many of Spain's elite—a mix of old money aristocrats and nouveau riche millionaires—were on the guest list.

He took a glass of champagne offered by a waiter and gave it to Juliet before he took a glass for himself. *'Salud.'*

She sipped her drink. 'Is it real champagne? I've only ever had sparkling wine.'

'Of course it's real champagne. My grandfather would not allow fizzy wine to be served at his eightieth birthday party,' he said drily.

'It's lovely.' She took another sip and giggled. 'It feels like the bubbles are exploding on my tongue.'

Rafael stared at her. He could not stop himself. Juliet was like a breath of fresh air, and he realised how stultifying and predictable his life had become until she had burst into it.

He did not know what to make of the feelings she stirred in him. The hot rush of desire that went straight to his groin was something he understood, but he felt possessive, protective, and a host of other emotions that had never troubled him before.

Juliet bit her lip and he realised that she had mistaken his brooding silence for irritation. 'I'm not sophisticated,' she mumbled, rosy colour running under her skin.

'Thank God,' he reassured her.

The band had started playing and he led her over to the dance floor, handing their empty glasses to a waiter before he drew her into his arms. Even in high heels she was so much smaller than him that he could rest his chin on the top of her head.

She danced with a natural grace that captivated him, and he swore silently when he felt the predictable reaction of a certain part of his anatomy to the sensation of Juliet's lithe body pressed up against his hard thighs. He was in trouble, Rafael acknowledged, seizing the excuse that the tune had finished to step away from her.

'Come and meet some people.'

He took her hand and felt her tense as he led her across the ballroom.

'Relax,' he murmured, bending his head so that his mouth was against her ear and his breath stirred the tendrils of her hair. 'Tio Alvaro and his wife Lucia are nice. Just be yourself.'

Rafael introduced Juliet to his aunt and uncle and fielded their curiosity about where and when he had met his bride. He was conscious of the simmering look Juliet darted at him when he explained that it had been love at first sight when they had met in London.

Lucia glanced at Juliet's hand. 'I see you are not wearing an engagement ring. Shame on you, Rafael.'

'We married quickly—there wasn't time to choose a ring,' he said smoothly.

'Alvaro and I will be visiting London next month,' Lucia said to Juliet. 'I want to visit Buckingham Palace. Did you live near it?'

'Not very near,' she replied without a flicker.

Rafael pictured the tower block in the rough part of London where Juliet had lived, and was fiercely glad that she and her little daughter would never have to go back there.

'Where else do you recommend we visit while we're staying in the capital?' Lucia asked.

'Well, if you like music, or ballet, I recommend booking tickets for the Royal Albert Hall. It's a wonderful venue to enjoy a concert. Or there's the Royal Festival Hall and the Royal Opera House. All are spectacular.'

'I suppose you worked as a cleaner in the Opera House?' a voice said sarcastically.

Rafael looked round and saw Hector was standing close by. His grandfather had obviously been listening to the conversation. Furious with the old man, he tightened his arm around Juliet's waist, hoping she was not upset. *Dios*, his grandfather was a snob.

'Abuelo...' he began tensely.

'Actually, I danced at all three venues,' Juliet said calmly. 'I was a ballerina, and in my very brief career I performed on stage at several of London's best concert halls.'

Shock ran through Rafael. He heard Hector give a disbelieving snort but Tia Lucia clapped her hands together and said excitedly, 'I *love* the ballet—especially *Swan Lake*.'

'That's one of my favourites too,' Juliet said with a smile. 'I once performed the Dance of the Cygnets.'

'Do you still dance?' Lucia asked.

Juliet shook her head. 'Not professionally. I was badly injured in an accident and couldn't continue with my ballet career.'

Hector walked away and Rafael made an excuse, leaving Juliet to chat to his aunt and uncle, while he strode after his grandfather.

'Abuelo.' He caught up with the old man and scowled at him. It occurred to Rafael that he had spent all his adult life trying to win Hector's approval—without success. He *was* the best person to take over running the Casillas Group—he knew it and so did his grandfather. But he could never escape his gypsy heritage and the prejudice and mistrust it evoked—not just in his family but in people generally.

'Do not *ever* treat my wife with disrespect again,' he told Hector savagely. 'You have no right to make judgements upon her. You know nothing about Juliet.'

Hector's bushy brows rose. 'Do *you*?' he challenged.

He stared at Rafael, and the curiosity in his expression slowly changed into something which might have been begrudging respect. But maybe he'd imagined it, Rafael thought. And then he realised that he did not care about his grandfather's opinion of him. His only concern was that Hector would treat Juliet with the consideration and courtesy she deserved.

As he threaded his way back across the crowded ballroom he was waylaid by his half-brother. 'How are you, Francisco?' he greeted the young man.

'I'm in shock,' his brother said with a grin. 'Mamà has told me that you have a wife, but she seems to think it is suspicious that you married so quickly.'

Rafael knew it was not his half-brother's fault that their mother favoured him, her youngest son, and would do anything to see him succeed Hector. He did not like deceiving Frankie, but he could not risk Delfina discovering that his marriage was fake.

'No one was more surprised than me when I fell in love with Juliet,' he murmured. It was odd how easily the lie fell from his lips.

'I can't wait to meet the woman who finally persuaded you up the aisle. She must be amazing.'

'She certainly amazes *me*,' said Rafael, thinking of Juliet's latest startling revelation. 'I'll introduce you to her when I find her.'

He frowned as he scanned the ballroom but failed to see a sparkly gold dress.

* * *

Juliet stepped through the glass doors leading from the ballroom onto a wide balcony. Immediately the buzz of chattering voices and the music from the band became muted. It was a clear night, and she tipped her head back and studied the stars glittering like diamonds against the inky backdrop of the sky.

The party wasn't as daunting as she had expected, and apart from an awkward moment when Rafael's grandfather had made an unpleasant comment to her she was enjoying herself.

She had never dreamed when she'd been cleaning floors in the shopping centre that she would ever wear a beautiful ball gown, drink champagne and dance cheek to cheek—well, cheek to chest, she amended—with her impossibly handsome husband.

She leaned her elbows on the top of the stone balustrade and stared out over the dark garden. The mingled scents of jasmine and bougainvillea filled the air and she breathed deep, trying to slow the frantic thud of her pulse as she remembered the expression on Rafael's face when she had walked down the stairs in her glittering gold ball gown.

He had looked stunned—as if he couldn't believe it was her. And she understood the feeling because when she'd seen her reflection in the mirror after Sofia had applied the finishing touches to her make-up she had hardly recognised herself.

'My brother is in for a shock,' Sofia had said in a satisfied voice. 'You look amazing.'

Juliet *felt* amazing. Rafael had told her she looked beautiful and her heart had leapt when she'd seen the unmistakable gleam of desire in his green eyes. It had restored her pride after he'd looked at her with such disdain on the day of their wedding, when she had walked down the stairs at Ferndown House wearing that hideous dress.

But none of this was real, she reminded herself. Oh, the ball gown which shimmered every time she moved was real, as were the dozens of new outfits—some formal, some more casual, but all of them exorbitantly expensive—that filled her wardrobe. She had new shoes too: numerous pairs of elegant high heels made of softest Italian leather in a variety of colours, with matching handbags, and accessories including silk scarves and some pieces of modern, chunky costume jewellery made from semi-precious stones. She had thrown away all her old clothes, apart from a couple of leotards and her pointe shoes that she'd kept as reminders of her life as a ballerina.

Juliet knew it would easy to be swept away by the magic that had transformed her from looking and feeling unattractive to a realisation that she looked quite nice in clothes that fitted properly. But she must not forget the reason why Rafael had married her, and she must not allow herself to be seduced by a self-confessed playboy who had made clear his scathing opinion of love.

Not that she would be foolish enough to fall in love with him, she assured herself.

'Why are you out here alone?'

Rafael's gravelly voice sent a prickle of awareness across Juliet's skin and she spun round and found him standing close beside her. Much too close. Heat exploded inside her when his thigh brushed against hers.

He looked incredible, in a superbly tailored black tuxedo, white silk shirt and a black bow tie. A lock of his hair fell forward across his brow, and the shadow of black stubble covering his jaw gave him a rakish look that was spine-tinglingly sexy. Memories assailed her of the way he had held her tightly against his strong body while they had danced together. She had felt the warmth of his skin through his shirt and seen the shadow of his black chest hair beneath the fine silk. She'd wanted so badly to tear open the buttons and run her hands over his naked torso…

'I came outside for some air.' She gave him a rueful smile. 'I am no more alone out here than in the ballroom, where I don't know anyone.'

'You know me.'

'Not really. We are strangers, thrown together in this crazy marriage.'

He frowned. 'We need to spend some time getting to know each other or we won't manage to convince my grandfather that our relationship is genuine. For a start, why didn't you mention before that you trained as a ballerina?'

'I didn't think you would be interested. You picked me to be your wife because you believed I was uncultured and came from a poor background.'

His jaw tightened. 'I have already apologised for the way I treated you.'

'You don't have to apologise when you're going to pay me five million pounds.'

If she kept reminding herself of the deal they had made she might find it easier to ignore the burning intensity in his gaze that made her wish their marriage was real in every sense.

Rafael exhaled heavily. 'The car accident that took your parents' lives also ended your dancing career, didn't it?'

'I had just danced the role of Giselle in London— one of the youngest ballerinas to have been chosen for the part.' Juliet hugged her arms around her. 'Mum and Dad died because of *me*,' she whispered. 'They were driving me to Birmingham, because the ballet was due to open next at the Symphony Hall there. I could have gone on the coach with the other dancers but my parents always came to my first night performances.'

'The accident was not your fault—you have to believe that,' Rafael said roughly. He pulled her into his arms and held her close to his chest. 'Thick fog and a speeding lorry—you had no control over those things.' He stroked his hand over her hair. 'It sounds as though your parents loved you very much.'

There was an odd note in his voice that Juliet could not define.

'They sacrificed so much so that I could follow my dream of being a ballerina,' she said. 'I won a scholarship to a boarding ballet school when I was eleven. The fees were paid but there were many other expenses, and my parents worked extra hours to buy my ballet shoes and cover all the costs.'

She sighed.

'I was the only scholarship student in my year and most of the other pupils were from wealthy families. I was made to feel that I didn't belong there by some of my peers because of my background. In the same way your grandfather made me feel that I was an outsider when you introduced me as your wife.'

Rafael's chest rose and fell. 'Why did you stay at the school if the other pupils upset you?'

'I was determined to be a ballerina and I didn't care about anything else. The other kids stopped teasing me when I consistently came top of the class in my dance exams. And I did make some friends. My best friend Chloe is the daughter of the famous art collector Derek

Mullholland. I used to stay with her in the school holidays and her father would show us around his private art gallery and talk about the paintings.'

Beneath her ear Juliet heard the steady thud of Rafael's heart.

'Chloe is a soloist ballerina. We keep in touch, but I am envious of her career,' she admitted.

He said nothing, but he tightened his arms around her as if he understood, as if he cared—*which of course he doesn't*, whispered her common sense.

'I plan to use some of your money to set up a dance school for children and young adults. My leg isn't strong enough for me to dance on the stage, but I can teach ballet and give other little girls the dream that I fulfilled for a short time.'

Juliet's heart missed a beat when she felt Rafael brush his lips over her hairline. Time seemed to be suspended and she did not know how long they stood there, with his arms wrapped around her and her cheek resting on his shirt front. But gradually she became aware of the hardness of his thighs pressing against her, and the heat of his body through his shirt.

The spicy scent of his cologne filled her senses, and when she looked up at him she discovered that he was staring at her with an intent expression that made her stomach swoop. She felt dizzy, as though she had drunk too much champagne, although she'd only had one glass.

He slid his hand beneath her chin and his eyes narrowed, gleaming with a sensual promise that set her pulse racing. Once again she had the feeling that none of this was real. It was a beautiful dream and she never wanted to wake up. Her eyelashes drifted closed and she felt Rafael's warm breath graze her lips.

'Open your eyes,' he commanded in a husky growl that sent a delicious shiver down her spine.

She obeyed, and as her gaze meshed with his she instinctively arched towards him as he angled his mouth over hers and kissed her. At first he kept it light, teasing her lips apart while he moved his hand from her jaw to cradle her cheek in his palm. He tasted divine and she pressed herself closer to him, wanting more, wanting...

'Oh!' Her soft gasp was muffled against his lips as he deepened the kiss, crushing her mouth beneath his so that her head was tilted back and she was powerless to resist his passionate onslaught.

Heat swept through her veins and a wildness bubbled up inside her as Rafael coaxed her lips apart in a kiss that transported her to a place where there was only sensation. He made a rough sound in his throat and moved his hand from her waist to the base of her spine, forcing her pelvis into contact with his so that she felt the powerful proof of his arousal.

Astounded that she could have such an effect on him, Juliet melted against him, lifting her arms to wind them around his neck while he pushed his tongue into her mouth and the kiss became ever more erotic.

Sparks shot through her. She hadn't known that a kiss could be like this: a conflagration that swept away her inhibitions and her uncertainty and compelled her to burn in Rafael's fire.

It took a few seconds for her to realise that the brilliant white lights she could see were not shooting stars but actual lights, which had been switched on to illuminate the balcony. Even more puzzling was the sound of applause.

Rafael lifted his mouth from hers and she turned her

head to discover that they were in full view of the party guests in the ballroom—including his grandfather.

Understanding brought with it a wave of humiliation at the realisation that Rafael had kissed her so publicly in a bid to prove to Hector that their marriage was real. He must have known that the balcony lights were about to be turned on—or maybe he had instructed the staff to switch them on. Either way, that kiss had been under the spotlight...but only one of them had been acting.

Juliet wished a hole would appear beneath her feet and swallow her. But Rafael tightened his hold on her waist, as if he guessed that she wanted to tear herself out of his arms and slap his face. He strode across the balcony, giving her no choice but to walk with him back into the ballroom.

'I want to go and check on Poppy,' she muttered, making the excuse so that she could leave the party.

She was such an idiot. Rafael was a playboy, highly experienced in the art of seduction. And she had betrayed her fascination with him when she had responded to his heart-stopping kisses with an eagerness that made her cheeks burn when she remembered how she had come apart in his arms.

'You can't leave now. My grandfather is about to give his speech,' he told her. 'The nanny will see to Poppy if she wakes up.'

Hector stepped onto a dais at one end of the room and looked around at the guests. 'As you all know, today I celebrate my eightieth birthday. The time has come for me to think about the future of the Casillas Group and consider who will be the best person to succeed me as Chairman and CEO. I believe that person is my eldest grandson Rafael.'

Juliet glanced around the room and was shocked by

the look of fury on Delfina Casillas's haughty face. She wondered why Rafael's mother favoured her youngest son, and why there was no sign of affection between her and Rafael.

'However,' Hector continued, 'I have decided to remain as head of the company for the coming year, while I work closely with Rafael to ensure a smooth transition to his leadership. Rafael knows there are certain areas where he will need to prove his suitability before I step down. In my opinion, whoever ultimately succeeds me should be prepared to show commitment in all areas of his life—which is something that, frankly, Rafael has not done in the past. But his recent marriage suggests a change of heart.'

Hector paused, and from across the room Juliet felt the old man's sharp black eyes flick from Rafael to her. She felt Rafael tighten his grip on her waist, pinning her to him.

'Perhaps,' Hector said thoughtfully, 'Rafael will be able to convince me to retire before the year is up.'

CHAPTER SEVEN

'Juliet—wait.'

The sound of Rafael's voice behind her spurred Juliet on to increase her pace as she tore across the lawn, heading away from the twinkling lights of the mansion. But she wasn't used to walking, let alone running in high heels, with a long skirt swirling around her ankles, and he caught up with her in front of the chalet-style summerhouse.

His hand curled around her shoulder. 'Where are you going?'

'Anywhere as long as I'm far away from *you*.'

He swore and caught hold of her other shoulder, spinning her round to face him. 'What's the matter?'

The impatience in Rafael's voice fanned Juliet's temper. 'You are an expert at this game, but I'm just a novice and I don't know the rules,' she muttered.

Moonlight slid over his face, highlighting his razor-edged cheekbones and hard jaw. The mouth that had lived up to its promise of heaven was set in a grim line and his brows were two black slashes on either side of his nose.

'What game? Why did you disappear from the ballroom while the guests were making a toast to my grandfather? People will think we have had a row.'

'I doubt it, after you made sure that everyone, including Hector, witnessed that X-rated snog on the balcony.' Juliet bit her lip. She felt such a fool. 'I opened up to you in a way that I have never done with anyone else,' she told him rawly. 'I thought you'd kissed me because— Oh, not because you *cared*, but I thought you liked me a little. I should have realised it was an ideal opportunity for you to act the role of a loving husband in front of your grandfather when you found me on the balcony. The stage was set and all you needed were lights and action.'

To her horror, her voice wobbled, and she cringed because she could not disguise her hurt feelings. Just because she was wearing a beautiful dress it did not change who she was. She was still a single mother from a council estate, and no amount of clever tailoring could give the illusion that she had the kind of curvaceous figure that Rafael preferred—if the newspaper pictures of his last busty blonde mistress were anything to go by.

She shrugged her shoulders, trying to throw off his hands, but he held her tighter. A muscle flickered in his cheek when she dashed a hand across her wet eyes.

'That was not why I kissed you,' he said harshly. 'It had nothing to do with my grandfather. I didn't know that those damn lights would come on.'

'You can't deny it was convenient that we were lit up like a Christmas tree. And Hector hinted in his speech that he might make you CEO in less than a year, so I can't complain. The sooner he hands you the company the sooner we can end our farce of a marriage.'

'I did not know that we would be seen by everyone in the ballroom.'

Rafael's voice was as dangerous as the rigid set of his

jaw. He trapped her gaze, and her breath hitched in her throat when she saw heat and hunger flash in his eyes.

'I kissed you because I couldn't resist you,' he said tensely. 'Because I'd wanted to kiss you since I watched you float down the stairs looking like a princess in that golden dress with your hair like amber silk. Looking like every red-blooded male's fantasy woman.'

She shook her head, not allowing herself to believe him. 'What man would fantasise about *me*?' she whispered.

'This man, *chiquita*,' he growled.

He jerked her towards him, taking her by surprise, so that she slammed hard into his chest and the air was forced out of her lungs. Before she could draw a breath he'd lowered his head and claimed her mouth in a kiss of blatant possession and savage passion.

Her brain told her to resist him. Insisted she would be a fool to believe him. But there had been something so stark in his voice. And she *wanted* this, Juliet admitted to herself. She wanted his mouth on hers, kissing her with an urgency that was too fierce to be fake.

The world spun on its axis as he swept her into his arms and carried her along the path to the summerhouse, shouldered open the door and kicked it shut behind him while his lips remained fused to hers.

Moonlight shone through the windows and filled the summerhouse with a pearly gleam. Rafael strode over to the sofa that took up one corner of the room and sat down, settling her on his lap. He traced his lips over her cheek, nuzzled the tender place behind her ear and then nipped her earlobe with his sharp teeth, sending starbursts of pleasure through her entire body.

And then his mouth was on hers once more and he was kissing her—unhurriedly at first, and then with increasing passion when she responded to him with a fervency that made him groan. His pressed his lips to the pulse beating erratically at the base of her throat before he kissed his way along her collarbone.

Juliet felt his hand on the bare skin of her back and only realised that he had tugged the zip of her dress down when the strapless bodice fell away from her breasts. The air felt cool on her heated skin and her nipples swelled and hardened beneath Rafael's avid gaze.

'No bra,' he said thickly.

'I'm too small to need one.' Her tiny breasts were a constant regret to her.

'You're perfect.'

Dark colour ran along his cheekbones when he cupped one breast in his hand. Reaction shivered through Juliet as he rubbed his thumb-pad across her nipple, teasing the sensitive peak so that she made a choked sound. The pleasure of his touch was so intense that she could not control the little quivers that ran through her. Rafael was a sorcerer and she was spellbound by his magic.

She held her breath when he lowered his head to her breast. Moonbeams danced across his dark hair and Juliet sank her fingers into the rich silk as he captured her nipple between his lips and flicked his tongue back and forth over the dusky tip.

Darts of pleasure shot down to the molten place between her legs. Her ability to think was lost in the wondrous sensations he was creating with his mouth and his hands on her body. She was startled to realise that the husky moans that bounced off the walls of the summerhouse were coming from her throat.

Rafael pulled the bodice of her dress down so that it bunched at her waist and then leaned his head against the back of the sofa, his eyes glittering as he subjected her to a slow appraisal.

'You are exquisite,' he said, in a rough tone that made Juliet ache everywhere.

He cradled the pale mounds of her breasts in his big hands and played with her reddened nipples. The ache deep in her pelvis became an insistent throb. When he shifted their position, so that she was lying on the sofa and he was stretched out on top of her, she gloried in his weight pressing her into the cushions. He nudged her legs apart with his thigh and she felt the hard length of his arousal press against her feminine core through the dress.

And all the while Rafael kissed her with a mastery that made her shake with an incandescent need that blazed and burned until she was only aware of the heat of his body and the sweep of his hands across her skin.

He lifted the hem of her dress and skimmed a path up to her thighs, tracing his fingers over her tiny lace panties. Lost in the sheer delight of his caresses, Juliet held her breath and willed him to move his fingers higher. She shuddered when he dipped into the waistband of her knickers and stroked his finger lightly over her moist opening.

It was a very long time since a man had touched her so intimately. There had only been one other man before Rafael and she didn't want to think about Bryan and her solitary, uninspiring experience of sex with him. But the word floated in her mind. Was that where this was leading? Did Rafael want to have sex with her?

He was as hard as a spike beneath his trousers, and she imagined him pulling his zip down and pushing the panel of her panties aside so that he could drive his erection into her.

She was eager for him to make love to her. But like this? A frantic coupling in the dark in a glorified shed before they returned to his grandfather's birthday party?

More importantly, she wasn't prepared for sex—and while she had forgiven herself for one accidental pregnancy, two would be utterly irresponsible.

Even so, the temptation she felt to allow Rafael to continue caressing her with his clever fingers was strong, and her body throbbed with unfulfilled longing when she tore her mouth from his.

'I'm not on the pill.'

Rafael froze as Juliet's words kick-started his brain, which until that moment had been clouded in a red haze of desire. His first reaction was frustration that he wasn't carrying condoms in his jacket, as he invariably did on evenings out in London. He saw nothing wrong with one-night stands if both parties understood the rules.

But Juliet was not a woman he had picked up in a nightclub—she was his wife. In name only. That was what he had assured her when he'd suggested their marriage deal, and in all honesty he hadn't expected that he would *want* to take his unappealing bride who had behaved like a sullen teenager at the register office to bed.

He had been blind to her beauty and unaware of her vulnerability, which was evident now in her wary expression as he lifted himself off her and offered her his hand to pull her up from the sofa. The shadowy interior of the summerhouse could not disguise the flush that spread over her cheeks as she dragged the top of her dress up to cover her breasts.

'Will you zip me up?'

She presented her back to him and his stomach

clenched as he pushed her silky fall of hair over one fragile shoulder so that he could fasten her dress.

'I can't face going back to the ballroom,' she said in low voice.

Rafael studied her kiss-stung lips and the betraying hard points of her nipples, visible through her dress, and it occurred to him that his grandfather would have no doubt that his marriage was real if he saw evidence that he and Juliet had slipped away from the party to indulge their passion for each other.

But he couldn't bring himself to humiliate her in front of his family, who had already judged her so harshly because of their misplaced belief that money and an aristocratic lineage made them better than a cash-strapped single mother.

He looked away from her, struggling to bring his rampant libido under control. 'You can go into the house via the kitchens and use the back staircase to go up to the apartment so that no one sees you. I'll say that you were feeling unwell and have gone to bed.'

'Thank you.'

Instead of walking out of the summerhouse when he opened the door she stood on her tiptoes and pressed her lips to his cheek. His pulse kicked when he breathed in her feminine fragrance—perfume mixed with something muskier that clung to his fingers—and he recognised the scent of her womanhood.

'Rafael...'

He did not want a post mortem on what had happened between them. What definitely should not have happened and what must not happen again.

'I should get back to the party before my absence is noticed,' he said.

The flash of hurt in her eyes at his abrupt tone convinced him that he should have listened to the warning voice in his head when she'd fled from the party and he had chased after her.

Rafael stayed in the ballroom until after midnight, when the last of the guests departed. His grandfather had retired to bed some time ago and it had given him an excuse to remain downstairs and act as host.

When he entered his private suite he headed straight for his study and spent another half an hour there, nursing a large cognac. Juliet would surely be asleep by now, he thought as he entered his dressing room and threw a pile of bedding onto the sofa.

His cufflinks hit the dressing table, followed by his tie. He shrugged out of his shirt and undid his trousers, wincing when the zip brushed against his manhood, which was still semi-aroused several hours after he'd nearly lost his sanity in the summerhouse.

'I only discovered today that this is where you have been sleeping.'

Juliet's soft voice came from the doorway between the master bedroom and the dressing room.

'I assumed there were two bedrooms in the apartment and you were using the second one.'

He glanced at her and felt his blood rush south, his erection instantly and embarrassingly hard. Juliet had shimmered in the sequined ball gown, but in a black satin chemise with semi-transparent lace bra cups that exposed a tantalising amount of her small but perfectly formed breasts she simmered with sensual promise.

Once again he wondered how he could have dismissed her as drab. The uncomfortable truth was that he had seen what he'd wanted to see, Rafael acknowledged. The irony of finding himself fiercely attracted to his little sexpot wife wasn't lost on him.

'There is only a master bedroom in my private suite. Obviously the house has other bedrooms—twenty-five, I believe, although I have never counted them. But we need Hector to think we are sleeping together.'

'I can't imagine that sofa is comfortable for someone of your height...' Juliet hesitated and a rosy stain ran under her skin. 'We could share the bed. I mean—it's huge. Big enough for us to keep to our own sides of the mattress...unless you want...'

Her voice trailed off and the shy look she gave him very nearly made him forget that she was off limits.

'No,' he said curtly. 'That would be a bad idea.'

The pink flush on her cheeks spilled down her throat and across the upper slopes of her breasts, tempting him to rip the confection of satin and lace from her body, sweep her into his arms and carry her through to the bedroom so that they could both enjoy that big, soft bed—but not to sleep in.

He knew it was what Juliet wanted him to do. Her pupils were dilated so that her eyes were dark discs rimmed with brilliant blue. But he suspected that she wanted her sexual gratification wrapped up in a romantic ideal that he was incapable of giving her.

'I didn't get the impression earlier tonight that you thought our sharing a bed was a bad idea.' Her tongue darted out across her bottom lip. 'In the summerhouse—'

'What happened between us there was a mistake.'

'You wanted to make love...and so did I.'

Dios, why not take what she was offering and satisfy his libido? Rafael asked himself. If Juliet expected hearts and flowers that was *her* problem.

But the nagging voice of his conscience insisted that he was responsible for her. She had no idea what he was. He had been born in the gutter and had grown up in a slum where every day had been a fight to survive. He knew how to keep himself together, but that was all he knew. There was nothing inside him but darkness and ruthless ambition.

Juliet had lost her parents when she had still been a teenager and he sensed her loneliness. She was looking for love, affection, caring—but he could not give her those things. How could he when he had never experienced them?

'I wanted sex,' he told her bluntly. 'To scratch an itch. And you happened to be there.'

The colour drained from her face as quickly as it had appeared. 'So you're saying that any woman would have done?'

Her eyelashes swept down, but not before he'd seen a wounded expression that gutted him.

Juliet was silent for a moment before her chin came up. Rafael though of all the other times she had picked herself up after life had delivered another knockout blow. Admiration curled through him when she met his gaze steadily. Only the faint tremor of her bottom lip betrayed her hurt, but she quickly firmed her mouth.

'Then there is nothing more to be said. But it's ridiculous for you to sleep on the sofa when I am so much smaller than you and will fit on it much better. You can have the bed and I'll sleep here.'

She turned towards the sofa and started to make up a bed. When she bent over to smooth out the sheet her satin chemise pulled tight across her pert derrière. Rafael swore beneath his breath. She would tempt a saint, let alone the sinner he knew himself to be.

He snatched a pillow out of her hands. 'Leave it,' he said savagely. 'Go—now—before I do something that we will both regret.'

Juliet's eyes widened. But she must have realised that his self-control was at breaking point and without another word she sped back into the bedroom and slammed the door behind her.

Juliet put off taking Poppy down to breakfast for as long as possible. She knew that Rafael was in the habit of drinking several cups of black coffee in the morning, while he sat on the balcony and glanced at the day's newspapers before he left for work at the Casillas Group's offices in Valencia. But she couldn't face seeing him.

She was mortified at the memory of how she had thrown herself at him and he had rejected her, so she read Poppy two more stories until the little girl hopped off the bed and ran over to the door.

'I'm hungry, Mummy.'

It was past nine o'clock—he must have left by now. 'Okay, munchkin. I'm coming.'

She followed her daughter into the kitchen and her heart leapt into her mouth when she saw that the bi-fold doors were open and Rafael was outside, sitting at the table with a newspaper propped against the coffee jug.

Poppy greeted him excitedly and climbed onto the chair beside him. 'Raf, will you read me *The Three Bears*?'

'Rafael has to go to work,' Juliet said quickly. She avoided his gaze and fussed over Poppy's breakfast. 'Would you like a peach with your yoghurt?'

'I'm not going to work today,' he told Poppy. 'And I'll

read the book if you eat all your breakfast.' He picked up the cafetière and looked at Juliet. 'Coffee?'

'Thank you,' she said stiffly, feeling her colour rise.

Her unsubtle suggestion that they should share the bed came back to mock her. She wished she didn't blush so easily. She wished Rafael wasn't wearing sunglasses which hid his expression. She wished she could prevent her eyes from straying to his broad chest and the denim shirt that was open at the neck, revealing a sprinkling of black chest hair.

Thankful that her body's reaction to his sexual magnetism was hidden beneath her robe, she hugged her coffee cup like a security blanket while Poppy chatted away to Rafael. His patience with the little girl surprised Juliet again, and made her wonder why he had been so vehement when he'd said he did not want children of his own.

She looked up when the nanny stepped onto the balcony. 'Would Poppy like to come and play with the twins in the garden?'

'Keep your sun hat on,' Juliet instructed as Poppy trotted off with Elvira.

She really did not want to be alone with Rafael, but just as she was about to rise from the table he pushed a plate of *churros*—little sticks of dough which had been deep-fried and sprinkled with sugar and cinnamon—towards her.

'You should have some breakfast.'

'I'm not hungry,' she muttered, her chair scraping on the stone floor as she stood up.

'Sit down and eat.'

Rafael's exasperated tone made Juliet feel like a naughty child. After a moment's hesitation she sank back down onto her chair.

'Sulking is not an attractive trait,' he drawled.

'I am *not* sulking.' Releasing her breath slowly helped to control her temper. 'I'm tired of the games you play. You blow hot and cold. I don't know where I am with you, or what you want from me, and frankly I don't care.'

She forced herself to look directly at him and ignored the leap of her pulse. Okay, he was so gorgeous that her heart did a flip every time she looked at him. *Get over it*, she told herself. He was also unbelievably arrogant and had an ego the size of a planet.

To her surprise, Rafael looked away first. 'We are having lunch with my mother and her husband Alberto. My dear *mamà* is desperate for my grandfather to choose my half-brother as his successor and she will do anything to discredit me.' His voice was emotionless. 'Delfina must not suspect that our marriage is fake.'

'I'll do my best to pretend that I think you're God's gift to womankind,' Juliet told him flippantly.

His heavy brows lowered. 'Do not test my patience, *chiquita*.'

'Or you'll do what?'

He pulled off his sunglasses and scowled at her. But the hard gleam in his eyes was not temper but desire, and the heat of it scorched Juliet even as it confused her.

Last night he had told her that he'd wanted sex with any woman who was conveniently to hand and it had happened to be her. But he was staring at her now as if she really was his fantasy woman—as if she was the only woman he wanted.

The air was so still that she could hear the rasp of his breath and the unevenness of hers. Awareness prickled across her skin. Sexual tension sizzled between them and suddenly she was afraid—not of Rafael, but of the way he made her feel. The way she made *him* feel if the hunger in his gaze was real...

She broke eye contact and took a deep breath. 'You said we should get to know each other so that we can convince Hector and other members of your family that we are genuinely a couple. I've told you a lot about me, but I know virtually nothing about you.'

He put his shades on again and leaned back in his chair, watching her. She had no idea what he was thinking.

'What do you want to know?'

'Why is there such animosity between you and your mother?'

He shrugged. 'A clash of personalities.'

'I assume your parents are divorced as your mother is remarried and you have a half-brother? Do you keep in contact with your father?'

'No.'

The word shot from him like a bullet.

Juliet said nothing, and he must have realised that she was waiting for him to continue because after a moment he muttered, 'My father died years ago.'

'I'm sorry.'

'Don't be,' he said harshly. 'I'm not.'

She could not hide her shock. 'That's a terrible thing to say about your own father.'

'He was a terrible man.'

Rafael shoved a hand through his hair, and although Juliet could not see the expression in his eyes she sensed that he was agitated—something she would not have believed possible for a man whose self-control was formidable.

'I suppose you will find out about my background at some point, so it might as well be now,' he muttered.

Juliet suddenly remembered that his sister had said something about how she and Rafael had felt overawed when they had come to live at the Casillas mansion.

'My mother eloped with my father because my grandfather disapproved of her relationship with him. Ivan Mendoza had a gardening job on the Casillas estate and apparently Delfina fell madly in love with him.' Rafael grimaced. 'I remember he could be charming to people when it suited him, but he was never anything other than violent and aggressive to me.'

She froze. 'Did your father hit you?'

'Frequently—until I learned to dodge his fists and run away when he undid his belt.'

'How old were you when he started hitting you?'

He shrugged. 'I don't remember a time when I wasn't afraid of him.'

Juliet felt sick, imagining Rafael as a little boy, perhaps no older than Poppy, being physically abused by his father. 'What about your mother? Didn't she try to protect you?'

'I don't know if my mother was aware when she married Ivan that he was involved in the drug scene. He was a petty crook, who worked when he could find a job, and had a sideline in drug dealing.' Rafael exhaled heavily. 'I think it's likely that my mother was a drug user then—probably encouraged into that lifestyle by Ivan. I have very few memories of her before she left. She was distant, uninterested—especially in me. I don't remember her ever showing me affection.'

'What do you mean when you say that your mother left?'

'She disappeared out of my life when I was about seven. Sofia would have been around two years old. I didn't find out my actual birth date until years later, when I saw my birth certificate,' he explained. 'My father never said where my mother had gone.' A nerve flickered in his cheek. 'I think my sister missed our mother at first and she clung to me.'

Juliet thought of her happy childhood, with parents who had adored her, and her heart ached for Rafael and his sister. 'Who took care of you and Sofia?'

He gave another shrug. 'My father was a *gitano*—a gypsy. The Roma community is tightknit, and *gitanos* have a strong sense of family. Sometimes the other mothers took care of Sofia and gave us food. But my father was always moving around and we didn't settle anywhere for long—which is why it was years before my grandfather found us.'

He caught Juliet's questioning look.

'My mother had returned to the Casillas mansion. Presumably she missed the wealth and status of belonging to one of Spain's foremost families,' he said drily. 'I don't know why she did not take us or at least my sister with her when she left. We ended up living with my father in a slum outside Madrid, where drugs were dealt openly on the streets and criminal gangs were in charge. We were there for a few years before Ivan was shot dead in a gang war and Sofia and I were placed in an orphanage. Once there was an official record of our whereabouts Hector managed to track us down, and he brought us to live at the Casillas mansion when I was twelve.'

Juliet was so shocked by Rafael's description of his childhood that she did not know what to say. It explained the toughness she sensed in him, and his obsessive determination to get what he wanted.

'Your mother must have been happy to be reunited with you and your sister...' she murmured.

He gave a short laugh. 'I was a surly teenager, with a chip on my shoulder and a hot temper. *None* of my relatives—including my mother—were pleased to have me around, although I'm glad to say that Sofia was made more welcome.' He gave a faint smile. 'My sister learned young how to smile and say the right things to people. I was far less amenable. But my grandfather saw something in me and pushed me to catch up on my education. Meanwhile my mother had married a distant cousin, and my half-brother Francisco is a *true* Casillas, in Delfina's opinion, and should be Hector's successor.'

Rafael picked up his coffee cup and swallowed its contents.

'You said you were made to feel that you did not belong at your ballet school by some of the richer pupils. I understand what it's like to feel like an outsider, because that's how I felt when I came to live here with my aristocratic family. Many of my relatives still think that a *gitano* is not good enough to be a Casillas.'

Juliet stared at him. 'Yet even knowing that your family would despise me, you brought me here and presented me as your wife. You didn't consider my feelings. Perhaps,' she said huskily, 'you thought I was too unintelligent to *have* feelings.'

His jaw clenched. 'I have never thought you unintelligent. I admit that when I first met you it crossed my mind that it would infuriate Hector if my bride was a single mother from a council estate…'

Juliet blanched and he swore.

'You have shown me that I was wrong to make assumptions about you based on the circumstances I found you in. But I won't lie to you. I needed to marry quickly, and your financial problems gave me the leverage to persuade you to be my wife.'

Rafael's voice was indecipherable, and his eyes were still hidden behind his sunglasses so that Juliet had no clue to his thoughts.

'Was my decision cold and calculating? Yes.' He answered his own question before she could speak. 'I told you once that my pursuit of power is a ruthless game, with no place for weakness or emotions—and nothing has changed.'

CHAPTER EIGHT

SOMETHING *HAD* CHANGED. Rafael suspected it was something inside him, but he refused to examine that unsettling thought and assured himself that the change was entirely in Juliet.

It was not only her appearance, he brooded, studying her where she sat opposite him at the dining table in his mother's over-fussy suite. The truth was that he hadn't been able to take his eyes off his wife throughout this tedious lunch with Delfina and her tedious husband.

Juliet looked deliciously cool and elegant in a pale blue silk sheath dress that skimmed her slender figure. The neckline was decorous, but cut just low enough to reveal the upper slopes of her breasts. Those perfect small handfuls that made Rafael's mouth water when he pictured the dusky pink nipples he had tasted once. He had come to the conclusion that he would *have* to lick and suckle them again—if his overheated body did not spontaneously combust first.

He forced his mind away from the erotic images and shifted in his seat in a bid to ease the uncomfortable tightness of his trousers stretched across his arousal. *Dios*, no other woman had ever made his heart pound the way Juliet did, nor made him feel like a hormone-fuelled youth instead of a self-confessed cynic who had become jaded with easy sex.

He was used to having whichever woman he wanted with minimum effort from him, but he had discovered that there was such a thing as too much choice, Rafael acknowledged sardonically.

Juliet's daughter was sitting beside her. Despite Poppy's young age she had behaved impeccably during lunch. She was a cute kid, he conceded. But like her mother Poppy had a way of looking directly into his eyes that disconcerted him. As if she saw something inside him that Rafael was quite certain did not exist.

'I did not expect that you would bring the child with you,' Delfina had said when he'd carried the little girl into the private apartment. Beside him, Juliet had stiffened as his mother had added coldly, 'Couldn't you have left her with the nanny?'

'Elvira offered to look after Poppy, but I like to spend as much time as possible with my daughter,' Juliet had replied calmly, but Rafael had caught the gleam of battle in her blue eyes.

Now Alberto was chatting to Juliet about three of Pablo Picasso's paintings, which he owned. Rafael knew his mother did not share her husband's interest in the famous Spanish painter, and she'd looked irritated when Juliet had revealed an impressive knowledge of the artist's work.

'Did your parents have professions?' Delfina asked during a lull in conversation.

'They both worked at a hospital.'

'Oh! Were they doctors?'

'Dad was a porter and Mum was a domestic assistant,' Juliet said cheerfully.

Delfina's brows arched in a supercilious expression. 'Domestic work seems to be a favourite in your family.'

'Madre...' Rafael said warningly. His mother could be a bitch and he would *not* allow her to upset Juliet.

'My parents worked hard so that I could follow my dream of becoming a ballerina. They were not rich, or particularly well educated, but they loved me and supported me.' Juliet looked directly at Delfina. 'They would never have abandoned me in a crime-ridden slum as you did Rafael and his sister when they were young children—Sofia just a baby and Rafael only seven years old.'

Delfina drew a sharp breath, but Juliet was continuing in a fierce voice.

'How *could* you have left your children with a father who was cruel and violent? You must have known that Ivan beat Rafael with his belt—'

Her voice cracked and a chink opened up in Rafael's heart.

His mother had paled and her highly glossed lips were a scarlet slash across her face. 'How dare you...?' Delfina breathed.

'I dare because I am Rafael's wife. And it is a wife's duty to stand by her husband. I was appalled when Rafael told me about how he suffered as a child, living in a slum.'

Juliet brushed her hand across her eyes and Rafael felt a jolt of something he could not explain when he saw that her lashes were wet.

'Hector brought him to the Casillas mansion to be reunited with you and his other relatives but he was made to feel unwelcome and unwanted. *You* did not defend him, but I will. Rafael is Hector's eldest grandson and *he* should succeed his grandfather as head of the Casillas Group.'

In the stunned silence that followed Rafael told himself that the pain he felt beneath his breastbone was indigestion...too much rich food. The ache could not be because Juliet had stood up for him, *fought* for him in a way that no one had ever done in his entire life. As if he mattered. To *her*.

His mother picked up her wine glass and drained it before she looked at Rafael. 'I was ashamed,' she said tightly.

'I know, Madre. You have always made it clear that you are ashamed of having a son who is part-*gitano*. I will never be the perfect son, like Francisco, but the CEO-ship *is* my birthright and I *will* claim my place within the family and the company.'

Delfina did not speak again, although as Rafael bade her goodbye and kissed the air close to her cheek he had an odd sense that she wanted to say something to him.

'Are you angry with me?' Juliet muttered as they walked through the house back to his apartment.

He glanced at her over Poppy's head. The little girl was walking between them and had insisted on holding his hand as well as Juliet's.

'Why would I be angry? You acted the role of supportive wife very convincingly.'

He opened the door of his apartment and as Juliet preceded him inside her long hair brushed against his arm and he breathed in the lemony scent of the shampoo she used.

Poppy spied her favourite teddy bear and ran across the room.

Juliet turned to him. 'I wasn't acting. What happened to you when you were a child was terrible. Your mother shouldn't have deserted you, and her failure to protect you has had a fundamental effect on you. I think it could be the reason why you have never allowed yourself to fall in love. You're afraid of being let down and abandoned, like Delfina abandoned you before.'

Her words opened that chink in his heart a little wider, and Rafael didn't know what to make of that—or her.

'I think you should stop trying to psychoanalyse me,' he said drily. 'And you should certainly stop looking for my redeeming features, because I don't have any.'

She shook her head. 'You took care of your sister—acted as a parent to her when you were just a child yourself. When I met you I thought you had only ever known wealth and privilege. The fact that you spent the first twelve years of your life in a slum doesn't make you less of a man, it makes you *more* of one—a better person than any of your pampered relatives who have no right to look down on you.'

'A better man would not have sat through lunch imagining stripping you naked and having wild sex with you on my mother's dining table,' he rasped.

Rosy colour winged along her high cheekbones, but she held his gaze. 'That itch still bothering you, is it?'

'You have no idea, *chiquita*…' He could not explain the restlessness inside him that seemed to get a whole lot worse when she smiled. 'I need to disabuse you of the idea that there is anything good in me.'

Juliet tilted her head to one side and looked at him thoughtfully. 'I wonder why you are so determined to do that,' she said softly.

Before he could reply—and the truth was that he did not *how* to respond—she walked away from him in the direction of her dressing room.

'Sofia has asked me to give Ana and Inez some ballet lessons. We're going to have our first dancing class this afternoon—unless there's anything else you want me to do?'

A number of highly erotic scenarios flooded his mind, which had an immediate and predictable effect on his body.

'I promised to play golf with Tio Alvaro,' he growled, his feet already taking him towards the door of the apartment and safety—away from the temptation of his wife who was not his wife. Not in any way that mattered. And Rafael was beginning to think that it mattered a lot.

Three hours spent on the Casillas estate's private golf course would ordinarily have given him time to clear his head.

'You seem to be distracted,' his uncle commented as they walked off the green. Alvaro was jubilant because he had won the game convincingly. 'I suppose you are thinking about business?'

Rafael hadn't spared a single thought for any of the business projects which until recently he had been obsessed with. The realisation that his new obsession with Juliet was interfering not just with his game of golf but with his focus on the company was disturbing. Work had always been his number one priority—the only mistress to command his fidelity.

The situation could not continue, he brooded. Juliet had got under his skin and there was only one way to deal with his unexpected fascination with her.

There was no one around when he entered the mansion. Most of his relatives and the household staff took a siesta in the afternoons, but as he walked across the entrance hall he heard music coming from the ballroom. Puzzled, he opened the door—and stopped dead when he saw Juliet dancing.

Rafael knew nothing about ballet, but he could tell instinctively that she was a talented ballerina. Dressed in a black leotard that revealed her ultra-slender figure, she seemed to glide across the floor on the points of her ballet shoes. Ethereal and graceful, strong and yet fragile. She did not simply dance to the music she lived it, breathed it, painting pictures in the air with each twirl and leap as if she had wings and could fly.

He stepped into the room and quietly closed the door, leaning against it while he watched her. He was utterly captivated...mesmerised. As a boy growing up in the slums he'd had no idea that such beauty existed. He could not take his eyes off her supple body, and his breath became trapped in his lungs as desire swept molten and hot through his veins, setting him ablaze everywhere.

Juliet danced with such passion, such fire, and he wanted all of it.

But her performance ended abruptly when she leapt into the air and seemed to land awkwardly. She gave a cry as she crumpled to the floor, trembling like a bird with a broken wing...a bird that could no longer soar into the sky.

Rafael's heart gave a jolt when he heard the sound of her weeping.

'*Dios, querida*, are you badly hurt?'

He was across the ballroom in seconds and kneeling on the floor beside her. 'Juliet, *cariño*,' he said huskily as she lifted her face and he saw tears streaming down her cheeks.

'My stupid leg.'

The words hung there, hurting him as much as she was hurting. Her voice ached with a depth of emotion he could barely comprehend. Loss—of her parents, and her ballet career, and more than that. The loss of the unique gift that Rafael had glimpsed when he'd watched her dance.

He had no idea what to say to her. 'You must miss dancing.'

'Ballet was my life,' she said, in a low voice that scraped his insides. 'It was like breathing—a necessary part of me. But now it's gone.'

'But you can still dance. You are incredible, *querida*.'

She scrubbed a hand over her eyes. 'I can manage for a few minutes, but I'll never be able to dance professionally. My leg isn't strong enough to cope with the relentless routine of rehearsals and performances, the pursuit of perfection. There's a reason why the life of a ballet dancer is called a beautiful agony.'

Her wry smile floored Rafael. The lack of self-pity in her voice humbled him, and that chink in his heart opened wider still.

'Come,' he said softly, lifting her into his arms.

'I can walk,' she protested as he carried her across the ballroom. 'I'll have a bath. It helps to relax the muscles in my thigh.'

'Put your arms around my neck,' he commanded, liking the feel of her small breasts pressed against his chest when she complied.

He strode up the stairs, and when he entered his apartment headed straight into the en suite bathroom and placed her on a chair. He ran a bath, tipping a liberal amount of scented bath crystals into the water.

He turned to find her watching him, and the lost look in her blue eyes, the shimmer of tears, evoked a reaction inside him that was too complicated for him to deal with right then.

Instead he knelt in front of her and curled his fingers

around the edge of her leotard. 'Let's get you undressed and into the bath.'

'I can manage. Please...' she whispered when he didn't move. 'I want to be alone. I don't need your help.'

Her rejection was no more than he deserved, Rafael acknowledged. But it hurt more than it should—more than he would have believed possible when he had prided himself for nigh on thirty years in not allowing anyone the power to hurt him.

He stood up and stared at her downbent head. Her hair was arranged in a classical bun that showed off the delicate line of her jaw and her slender neck.

'Don't lock the door,' he said tautly. 'I don't want to have to break it down if you have a problem.'

Juliet lay back in the roll-top bath and felt the ache in her thigh start to ease in the warm water. She had been an idiot to dance on points, she thought ruefully. But giving a dancing lesson to Rafael's nieces had reminded her of how she had fallen in love with ballet when she had learned those first simple steps as a child.

After the class Sofia had taken the twins and Poppy to play in the garden, and Juliet had found the temptation to dance in the huge ballroom too strong to resist.

She closed her eyes and allowed her mind to run over the other events of the day. Rafael's shocking revelations about his childhood, when his mother had abandoned him to his fate with his violent father. It had made her want to cry when he'd told her his story, and she hadn't been able to control her anger when they'd had lunch with his mother.

She did not care about Delfina's haughty disdain of her, but Rafael deserved better than to be treated like an outsider by the Casillas family.

The water was cooling and she rested her arms on the edge of the bath while she levered herself upright. Her thigh muscle spasmed and she couldn't hold back a yelp of pain.

Immediately the bathroom door flew open and Rafael appeared, glowering at her. 'What happened? Your leg…?'

'It's fine. It just twinged a bit.'

She caught her bottom lip between her teeth when it belatedly occurred to her that she was naked, standing there in the bath with water streaming down her body. Rafael was staring at her with an intensity that caused her stomach to swoop, and now his gaze dropped down from her breasts to the neatly trimmed triangle of pale red curls between her legs.

Her skin, already pink from being immersed in hot water, flushed even pinker, and there was nothing she could do to prevent her nipples from hardening so that they jutted provocatively, as if begging for his attention.

'Go away…' she muttered.

'You've got to be kidding.'

His rough voice rasped over her, setting each nerve-ending alight. The fierce glitter in his eyes caused her heart to kick in her chest as he walked purposefully across the bathroom.

She licked her dry lips and saw his eyes narrow on the movement of her tongue. 'Will you pass me a towel?'

He took a towel from the shelf and held it out to her. But when she unfolded it, she discovered that it wasn't a big bath sheet but a hand towel that was too small to cover her nakedness. *Seriously?*

His mouth curved into a wicked grin that destroyed her flimsy defences like skittles tumbling after a strike.

Modesty dictated that she should at least hold her hands in front of the pertinent areas of her body, to hide them from his hot gaze. But instead she burned in the fire that danced golden and bright in his green eyes.

'Rafael...' she whispered, with so much longing in her breathy voice that he gave a chuckle as he settled his hands on either side of her waist and lifted her out of the bath. 'I'll make you wet.'

She caught her breath when he settled her against him, so that one of his arms was around her back and the other beneath her knees, and carried her through to the bedroom.

'Not as wet as I am about to make you, *chiquita*.'

The promise in his voice echoed the desire in his eyes. His skin was stretched taut over the blades of his cheekbones, giving him a feral look that sent a quiver through Juliet. She felt boneless, and when he bent his head and angled his mouth over hers she parted her lips and gave herself up to the sweet seduction of his kiss.

The room tilted as he lowered her onto the bed and leaned over her, running his hands over her body from her hips up to her breasts, scalding her skin wherever he touched. She wanted him to surrender to the passion that she sensed he was controlling with his formidable willpower. What would it be like to see that control shatter? Would she survive the tsunami?

'You said that any woman would do,' she reminded him.

'I lied.'

His husky admission dispatched her doubts. He stopped nuzzling her neck and claimed her mouth once more, gentle seduction replaced by hungry demands that she was powerless to deny. He had fascinated her from the start, and she shuddered with delight when he moved down her body and flicked his tongue across one pebble-hard nipple and then the other, again and again, until the pleasure was too intense and she gave a keening cry.

Eyes closed, she felt the scrape of his beard over her belly—her thighs. Her eyelashes flew open. 'What are you doing?'

He lifted his head, amusement and something else that made her stomach muscles contract glinting in his narrowed gaze. 'What do you *think* I am about to do, *chiquita*?'

'I have no idea.'

His low laugh rolled through her and she tried to twitch her thighs together, to hide the betraying dampness of her arousal that scented the air.

'You cannot really be so innocent,' Rafael said half beneath his breath as he pulled her hips towards him, so that her bottom was on the edge of the bed, and dropped to the floor on his knees.

A suspicion finally slid into her mind. 'You can't...' she whispered, appalled yet fascinated, and excited when he pushed her legs apart and lowered his head to her feminine core.

'Want to bet on it?'

His accent was thicker than usual, and his breath fanned the sensitive skin on her inner thigh. One strong hand curled around her ankle. He lifted her leg and draped it over his shoulder. And then he simply put his mouth against her centre and ran his tongue over her opening, making the ache she felt there so much worse, so much *more*.

Juliet glanced down at his dark head between her thighs and knew there was a part of her that was horrified for allowing him to pleasure her in such a way. But she could not deny that he was giving her the most exquisite pleasure as he teased and tormented her with his tongue. She sank back against the mattress, twisting her head from side to side as the heat and the fire and the terrible need inside her built to a crescendo.

Nothing had prepared her for sheer delight of Rafael's intimate caresses, or his soft murmurs of approval when she arched her hips and offered herself to him. She was aware of a coiling sensation low in her pelvis that wound tighter and tighter, until she was trembling and desperate for something that hovered frustratingly out of reach.

And then it happened.

He flicked his tongue across the tight nub of her clitoris and the coil inside her snapped, sending starbursts of pleasure shooting out from her core in a series of exquisite spasms that made her internal muscles clench and release, clench and release, flooding her with the sticky sweetness of her earth-shattering climax.

Her first.

She would remember it long after their marriage was over.

Her heart contracted painfully as the thought slid like a serpent in paradise into her mind.

In the aftermath, as her breathing slowed, she realised that the most amazing sexual experience of her life could not have been satisfactory for Rafael. When he leaned over her and kissed her lingeringly on her mouth she tasted her own feminine sweetness on his lips and wondered if he expected her to afford him the same pleasure he had given her. But how to suggest it?

She felt frustrated by her inexperience. 'I—' She broke off, at a loss to know what to say. He had taken her apart utterly and she didn't know how to put herself back together again, or if she even could.

She watched him uncertainly when he stepped away from the bed. 'I can hear Poppy,' he murmured.

Her daughter! How could she have forgotten?

She scrambled off the bed when she heard voices from somewhere in the apartment and guessed that Sofia had returned Poppy after she'd spent the afternoon with the twins.

'I'll go and see her while you get dressed,' Rafael said, kissing the tip of her nose before he strolled out of the room.

It took Juliet seconds to slip into the blue silk dress she had worn at lunch. Silently cursing the tell-tale flush on her cheeks, she hurried through the apartment.

As she entered the sitting room Poppy ran towards her. 'Mummy, can I have my pyjamas?'

'It's not bedtime.'

Sofia laughed. 'The twins would like Poppy to come to us for a sleepover.' She glanced at her brother. 'Rafael has explained that you have a dinner engagement in Valencia this evening, so it's perfect timing.'

It was the first Juliet had heard of a dinner engagement, but Rafael seemed determined to avoid her gaze.

For the next ten minutes she was busy packing a bag with Poppy's pyjamas, toothbrush and an assortment of cuddly toys. She gave her daughter a big hug and felt a pang when Poppy trotted off happily with Sofia. Her baby was growing up so fast.

When they had gone she turned to Rafael. 'Who are we meeting? Some more of your relatives? Or is it a business dinner?' She did not relish the thought of either. 'What should I wear?' She frowned when he didn't answer. 'Is it a formal function?'

'It's a date.'

'A *date*?' Her confusion grew as dull colour ran along his cheekbones. 'I don't understand.'

'It's quite simple, *chiquita*,' he said, strolling towards her. 'I'm taking you to dinner, away from the Casillas mansion, so that we can spend some time alone.'

'I thought the point was for us to stay here in the house under your grandfather's nose so that we can convince him our marriage is real?'

Instead of replying, Rafael tucked a tendril of hair that had escaped from her chignon behind her ear. The unexpectedly tender gesture tugged on Juliet's heart.

'I would like to explore the attraction between us and I think you would like to do that too,' he said quietly.

She did not deny it and a heavy sigh escaped him.

'We have done everything in the wrong order—married before we had even spent a day together. I was arrogant enough to believe that it didn't matter. But I would like us to start again. So, *bella Julieta*, will you have dinner with me?'

She nodded, feeling suddenly shy, but excited too— and apprehensive, and a host of other emotions she was afraid to define. Rafael had made it clear that he desired her, and although it felt as if she was about to jump from the top of a precipice she was ready to leap into the unknown.

'I'd love to.'

'Good.' He dropped a swift, hard kiss on her mouth that left her lips tingling. 'I have some work to do in my study and we'll leave in an hour.' He paused on his way out of the room. 'By the way, you'll need to bring an overnight bag as we'll be spending the night at my penthouse in the city. Oh, and wear something sexy, *amante*.'

Juliet's heart missed a beat. *Amante* meant lover.

CHAPTER NINE

'WE COULD SKIP dinner and go straight to the penthouse.'

Rafael's voice was oddly hoarse and it sent a shiver across Juliet's skin. She tore her gaze from the unholy gleam in his eyes and glanced around the restaurant, which he'd told her was one of the best places to eat in Valencia. Situated in a charming little square in the old part of the city, it had plenty of atmosphere, and a band was playing traditional Spanish music.

He had promised her a date. 'I'm hungry,' she told him, unfolding her napkin.

'Same here,' he growled. 'You look incredible in that dress. Good enough to eat.' His accent thickened. 'I am looking forward to tasting you again later.'

Heat scorched her cheeks at the memory of how he had pleasured her with his tongue, and she buried her face in her menu. A black velvet dress clung to her slender figure and the low-cut neckline pushed her breasts up to give her a cleavage. Sheer black stockings and high-heeled strappy sandals completed the outfit, and she had left her hair loose, with just the front sections drawn back from her face with diamante clips.

She'd worn a lightweight wool coat when they had left the Casillas mansion, so Rafael had only seen her dress when they'd arrived at the restaurant. The sizzling look he'd given her had made her feel like a sex goddess and boosted her confidence.

When the waiter had taken their order Juliet sipped her champagne cocktail and gave a small sigh. None of this was real. She still expected to wake up in her flat in the tower block and find it had all been a dream. Especially Rafael.

Her eyes were drawn across the table to him. In tailored black trousers and a black silk shirt, casually open at the throat to reveal a vee of bronzed skin, he was darkly gorgeous, and the black stubble on his jaw gave him a dangerous sexiness that sent her heart clattering against her ribs.

'Were you in love with Poppy's father?'

Startled by his question, she gave him a wry look. 'I thought I was. I met him at a party given by some friends of my cousin. Bryan was good-looking, and he knew it, and I was naïve and grieving for my parents. I was flattered that he'd noticed me. But after we'd slept together he told me he'd only wanted sex.'

She sighed.

'I had been taking the contraceptive pill to regulate my periods, and I stupidly agreed to have sex with him without a condom. I'd been taking a herbal remedy to help with my feelings of depression following my parents' deaths and I had no idea that it could decrease the effectiveness of the pill. When I discovered I was pregnant Bryan wasn't interested, and he refused to support his child, although he did agree to have his name on Poppy's birth certificate.'

'He sounds like a jerk. It's Bryan's responsibility to make a financial contribution towards his daughter's upbringing.'

Juliet stared at Rafael. 'Would you support *your*

child? You're a renowned playboy, but if one of your mistresses became pregnant what would *you* do?'

'It won't happen because I always use protection,' he told her smoothly. Seeing her frown, he added, 'But in the extremely unlikely event that it did, I would make a settlement to ensure the child had financial security for life.'

She grimaced. 'Money isn't everything. A child needs to be loved and nurtured. My parents had little money but I had a wonderfully happy childhood, with the security of knowing they loved me.'

'I had a miserable childhood, living in poverty—and, believe me, money would have made a huge difference to my life and my sister's.' A nerve flickered in Rafael's cheek. 'The best thing—no, the *only* thing I could give a child of mine is access to my wealth.'

His harsh tone warned Juliet to drop a subject that was clearly contentious, but she couldn't. 'Are you saying you wouldn't want to be involved in your child's life? You wouldn't *love* your child?'

'The question is irrelevant,' he said coldly.

His expression was as haughty as his mother's, Juliet thought. Centuries of his family's aristocratic heritage were stamped on his hard features and revealed that he was every bit a Casillas. No doubt some of his noble ancestors had been as ruthless as Rafael was.

It was a relief when the waiter arrived at their table to serve the first course. When they were alone again Juliet stayed silent while she ate her grilled scallops with chorizo. The food was delicious, but tears pricked the back of her eyes at the thought that she had spoiled the evening.

Rafael sipped his wine. 'I thought you might like to visit the Museum of Fine Arts tomorrow. The building is very beautiful, and worth visiting simply to see the baroque architecture. It houses the second most important art collection in Spain.'

'I'd love to go.'

His mention of 'tomorrow' reminded her that they would be staying at his apartment in the city tonight.

'But what about Poppy? I'll need to get back for her.'

'My sister is planning to take all three girls to the beach, and she will have the nanny to help out. Valencia is a beautiful city and I think you would enjoy the City of Arts and Sciences and the aquarium—although both are a day's visit. But we don't have to do everything in one day. There will be plenty of time in the year ahead for you to enjoy all that Valencia has to offer.'

Rafael's words were a timely reminder of why she was there with him. Their marriage was a temporary arrangement and she would be a fool to hope for more than he was offering.

Why not use this opportunity to explore her sensuality and enjoy great sex, free from the expectations that came with a normal relationship? Juliet asked herself while the waiter cleared away her plate and served her main course. Life had taught her to seize the moment, and she would regret it for ever if she did not make love with Rafael. As long as she remembered that *love* wasn't involved.

She looked up, and her heart leapt when she found him watching her. His mouth crooked in a sexy smile that made her pulse race and her spirits soar as the awkwardness between them disappeared. For the rest of the meal they chatted with an ease that surprised her. Rafael had travelled widely and she was fascinated to hear of the places he had visited.

'I've only been to Australia—and now Spain,' she admitted.

'I have to go to New York for a few days next month. I'll take you with me.'

Going to New York was another dream of hers that she had never imagined she would fulfil when she had lived in the tower block.

Juliet licked the last morsel of the chocolate mousse she had chosen for dessert from her spoon. The light-as-air mousse felt sensual on her tongue and she closed her eyes while she enjoyed the sensory experience.

'Dios...' Rafael growled. 'Do you do that on purpose?'

Her eyes flew open. 'Do what?' she asked innocently.

Instead of replying, he dipped his spoon into his own dish of mousse and leaned across the table to hold the loaded spoon against her lips. 'You would tempt a saint, *bella*, and piety is not my strong point. Open your mouth,' he ordered softly.

Juliet could not resist the rich mousse, or Rafael, and she obediently parted her lips and licked the dessert from his spoon. He made a thick sound in his throat that provoked a flood of molten warmth between her legs.

She watched him dip the spoon back into his bowl and then lift it to his own mouth. She could not tear her gaze from his tongue as he licked his spoon clean. It was incredibly erotic, and heat coiled through her as she imagined him using that wicked tongue on her body.

She swallowed, searching her mind for something—anything—to say that would break the sexual tension that crackled between them.

'I've heard this music before,' she murmured, recognising the tune that the band were playing. 'My uncle

Carlos is a brilliant acoustic guitarist and he used to play this.'

Rafael pushed back his chair and stood up. 'Dance with me,' he said, holding out his hand to her. 'This music is flamenco. It originated in the gypsy communities in southern Spain and is as fiery and passionate as the people who created it.'

Dazedly Juliet put her hand in his and allowed him to lead her to the small dance floor in the centre of the restaurant, where a few other couples were already dancing. Rafael drew her into his arms and placed one hand in the small of her back, holding her so that her pelvis was pressed up against his. A tremor ran through her when she felt the bulge of his arousal through his trousers.

He danced with a natural grace and Juliet matched his rhythm, swaying her hips in time with his as the dance became a seduction of her senses. Nothing existed but the music and this man whose green eyes gleamed with a naked hunger as he lowered his head towards her, compelling her to slide her hand around his neck and pull his mouth down to hers.

She was drowning in the whirlpool of sensations that he was creating with his mouth as he plundered her lips in a kiss that left her trembling. He threaded his fingers through her hair while he trailed hot kisses along her jaw. Need clawed inside her, obliterating every sane thought and leaving a kind of madness, a wild restlessness that only Rafael could assuage.

And all the while they danced together to the music of the flamenco as the tempo quickened and became more intense.

'We need to leave,' he growled close to her ear.

Minutes later he'd settled the bill and escorted her out

of the restaurant to where his car was parked. Neither of them spoke on the short journey to his city apartment. The sexual tension in the car and then in the lift on the way up to the penthouse was tangible, and Juliet's heart pounded as Rafael leaned against the wall of the lift and studied her with a brooding intensity.

The penthouse was ultra-modern and stylish. A bachelor pad, Juliet thought as she took in the pale wood floors, white leather sofas and colourful modern art on the walls of the open-plan living space. She bit her lip as she wondered how many of his mistresses he had brought here.

'Would you like to take a look around the apartment?' Rafael offered, standing behind her to take her coat when she slipped it off her shoulders.

She felt his hand smooth her hair. 'Not really,' she said huskily.

'Can I get you a drink?'

'No, thank you.'

He placed her coat over the back of a chair and came to stand in front of her, his glittering gaze making her stomach swoop. 'What *would* you like, *chiquita*?'

'You.'

The word burst from her. She couldn't help it. He had driven her crazy with longing all evening with every smile he'd sent her as they had lingered over conversation and champagne—flirting with her, she realised.

He laughed, and the sound filled her with golden light and a fire that burned hotter still when he opened his arms wide.

'Have me, then, *bella Julieta*.'

His laughter stole around her as she literally threw herself into his waiting arms and he lifted her off her feet.

'Wrap your legs around me,' he told her, and when

she obeyed he gave a groan as her pelvis pressed hard against his arousal.

He carried her into the bedroom and set her down next to the bed. She was vaguely conscious of muted lighting and décor of black and gold, a printed throw on the bed. But then he bent his head to claim her mouth and she was only conscious of Rafael: the slide of his lips over hers, the heady scent of his cologne mixed with the indefinable musk of male pheromones, the heat of his body beneath her palms as she ran her hands over his chest and tugged open his shirt buttons.

He undressed her, taking his time to slide her zip down her spine and peel her dress away from her breasts, baring her to his hot gaze. But he didn't touch her breasts yet, focusing instead on tugging her tight-fitting dress over her hips so that it fell to the floor and she stepped out of it.

'*Dios,*' he said roughly as he stared at her sheer black stockings. 'If I'd known you were wearing these...' he traced his fingers over the wide bands of lace around the tops of her thighs '...we wouldn't have made it past the starter.'

He knelt to remove her shoes and then slowly drew one stocking down her leg, then the other, pressing his lips along her white scar, his gentle kisses healing the deeper scars inside her.

'You are so beautiful,' he murmured, and there was nothing but truth and hunger in his eyes when he stood and drew her into his arms.

He made her feel beautiful. And, oh, he made her want him when he kissed her as if he could not have enough of her, when he cupped her breasts in his palms and stroked his thumbs over her nipples so that they peaked and she shuddered beneath the pleasure of his touch.

His hands skimmed down to her panties and he hooked his fingers in the waistband to draw them down her legs.

'So beautiful,' he said again, his low tone aching with need, making the ache between her legs even more acute.

He stripped with an efficiency that caused her a tiny flicker of doubt. Rafael had done this a thousand times or more—perhaps he would be disappointed by her inexperience. But then he took off his boxer shorts, and the sight of his erection jutting so big and bold turned her insides to liquid.

Did he see the flash of uncertainty in her eyes when she viewed the awesome size of him?

He slipped his hand beneath her chin and tilted her face to his. 'We'll take things slowly, *cariño*,' he promised, rubbing his thumb across her lower lip. And then he lay down on the bed and pulled her on top of him, arranging her so that she sat astride him and the hard ridge of his arousal was *there*, pressing against her opening.

But he didn't push any further forward, and it was his finger that stroked over her moist vagina, gently parting her and easing inside her, swirling and twisting, making her gasp and rock her hips against his hand. A second finger joined the first, testing her, stretching her, while his other hand cradled her breast and he tugged her down so that he could close his lips around her nipple and suck hard, so that she gave a moan and molten heat pooled between her legs.

Juliet pushed herself upright and ran her hands greedily over his torso, loving the feel of his satin skin and the faint abrasion of his chest hair beneath her palms.

'Kiss me,' he ordered, and all that arrogance of his

was there in his gravelly voice and in his eyes that gleamed fiercely beneath his half-closed eyelids.

She did not hesitate—simply placed her hands flat on the bed on either side of his head and lowered her mouth to his. He might be arrogant but he wanted her— badly—and she kissed him with all her passion and need, with all her heart and soul, because she was intrinsically honest and her lips could not lie as they clung to his.

'*Querida...*' he groaned, and set her away from him while he reached across to the bedside drawer and took out a condom.

She watched him roll it down his hard length and her heart hammered in her chest, anticipation and the faintest apprehension causing her to catch her breath.

His gaze sought hers and she was entranced by the darkness of desire that had turned his green eyes almost black. She read the unspoken question in his eyes and her breath escaped her on a soft sigh of assent.

He lifted her into position above him and then pulled her slowly down so that his erection nudged her opening. Holding her hips, he guided her, his eyes locked with hers as his swollen tip stretched her and pressed deeper, deeper, filling her inch by inch, and it was so impossibly intense that she thought she would die in the beauty of his possession.

The feel of Rafael inside her was perfect—beyond anything she could have imagined as he began to move, thrusting into her with steady strokes while he slipped his hands round to cup her bottom. His head was thrown back against the pillows, his black hair falling across his brow, his eyes blazing into hers.

'Dance for me,' he said thickly.

And she did. Catching his rhythm, she closed her

eyes and lost herself in the magic of an age-old dance, arching her supple body above him, throwing her head back as they moved together in total accord and flew ever upwards towards the pinnacle.

It couldn't last. Fire this bright had to burn out.

The power of him moving inside her stole her breath and the perfection of each devastating thrust broke her heart. This was not just sex. Not for her. Deep down, she'd known it would be more, that *making love* with Rafael was exactly what she was doing.

She leaned forward so that her nipples brushed across his chest, making him groan and increase his pace. She kissed his mouth and her heart flipped when he pushed his tongue between her lips. The storm was about to break and she arched her body backwards, shaking her hair over her shoulders as the pressure built deep in her pelvis.

'*Dios*, what you do to me...' he muttered—raw, harsh, as if the words were torn from him.

His jaw was clenched and she sensed he was fighting for control—a battle he lost spectacularly when he exploded inside her at the same moment that she shattered. Her sharp cry mingled with his deep groan as they rode out the storm together, and she felt the flooding sweetness of her orgasm and heard the uneven rasp of his laboured breaths.

In the aftermath she lay sprawled across his chest, too exhilarated, too empowered, too *everything* to be able to move. But the idea that he would think she was clingy and needy finally stirred her and she attempted to roll off him—only for him to tighten his arms around her.

'Stay.'

The word rumbled through his chest and tugged on

Juliet's heart. She heard in his low tone the boy who had been abandoned by his mother. She heard the teenager shunned by his rich relatives because they believed his background was shameful, when it was they who should have been ashamed.

Don't, she told her heart sternly when it leapt at the feel of his hand stroking her hair. She must not allow the idea that Rafael was in any way vulnerable to breach her defences.

But when he rolled them both over so that she was beneath him, and he sought her mouth in a kiss of beguiling sweetness and the renewed flowering of passion, she knew that the warning was too late.

Something had changed and now Rafael knew it was him. It had started when he had told Juliet about his boyhood, which he had never spoken of to anyone—not even to Tio Alvaro, to whom he was closest out of all his relatives.

But perhaps it had started before that—when he had watched Juliet descend the stairs at his grandfather's birthday party, a vision of ethereal loveliness in that golden dress.

His wife.

He wasn't comfortable with the possessive feeling that swept through him, nor did he understand it. Rafael knew what he was—knew better than to think he could be a better man. The kind of man a woman might love. It was hardly likely when his own mother hadn't loved him and his father had used any excuse to beat the life out of him. A few times he had very nearly succeeded.

Rafael hated the name Mendoza, but he'd kept it because it reminded him of what he was—what he feared he could be. Tacking Casillas on to his name did not make him a member of the family, his grandfather had told him more than once. Which meant that he was no one—nothing.

Why, suddenly, did it matter? Why did he care? And, even worse, why did she wish that he could overcome the legacy of his past?

The answer to those questions circling like vultures in his mind was curled up beside him, sleeping as only the innocent could sleep, with her hand tucked under her cheek and her lips slightly parted so that when he put his face close to hers her sweet breath whispered across his skin.

It astonished him that he had once thought her plain. He wondered if she'd felt victorious when he'd come so hard inside her, three times the previous night, that his groans had echoed around the bedroom. Now the pearly grey light of dawn filled the room, and the only way to resist the temptation to pull her beneath him again was to get out of bed.

Juliet needed to sleep after he'd kept her awake for much of the night with his demands—which she had enjoyed, he reminded himself as he pulled on a pair of sweatpants. They were mercifully loose around his erection, which had sprung to attention when he'd pushed back the sheet and unintentionally exposed one of Juliet's pale breasts, tipped with a nipple that was rosy red from the ministrations of his mouth.

Rafael walked through the penthouse and made a jug of coffee. Then he stood in front of the glass doors and watched the sun rise over Valencia. Nothing had changed, he decided. He felt in control of himself once more as the caffeine entered his bloodstream. In a year he would achieve his goal of becoming CEO, and by then his fascination with Juliet would have faded. Desire was always transient, but for now she was his.

He shoved a hand through his hair, remembering her hungry little cries when they'd shared a bath last night and he'd made her come as he'd eased his long fingers inside her. Never before had he taken such delight in giving a woman pleasure. Juliet's curious mix of innocence and heart-stopping sensuality intrigued him.

'Rafael?'

Her voice sounded from behind him and he turned, frowning when he saw her wary expression, the vulnerability that she successfully hid from most people but not from him.

'I woke up and you'd gone, and I thought…'

She'd thought he had used her for a night of sex, in the same way that the father of her child had done.

Rafael did not question why he felt a tugging sensation beneath his breastbone. He simply strode across the room and pulled her into his arms. 'I'm an early riser,' he said lightly, aware of another tug in his chest when relief flashed in her eyes.

That's very apparent,' she murmured drily, moving her hand over the tell-tale bulge beneath his sweatpants.

He laughed. He couldn't help it. And it felt so good, so carefree, that he laughed again as he scooped her into his arms and carried her back to the bedroom.

Her impish smile stole his breath. 'Are we going back to bed? Because I've had enough sleep…'

'Who said anything about sleeping, *chiquita*?'

CHAPTER TEN

'Where are you going?'

Rafael's gravelly voice halted Juliet's attempt to wriggle over to the edge of the bed. They were in the bedroom of his private suite at the Casillas mansion. It was a huge bed, and for the past few weeks she hadn't slept in it alone. His stretched out his arm and hauled her back across the mattress.

'I was trying not to wake you,' she mumbled, pressing her face against his warm chest and listening to the steady thud of his heart.

'I've been awake for a while.' He chuckled. 'Did you really think I would remain asleep while you were taking liberties with my body, *querida*?'

'Oh.'

She burrowed closer to him to hide her hot face. She'd had no idea that Rafael had been aware when she'd pulled back the sheet and made a detailed study of his naked body with her eyes and hands. He was a work of art: lean and yet powerfully muscular, his bronzed skin overlaid with black hair that arrowed over his flat stomach and down to his impressive manhood.

'I'd like to know what you intend to do about *this* as you're responsible for it,' he drawled, flipping her over onto her back and settling himself between her thighs so that his rock-hard erection jabbed her belly.

'I was going to make coffee,' she said breathlessly. 'Don't you have to get up for work?'

'I'll go into the office late.'

'But you're coming back early for the twins' birthday party,' she reminded him, catching her breath when Rafael flicked his tongue across a turgid nipple.

'Mmm... There has definitely been a drop in my productivity since I married you.'

'I have no complaints about your performance,' she said, and gasped as she wrapped her legs around his hips and he surged into her.

He grinned and her heart contracted. She loved it when he smiled, and lately he'd smiled a lot. *She loved him*, whispered a voice inside her, but Juliet didn't want to admit that dangerous truth to herself, let alone to Rafael.

Much later, after they had shared a shower and he'd given her another bone-melting orgasm while she'd been bent over the side of the bath, he finally went to work. It was lucky that Poppy now slept in the nursery with Sofia's twins, Juliet mused as she stepped onto the balcony and found her daughter eating breakfast with the nanny.

Poppy had formed a real bond with Elvira, as she had with Sofia and Ana and Inez. It would be a wrench when she took Poppy back to live in England.

The thought sent Juliet's heart hurtling down to her toes. She had never imagined when Rafael had brought her to the Casillas mansion that she could be this happy and feel so settled. Some of his relatives had been cool towards her at first, but others, like his aunt Lucia and uncle Alvaro, were friendly and made a fuss of Poppy.

Rafael's mother had kept her distance since that explosive lunch, but Juliet didn't regret the things she'd said to Delfina. Rafael had told her more about his terrible childhood in the slum, and Sofia had also spoken to her about their early life.

'I don't remember much about the slum or my father,' she'd told Juliet. 'My brother took care of me and I felt safe with him.'

But no one had taken care of Rafael and protected him from his violent father—least of all his mother, who had abandoned him and then spurned him, or his grandfather, who had found him but refused to acknowledge Rafael as his successor.

Juliet knew she must not forget the reason why Rafael had married her, but over the past weeks she had felt closer to him than she'd ever felt to another person. Even though she had adored her parents and known they loved her, their love for each other had come first. But it would be the worst folly to start believing that Rafael was hers, or that he too felt a connection between them that went beyond the passion they shared.

Pushing her complicated thoughts to the back of her mind, she sat down at the table with Poppy and Elvira and poured herself a cup of coffee. A feeling of nausea swept over her and she set her cup down without taking a sip. She was probably hungry, she decided. But the sick feeling grew worse after she'd eaten some yoghurt and she hoped she wasn't coming down with another gastric virus.

Luckily the sensation of nausea soon passed, and she spent the morning at the pool with Poppy before Elvira took the little girl back to the house for lunch.

Juliet was aware that Rafael's grandfather had come to sit beneath a parasol on the pool terrace. She had barely spoken to him since he had been so unpleasant to her when Rafael had introduced her as his wife, but she had left her book on the table where Hector was now sitting.

Steeling herself for more of his rudeness, she walked over to him, puzzled to see two copies of a psychological thriller by a popular author on the table.

'Are you enjoying the book?' she asked as she picked up her copy.

Hector shrugged. 'It is good, but I have not read very much of it. My eyesight is poor because I have cataracts in my eyes which impair my vision. A surgical procedure could resolve the problem, but I also suffer from a heart condition and my doctor has advised me against having an anaesthetic.'

'I'm sorry. You must find it frustrating not to be able to read. I know I would.' Juliet hesitated. 'I could read to you, if you like.'

After a moment he nodded, and said rather stiffly. 'Do you have time? Your little daughter keeps you busy.'

'Oh, Poppy will have a nap after lunch.' Juliet picked up Hector's copy of the thriller and opened it at the page he had bookmarked. 'It's lucky this is the English edition. I'm not very good at reading in Spanish.'

'But you speak the language fluently.' He sighed. 'I must apologise for the reception you received when my grandson brought you here.'

Juliet was not one to hold a grudge. 'That's all right. I wasn't what you were expecting. I'm not the kind of wife you hoped Rafael would marry.'

'No,' Hector admitted. 'But I have watched you with Rafael and I think you are a good wife to him. You love him, don't you?'

She flushed. Were her feelings for Rafael so obvious? If so, had he guessed how she felt about him?

She met his grandfather's knowing gaze. 'Yes,' she said huskily.

It occurred to her that she was supposed to be trying to convince Hector that their marriage was genuine, but she didn't have to pretend that she had feelings for Rafael.

She looked down at the book in her hand. 'Chapter Four…' she began.

The Valencian sun grew hotter as the summer progressed, and Juliet spent much of her time slathering sun cream on herself and Poppy, cursing their pale Anglo Saxon skin that burned so easily. Even so she had developed a light golden tan, and Poppy brimmed with energy and had learned to swim without water aids.

Life couldn't get much better than this, she thought one afternoon. A few days ago she had received a letter from the Australian law firm informing her that Bryan was no longer seeking custody of Poppy.

The reason he'd given for dropping his claim was that he felt reassured that Poppy was now growing up in a stable family environment since Juliet's marriage. But her cousin in Sydney had heard that Bryan's heiress girlfriend had dumped him. Juliet had emailed, offering Bryan phone contact with his daughter, and possibly visits when Poppy was older, but she'd had no response.

It was a huge relief to know she would not lose Poppy. She looked over at where the little girl was busy building a sandcastle. They had spent the day at the Casillas estate's private beach—her, Rafael and Poppy, and Sofia, her husband Marcus and the twins. They had swum in sea that was as warm as a bath, and now the men were tending to a barbecue while the children played and she and Sofia had a chance to relax.

They must look like a typical family group, Juliet thought, looking over at Rafael and finding him staring at her. Their eyes met, held, and he smiled, his teeth flashing white in his tanned face, causing her heart to skip a beat.

It was tempting to believe that it was all real: the lingering looks he gave her when she glanced up from her book, his smile which was the first thing she saw when she opened her eyes every morning, the way he held her close after sex. And the sex... She bit her lip, thankful that her sarong hid the hard nipples jutting beneath her bikini top as she remembered how he had made love to her on this very beach the previous evening, after they had walked hand in hand along the shoreline at sunset and he'd tumbled her down onto the sand.

Rafael had told her that he would not fall in love with her. He didn't believe in love, only lust. But was it foolish to think, to hope, that he might see her as more than his public wife and private mistress?

Juliet sighed as her mind turned to the niggling worry that had the potential to shatter the fairy tale. Her period was late. Only by a few days, but it was enough for her to feel concerned. It had got her thinking about her period last month, which had been unusually light. She'd put it down to the gastric virus she'd had when she'd arrived in Spain. The feeling of nausea when she smelled coffee was another red light, but it was probably all in her imagination.

To put her mind at rest she'd bought a pregnancy test, and if her period didn't start in another couple of days she would take it. She closed her eyes and an image popped into her mind of a chubby olive-skinned baby with a mop of black hair and green eyes like his father's.

Startled, she jerked upright and blinked at Rafael as he dropped down onto the sand beside her.

'You fell asleep in the sun,' he murmured, brushing his lips across hers in a lingering kiss. 'What's the matter, *querida*, did you have a bad dream?'

She swallowed. 'Something like that.'

'Well, Madre, what is this about?'

Rafael did not hide his impatience. He didn't want to be cooling his heels in his mother's cushion-stuffed sitting room when Juliet was waiting for him in his own apartment. Hopefully she would already be in bed, but if not he would soon take her there.

An early-morning meeting meant that he'd left for the office before Juliet had woken up. Usually they had sex first thing, and he'd missed it—missed *her*, if he cared to admit it. Which he did not.

'I want to talk to you.' Delfina was twisting her hands together and seemed hesitant. 'When you brought your wife to lunch…it must be three months ago now… I told you that I was ashamed, and you assumed that I meant I was ashamed of *you*.'

'An easy assumption to make as you have barely been able to look at me for the past twenty-three years,' he said sardonically.

'I was ashamed of myself. I *am* ashamed of what I did to you,' Delfina whispered. 'When Juliet accused me of abandoning you, leaving you with your violent father, I saw the condemnation in her eyes and knew I deserved it. I knew what Ivan was like…the monster he was.'

She sighed.

'I had led a sheltered life and he was dangerously attractive. Within months of running away with him he'd persuaded me to take drugs. It was his way of controlling me, and as my life with him spiralled ever downwards I took more drugs to block out the grim reality of life with him.'

Delfina dropped her face into her hands.

'I don't even remember giving birth to you or your sister. I felt half alive. But then one day I saw my father on the television and all I wanted was to go back to my *papà*, who had always protected me. I took some money out of Ivan's wallet and somehow I made it back to my family.'

'*I* was your family,' Rafael said harshly. 'Me and Sofia. Your *children*. And you left us with him.'

His mother was crying. He had never seen her cry before and he was angry that her tears hurt him. She hadn't cared about *him*.

'I was afraid of him.'

'Do you think *I* wasn't? You called him a monster and that's exactly what the man who fathered me was.' A monster whose blood ran through *his* veins, Rafael thought, and something bleak and hopeless lashed his heart.

'I'm sorry,' his mother sobbed. 'I know you must hate me. I never knew how to try and reach out to you. When Hector brought you here you were so angry. And as you grew older you were cold and hard, and I knew it was my fault that you never smiled with your eyes.' Delfina took a shaky breath. 'This girl you've married...'

'Juliet,' Rafael gritted. 'My wife's name is Juliet.'

'She is a brave young woman,' his mother said quietly. 'She is good for you. She makes you smile.'

Delfina put her hand on Rafael's arm. It was the first time they'd had any sort of physical contact since— He frowned, unable to remember a time when his mother had touched him, let alone hugged him, unlike Juliet, who constantly hugged and cuddled her daughter.

'Rafael, I am reaching out now,' Delfina said in a trembling voice. 'I cannot expect you to forgive me, but I wish that some day we can be…friends.'

He should tell his mother to get lost and walk away. A few months ago he probably would have done, Rafael acknowledged. But life was short, as Juliet often said. Juliet, his wife, who had more courage in her tiny body than the tallest giant. Right now he didn't know if he could forgive his mother, but he found that he didn't want to walk away, so he placed his hand over Delfina's and gently squeezed her fingers.

'It's all right, Madre.'

Juliet did much more than make him smile, Rafael thought, recalling his mother's words as he entered his apartment. Juliet intrigued him, fascinated him, drove him crazy with her stubbornness and evoked an ache inside him that defied explanation when he watched her with her little daughter. She was an amazing mother and an amazing lover, and if he was a different man he might have hoped for things that he'd long ago accepted he could never have.

But he could not escape his past. He could not be a different man. So he would settle for having her in his bed, and if the nine months that were left of their marriage seemed not enough—not nearly enough—he would bury that thought and live for the day, which was how he had survived his childhood.

He found her standing outside on the balcony. She was wearing a simple white dress made of a floaty material that skimmed over her slender figure like gossamer, and her hair was loose, falling down her back like a river of amber silk.

'There you are,' he said, and there was satisfaction in his voice as he thought of the evening ahead and an early dinner and an early night—not necessarily in that order.

He waited for her to turn around and give him one of her smiles that lit up her face and did something peculiar to his heart rate.

But she seemed to stiffen before she swung round, and she didn't smile. Her eyes were very blue—as blue as the summer sky.

'I have something to tell you.'

Out of nowhere Rafael felt sick with dread. It was the same feeling he'd had when he was a boy and he'd heard the swish of his father's belt. The hairs on the back of his neck prickled with foreboding.

'So tell me,' he said evenly, while his heart thudded.

Juliet lifted a hand and let it fall to her side again. 'I'm pregnant.'

Silence. So intense it pressed on him. And then a roaring in his ears.

Every muscle in his body clenched in rejection of something that he knew from her face was true. But he rejected it anyway. 'You can't be. We've always been careful. Even on the goddamned beach I made sure I had condoms in my pocket.'

'It was before then.'

She swallowed and he saw her slender throat convulse.

'The test shows that I'm nine weeks.'

He shook his head. 'That's more than two months. How didn't you know before?'

Not that it mattered, Rafael thought grimly, turning

away from her and gripping the balustrade before his legs gave out. Juliet was expecting his baby. *Dios.* How could *he* be a father? The son of a monster? He'd decided long ago that his bloodline—the Mendoza bloodline—had to end with him.

'I know it's not what you had planned,' she said in a low voice.

He closed his eyes as her words struck him another blow. *What he had planned.* A fake marriage so that he could claim the CEO-ship. His arrogance mocked him and he felt ashamed of the ambition that was all he had, all he was.

He knew what he had to do. For Juliet's sake and for the child she carried. Especially for the child's sake.

'No,' he said unemotionally. 'A baby was not in my plans nor what I wished for.'

'Here's a newsflash, Rafael. Your wishes no longer matter.'

The bite in her voice made him turn his head and he saw anger on her face—and something else…something fiercely protective. A lioness defending her cub, he realised, and admiration joined the swirling mix of emotions he was trying to control.

'Like it or not, I am going to have your baby.'

He nodded and turned away from her again, to stare unseeingly across the gardens to the sea beyond. When this was done he would go for a run along the beach, but he knew he wouldn't be able to outrun his demons. They would sit on his shoulders, terrible and ugly, reminding him of why he dared not deal with this situation differently. Why his child and Juliet would be safer without him.

'I will ask my lawyers to begin divorce proceedings,' he told her flatly. 'Spanish law allows couples to seek a no-blame divorce after three months of marriage, a fact of which my grandfather is unaware. And I'll make immediate arrangements for you and Poppy to return to England. Ferndown House will be made over to you and five million pounds transferred into your bank account as per our agreement. I will also make further provision for Poppy and the child you are carrying.'

'*Your* child,' Juliet said fiercely. 'I am carrying *your* child.'

Rafael felt the glare she sent him but he didn't look at her, and after a moment she gave a heavy sigh.

'You know we can't divorce until we have been married for a year—your grandfather insisted on that before he will make you CEO.'

'Then I won't be CEO.'

If he allowed her to live at the Casillas mansion until their first wedding anniversary he would see her body change as her pregnancy progressed and he'd be tempted to hope for a miracle. If she was already two months pregnant the child would be born seven months from now, but their marriage had nine months to run, which meant that some sort of involvement with his child would be unavoidable. He couldn't risk it.

Juliet's silence compelled Rafael to look at her. He watched the tears roll down her face and hardened his heart. She would never know how much it was costing him to send her away. He was only just starting to realise that despite his best efforts to avoid this kind of situation, this level of pain, he had been reckless when he'd allowed Juliet close. All he could do now was try to limit the damage.

'Do you hate the idea of having a child so much that you're willing to give up your claim to be your grandfather's successor and head of the Casillas Group?'

Juliet stared at him, and when she spoke again her voice was cold—as cold as the ice around his heart.

'In that case the baby will be better off without any father rather than growing up with a father who does not love him.'

Rafael's jaw clenched and despite himself he was curious. 'Him? You know it's a boy?'

'It's too early for a scan to show the baby's gender, but I am sure I'm having a boy.' She reached out her hand towards him and let it fall again. 'Rafael... It doesn't have to be like this. I understand if you don't want me. That you might feel trapped—' Her voice cracked. 'But your son needs his father.'

'And what if I am my father's son?' he said harshly. 'No child needs a father like mine.'

He saw shock on Juliet's face, confusion. The wounded expression in her eyes felt like an arrow through Rafael's heart. He did not trust himself to be near her and without another word he walked away.

CHAPTER ELEVEN

JULIET CURLED UP in a tight ball in the bed that was much too big for her alone and cried until her head hurt and her eyes burned. Some time around dawn she slept fitfully, and when she woke she cried again because Rafael's head wasn't on the pillow beside her, He wasn't there to greet her with a smile that promised it would be another beautiful day.

Maybe there would never be another beautiful day. Just grey, sad days, like the days and weeks and months after that lorry had wiped out everything she'd cared about when she was a teenager.

She stumbled into the bathroom and splashed water on her puffy face. All that crying had made her look like a frog. It was lucky there was no chance that Rafael would see her.

He hadn't come back to the apartment after he'd stormed out the previous night, but he'd sent her a text telling her that he had gone to his penthouse in Valencia and would arrange for the Casillas private jet to take her and Poppy back to London.

More tears came into her eyes but she blinked them away. She had managed as a single parent when Poppy was born and she would manage just fine having this baby without Rafael's involvement, she told herself firmly. Being financially secure would help.

She'd considered refusing the money he'd agreed to pay her, but although it might restore her pride, which had taken such a battering, she could not let her children grow up in poverty. Rafael had made it clear he did not want his baby, but he was prepared to provide financial support.

His rejection of his child had forced her to accept that the closeness she'd sensed between them had been an illusion. By rejecting their baby he had also rejected her, and it hurt even though she knew she should have expected it. At the start he had warned her not to fall in love with him, and it was her own fault that she'd given him her heart only for him to trample all over it.

Refusing to wallow in any more self-pity, she went to find Poppy in the nursery. Sofia was there, with Ana and Inez, and she looked shocked when she saw Juliet.

'Has something happened? You look terrible.'

So Rafael hadn't told his sister.

Juliet forced a bright smile. 'I must be coming down with a cold—or maybe hay fever has made my eyes red.'

Sofia looked unconvinced, especially when Juliet went on to explain that she was taking her daughter back to England.

'Poppy is due to start nursery in a month, and I think it will be better for her to begin her schooling in England.'

'Is Rafael going with you?'

'You'll have to ask him.' Juliet avoided her sister-in-law's gaze and started taking Poppy's clothes out of the drawers, ready to be packed.

'I don't know what's happened between you and my

brother,' Sofia muttered while the children played. 'But I do know that Rafael has never been as happy as he has for the past months. He needs you, Juliet.'

Juliet bit her lip, fighting back tears. 'He doesn't need anyone. Rafael is…'

'A flesh and blood man—even though he lets people think he has ice in his veins. I *know* him,' Sofia said intensely. 'He bleeds when he is wounded, the same as the rest of us.' She grimaced at Juliet. 'I thought you were different from the other women. I thought you would fight for him—but you're giving up on him.'

Now was not the time to tell Sofia about the baby, Juliet thought wearily as she stood in her dressing room and picked out a few clothes to take with her. Her flight to London was later that afternoon and Rafael had said in his text that he would have the bulk of her belongings sent to Ferndown House.

Not that she would be needing ball gowns or the sexy negligees that she'd bought to replace her horrible old pyjamas. She would only need maternity clothes in the months ahead.

Her hand strayed to her flat stomach. It was hard to believe that a new life was developing inside her. Despite everything, her heart clenched with love for this baby. Another little one who would need her to fulfil the roles of both parents.

The positive pregnancy test had made her sink to her knees on the bathroom floor, her shock mixed with trepidation about Rafael's reaction to the news. She'd guessed he might be angry for a while, but he had been so much worse, so grimly adamant that he didn't want this baby.

She frowned, thinking of that strange comment he'd made. *'What if I am my father's son?'* She did not understand what he'd meant, and she was too tired and defeated to try and work it out.

She looked at the clock and realised that Hector would be waiting for her in his study. She read to him every day, and they were on the final chapter of the latest book they had enjoyed. It would be the last time she would read to him and her eyes brimmed again.

Never would she have believed when Rafael had brought her to the Casillas mansion that she would become fond of the elderly man.

Hector was in his study, but he shook his head when she picked up the book from his desk. 'Rafael came to see me last evening.' His shoulders sagged and he suddenly looked old and frail. 'I was shocked by what he told me.'

Juliet waited for Hector to mention her pregnancy, but what he said next sent a judder of shock through her.

'He explained why he married you. That it was a fake marriage to meet my stipulation that he must be married before I would make him CEO. I suspected as much,' Hector said heavily. 'But I could not really believe that Rafael's ambition would drive him to such an action.'

'We did a terrible thing,' Juliet whispered, shame rolling through her. 'I agreed to the marriage deal because I needed the money. It wasn't only Rafael. I am as much to blame for pretending that our marriage was real.'

His grandfather looked at her closely. 'You defend him?'

'I am his wife. It is my duty to defend my husband.'

Hector nodded. 'And for you the marriage wasn't fake, was it?'

'No.' To her horror Juliet heard her voice crack and she couldn't hold back her tears. 'Thank you,' she choked when Hector handed her a box of tissues.

'I do not think it was fake marriage for my grandson either. Last night Rafael looked more troubled than I have ever known him to be.' Hector sighed. 'I was wrong to insist that he choose a bride. I do believe that Rafael is the right person to succeed me, but any position of power can be a lonely place. I was lucky enough to have the support of my dear wife, until her death three years ago. Rafael had no one. I hoped that by forcing him to marry I could make him realise that there is more to life than his ruthless ambition.'

Hector patted Juliet's hand.

'Clearly something has happened to cause a rift between you. Is there no way to resolve the issue?'

She shook her head, remembering Rafael's look of abject horror when she'd told him she was pregnant. 'He doesn't want me and he certainly doesn't love me.'

'How can you be so sure?'

'He's never said so.'

But she thought of the vase of roses he had placed by her bed yesterday morning. He must have picked them from the garden before he'd gone to work, while she had been asleep. And last week he had spent two hours helping her search for the gold locket containing photos of her parents that she'd lost. When he had eventually found it on the pool terrace he had painstakingly fixed the broken clasp on the chain. But did those kind gestures and dozens more like them mean that he cared about her?

'Have you told Rafael how you feel about him?' Hector asked gently.

Even if she did find the courage to admit her love to Rafael he wouldn't want her now that she was pregnant, Juliet thought as she left Hector's study. Perhaps he was so against having a child because he thought he would feel trapped. He had looked so furious, but as she thought back to when she had announced her pregnancy she remembered there had been another emotion in his eyes. There had been fear.

'What if I am my father's son?'

She frowned. His father had been a violent bully who had beaten Rafael when he was a little boy. Surely he couldn't think…?

Rafael ran his hand over the thick stubble on his jaw. He guessed he should shave, maybe change out of the clothes that he'd worn for the past twenty-four hours. He tipped the last of the cognac out of the bottle into his glass and contemplated the effort of getting out of his chair, where he had been sprawled ever since he had walked into the penthouse, and decided that the only way to escape his personal hell was to drink himself into oblivion.

Hell had got even blacker when he'd looked at his watch a couple of hours ago and realised that Juliet would be on the Casillas jet heading for London. Heading away from him, and a good job too. She and her cute little daughter would be fine living at Ferndown House without him. And as for the baby. *His baby.* It… he—Juliet was sure she was expecting a boy, and maybe she had an instinctive mother's knowledge—would be well provided for.

Rafael had his own money from the property portfolio he'd built up. His fortune didn't match his family's billions, but he didn't much care right now. Besides he wasn't a Casillas. And he sure as hell didn't want to be a Mendoza. The truth was that he was a mess.

He moved his hand up from his jaw to his cheek and swore when his skin felt wet. He'd get over this, he assured himself. He'd get over *her*. Although it would help if he wasn't being haunted by a vision of her standing by the window, silhouetted against the fading light.

The vision came closer to him and wrinkled her pretty nose. 'Are you drunk?'

'If I am, it's no business of yours,' he growled. 'You should be on a plane.'

'About that…'

She knelt in front of his chair and pushed her long hair over her shoulders. Her perfume stole around him and he gripped his glass so tightly in his fingers that he was surprised it didn't shatter.

'I've decided to stay.'

He glared at her, because it was that or kiss her, and kissing her led to all sorts of trouble—like making love in the shower the one and only time he'd forgotten to use protection.

'Stay where?'

'At the Casillas mansion—or here.' She shrugged. 'A tent on the beach? I don't know. It doesn't matter as long as I'm with you.'

Rafael felt his heart kick hard in his chest. *Fear*, he recognised. Fear that he wasn't strong enough to send her away even though he knew he must.

'The only problem with your plan, *chiquita*,' he drawled, 'is that I don't want you. Surely you've realised that by now?'

'I've realised a great many things,' she told him seriously. 'For one thing I've realised that you are a liar.'

He swore, but it didn't stop her leaning forward until her face was inches from his and putting her hands flat on his chest.

'You are making a fool of yourself,' he said harshly.

'Are you really going to beg on your knees for me to take you back?'

'If I have to. But as I never left you can't really take me back.'

There was a hint of laughter in her voice. *Laughter.* He'd accepted that he would never laugh again, and he would have told her that grim truth if she hadn't pressed her lips to his mouth so that he couldn't speak, couldn't think. He couldn't do anything but keep his mouth tightly closed until she got the message.

But it got harder and harder to resist the sweet seduction of her lips. He dropped the glass and put his hands on her shoulders to push her away. How, then, did she end up sitting on his lap, her hand holding his jaw, his hands tangled in the silken fall of her hair?

Her mouth was his downfall and his delight, and with a savage groan he took charge of the kiss and drank from her as if he had been lost in a desert and she was life-giving water.

'I love you.'

Dios. He stared into her eyes and watched a tear slide down her cheek. 'I told you not to. Why didn't you pay attention, you little idiot? I'm no good for you, and I'm certainly no good for that baby of yours.'

He tried to set her away from him but he was trapped by her hair wrapped around his fingers and by something invisible that wrapped itself around his heart.

'The baby is yours too. *Ours.*'

He sat upright and cupped her chin in both his hands so that she couldn't look away from him. 'I've told you what my father was—what he did to me. Suppose I am like him? I have a temper like Ivan did. I've learned to control it, but what if I *lose* control? What if I lash out and hurt the baby? Or you?'

'You won't.'

'I won't take the risk.'

Juliet stood up and walked across the room.

Finally, Rafael thought bleakly. *Finally she sees the monster.*

'Do you think I would risk my children's safety and wellbeing?' she said fiercely. 'I have seen you with Poppy and your nieces—your patience and your caring. You are not the evil man your father was.'

'How do you *know*?' he said, struggling to speak past the lump in his throat. 'How can you have such faith in me?'

She smiled and he rocked back on his heels, blinded by her beauty, humbled by her courage.

'Because I *know* you. I know you are capable of love and I understand why you are afraid. You are a good man, Rafael. You don't need to prove yourself to anyone, least of all me. I love you with all my heart. I need you, and so does our baby.'

He stared at her while his thoughts rearranged themselves and hope slipped stealthily into his heart. When he walked towards her he saw a shadow of vulnerability in her eyes that killed him.

'Say something,' she whispered. 'Can you love me just a little?'

'*Querida*—' His voice broke and he reached for her, hauling her into his arms and holding her against his chest where his heart was doing its best to burst through his skin. '*Te amo, mi corazón.*'

He kissed her wet eyelashes, the tip of her nose, her lips that parted beneath his as she kissed him back with all that sweetness and light that was his wife, the love of his life.

'I don't know when it began,' he said, resting his

chin on the top of her head. 'You got to me in a way no other woman had ever done. You defended me, and no one had ever done that before.'

'It wasn't love at first sight, then?' she said ruefully.

'I was a blind fool—but you showed me that you are beautiful, inside and out.' He looked into her eyes and read her unspoken question. 'It ripped my heart out when I sent you away but I thought it was for the best.'

His heart gave another kick when she held his hand against her stomach, where the new life they had created together linked them inextricably.

'I will love our baby, and Poppy, but more than anything I will love *you, mi Julieta*, for the rest of our lives. For always and for ever.'

EPILOGUE

RAFAEL STOOD IN the hallway of Ferndown House and watched a troop of small girls wearing pink leotards run out of the room which Juliet had turned into a dance studio. Their parents were waiting in the lobby and there was general chaos while coats were found and ballet shoes were swapped for trainers.

'Your last class for a while,' he said to his wife when the house was quiet again.

'Yes, it will be nice to have a few weeks off, and the babies should arrive any day now.' She patted her swollen belly. 'In a couple of years' time I'll have two more pupils.'

He shook his head. 'I can't believe there will be another set of twin girls in the family besides Sofia's girls. Can you imagine the mayhem when we all get together at Christmas?'

Rafael looked at his son, who had run in from the garden holding a football. Diego Casillas was three years old, and chasing him was his big sister Poppy, who had just turned seven.

'Your grandfather will enjoy having the whole family to stay. You know how he dotes on all the children. And your mother will spoil them,' Juliet said serenely.

She was tired now, at the end of her third pregnancy, but Rafael thought she had never looked more beautiful.

They had made the decision to live in England after Diego was born. When Rafael had become CEO of the Casillas Group after Hector had retired he had insisted on sharing the role with his half-brother. Francisco now worked from the company's offices in Valencia, and Rafael was based in London. He and Juliet wanted their own home, where they could bring up their growing family, and Ferndown House was filled with love and laughter.

Especially love, Rafael mused as he drew Juliet into his arms and she lifted her face for his kiss. He adored her, and told her so daily. The bright blue sapphire and diamond ring he had slipped onto her finger next to her wedding band was just one token of his deep and abiding love for this woman who had brought him out of the darkness into her golden light.

'It feels like there's a riot going on in there,' he murmured when a tiny foot kicked his hand where his fingers were splayed possessively on Juliet's bump.

'Yes, I think your new daughters are ready to meet their daddy.' She looped her arms around his neck. 'You know what's supposed to bring on labour…?'

'Señora Casillas—are you suggesting that we…?' He whispered the rest of the sentence in her ear and she giggled.

'Yes, please, Señor Casillas, my love.'

Love and laughter. He couldn't ask for more, Rafael thought.

And three days later, when he held two little bundles whom they'd named Lola and Clara in his arms, he knew he was the luckiest man in the world.

* * * * *

COMING SOON!

We really hope you enjoyed reading this book. If you're looking for more romance be sure to head to the shops when new books are available on

Thursday 28th August

To see which titles are coming soon, please visit
millsandboon.co.uk/nextmonth

MILLS & BOON

FOUR BRAND NEW BOOKS FROM
MILLS & BOON MODERN

The same great stories you love, a stylish new look!

OUT NOW

Eight Modern stories published every month, find them all at:

millsandboon.co.uk

afterglow BOOKS

Afterglow Books is a trend-led, trope-filled list of books with diverse, authentic and relatable characters, a wide array of voices and representations, plus real world trials and tribulations. Featuring all the tropes you could possibly want (think small-town settings, fake relationships, grumpy vs sunshine, enemies to lovers) and all with a generous dose of spice in every story.

@millsandboonuk
@millsandboonuk
afterglowbooks.co.uk
#AfterglowBooks

For all the latest book news, exclusive content and giveaways scan the QR code below to sign up to the Afterglow newsletter:

SCAN ME

afterglow BOOKS

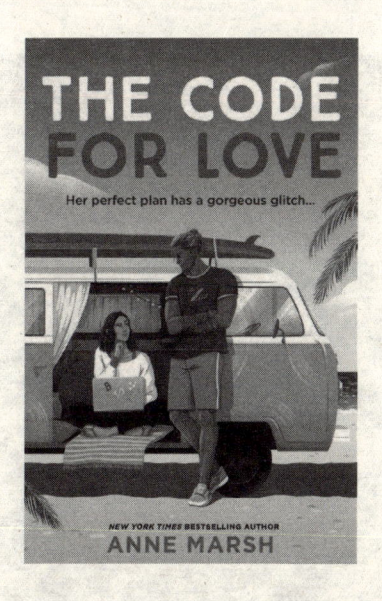

THE CODE FOR LOVE

Her perfect plan has a gorgeous glitch...

ANNE MARSH
NEW YORK TIMES BESTSELLING AUTHOR

✈ International

⛅ Grumpy/sunshine

Fake dating

OUT NOW

To discover more visit:
Afterglowbooks.co.uk

OUT NOW!

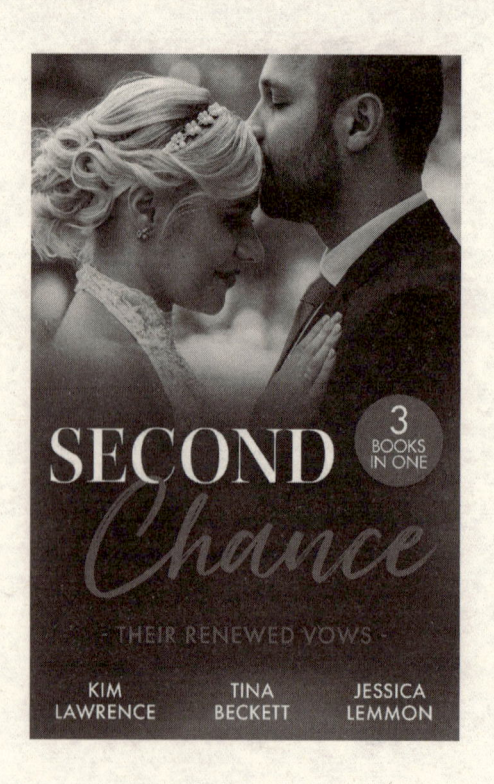

SECOND Chance
THEIR RENEWED VOWS

3 BOOKS IN ONE

KIM LAWRENCE TINA BECKETT JESSICA LEMMON

Available at
millsandboon.co.uk

MILLS & BOON

OUT NOW!

THE TYCOON'S AFFAIR COLLECTION

TEMPTED BY DESIRE

USA TODAY BESTSELLING AUTHOR
ABBY GREEN

Available at
millsandboon.co.uk

MILLS & BOON

OUT NOW!

A DARK ROMANCE SERIES

Thorns of Revenge

TARYN LEIGH TAYLOR • ABBY GREEN • JACKIE ASHENDEN

Available at
millsandboon.co.uk

MILLS & BOON

MILLS & BOON

THE HEART OF ROMANCE

A ROMANCE FOR EVERY READER

MODERN — Prepare to be swept off your feet by sophisticated, sexy and seductive heroes, in some of the world's most glamourous and romantic locations, where power and passion collide.

HISTORICAL — Escape with historical heroes from time gone by. Whether your passion is for wicked Regency Rakes, muscled Vikings or rugged Highlanders, awaken the romance of the past.

MEDICAL — Set your pulse racing with dedicated, delectable doctors in the high-pressure world of medicine, where emotions run high and passion, comfort and love are the best medicine.

True Love — Celebrate true love with tender stories of heartfelt romance, from the rush of falling in love to the joy a new baby can bring, and a focus on the emotional heart of a relationship.

HEROES — The excitement of a gripping thriller, with intense romance at its heart. Resourceful, true-to-life women and strong, fearless men face danger and desire - a killer combination!

afterglow BOOKS — From showing up to glowing up, these characters are on the path to leading their best lives and finding romance along the way – with plenty of sizzling spice!

To see which titles are coming soon, please visit

millsandboon.co.uk/nextmonth

LET'S TALK
Romance

For exclusive extracts, competitions and special offers, find us online:

- **f** MillsandBoon
- **X** @MillsandBoon
- **◉** @MillsandBoonUK
- **♪** @MillsandBoonUK

Get in touch on 01413 063 232

For all the latest titles coming soon, visit
millsandboon.co.uk/nextmonth